PENGUIN BOOKS

BOUND BY BLOOD, BRIDGED BY LOVE

Journal Kyaw Ma Ma Lay, often regarded as one of the foremost Burmese writers of the 20th century, authored nearly twenty books along with numerous articles and short stories. Many of her contemporaries, as well as younger writers, recognize her as a literary genius who won two top Burmese Literary Prizes and had a unique gift for transforming everyday events into compelling narratives. Her works reflect the lives, struggles, and aspirations of modern Burmese society, resonating deeply with readers across generations. Ma Ma Lay, being one of Burma's few prominent female authors, became the president of the Writers Association in 1948.

San Shwe Baw holds a BA in English from the Institute of Education, Yangon, Burma, an advanced Diploma in English Language Teaching (DELT) from the University of Leeds, UK, and an M.A. in Teaching English to Speakers of Other Languages (TESOL) from St. Michael's College, USA. He retired as an assistant professor at the Theodore Maria School of Arts, Assumption University, Thailand, where he served for nearly three decades. Before moving to Thailand in 1994, he spent twelve years as an English tutor at Yangon University and Sittwe College. His English language teaching articles have been published in both Thailand and USA.

San Shwe Baw is the author of four acclaimed novels—*The Astrologer's Predictions*, *Enslaved by English*, *Love by Fate*, and *A Candle in Darkness*. In addition to his original works, he has brought notable Burmese classics to English readers through his translations, among them *I Gave My Life for Thee*—the English rendering of *Myay Si Mel Mel Thway Yel Yel* by Phoe Kyawt—*Ah Phyu*, *She*, and *Six Timeless Short Stories*, all by the celebrated writer Journal Kyaw Ma Ma Lay. *I Gave My Life for Thee* was honoured with the prestigious 10th Mekong Literary Award. His books have been published in Myanmar by Myat Su Mon Sarpay, Global Ahlin, Myanmar Book Centre, Seikku Cho Cho, Juty Sarpay, and Thihayadanar Sarpay.

ADVANCE PRAISE FOR *BOUND BY BLOOD, BRIDGED BY LOVE*

'As a writer and admirer of Burmese literature, I am deeply moved by this English translation of *Blood* (published as *Bound by Blood, Bridged by Love*), the classic novel by our esteemed author Journal Kyaw Ma Ma Lay. Translated with remarkable sensitivity and literary care by San Shwe Baw—himself a novelist and translator—this edition preserves the delicate threads of family, memory, and identity that make the original so timeless.

Blood is more than a story; it is a meditation on the invisible bonds that endure even in war's aftermath. Through Yumisan, a young Japanese woman searching for her Burmese brother, we embark on a journey both intimately personal and profoundly universal. San Shwe Baw's translation captures the emotional depth of Journal Kyaw Ma Ma Lay's prose, reminding us of the strength of kinship and the healing power of love.

This book is a gift: a bridge between cultures, languages, and hearts. I recommend it without reservation.'

—Mya Kyar Ngyone, winner of the 11th Mekong Literary Award

Bound by Blood, Bridged by Love

Journal Kyaw Ma Ma Lay

Translated by San Shwe Baw

PENGUIN BOOKS
An imprint of Penguin Random House

PENGUIN BOOKS

Penguin Books is an imprint of the Penguin Random House group of companies whose addresses can be found at global.penguinrandomhouse.com

Published by Penguin Random House SEA Pte Ltd
40 Penjuru Lane, #03-12, Block 2
Singapore 609216

First published in Penguin Books by Penguin Random House SEA 2025

10 9 8 7 6 5 4 3 2 1

ISBN 9789815323696

Typeset in Merriweather by MAP Systems, Bangalore, India

www.penguin.sg

1

May 9, 1967

Yumisan had been nervous ever since the announcement instructed passengers to fasten their seat belts for the landing at Yangon Airport. As the plane descended, she looked out the window and took in everything she saw, feeling a flutter in her chest at the knowledge that she was getting closer to the ground. Her heart beat faster as the plane's wheels touched down. When the wheels finally made contact with the ground, she instinctively exclaimed, '*Bhiruma!*' The fatigue from the long overnight flight suddenly vanished, replaced by an inexplicable surge of energy. She cried out 'Bhiruma!' with renewed vigour.

As the plane came to a stop, Yumisan's face glowed with pure delight, her expression sweeter and more radiant than that of any other passenger. Around thirty years old, she was dressed entirely in white—a white hat, blouse, gloves, and shoes—exuding an aura of pristine elegance. Her delicately pink face, framed by a straight nose and slender eyebrows, enhanced her striking beauty.

For a Japanese woman, she was not at all short. Of medium height and build, her figure was graceful and well-proportioned. Her eyes, luminous and glistening, shone with a striking vividness.

She was among the last passengers to disembark. The fresh, sweet breeze blowing in from the airplane's exit was refreshing. Inhaling this sweet air, she descended from the plane, looking around in wonder. *Bhiruma*! Yumisan had finally arrived in Myanmar, a place she had longed to visit. This evening was particularly pleasant. The sky was clear and bright without a trace of clouds.

As Yumisan's feet touched the ground of Myanmar, she felt warmly welcomed, embraced by the land. There was a sense of warmth and comfort within her heart.

As she walked towards the airport building, she moved with liveliness, her bright eyes shining with enthusiasm. She brushed away the strands of hair that had fallen across her forehead and gazed at the crowd inside the airport building. It seemed as though the crowd, composed of men, women, the old, and the young, was there to welcome her. She felt an inexplicable sense of familiarity, as if these strangers were her own relatives and friends. She smiled warmly and looked around as she entered the airport building.

She had finally arrived in Myanmar. She felt a deep sense of satisfaction and relief, thinking that her journey would only be worthwhile if she succeeded in achieving her goals here.

The belief that she would someday arrive in this country had begun when she had been fifteen years old. From the day she'd first seen the image of the Shwedagon Pagoda, she prayed to be called to Myanmar by the power of the Shwedagon.

After obtaining significant university degrees, she continued her studies at the Osaka University of Foreign Studies. There, she focused on Myanmar language studies for four years, working diligently to earn a BA degree. After completing that degree, she pursued an MA in Linguistics. During this time, she also worked as a temporary teacher while striving to attend a postgraduate Myanmar language course at Yangon University.

Fortunately, she was offered a position as a Japanese language teacher at the Institute of Foreign Languages in Myanmar, and she came to Myanmar with great joy and enthusiasm.

Before leaving Japan, the prospect of going to Myanmar had filled Yumisan with immense anticipation and excitement. Ever since she was fifteen, her desire to visit Myanmar had been overwhelming. She had constantly vowed that one day she would make it there. Yet, she had never imagined that this day would arrive so easily and smoothly.

Responding in Burmese to the airport officer's question in English, Yumisan caused the customs officer inspecting her passport to look up at her face in surprise.

As her belongings were being inspected, a Japanese embassy official arrived in the room to meet her. Although she had never met this official before, Yumisan felt delighted to encounter a fellow countryman in a foreign land. She smiled sweetly and greeted him with a slight bow.

The embassy official welcomed Yumisan and informed her that they would notify the Myanmar Government's Education Department of her arrival the next day. They then took her to their residence. As the car left the airport, Yumisan recited in her mind the words her father had spoken before he passed away: 'Mingaladon, Bago, Phayalay.'

When Yumisan asked about Mingaladon, the embassy official took a detour and pointed out the military buildings. Yumisan gazed at the military structures on the way back from Mingaladon, wondering which buildings her father had stayed in during the wartime.

Her father, Major Yoshida, was a Major from an armoured unit stationed at Mingaladon during the war in Myanmar. For her fifth birthday, he had taken a photograph of himself in Mingaladon and sent it to her in Japan. Along with the photo, he had sent a poem titled ‘Mingaladon’, which Yumisan had memorized by heart and remembered to this day.

Yumisan recited the poem in her mind, and, without realizing it, she bowed slightly, closing her eyes out of respect for the place where her father had once lived.

Yumisan’s long, fluttering eyelashes cast shadows over her puffy eyelids as she silently prayed in calm composure. Her father, Major Yoshida, was a distinguished figure in both poetry and painting. After giving birth to Yumisan in Osaka, Japan, her mother passed away in the hospital, leaving her motherless. Major Yoshida, needing to leave for the war in Myanmar, had entrusted young Yumisan in the care of her grandparents. Every time he missed his daughter during his time in Myanmar, he would write poems to ease his longing.

The photograph that Major Yoshida had taken and sent from Mingaladon was in Yumisan’s handbag. She took it out and looked at it, then showed it to the embassy official.

'When I was five years old, my father took this photograph in Mingaladon and sent it to me,' Yumisan said.

The embassy official nodded in surprise and took the photograph to look at it. The photo, faded with age, depicted her father in a full Japanese military uniform with a gentle and delicate demeanour, which contrasted with the sternness of the attire.

'Oh . . . so your father was in the military?'

'Yes.'

'Is he still in Japan now?'

Yumisan, with a slight, melancholic smile, replied, 'No, he passed away.'

'Oh . . . did he die in Myanmar?'

'No, he passed away in Japan.'

'Oh . . . I see.'

The embassy official looked at the photograph again before returning it to Yumisan. She took one last, thoughtful look at the photograph, as if reflecting on her father's time in this place, before putting it back into her bag.

The golden sunlight from the western sky gently descended onto Mingaladon Road. Ahead, she saw the golden stupa of Kyaikkalo Pagoda standing on a quiet, tree-covered hill. The serene view was tinged with melancholy. Walking silently beside the embassy official, Yumisan pondered the strange and winding path her life had taken.

She felt as if her blood in Myanmar was calling out to her, waiting for her to arrive today. She believed that if she came to Myanmar but didn't meet her blood, it would be a great disappointment. She wondered how she would go about finding her blood, who was said to be in Myanmar.

Having made the effort to reach Myanmar, Yumisan pondered over her destiny and what it held for her. The embassy official turned and drove towards a building, parking the car.

'This is the Institute of Foreign Languages where you will be teaching. It's currently closed,' he said.

Yumisan got out of the car and looked at the school she would be teaching at. The entire campus was calm and peaceful. It was a long, two-storey building facing a green lawn. This school, where French, German, Japanese, Chinese, Russian, and English literature were taught, was filled with the prestigious atmosphere of a multinational cultural institution.

Yumisan was impressed by the school grounds and the shape of the building. She might have felt differently if the structure had been large and old-fashioned. However, the school building appeared neat, majestic, and beautiful, embodying a modern aesthetic while also evoking a sense of a peaceful retreat. Yumisan found herself immediately drawn to it. She felt a strong desire to meet the Myanmar students who would be learning Japanese literature and language at this institute.

Yumisan asked the embassy official to take her to the Shwedagon Pagoda that very day. Having first seen a picture of the Shwedagon Pagoda at the age of fifteen, her interest in Myanmar had been piqued, and she had longed to visit it. The embassy official obliged and soon they arrived at the grounds of the grand Shwedagon Pagoda.

The pagoda grounds were bustling with devotees. With the clear sky as a backdrop, the magnificent Shwedagon Pagoda towered majestically, akin to a sanctuary building. This sight deeply impressed Yumisan.

Against the backdrop of a pale blue sky, the towering Shwedagon Pagoda, coated in layers of gold and rising proudly into the heavens, presented a sight of unparalleled beauty that left Yumisan in silent awe.

Shwedagon Pagoda, I have arrived today, drawn by your presence, and paid my homage. Please continue to protect me and help me achieve all my desires, she silently prayed in Burmese for the first time, standing quietly with her hands folded in reverence.

Yumisan walked around the pagoda grounds, observing it. Myanmar's artistic carvings and sculptures left her in endless awe, filling the entire pagoda hill with things to see and admire. She was especially impressed by the exquisite craftsmanship. She continued to walk and look at the splendid carvings, noting the intricate floral motifs and the fine details on the grand statues. This gave her a sense of how rich Myanmar's cultural heritage was.

The statues within the grand pagodas were each distinct, showcasing the varied and precise architectural styles of Myanmar, making Yumisan reluctant to look away as she observed them with deep admiration. She encountered unfinished carvings and floral vines that were so beautifully crafted, they appeared almost real. The ancient sculptures and floral motifs around the pagoda made her fall in love with the artistic richness of Myanmar, leaving her mesmerized.

She was captivated by the ancient paintings depicting the life of the Buddha. Even in college, Yumisan had studied painting as an additional subject. She had followed in the footsteps of her father, Major Yoshida, who excelled in the arts.

She had trained under the famous Japanese painter Nakakawa Kiwain, becoming his prized student. Whenever her work met his approval, he would arrange special solo exhibitions to showcase her paintings, taking pride in his pupil.

Yumisan realized that if she could regularly visit and explore the Shwedagon Pagoda, Myanmar's artistic heritage in painting and sculpture would offer her an endless source of inspiration. She resolved to paint a picture of the Shwedagon Pagoda using oil paints. Moreover, she was determined to write a book on Myanmar's arts in Japanese. Before leaving the pagoda hill, she promised herself she would take on this challenge.

2

When additional Japanese household items, including porcelain dishes and cups, arrived by ship from Japan, Yumisan became more settled in Myanmar. The Myanmar government provided her with a house to live in. The house was spacious enough for her to live alone, with a bedroom, living room, and dining room. They also provided her with a driver and a car for her to use for school commutes.

Though the embassy suggested she could easily hire an Indian housekeeper, Yumisan preferred to have a Myanmar woman. She believed that living with a woman from Myanmar would help her better understand and become proficient in Myanmar's customs, culture, and language.

She hired Daw Aung May, who was around fifty years old, as her housekeeper. Daw Aung May was the kind of Myanmar woman Yumisan desired. Despite her age, she was very much to Yumisan's liking because of her cleanliness and organized nature.

Yumisan appreciated these qualities and considered them to be the habits of older individuals.

Yumisan had never lived with her mother. She had been raised by her grandparents. Therefore, she did not see Daw Aung May merely as a housekeeper but developed a fondness for her as one would for a maternal figure. With a sense of closeness, she affectionately called her '*Obasan*' (auntie in Japanese).

In the morning, Daw Aung May would be seen with a small bun on her head, wearing a clean white blouse and traditional wrap, with *thanaka* on her face. This appearance always pleased Yumisan. Daw Aung May was someone who preferred to stay busy with work, never stopping to rest.

Her demeanour was calm, and she was articulate and lively in her speech. Being a native of Mandalay, she spoke with elegance. Having spent time with her grandmother, who was a nun in the Sagaing Hills, she was well-versed in Myanmar literature. After her mother passed away, she was placed under the care of the head nun at Pyin Oo Lwin Convent, and she spent her life navigating various social strata. Fluent in English, she earned a good salary working for foreign embassy households, gaining a reputation as an excellent housekeeper.

Working in the home of a young Japanese teacher, who was closer in culture to the East, felt far more peaceful and comfortable than working in other foreign households. Without any pride, she spoke fluent Myanmar and treated Yumisan, who was warm and friendly, like her own daughter. She cooked a variety of dishes daily, catering to Japanese, Chinese, Western, and Burmese tastes, with sincere dedication. Yumisan often remarked, 'Living with Obasan is a blessing.' The Japanese professor from Yumisan's department also appreciated Daw Aung May's capabilities and diligence, valuing her as a reliable assistant.

* * *

On the first day of school, the principal and the Japanese professor escorted Yumisan to the Japanese language classroom. They crossed the French and German language classrooms, located on the west side of the school building, to reach the Japanese language classroom.

The classroom had large windows fitted with glass, allowing plenty of light to enter. It could accommodate about forty students. At the front of the Japanese classroom, a large map of Japan was hung.

The room was decorated with grand and beautiful pictures showcasing Japanese culture and industry, such as the capital city Tokyo, traditional Japanese tea ceremonies, and other cultural aspects, making the atmosphere distinctly Japanese.

The students in the Japanese classroom were not just young schoolchildren but included adults and middle-aged individuals, and some were even office workers and employees. Yumisan was eager and enthusiastic to teach Japanese to her students in this classroom. Since many of her students were older or the same age as her, with only a few being younger, Yumisan initially felt slightly embarrassed. She realized that those in the Japanese classroom were eager to learn the Japanese language and literature. It was only after she started teaching that she fully understood their dedication.

On the first day she began teaching in the Japanese classroom, she heard her students repeating after her in unison. Among their voices, she thought she detected a familiar tone, as if it belonged to someone she was searching for with great hope—her half-brother, a younger brother with the same father but different mothers.

The thought that she had a younger brother in Myanmar was a deeply concealed emotion within Yumisan. She did not know who he was, where he lived, or even if he was alive. She had only learned of his existence five years after the war, when her father, Yoshida, had told her about him. By the time she reunited with her father at the age of fifteen, he had been bedridden and chronically ill for a long time.

Before Yoshida passed away, he had revealed that Yumisan was not alone in the world; he had married a Burmese woman and had a son in Myanmar. This was the revelation that had made Yumisan aware that she had a younger brother in Myanmar.

Yumisan had always thought of herself as an only child, but now she knew she had a brother. From the moment she learned this, she developed a keen interest in Myanmar. On the day her father told her, she tried to calculate her younger brother's age. She had also realized how much her father had loved his son. She often wondered what her brother looked like. The voice, gestures, demeanour, and overall presence of her younger brother had deeply etched themselves into Yumisan's mind. Though she tried to imagine and picture him, it was always an elusive image, never a concrete one.

This shadowy figure, which had become a focal point of her thoughts, grew closer to her with each passing year. It didn't fade away but rather became more defined, clinging to her as an inseparable companion, intensifying her longing and affection.

Much like she had been separated from her father before fully understanding the world, her younger brother had also been separated from their father at an early age. However, unlike her, he had never had the chance to reunite with their father, a fact that filled Yumisan with compassion and sympathy for him.

Whenever she thought about the similar fate they both endured, her desire to meet and see her brother, whom she had never met, grew stronger. The incomplete address given to her by her father before his death was her only clue: 'Daughter of the headman of Phayalay village near Bago, nurse in training at Bago Hospital named Ma Htway Htway.' This was the address she had memorized, and it was her main hope for finding her brother.

According to Major Yoshida, he had met Ma Htway Htway at Bago Hospital, and they had gotten married officially with the consent of Ma Htway Htway's father, the village head of Phayalay village.

When he was forced to retreat from Myanmar due to the defeat in the war, Yoshida could only inform Yumisan that he had left behind a ten-month-old son with Ma Htway Htway. From the moment she heard this, Yumisan began to keep track of her younger brother's age year by year. By the time she arrived in Myanmar, she calculated that her younger brother would be twenty-two years old. It took Yumisan about three months after arriving in Myanmar to start investigating Bago and Phayalay village.

Yumisan wanted to take her time and carefully investigate this matter. She was worried that the brother she found might not be her real brother but an imposter. She first sought the help of her Japanese language instructor, Daw Khin Win Mu, who worked under her at the school, to find out if Phayalay village existed near Bago. Within a week, Daw Khin Win Mu informed her that there indeed was a village by the name of Phayalay near Bago. Curious about why Yumisan was asking, Daw Khin Win Mu inquired further.

'Why are you interested in Phayalay village, *Sayama*?'

Yumisan had to think for a moment before answering that question without hesitation.

'A friend of mine from Tokyo asked me to check. His wife's name is Ma Htway Htway, and she lives in Phayalay village. He wanted to know if she still lives there.'

'Was your friend a soldier or an officer who married Ma Htway Htway during the war?'

Daw Khin Win Mu kept asking questions. From the moment she heard the name Ma Htway Htway from Phayalay village, she suspected it might involve an ordinary Japanese soldier rather than an officer.

Yumisan smiled slightly and replied.

'No, not a soldier, but an officer. Ma Htway Htway is said to be the daughter of the village headman of Phayalay village.'

Whether she said officer or soldier, in truth, Daw Khin Win Mu had a preconceived notion and little regard for Myanmar women who had married Japanese officers or soldiers during the Japanese era. So, she replied indifferently.

'It's been over twenty years since the war ended, Sayama. How could anyone know if Ma Htway Htway is still there or not?'

Yumisan realized that Daw Khin Win Mu was speaking dismissively, trying to make it easy to drop the matter. To engage Daw Khin Win Mu's interest and willingness to help, Yumisan tried again.

'While I'm in Myanmar, I need to find out if Ma Htway Htway is still there. Her husband sent some things for her through me. He passed away before I came to Myanmar.'

'Really? What are the things?'

Only then did Daw Khin Win Mu's curiosity spark, as she fluttered her eyelashes.

'The deceased left some clothes. He asked me to deliver them. It would be good if I could find her, wouldn't it, Daw Khin Win Mu?'

Yumisan looked intently at Daw Khin Win Mu's face and spoke earnestly.

'Oh . . . I see. In that case, you're right, Sayama. If Ma Htway Htway is still living in Phayalay village, especially in poverty, then clothing would be of great value to her,' Daw Khin Win Mu remarked. Despite hearing that Ma Htway Htway might be a Japanese wife, Daw Khin Win Mu felt a sense of sympathy and compassion as a fellow Burmese. She was pleased that a Japanese man who had taken a Myanmar woman during the war had remembered and valued her, considering her as his wife.

'I'll slowly inquire and investigate, Sayama. We have a saying in Myanmar: "If the dead are long gone, they are forgotten, but if the missing are searched for, they will be found." One day, she'll surely be found. I'll try my best to help. Don't worry, Sayama,' she said.

Yumisan felt a growing anticipation and eagerness to hear news about Ma Htway Htway from Daw Khin Win Mu every time she came to school. While waiting to meet her younger brother, she was in a situation where she couldn't yet express how eagerly she wanted to meet Ma Htway Htway. As a result, she wanted to ask but kept holding back. She refrained from asking too many questions for fear of spreading rumours and encountering someone posing as Ma Htway Htway. To ensure the truth, she kept crucial information private, such as the fact that Ma Htway Htway had a ten-month-old son when separated from her father. This detail would serve as a reliable indicator if Ma Htway Htway truly had a child, and so Yumisan chose to withhold it for now.

Every morning and afternoon when she came to school, Yumisan met with the young Japanese language instructor, Daw Khin Win Mu. Although Yumisan wanted to ask her about the news, she held back and waited for Daw Khin Win Mu to bring it up. Days turned into weeks, and weeks into months—two months passed this way. Yumisan was busy during this period with tasks such as exam preparations, setting exam questions, and grading answer sheets, which kept her from bringing up the topic.

One Sunday, Daw Khin Win Mu and a young woman unexpectedly came to Yumisan's house. Following Japanese customs, Yumisan greeted them with a slight bow and joyfully ushered them into the living room.

'Obasan, the teachers from my school are here. Please bring some food,' Yumisan called out to Daw Aung May in the inner room.

Noticing Yumisan's use of the word '*kyunma*' (my) in her speech, Daw Khin Win Mu realized that

Yumisan's Burmese had significantly improved over the past four to five months.

'Sayama, I've come to discuss the matter you mentioned about Bago,' Daw Khin Win Mu said, sitting down in the living room only after sharing the news.

'Oh, really? What interesting news do you have? Please tell me, I'm eager to hear,' Yumisan said excitedly as she sat down on a cushion.

'Sayama, this is a university student from Yangon University. She lives near my house, and her parents live in Bago. She said she can take you to her father. He might be able to find out about Ma Htway Htway for you.'

As Daw Aung May arrived carrying a tea tray into the living room, Yumisan worried that Daw Aung May might overhear. To prevent this, Yumisan switched to Japanese and spoke to Daw Khin Win Mu.

'*Watashi wa ureshī watakushi wa ikemasu ka? Ikemasu, Bago no mura ni tomaru nodesu ka*? ('I'm so happy. Can I go? Will we stay overnight in the village?')

Daw Khin Win Mu replied in Japanese—without switching back to Burmese—saying that they could make it a day trip if they left early in the morning.

'Hai, hai. Yes, yes, then next Saturday. Daw Khin Win Mu, can you come along?'

Nu Nu, who had accompanied Daw Khin Win Mu, smiled as she watched Yumisan switching between Burmese and Japanese.

'Sure, Sayama. I'll join if I can.'

Yumisan, noticing Nu Nu's neat appearance with long, well-kept hair, asked, 'What is your name?'

Upon seeing Nu Nu, Yumisan instantly took a liking to her. She noticed the stark difference between Nu Nu's traditional, refined attire and Daw Khin Win Mu's more Westernized, modern look.

Nu Nu wore her hair neatly, with her bangs cut straight and the rest tied into a simple knot at the back, leaving a long, loose strand down her back. This style, along with her traditionally embroidered *htamein*, perfectly complemented her, exemplifying the true essence of Burmese elegance, which Yumisan deeply appreciated.

Since arriving in Myanmar, Yumisan had been particularly attentive to the traditional attire and grooming of Myanmar's women. She occasionally encountered the pure beauty of Burmese culture and tradition in individuals like Nu Nu.

Because Yumisan spoke Burmese as quickly as Japanese, Nu Nu seemed initially puzzled by her sudden question, while Daw Khin Win Mu understood her perfectly, having heard her speak Burmese every day. Realizing that Nu Nu hadn't fully understood,

Yumisan repeated her question slowly until Nu Nu comprehended.

'My name is Nu Nu.'

'Oh, Nu Nu, what major are you studying at the university?'

'I'm in my final year of a BA programme, majoring in History.'

'Are there foreigners at the university taking postgraduate courses in Burmese?'

'Yes, there are.'

'I really want to take a postgraduate course in Burmese.'

'How long did you study Burmese language and literature in Japan?' Nu Nu asked Yumisan with genuine interest.

'There's a foreign language studies university in Osaka, and there's one in Tokyo as well. At this university, it takes four years to earn a BA degree. Among the fifteen different languages offered, you can choose whichever you prefer. At Osaka University, I majored in Burmese. I also took Spanish and French. However, these two languages weren't as intensive as Burmese.'

'What subjects do you study in Burmese?' Daw Khin Win Mu asked, wanting to know more details.

'We don't just learn the language; we also study history and culture. In history, we learn about

Anawrahta, Kyansittha, Alaungpaya, and Bayinnaung. After four years at the university, I can read Burmese newspapers and magazines quite well. I graduated from Osaka University with a degree, then pursued an MA in Linguistics, and became a teacher. I applied and worked hard to come to Myanmar because of my passion for the language I studied.'

Although Yumisan seemed to have finished speaking, she was inwardly holding back something important she wanted to say: '*I also have a brother in Myanmar whom I wish to meet.*' She stopped, wearing a slightly pensive expression.

Nu Nu gazed at Yumisan with bright, curious eyes. She felt delighted hearing words like Anawrahta, Kyansittha, and Bayinnaung spoken by a foreign woman.

Because Yumisan said she had studied Burmese at Osaka University, Nu Nu saw Yumisan as a Burmese girl rather than a Japanese girl. The blue silk dress Yumisan wore highlighted her slender waist, full hips, and smooth, white legs. The blue dress contrasted beautifully with Yumisan's fair skin. She wore Japanese slippers and had her dark hair neatly tied with a leather band. Her bright, dark eyes with a straight nose made her even more beautiful, and her always cheerful face made her even more attractive. Anyone who saw her would instantly like her.

'I've never been to Bago before. Do you go back to Bago every day, Nu Nu?'

Nu Nu laughed.

'No, I don't go back every day. I go once a week.'

'Have you been to the Phayalay village near Bago?'

'No, I haven't. But my father's acquaintance who lives in Pagoda village often comes to see my father. If you ask him about Ma Htway Htway, I'm sure you'll get to know her. When are you going to Bago next Saturday? I'll accompany you when you go to my house.'

'Oh . . . if that's the case, I'd like to go at six in the morning.'

Daw Khin Win Mu and Nu Nu laughed together.

Yumisan wondered why they were all laughing at what she had said. Daw Khin Win Mu laughed and then said, 'Six o'clock is too early, Sayama. Let's do this instead: Nu Nu and I will be waiting at the school at seven o'clock in the morning. You can come to the school at seven, and we will meet there.'

Yumisan said 'hai hai' in her usual straightforward manner, and then asked, 'What does "*sone*" mean?' She often asked immediately about words she wanted to remember when she heard unfamiliar terms.

'"Sone" means to gather together to go somewhere,' Daw Khin Win Mu explained clearly to Yumisan.

'There are many similar-sounding words in Burmese. There's still a lot I don't know yet,' Yumisan remarked.

Nu Nu listened to Yumisan's imperfect yet sweet, clear voice speaking Burmese, and thought it sounded wonderful.

'Since you arrived from Japan, your Burmese has improved a lot in the last three or four months,' Daw Khin Win Mu cut in. 'You speak more fluently and confidently, and you use many new words. Are you still continuing your lessons with a Burmese teacher here?'

'To speak well, I don't need a teacher, Daw Khin Win Mu. I have Obasan to help me. Every day, she patiently corrects me until I speak perfectly. If I make mistakes, she has me repeat until I get it right,' Yumisan said, laughing sweetly.

'How convenient! This lady looks adorable. Who helped you hire her?' Daw Khin Win Mu asked.

'With help from the embassy, I got Obasan. I'm very fortunate. I don't have to look after any household chores because she does everything so well. I really like how clean she keeps everything.'

'How much is her salary?' Nu Nu inquired.

'I pay her 150 kyats per month.'

'That's a good salary. The house is always spotless. Does she do all the housework alone, Sayama?'

'We have an Indian girl who helps with laundry and taking out the trash. Obasan handles the grocery shopping, cooking, and house cleaning. She even sews well. I don't have to do anything.'

'That's quite a set-up,' Daw Khin Win Mu said, glancing at Nu Nu before continuing. 'While you're living in Myanmar, you even have a Myanmar auntie.'

'When she first came, she treated me like her boss. I called her Obasan, but I didn't like her calling me "*Sayamagyi*", so I told her to just call me by my name. Now, she calls me *Ma* Yu. Isn't this Myanmar name nice? Sometimes she even calls me May Min Gyi Ma Lay,' Yumisan said.

Nu Nu and Daw Khin Win Mu appreciated Yumisan's charming demeanour and manner of speaking, along with her gentle and polite nature, and they all laughed together happily.

'The Shwedagon Pagoda painting is really impressive. Where did you get it? Who painted it?' Daw Khin Win Mu admired the decoration in the living room, especially the large painting of the Buddha at the top of the room.

'I painted it. I went to the pagoda every day with Obasan and painted it. It was finished not long ago.'

'Oh, Sayama, your painting is excellent,' Daw Khin Win Mu said, standing up to get a closer look at the painting. Nu Nu also stood up to admire it. Nu Nu felt a growing respect for Yumisan. She admired the fact that, among the Japanese people—especially among Japanese women—there were many accomplished women, exemplary and worthy of respect, who were well-versed and proficient in the various fields of women's arts.

'There are many things to paint while I am in Myanmar. I'll go to Bagan and Mandalay. I'm very interested in Myanmar's arts,' Yumisan said.

Nu Nu, who was studying history, reflected on herself. She wondered if she had as much interest and appreciation for her own country's heritage as Yumisan did. She questioned whether she valued and understood her own culture and history to the same extent. Her initially carefree and light-hearted spirit was unsettled when she met Yumisan, causing her to reflect and find herself somewhat disappointed in herself. She realized that she must visit Bagan, a place she had never been to, to truly understand its significance.

When Ma Khin Win Mu and Nu Nu left, Yumisan sat quietly in the living room. Her face showed signs of deep contemplation, her brows furrowed, and her heart pounding with thoughts. However, her expression soon changed to a cheerful smile.

Thinking about her trip to Bago, Yumisan pondered how she would go about gathering information about her younger brother. She wondered how she would act if she met him. These thoughts often intruded into her mind, considering whether she would cry with joy when she revealed that she was his sister or if she would be hurt if he reacted negatively.

Even though they did not share the same mother, they had the same father. As his sister, she had always cared for him. She wondered if he would feel the same affection and significance upon meeting her.

Yumisan pondered deeply about her younger brother. Regardless of her feelings, he would always be her brother, sharing the same father. As she thought about the stepmother who came between them, she felt that the stepmother, who wasn't related to her by blood, was just an outsider.

Has my younger brother already started a family? Is he working? These thoughts occupied her mind until dusk, yet she continued to sit and ponder in the living room.

'Would you like to take a bath, Ma Yu?' Daw Aung May called out from afar, observing Yumisan sitting alone in the living room, deep in silent contemplation.

Upon hearing Daw Aung May's voice, Yumisan turned to look at her. At that moment, she was momentarily startled, feeling as if she had seen her younger brother's mother, Ma Htway Htway, in Daw Aung May. She wondered if Ma Htway Htway would be of the same age as Daw Aung May as she continued to gaze at her.

Noticing that Yumisan's gaze was different from usual, Daw Aung May asked, 'Ma Yu, what have you been thinking about for so long?'

'Let me ask you, Obasan. In Myanmar, when siblings have the same father but different mothers, do they love each other as much as those who share the same mother and father? I want to know,' Yumisan replied.

Daw Aung May nodded thoughtfully and smiled as she listened.

'In Myanmar, it's like this, Ma Yu. The love between siblings who share the same mother and father is different from the love between those who share the same father but have different mothers. It's not quite the same because the blood ties are different. But it's not something that can be generalized just like that,' she explained. 'The number of siblings also makes a difference. If there are only two siblings, whether sisters or brother and sister, they love each other like siblings born of the same mother and father. How is it in Japan?'

Yumisan replied enthusiastically in her soft voice. 'In Japan, children born from a second marriage after a parent's death are loved by their half-siblings as if they were full siblings, Obasan,' Yumisan explained.

'In Myanmar, it's similar to Japan, Ma Yu. When children are born from a second marriage after the death of a parent, they are regarded and loved as true siblings. However, if children are born from a second wife while the first wife is still alive, even if they share the same father, the love and affection can be more distant,' Daw Aung May elaborated.

Yumisan, with a pleased smile and bright eyes, asked, 'For example, if Obasan's mother passed away and Obasan's father remarried and had more children, wouldn't you love those children?'

'If they are born after my mother has passed away, of course, they would be loved, Ma Yu. Suppose I am the only daughter and the second marriage results in a son, we would become brother and sister, and we would love each other more as siblings,' Daw Aung May responded.

Daw Aung May's response, like oil seeping into cotton, filled Yumisan's entire being with a deep sense of contentment.

'Obasan, between a brother and sister, does the brother love the sister more, or does the sister love the brother more? Please tell me,' Yumisan asked, eagerly leaning forward and gripping Daw Aung May's shoulders to emphasize her curiosity.

Daw Aung May, finding Yumisan's earnest questioning endearing and childlike, answered gently, 'Isn't the sister older than the brother? Since she's older, she's like a mother. The sister is supposed to love the brother more, Ma Yu.'

Yumisan, feeling both her mind and heart comforted by this answer, exclaimed, 'That's right . . . that's right.' Then she continued, 'There are many similarities in traditions between Japanese and Myanmar people from the East. In Japan, an elder brother takes the father's place, and an elder sister takes the mother's place. It's very similar in both Japan and Myanmar.'

Daw Aung May did not find today's series of questions from Yumisan extraordinary. Every day, Yumisan inquired about different aspects of Myanmar's culture and customs. Daw Aung May always took care to explain the meanings clearly to Yumisan.

Eastern cultures that follow Buddhism tend to have similar traditions and customs. Then Daw Aung May asked, 'Ma Yu, do you love your father . . . or your mother more?'

'My mother passed away right after giving birth to me. I don't have a mother. I only love my father. What about you, Obasan?'

Daw Aung May chuckled and then, assuming a serious look, replied, 'Oh, dear little May Min

Gyi Ma, it's time to take a bath. It's already seven o'clock.'

As usual, Daw Aung May, with her disciplined manner, instructed Yumisan about the time and schedule, and Yumisan complied respectfully.

In truth, Daw Aung May was not just a housekeeper for Yumisan. She could be considered Yumisan's aunt. More accurately, she was like a guardian who raised and looked after a child, much like a nanny.

3

The month of Tazaungmone had arrived. Early in the morning, the main asphalt road was dampened with fog and dewdrops. The northern wind, whispering through the thin layer of fog, brought a refreshing coolness. As Yumisan looked into the distance from the moving car, she saw the horizon shaded by clusters of trees. Soon, the sun emerged through the canopy of the oak trees, piercing through and illuminating the road.

As Yumisan travelled towards Bago, she experienced a profound sense of peace and joy, unlike anything she had felt before. Her thoughts drifted like clouds across the sky, mingling with the floating mist, continuously wandering. Amid those thoughts, she felt a profound sense of anticipation. Yumisan had come to meet her stepmother and younger brother, whom she had never seen before. Despite having never met them, she felt an extraordinary sense of going to her own family, her own place, and her own home.

She became accustomed to the sights of the fields bathed in sunlight, the occasional tall tree here and there, the frequent small bridges over canals, and the pagodas whitewashed with lime at the village entrances as she travelled.

Nu Nu sat silently next to Yumisan, perhaps lost in thought, imagining herself taking a foreigner to her home. She didn't talk much, as Daw Khin Win Mu couldn't accompany them on this trip due to an urgent matter.

As the car sped along the straight asphalt road past Inntakaw, Yumisan whispered to herself, '*Little brother, your sister has come. I brought your father's photo for you. We're almost there, little brother.*'

Just as she saw the grand Shwemawdaw Pagoda in the distance, slicing through the horizon, Nu Nu finally broke the silence.

'We're almost in Bago,' Nu Nu said. Yumisan's heart swelled with anticipation.

'In Yangon, it's Shwedagon, in Bago, it's Shwemawdaw—both are historically significant and revered pagodas, Sayama,' Nu Nu explained, announcing the name of each village they passed and marking the mileposts. She could sense when

Yumisan wanted to talk and when she wanted to follow her own thoughts and imagination.

As they entered Bago, Yumisan read the large sign saying 'Welcome'. Soon, the grand Shwemawdaw Pagoda, glowing golden, came into view. Mimicking Nu Nu, Yumisan placed her hands together on her forehead in reverence.

She understood that this gesture from the car was a form of worship and prayer. After entering Bago city and crossing the large bridge, they turned off onto a side road. They navigated past parked cars and horse-drawn carts, driving carefully.

They stopped in front of a two-storey house with a fenced yard. Nu Nu directed the driver to enter the yard. Nu Nu's father, U Thaung, and mother, Daw Hla Shwe, warmly welcomed them at the entrance. Because Nu Nu had informed them in advance, the house was clean and well-prepared, with a variety of Myanmar's snacks and food.

Yumisan respectfully bowed and greeted them. Daw Hla Shwe, seeing Yumisan's sweet smile, couldn't help but think to herself how endearing she was.

'She can speak Burmese well, father,' Nu Nu said, introducing Yumisan to her parents.

'When we got Nu Nu's letter saying you were coming, our whole family was delighted. Please consider us as your close friends,' U Thaung said warmly, making Yumisan feel at ease despite the long journey. She repeatedly expressed her gratitude both verbally and through her demeanour.

They then led Yumisan to the living room.

'Please sit down, Sayama. We'll go to Phayalay village after having some coffee,' Nu Nu said.

As Yumisan was about to sit on a chair, her eyes were drawn to two objects in the corner of the living room. Pointing with her finger, she asked Nu Nu, 'What are those called?'

'They're called "*patala*" and "*saung*", Sayama,' Nu Nu replied.

Yumisan went to inspect the bamboo patala (xylophone) and the large saung (harp) decorated with gold leaf.

'I've seen a saung before. I've watched a Myanmar saung performance in Japan, but I've never seen one up close,' Yumisan said, gently touching the strings of the saung with her finger. Nu Nu, standing nearby, demonstrated how to play the patala.

'Can you play it, Nu Nu?'

'I'm learning to play it, Sayama,' Nu Nu replied.

With her appreciation for art and music, Yumisan felt a growing desire to hear the music that these instruments could produce.

'I also have a passion for music. I can play the piano. But I haven't heard this sound before. Will you play a little bit?'

Nu Nu expertly played the patala. As Yumisan listened, she was captivated by the gentle and soothing sounds of Myanmar music, allowing herself to be completely absorbed and momentarily forget all other matters.

'That's really beautiful. I want to learn to play it. Do you think I can play it if I learn?'

Nu Nu's family, who had gathered around, were fascinated by the Japanese girl speaking Burmese. They watched and listened with curiosity and admiration.

'If you hire a teacher in Yangon, you should be able to learn it, Sayama. If you already play the piano, this should be easy for you. With dedicated learning, you could master it within a year,' U Thaung offered his suggestion in a friendly manner.

That morning, Nu Nu's family treated their guest to coffee, plain tea, and a variety of Myanmar snacks. U Thaung mentioned that he had a student in Phayalay village, who could find Ma Htway Htway, the stepmother she wanted to meet. Yumisan was not only filled with satisfaction at this assurance but also delighted in tasting the Myanmar snacks she had never had before. The family urged her to try one snack after another, making the tea session lively and enjoyable. After breakfast, they set off to Phayalay village by car.

The car bounced along the dusty road filled with potholes. As the sun rose higher, its heat bore down intensely on Yumisan. Along the way, they passed several villages. (The small houses, and huts on both sides of the road revealed the impoverished state of the village.) They arrived at Phayalay village just before 10 a.m. U Thaung had the car stop by the roadside. Everyone got out of the car and walked down the cart track from the paved road. In front of a broken-down bamboo fence, U Thaung moved aside a bamboo pole and said, 'Please enter, Sayama,' as he led Yumisan inside.

'Phoe Thike,' U Thaung called out from the gate. A man around forty years old, shirtless, with a sarong tied at the waist, and a shawl covering the head, appeared at the entrance.

'Oh . . . *Saya*. Please, come in.'

Phoe Thike looked with surprise at Yumisan, who was following Nu Nu. Seeing her in a blue skirt, a white sports shirt, and sunglasses, he thought she might be Chinese.

The small house was old, supported by three poles with a zinc roof, wooden walls, and a floor. In front of the house, gourds, squash, and various greens were piled up, and a scale hung from a nail. An elderly woman sat nearby. The bamboo floorboards were cracked, and there were patches of mould and signs of wear. Like the others, Yumisan removed her shoes before stepping inside. The old woman stood up and laid out a woven mat. Yumisan knelt and sat on the mat with a straight posture.

Ko Phoe Thike suddenly became flustered and unsure of what to do. While attempting to sit, he said, 'Saya, you should have informed us beforehand if you were coming.'

The elderly woman seemed unfamiliar with the guests. Ko Phoe Thike explained, 'She is the daughter of my teacher named Nu Nu.' Then, he glanced back at Yumisan with some hesitation.

'She's a Japanese teacher from Yangon. We're here because she has something to inquire about in this village,' Nu Nu cut in.

'Ah, I see,' Ko Phoe Thike said, finally managing to sit down on the floor.

Yumisan looked around, contemplating the environment. She wondered what the house and the area were like when her father came to this village for his wedding. Nostalgia and longing for her father swept over her.

'This is how it is, Phoe Thike. This teacher wants to meet the daughter of the village head from this village during the Japanese era, so we brought her here.'

The old woman spoke before Ko Phoe Thike could respond. 'During the Japanese era? That was a long time ago, over twenty years. There are no old folks left in this village, only new residents. Even I've only been here for five years.'

'Mother, why don't you ask U San Aye? This old man is a long-time resident of this village,' Ko Phoe Thike suggested more confidently.

Yumisan felt a moment of relief at Ko Phoe Thike's suggestion after being discouraged by his mother's words.

'Where does the old man live? Should we go get him?' U Thaung asked energetically.

'The old man is seventy years old. He can't walk well. He lives in a hut at the edge of the village,' replied the old woman.

'What does this young lady want to meet the daughter of the village head for?' the old woman asked with a trembling voice.

'They say that that woman married a Japanese man during the Japanese era. The Japanese husband of that woman met this teacher and asked her to come and look for her,' Nu Nu explained to the old woman.

Yumisan, who had been silent the entire time, spoke to Nu Nu, 'Shouldn't we go to the old man's house?'

'Yes, Sayama. We'll go. Let's go, Phoe Thike,' U Thaung said, standing up first. Nu Nu, feeling a bit embarrassed to show the Japanese teacher the dirty and miserable life of the villagers, reluctantly stood up.

They walked through the narrow, winding paths between the huts and houses, heading towards the back path. Yumisan walked briskly, ignoring the dust, the smell of pig and cow dung, and the unpleasant environment, as if nothing bothered her.

Women from the huts along the path peeked out, carrying their children, to catch a glimpse of Yumisan and her group.

At the edge of the village, they found a small hut next to a cattle pen. Phoe Thike led the way up to the hut.

'Hi, Ah Ba,' he called.

Outside the hut, there was a worn mat and a small stool. On the stool sat a clay pot. From the inner room, along with the sound of coughing, emerged an old man, who looked quite alarming. His body was emaciated, with sunken cheeks and skin tightly stretched over his bones. His elbows and knees were covered in sores, making it a pitiable sight.

Apart from Phoe Thike, no one else had climbed up to the hut; the rest stood gathered in front.

'Phoe Thike . . . who are those people?' the old man asked, shielding his eyes with his hand as he looked towards the front of the hut.

'How are you, Ah Ba? How are your grandchildren?' Phoe Thike inquired.

'Today is the first day my swelling has subsided a little, so I could get up. They're tending to cattle. Who are these people?' the old man replied, shielding his eyes again and peering out.

'Please come up, *Sayagyi*. These are guests from Yangon who have some questions for you, Ah Ba,' Phoe Thike said, inviting U Thaung and the others to come up to the hut.

'Hey,' the old man said as he steadied himself on the bamboo post of the hut to sit down. Phoe Thike assisted him, helping him to sit. The old man squinted at the visitors on the hut, looking amazed.

Yumisan worried that the creaking bamboo floor might give way under her as she sat down.

'What brings guests from Yangon to see me?' the old man asked.

'They came to ask if you know about the headman of this village during the Japanese era,' Phoe Thike began, turning to U Thaung and his group. 'What was his name?'

'I don't know his name, but I know his daughter's name,' Yumisan interjected.

'The headman during the Japanese era was U Saing. Why do you ask?' the old man turned his squinting eyes towards Yumisan, straining to see her better.

'The matter is this, Ah Ba: This Japanese teacher wants to find the headman from the Japanese era in this village. His daughter married a Japanese man during that time, and she wants to find her in this village,' Phoe Thike explained.

'Oh . . . oh . . . yes, U Saing's daughter . . . Htway Htway,' the old man muttered, recalling the name with a sense of nostalgia.

'Yes, that's right . . . that's right,' he continued.

Before Yumisan could reveal the name Ma Htway Htway to the old man, he had already mentioned it, making her immensely relieved.

'Where are they, Ah Ba? Are they still living in this village?' U Thaung asked eagerly.

Seeing Yumisan's joyful expression, Nu Nu also felt encouraged in her role as a helper. The old man looked intently at Yumisan, his lips quivering.

'This girl is Japanese?' he asked.

'Yes, she is.'

'Ah . . . U Saing and his family are all dead. They're not here any more.'

'And . . . Ma Htway Htway?' U Thaung inquired further.

Yumisan's heart pounded at the mention, and she held her breath, anxiously awaiting the old man's answer.

'Htway Htway, U Saing's daughter, is also gone. Near the end of the war, she returned to Bago and on the way to Yangon, she got caught in a bombing. However, her son was left behind with the village head here.'

'Is the child still alive? Is he here now? Where can we find him?' Yumisan asked, her eyes bright with anticipation, her voice trembling with urgency as she struggled to keep from losing composure.

As the old man couldn't clearly catch Yumisan's words, U Thaung repeated the question for him.

'The child is not here now. During the Japanese occupation, the village was destroyed, and the headman fled to Kadote village, taking the child with him. After the war, the headman died there, and his brother-in-law, Htun Maung, took the child to the Kyaik Sakaw Monastery.'

'What is the child's name? Would he still be at that monastery now?'

'He was sent there when he was very young. I don't know if he is still there now. The child is called "Japan". Everyone in the village calls him "Japan", so he doesn't have a Burmese name.'

The old man paused, reminiscing about the past before continuing.

'Though U Saing was originally from this village, he spent much of his time in Bago, where he settled with his family. Htway Htway lived there and attended an English school. During the Japanese occupation, she worked as an assistant nurse at a hospital, where she met the boy's father, a Japanese military officer. They got married here in the village. I remember it well. Sugar was scarce back then, and the whole village celebrated with coffee. I attended the wedding too. Later, before the Japanese left, Htway Htway brought her son, about ten months old, named Japan, to the village to stay with her father. When the Japanese left, Htway Htway went to Yangon. Unfortunately, she died in a bombing there.'

Yumisan remained silent the entire time, pretending as if she learned about the child from the old man without asking anyone.

Feeling confident that this child was indeed her father's son, Yumisan became determined to find him immediately. Her desire to meet her brother grew stronger with each passing moment.

'Is Kyaik Sakaw village far from here?' Yumisan asked U Thaung.

'It's not far from this village. We can reach it in about an hour. Would you like to go? If you want, I can take you there,' he replied.

'Father, let's take her there right away,' Nu Nu suggested.

Yumisan felt immense gratitude towards the old man and wondered if he had been waiting his whole life just to share this information with her.

Her appreciation and affection for him deepened. She took out 50 kyats from her bag and handed it to Ko Phoe Thike, expressing her thanks and wishing the old man good health.

'Here, Ah Ba. The lady is donating 50 kyats for you for your medical expenses. Here, take it,' Ko Phoe Thike said.

The old man's weary eyes brightened. With all his remaining strength, he spoke loudly enough for everyone to hear, 'How generous . . . Phoe Thike, 50 kyats is a lot! Thank you . . . thank you. May you be healthy, wealthy, and may all your wishes come true.'

Yumisan and her companions then set off from Phayalay village to Kyaik Sakaw village.

Before reaching Kyaik Sakaw village, they stopped at Pyin Pone Gyi village to buy packets of noodles. Because it was almost time for lunch in Bago, Yumisan had to suppress her impatience and wait while they shopped.

They arrived at Kyaik Sakaw village and stopped the car in front of an ancient, ruined pagoda on a small tar road. U Thaung got out of the car and looked around before getting back in and directing the car to turn off the main asphalt road and onto a cart path. The car then climbed a hillock towards the pagoda and stopped in front of a monastery.

Having no acquaintances in Kyaik Sakaw village, they had headed straight for the pagoda where two old monasteries were located—one to the south and one to the north. Unsure of which one to go to, they were momentarily confused.

'Please wait here for a moment,' U Thaung said as he got out of the car and walked towards the southern monastery. He encountered a monk around the pagoda and asked him some questions before returning to the car.

Yumisan was anxiously waiting to hear what U Thaung would say. Since U Thaung had gotten out of the car, she had been restless and unable to sit still.

'The abbot of the monastery over there has gone to town and isn't available. But the abbot of this monastery has just recently returned. We'll inquire with him. All right, let's get out.'

Under the blazing sun, Yumisan walked barefoot on the broken brick path, with the heat from above and the sharp stones below, causing her to hop and skip along uncomfortably. The heat from above and the sharpness below made Nu Nu shout from behind, 'Sayama, run, run!' Unable to endure the heat any longer, Yumisan ran towards the monastery steps.

It was noon, and the large monastery, shaded by bamboo groves, was eerily silent, as if no one was there. The large, sturdy wooden monastery was surrounded by other small structures.

Yumisan had never been to a Burmese monastery before. Being in an unfamiliar place made her feel as if she had entered a new world and had become a stranger to herself. As they entered the monastery, they saw a magnificent Buddha statue on an altar at the end of the main hall. The floors gleamed, having been polished many times.

On one side of the main hall, there was a room. In front of the room, reed mats were spread out. Along the walls of the room, there was a large row of bookshelves filled with Buddhist scriptures.

Everyone stood at the top of the stairs, hesitating whether to call out or not before climbing up to the monastery. They heard movement from inside the room and waited. Soon, a monk about seventy years old appeared at the door, holding the cloth curtain. He looked healthy and robust, with a tall stature, and was wearing a pair of plastic-framed glasses. His appearance was dignified, gentle, and calm. After glancing at the group, he slowly walked towards the mat.

Yumisan, like U Thaung and Nu Nu, quietly climbed up to the monastery, making sure not to make any noise. They bowed three times in a kneeling position, Yumisan following their lead.

She remained silent, watching the surroundings and observing the customs of the Burmese monastery and culture.

'Where are you all from?' the monk asked as he sat on the reed mat, looking at them with a calm demeanour.

'*Ahshin* Phaya, we are from Bago, from the village of Phayalay. We have come here because we heard that the child of U Saing's daughter, Ma Htway Htway, and a Japanese officer, used to stay at this monastery. Ma Htway Htway's husband asked this Japanese teacher here to find out if Ma Htway Htway is still in Phayalay village, so we came to search for her.'

The monk, who had remained composed and serene, suddenly tensed his shoulders slightly. He fixed his gaze on Yumisan, attentively listening to U Thaung's explanation.

When U Thaung finished speaking, the monk seemed to regain his composure, setting aside his initial surprise. He then spoke, his voice calm but filled with astonishment.

'Amazing . . . truly amazing,' the monk remarked, nodding his head slightly.

'These events from over twenty years ago, I thought they had faded and disappeared. Hearing about them now even makes me tremble. Does this Japanese teacher here speak Burmese?'

'Yes, Ahshin Phaya, she does,' U Thaung replied, bowing his head.

'Really? I see. It's true that one's lineage cannot be easily erased; it persists through generations,' the monk continued, deep in thought.

Yumisan listened intently to every word the monk spoke, feeling both anxious and hopeful as the monk had yet to mention anything specific about her younger brother.

'When Tun Maung brought Japan, Ma Htway's son, here, the boy was already ten years old and hadn't been initiated as a novice monk yet. He knew his father was Japanese because people talked about it. However, he didn't seem to understand much about his father's life or background. Let's say the boy was hurt and ashamed that his father was Japanese. Whenever someone mentioned his father being Japanese, it troubled him greatly.'

The monk's words caused Yumisan a deep, indescribable pain in her heart.

'He had never seen his Japanese father and didn't know anything about him, yet he harboured a hatred for him. In the Burmese village, he felt shame because his father was Japanese. He was affected by the cruel legacy of the war in a pitiful way.'

Yumisan bowed her head in sorrow. The monk fell silent, and everyone else remained quiet as well, creating an eerie stillness in the air.

'Where is he now?' Yumisan asked, raising her head and bowing slightly. Her voice broke the silence, bringing life back to the surroundings.

'All right. I'll tell you. I'll tell you,' the monk replied, clearing his throat before continuing.

'About a year after Japan's arriving here, he met Maung Thet Lwin, a tutor in Yangon University and the son of a devotee of this monastery. He had a passion for painting and would come to this village during holidays to paint peacefully. When he saw Japan here, he took pity on him. The boy didn't get along with anyone in this monastery. Whenever his Japanese father was mentioned, it caused trouble. Everyone knew he was ashamed of his Japanese heritage, and that's how the conflicts started. One day, after a fight, the boy told Maung Thet Lwin he didn't want to stay at this monastery any more, so Maung Thet Lwin took pity on him and took him away.'

'Ahshin Phaya, so are the boy and the teacher in Yangon now?' U Thaung asked.

'When Maung Thet Lwin took the boy, he was working at Mandalay University as a tutor. So, he said he would leave the boy in Yangon to attend a school there. Shortly after they left, my elder brother passed away in Pakokku, and I went there to take over the monastery. I haven't been back long. I was told that Maung Thet Lwin and Japan came here once while I was away. I haven't seen them since. I heard the news that Maung Thet Lwin transferred from Mandalay to Yangon University.'

Yumisan felt immense gratitude towards the teacher who had saved her younger brother. She thought to herself, *Thank you so much, teacher*. She felt content and happy, thinking that if the teacher had taken him, he would have received a good education.

'Father . . . if it's U Thet Lwin, an assistant lecturer at the University's Myanmar Department, I wonder if it could be him. Yes, it must be him,' said Nu Nu enthusiastically after hearing the monk's words.

Yumisan couldn't hide her joy and said, 'Oh dear . . . I'm so happy!'

'Where in Japan did Japan's father live? What is he doing now?' the monk asked, inquiring about the origins of Japan's father.

Since she had never spoken extensively with a Burmese monk before, Yumisan carefully answered to avoid making mistakes. She spoke slowly and clearly, managing her intonation carefully.

'His father is no longer alive. He passed away before I came to Myanmar.'

'Hmm . . . but didn't he say he had a son before he died?' the monk asked pointedly. Yumisan felt pressured to answer in front of everyone. Her emotions, which she had kept hidden, were now difficult to conceal.

'He did say he had a son and asked me to find Ma Htway Htway.'

'Did he leave any message for the mother and son before he died?'

'He asked me to take care of Ma Htway Htway and her son when I arrived in Myanmar. I also brought some clothes for Ma Htway Htway.'

Since Yumisan had come as someone to investigate and find out about her, she spoke in line with her stated role.

'By inquiring at Yangon University, you will find out. Whether Japan is with Maung Thet Lwin now, I don't know. If you inquire about Maung Thet Lwin, you'll know.'

'Yes, Ahshin Phaya, my daughter can find them out easily,' U Thaung replied.

Following U Thaung's example, Yumisan bowed respectfully to the monk and said, 'I am especially grateful, Ahshin Phaya.'

The monk, pleased with the Japanese girl's politeness, composure, and quick learning, smiled and said, '*Sadhu* . . . Sadhu.'

After 3 p.m., they left Kyaik Sakaw Monastery. They opened the noodle packs they had brought along and had their breakfast in the car. The sun was low on the horizon as they entered Bago, and Yumisan dropped off U Thaung and Nu Nu at home, thanking the entire family once again before heading back to Yangon.

The return trip from Bago was markedly different from the journey to Bago. The trip from Yangon felt like a dream for her. The return trip, however, felt like watching an engaging movie in which she herself was an active participant.

She thought in amazement of the old man from Phayalay village, who was waiting to tell her about her younger brother without passing away. She felt immense gratitude towards the monk who had been so helpful to her. While searching for her younger brother in Myanmar, she concealed her identity as his sister and embarked on the journey in secret. As her adventures unfolded, they felt like part of a story, and she was surprised by what she discovered.

Thinking about the compassion and kindness of the teacher who had saved her solitary, parentless brother—who had to live in shame among the Burmese people—she developed a deep respect for him even before meeting him. The goal of meeting her brother was now within reach, and nothing seemed to be an obstacle any more. On the return journey, Yumisan felt light-hearted and full of joyful energy.

'Drive faster, Sarmi,' she said.

The car, under the owner's command, sped along at fifty miles per hour.

4

By Saturday afternoon, Yumisan arrived at the office of the assistant lecturer at Yangon University's Department of Burmese. Following Yumisan's instructions, Nu Nu had not yet informed U Thet Lwin about the real reason for their meeting. Instead, she had requested an appointment for a Japanese female lecturer to inquire about Burmese language teaching matters.

Assistant lecturer U Thet Lwin, who taught Burmese to foreign students at the university, assumed that the Japanese teacher was coming for academic purposes. Upon seeing Yumisan enter the office, U Thet Lwin smiled warmly. His smile brought a sense of peace to Yumisan.

'Please sit down, Sayama. Nu Nu has informed me beforehand that you can speak Burmese well. How can I assist you today?'

U Thet Lwin was extremely friendly. His warm smile and amiable demeanour were evident. Yumisan estimated he must be around forty years old. He had a strong build and dressed neatly, giving the impression of someone willing to help. Smiling with an endearing smile, Yumisan respectfully bowed in the Japanese manner and then sat down on the chair.

'Thank you for allowing me to meet you, Saya. Let me first express my gratitude upon meeting you. Thank you very much.'

The sound of Yumisan speaking Burmese struck U Thet Lwin as quite extraordinary. Her voice, with its unique accent, resonated in his ears like a musical note, lingering in his mind. Intrigued by her voice, he began to observe her closely.

Among the various forms of beauty characteristic of East Asian women, he perceived her beauty as uniquely striking. Imagining her in a traditional Japanese kimono rather than the silk gown she wore, he envisioned her appearance becoming even more graceful and elegant.

After expressing her initial words of gratitude, Yumisan smiled warmly. U Thet Lwin continued speaking, wanting to see her satisfied.

'How can I assist you, Sayama? Are you interested in enrolling in a Burmese language graduate course?'

'I studied Burmese in Japan for four years. While I'm here in Myanmar, I'd like to continue learning

Burmese if I have the time. However, my current visit is not related to the Burmese language. I am here for a personal matter.'

'What kind of matter is it, then? Do you want to write a book about Myanmar?'

U Thet Lwin smiled as he spoke. Yumisan, trying to remain calm, was about to explain her reason for visiting but responded to his question first.

'I've always wanted to write a book about Myanmar's culture. But at the moment, I'm not free to do so, Saya. The reason I wanted to meet you is to inquire about the Japanese child you took from Kyaik Sakaw Monastery. Do you know where he is now, Saya?'

Yumisan's voice was gentle as she asked her question directly. U Thet Lwin was momentarily taken aback, feeling as if he had been struck by lightning, his entire body tensing up. With wide eyes, he looked back at Yumisan. Despite his initial shock, he regained his composure and responded.

'I'm surprised, Sayama. How did you find out that I took Japan from Kyaik Sakaw Monastery?' U Thet Lwin stared intently at Yumisan.

'When I inquired at Phayalay village, the old man there directed me to the Kyaik Sakaw Monastery. The monk there told me that if I asked you, I would find out more.'

'Wait, Sayama . . . wait. What's your connection with this child?' U Thet Lwin interrupted Yumisan, urgently asking his question.

'This child is my younger brother. We have the same father, Saya.'

Yumisan revealed the 'key' secret she had kept hidden in her heart, feeling a great sense of relief and lightness.

'Oh . . . so he is your younger brother, Sayama?' U Thet Lwin could barely continue speaking, his lips trembling.

Japan was brought from the monastery when he was ten years old. In the twelve years they had lived together, no information about Maung Maung's background had surfaced. Now, unexpectedly, Yumisan had come and unveiled it all, leaving U Thet Lwin greatly shaken and astonished.

Because Yumisan had disclosed that the boy was her brother, the words 'brother and sister' kept echoing in U Thet Lwin's ears. He tried to calm himself before he spoke.

'I'm surprised, Sayama. I'm also happy. When he came to the monastery, he was only ten years old. Now he is twenty-two. We call him Maung Maung.'

Yumisan repeated the name 'Maung Maung' and said, 'I'm so happy, Saya.'

'Is Maung Maung's father in Japan?'

'No, Saya, he has passed away. I didn't see him right after the war. He was imprisoned in Myanmar for three years as a war criminal, then sent to Singapore for two years before returning to Japan, where I met him again. When he came back, he was not well. He told me about my younger brother in Myanmar. He loved his son very much and often talked about him. He became discouraged, knowing his health wouldn't allow him to see his son again. My father's wife, a nurse named Ma Htway Htway, took the child to Phayalay village near Bago when he was ten months old, and my father never saw them again.'

'What is Maung Maung's father's name?'

'His name is Mr Yoshida, Saya. He was a Major in the army when he married Ma Htway Htway, and he was promoted to Lieutenant Colonel before the end of the war.'

'So, Maung Maung's father was still in Yangon prison after the war. Maung Maung didn't even know his father's name, but he had seen a photo of him when he was young.'

'Really, Saya? He has seen it?'

'Not just him, Sayama. I've seen that photo too.'

'I brought my father's photo with me, Saya. It was taken in Mingaladon and he sent it to me.'

Yumisan took a photo out of her bag and handed it to U Thet Lwin, who looked closely at it. It was indeed the same photo of Maung Maung's father that U Thet Lwin had seen and sketched at the monastery.

U Thet Lwin's face visibly paled as he looked at the photo.

'Yes, this is it, Sayama. He tore the photo when he was young because he was ashamed, so I kept it and even made a sketch.'

'Why did he throw it away, Saya? He knew it was his father's photo, didn't he? Why?'

Yumisan's questions came in rapid succession, and U Thet Lwin felt increasingly uneasy. He was hesitant to explain openly but felt compelled to speak.

'He knew it was his father's photo, but he tore it out of shame because the other students at the monastery teased him.'

'Oh . . .'

The soft, drawn-out sound of 'oh' lingered. After the sound faded, the blood drained from Yumisan's face, and her expression turned sorrowful. The grim cruelty of the past war was truly frightening. Yumisan thought about how she and her brother had each faced the aftermath of the war's horrors in their own ways, feeling like remnants left on the shore by the receding tide.

U Thet Lwin sighed and continued, his voice heavy with emotion.

'Maung Maung was so ashamed that his father was Japanese, and I felt so sorry for him that I took him in from the monastery.'

'Is Maung Maung still living with you?' Yumisan's voice was soft, her body cold.

'From the day I took him in, he's been with me, Sayama. I brought him to attend a school in Yangon, and now he's studying at the university. He sees me as his older brother, and he is like my younger brother.'

Yumisan looked at U Thet Lwin's face through teary eyes.

'Thank you, Saya. I've been grateful to you even before I met you. That's why, as soon as I saw you, I had to express my gratitude. I understand what would have happened to his life if you hadn't taken him in. Since the day I found out he was alive, I've been eager to meet him. I learned Burmese so I could come to Myanmar and find him. Please let me meet Maung Maung.'

U Thet Lwin took a deep breath.

'You will meet him, but I think it's best not to tell him immediately that you're his sister. Build a relationship first, and then gradually tell him. He still harbours resentment about his Japanese father.

When I took him in, I promised him I wouldn't tell anyone about his father's identity. To this day, I've kept that promise. Since he came to live with me, he's forgotten his past. I'm sorry to say this, but I think it's best to proceed slowly.'

U Thet Lwin really felt a deep sense of discomfort, almost unable to look Yumisan in the eye. Yumisan forced a faint smile, swallowing her sadness.

'I understand, Saya. It's better for him to learn that I'm his sister only after he's grown to like and trust me. I'll do my best to make that happen. To achieve this, I'll need to meet him often.'

'That can be arranged, Sayama. You can come to my house under that pretence that you're writing a book about Myanmar culture. That way, you'll get to see Maung Maung frequently.'

Yumisan's face, which had been weary, visibly brightened. Her emotions, previously swirling within her chest, were now surging.

'Your suggestion is great, Saya. When should I start coming? Please set a date for me. And give me your address.'

Seeing Yumisan's renewed energy, U Thet Lwin felt relieved. He wrote down his address on a piece of paper and arranged for her to come and meet Maung Maung at his house the following Saturday at 4 p.m.

As Yumisan left the room feeling lighter, U Thet Lwin remained with a heavy heart, his mind preoccupied with thoughts of Maung Maung. When he reached home, it was Maung Maung who opened the door for him.

Just as he typically did every evening after school, Maung Maung opened the door, clad in his karate uniform. Seeing Maung Maung in his karate uniform, U Thet Lwin felt a pang in his heart. Today, seeing Maung Maung in this outfit made U Thet Lwin see Maung Maung not just as a young man in karate attire, but as a Japanese boy, the brother of the Japanese lady, Yumisan. For the first time, he saw Maung Maung through a new perspective, as the Japanese child he truly was.

'Huh . . . *Ahkogyi*, you're back early. Are you feeling unwell?' Maung Maung asked, noticing U Thet Lwin's pale face.

Seeing Maung Maung's concern, U Thet Lwin found it hard to keep up the pretence. He wanted to tell him, '*Your sister from Japan has arrived*,' but the words were stuck in his throat. He forced a smile and said, 'I'm just feeling a bit feverish and weak, so I came back early.'

U Thet Lwin then struggled to take off his top shirt, and Maung Maung helped him, hanging the shirt up. He followed his older brother into the bedroom.

'Why don't you lie down for a while, Ahkogyi? Ko Mya Phay just went out to the market. I'll boil some betel leaves for you to help you sweat it out,' Maung Maung suggested.

After helping U Thet Lwin lie down on the bed and covering him with a blanket, Maung Maung left the room. U Thet Lwin glanced sideways at Maung Maung's face, then closed his eyes and let out a deep sigh.

Maung Maung, with his short stature, brown skin, prominent nose, and well-defined thin lips, had a pure, childlike smile that lit up his face and made his eyes sparkle when he smiled. U Thet Lwin's heart swelled with emotion, almost making him feel feverish, and he let out a deep sigh.

Soon, Maung Maung returned to the room after making a betel leaf concoction in the kitchen.

'Ahkogyi, drink this while it's hot.'

Though U Thet Lwin had no desire to drink the concoction, he closed his eyes and obediently sipped the betel leaf concoction that Maung Maung blew on and handed to him.

'Ahkogyi, I got the military reserve uniform today. I'll show it to you soon.'

Maung Maung spoke excitedly while helping U Thet Lwin drink the concoction. U Thet Lwin couldn't help but notice Maung Maung's determined and gentle manner as he blew on the concoction.

He realized the bond between him and Maung Maung was so strong that no one could break it.

Throughout his life, Maung Maung had depended on him and loved him deeply, and U Thet Lwin had reciprocated that love and care. Knowing that there would now be another person who cared for Maung Maung, he felt both joy and relief for Maung Maung. He wished the time would come soon when he could tell Maung Maung that he was no longer alone in this world.

Maung Maung helped U Thet Lwin drink the betel leaf concoction, urging him to lie down and covering him with a blanket. He touched U Thet Lwin's forehead, saying, 'You don't have a fever, Ahkogyi.' Then, smiling, he walked over to the wardrobe and opened it. He took out his military uniform, removed his karate outfit, and started putting on the uniform.

U Thet Lwin watched Maung Maung change clothes with a focused gaze. Maung Maung dressed in the military uniform and finally put on the military cap. 'Ahkogyi, look at me. Don't I look good in the uniform?' he said.

Seeing Maung Maung in the army uniform, U Thet Lwin felt a wave of emotion. The image of Maung Maung in the military outfit reminded him of the picture of Major Yoshida shown to him by Yumisan earlier in the day.

Maung Maung then performed a mock salute and laughed at his own actions. U Thet Lwin could only manage a faint smile in response to Maung Maung's cheerful demeanour.

'Our Captain instructor said that after four years in the reserve force, I can go straight to officer training school, Ahkogyi. When my four years are up, I want to go to officer training school. Should I go?'

'Why do you want to join the military, my brother? Don't you want to be a teacher like me?'

'I want to join to protect our country and people, Ahkogyi. If fascist invaders dare to come to Myanmar again, I'll fight them.'

The mention of 'fascists' by Maung Maung, implying the Japanese, caused U Thet Lwin's face to fall. Noticing this reaction, Maung Maung felt a pang of regret and anxiety, realizing he had unwittingly revealed a buried pain. His expression showed that he hadn't forgotten the trauma, even at his age. This realization made U Thet Lwin more anxious about the upcoming meeting with Yumisan.

U Thet Lwin now wanted Maung Maung's father, Colonel Yoshida, to see and hear Maung Maung in his soldier's attire. How would Colonel Yoshida react if he could witness this scene?

These thoughts were continually revolving in U Thet Lwin's mind. He did not sleep well that night. Burdened by heavy thoughts and feelings, he pondered deeply over the significant issues weighing on his mind. Staring into the darkness with wide eyes, he heard the snoring of Maung Maung, who was asleep on the other side of the bed. Maung Maung's past loomed vividly.

5

In the evening, as usual, the earth heated up, and the smell of the soil permeated the air. The rustling of the bamboo leaves around the monastery compound was loud and constant. The ancient, ruined Kyaik Sakaw Stupa stood on a hill, providing a clear view of the small railway station and tracks to the west. Ko Thet Lwin descended from the hill of the stupa, walking along the path towards the railway tracks. From the other side of the tracks, he saw a group of monastery boys emerging from the rear of the village. The two at the front were carrying a pot of food with a bamboo pole. A few paces behind them, three or four more were marching in step, chanting:

Sein Kyi, oh Sein Kyi,
wed without a clue, oh my,
master went back to Tokyo,
left her with a belly round.
Birthed a boy, small and short,

monastery's now his retreat,
wai . . . hey . . . hey.

After finishing the chant for the third time, the boy carrying the food pot suddenly placed it on the ground, removed the bamboo pole, and then sprinted back towards his friends.

'Hey . . . here he comes . . . the vile Japan is coming!'

The students were ready to punch the approaching Japan with clenched fists. As Japan reached the student nearest to him, the student hit Japan in the face. Despite being outnumbered four to one, Japan did not back down, landing heavy punches that left two boys' faces bruised. When two other boys surrounded and attacked him from behind, he retaliated, wrestling one to the ground and beating the boy severely before escaping. The boys who had been attacked dared not chase after him but hurled insults from a distance. *Hey Mu Tuu . . . hey shortie . . . hey wicked Japanese. Where is your Japanese father?*

Ko Thet Lwin witnessed this scene on his first day at the monastery, near the back gate. Japan's face was covered in bruises. Though he appeared stern, the deep sorrow stirring within was evident in his eyes. He walked past Ko Thet Lwin and descended the road, returning to the monastery near sunset.

Ko Thet Lwin, who had come to Kyaik Sakaw Monastery for his summer break, saw that fight as he descended the hill to relieve his fatigue after speaking with the abbot. He had often seen minor quarrels among the monastery boys, but this incident stayed with him. The old war song ('Than Gyat' or traditional folk verse) sung by the monastery boys echoed in his mind, fuelling his curiosity.

On his return, he found himself searching for Japan on the monastery grounds before heading to the dining hall of the monastery.

In the dining hall, he noticed Japan, sweat glistening on his forehead as he drank from a jug of water. When Japan saw Ko Thet Lwin, he looked up with a smile in his eyes, but then, feeling a bit embarrassed, quickly set the cup down and hurried down the back stairs.

At that moment, U Sa, the caretaker, was arranging tables for the dawn meal. Hearing Japan's hurried footsteps, he looked up and saw Ko Thet Lwin.

'Please, *Sayarlay*, have a seat,' he said, pulling out a small mat for Ko Thet Lwin to sit on.

'U Sa, is that boy who just drank water Burmese?' asked Ko Thet Lwin.

U Sa chuckled, revealing his toothless grin.

'He's Japanese, Sayarlay. Not entirely Burmese. His father was Japanese, and his mother Burmese.'

Ko Thet Lwin's curiosity deepened.

'How did he end up at this monastery?'

'He's not from this village, teacher. He's from Phayalay village. His mother is Burmese. During the Japanese era, she married a Japanese soldier. When the Japanese retreated, she was left with a kid,' explained U Sa, with a smirk on his face.

'Is he here because his mother brought him, U Sa?'

'Sayarlay, he no longer has a mother—she passed away. He has no siblings, and his uncle, burdened with a large family and living in poverty, couldn't care for him. That's why he was left here at the monastery.'

'Does he know his father was Japanese?'

'Of course, Sayarlay. But he's never seen a Japanese. His name is Japan, so everyone in the village teases him. He's quite a troublesome kid, always getting into fights. The moment he's provoked, he starts punching. Just like the stories about the Japanese soldiers during the war.'

U Sa continued to speak ill of Japan, criticizing and blaming him for everything. From that day, Ko Thet Lwin watched Japan more closely. He noticed that, besides the abbot, no one in the monastery cared for the boy. This lack of care and affection made Ko Thet Lwin feel a bit of compassion for him.

One afternoon, while the abbot was taking a nap, Ko Thet Lwin sat under the monastery building, drawing. Two young novice monks, surrounded by other monastery boys, were watching him closely.

Though Japan didn't come closer, he leaned against the monastery pillar, watching them from a distance.

'Hey, come here, kid,' Ko Thet Lwin called out to him.

Japan, blushing shyly, leaned against the monastery pillar, circled around it, and then turned his back towards Ko Thet Lwin's direction.

'Hey, Japan . . . he's calling you. Come here!' a novice called out.

Japan looked back but didn't join them. Instead, he ran up the monastery steps.

'This kid is wild, *Dagagyi*. He never comes near people. His father was a Japanese,' the novice monk said in a mocking tone. The monastery boys jeered at Japan, laughing as he ran up the steps.

As Ko Thet Lwin painted, he grew irritated by the commotion. He put down his brush, feeling a pain in his chest and his face flushing red. Glaring at the children around him, he scolded them fiercely.

'Don't talk like that. He has no parents. So what if his father was Japanese? Is that his fault? Is that something to be ashamed of? He has no fault, and there's nothing to be ashamed of. He's not wild. If anything, you all are the wild ones.'

As Ko Thet Lwin was sternly reprimanding them, the two novice monks shyly slipped away from his side. The other children, unable to face Ko Thet Lwin, either hung their heads or turned away, looking ashamed. They did not listen to his words until the end but instead, one by one, quietly slipped away.

Once everyone had left, Ko Thet Lwin picked up his brush and resumed his painting.

At that moment, muffled sounds of wrestling and struggling came from upstairs. Ko Thet Lwin tiptoed up to the school and peered into a room where the noise was coming from.

In the room, Japan was struggling with a novice monk over a photograph. Another novice and two boys were trying to pull Japan away to separate them.

'Let go . . . let go,' the novice monk muttered as he struggled to keep the photograph from Japan's grasp. Japan finally managed to snatch the photograph and tore it up.

'Hey . . . hey!'

Ko Thet Lwin entered the room. The boys, who had been scrambling to pick up the torn pieces of the photograph, froze and moved aside upon hearing his voice. Ko Thet Lwin picked up the two torn halves of the photograph and examined them.

'What's going on here? Tell me,' he demanded.

Japan remained tight-lipped, his face set in a hostile glare. His eyes flashed with anger, and his nose flared with each audible breath.

'He claimed his father wasn't Japanese, so I secretly took this photo from the abbot's chest to prove it to him. But he tore it up!' the novice exclaimed.

Ko Thet Lwin carefully looked at the joined pieces of the photograph. The image of a Japanese military officer in uniform etched itself permanently into his memory.

'Why did you tear up your father's photograph?' Ko Thet Lwin asked gently, looking at Japan with a concerned expression.

'That man isn't my father. They're showing me this picture just to get under my skin,' Japan retorted, his voice sharp and unwavering, eyes narrowing. Ko Thet Lwin felt a deep sense of pity for the boy, feeling his pain resonate within his own heart.

'Why wouldn't it be? The monk kept it; that's a genuine photo of your Japanese father. I took it out to show you because you said your father wasn't Japanese.'

Before the novice monk finished speaking, Japan angrily interrupted, 'It's not true! Don't believe it. That's not my father's photograph. They're just shaming me.'

Japan's words were met with derisive laughter from the novice monk and two monastery boys, and just as he moved to punch the novice monk, Ko Thet Lwin firmly restrained him by holding his arm.

'Don't hit him, my brother. Even if that is your father's photograph, so what? At least you have a father. It's not something to be ashamed of. Your father was a great military officer.'

Japan, trying to break free from Ko Thet Lwin's grip, said with a mix of anger and distress, 'My father isn't Japanese. My father is U Saing from Kadote village. He's dead now.'

'Hey . . . U Saing is your grandfather, not your father. Ha ha ha,' one of the boys teased.

'Who told you that U Saing is not my father?' Japan asked, clenching his small fist and biting his lower lip.

'U Sa the caretaker told me. U Saing is your grandfather. If you don't believe me, go ask the caretaker yourself.'

'Hey . . . hey . . . stop it. All of you, stop talking. Go away. Leave him alone,' Ko Thet Lwin ordered, driving the boys and the novice out of the room. Once they had left, he turned to look at Japan.

Japan's face was still tense as Ko Thet Lwin approached him.

'Keep this photo,' he said, offering it to the boy.

'I don't want it. Don't give it to me,' Japan replied curtly and left the room, his face flushed.

When the abbot woke from his rest and stepped outside, Ko Thet Lwin explained the earlier incident and showed him the torn photo of Japan's father.

'This is his father's photo. His uncle, Tun Maung, gave it to me when he brought the boy to the monastery. The novice must have seen it then.'

'Did you ever show it to him, Ahshin Phaya?' Ko Thet Lwin asked.

'I did, but he barely looked at it. Because everyone mocked him about his Japanese father, he felt ashamed. It's pitiful,' the abbot replied.

Ko Thet Lwin wanted to piece the torn photograph back together, so he asked the abbot for permission to keep it with him. He carefully placed the two pieces on paper and began sketching a copy. To keep the portrait of Japan's father hidden from others, he worked in a quiet, secluded spot. Anticipating that the original photograph would eventually wear and fade, he secretly made a copy, believing it would be wise to preserve it.

One day, Ko Thet Lwin went to a quiet, shady area at the edge of the village to finish his paintings and meticulously work on the duplicate of Japan's father's photo.

Under the golden sunlight, Ko Thet Lwin found himself admiring the swaying golden Ngu flowers in full bloom that he had drawn. As he took pride in his work, he suddenly heard the familiar sounds of buffalo boys singing a traditional folk verse ('Than Gyat') as they returned from the fields.

Sein Kyi, oh Sein Kyi,
wed without a clue, oh my,
master went back to Tokyo,
left her with a belly round.
Birthed a boy, small and short,
monastery's now his retreat.

Hearing this, Ko Thet Lwin realized that Japan must be nearby. Rising from the base of the tree, he looked towards the group of buffalo boys. He saw Japan swimming in the stream, trying to run out of the water. One boy approached and Japan punched him in the face. These buffalo boys were not as young as novice monks but much older, stronger boys, including caretaker U Sa's grandson, Tun Shwe.

Japan was outnumbered four to one. Seeing the distant scene of Japan being surrounded and beaten, Ko Thet Lwin's heart raced. He ran towards the fight, shouting as he ran, 'Hey, boys, stop it . . . stop it!'

The buffalo boys, upon seeing Ko Thet Lwin, dispersed. They ran away while shouting insults at Japan, pleased with their victory. Among the loudest was Tun Shwe's voice. Japan was left with a swollen, bruised face and blood trickling from his bitten lip. He showed no pain, nor did he shed any tears, gritting his teeth the whole time.

'Look, your mouth is bleeding. How long have you been swimming?' Ko Thet Lwin asked Japan as he approached him.

'Not long. They saw me and provoked me into a fight,' Japan replied.

'Alright, I don't want to talk about it any more. If I hadn't been here, you'd be in worse shape. Go wash the blood out of your mouth.'

Japan walked to the stream, scooping water with his hands to rinse out his mouth, which turned the water bright red.

Seeing Japan's suffering, Ko Thet Lwin felt deep compassion. Japan changed into dry clothes and prepared to return to the village.

'Come with me,' Ko Thet Lwin said, leading Japan to his painting spot. Quickly, he covered the unfinished portrait of Japan's father with another canvas to keep it hidden. He had Japan sit down, then he took a white handkerchief from his bag, exhaled warm breath into it, and gently pressed it against Japan's swollen eye. Japan, who had never experienced such an act before, felt deeply touched by this gesture. As he quietly endured it, a sense of calm and warmth filled his heart. Throughout his life, the only person who had ever shown him such tenderness was Ko Thet Lwin. So, he found himself taking unexpected comfort in the warmth of Ko Thet Lwin's hot breath against his swollen wound.

'Does it hurt, Japan?' Ko Thet Lwin asked.

'Not much now, Ahkogyi,' Japan replied.

'I can't imagine how much harder your life will be when I return.'

'I don't want to stay here any more, Ahkogyi.'

'If you leave, where will you go?' Ko Thet Lwin asked.

'I want to run away from this village. Everyone here mocks me, calling me the son of a Japanese. Even at the monastery, I'm always getting into fights. Tun Shwe provokes me, and when I fight back, *Bagyi* Sa punishes me with a broom. He only scolds me, never his grandson Tun Shwe, even though he starts it. He's taught everyone the "Sein Kyi" song, and I hate it; I can't stand hearing it any more. That's why I don't want to stay here.'

Ko Thet Lwin looked at Japan with silent, compassionate concern.

On the outside, Japan might appear to be a tough kid, but Ko Thet Lwin discerned that he was actually a good-hearted boy.

'How do you think you can run away at your age? If you really don't want to stay in this village, how about coming with me when I go back to the city?'

'Really?' Japan replied excitedly. His eyes gradually brightened, and his face lit up. Though he was overjoyed at the invitation, he was hesitant to commit, showing a mix of excitement and uncertainty.

'What's the matter? Are you coming or not?' Ko Thet Lwin asked.

'If I go with you and people find out I'm the son of a Japanese, it'll be so embarrassing. I'm really ashamed. I want to go somewhere no one knows I'm the son of a Japanese,' Japan responded, staring intently at Ko Thet Lwin, waiting for his reaction.

Touched, Ko Thet Lwin reassured him, 'Who would know you're the son of a Japanese if I don't tell anyone? If you don't want anyone to know, I'll keep it a secret. I'll tell them you're my younger brother. We'll even change your name. You won't be Japan any more. How about we call you Maung Maung? So, what do you think, little brother? Will you come with me?'

Japan moved closer to Ko Thet Lwin. With Ko Thet Lwin's voice full of compassion and kindness, Japan knelt beside him, lips trembling and tears streaming down his face. With tear-filled eyes, he said, 'If that's the case, I'll go with you, Ahkogyi. I'll be your little brother Maung Maung, and you'll be my elder brother. I'm no longer Japan.'

As Japan spoke, his voice quivered and he began to cry, unable to control his emotions. Tears poured down his cheeks as he sobbed uncontrollably. Ko Thet Lwin, feeling deeply moved, tightly gripped Japan's shoulders.

* * *

U Thet Lwin's eyes were fixed intently on the sleeping Maung Maung beside him, recalling how he brought the boy from Kyaik Sakaw village and raised him as his own younger brother. Maung Maung had forgotten his past and now relied on Ko Thet Lwin as if he were his true brother.

When he first brought Maung Maung from the village, his intention had been to enrol him in an orphanage for boys in Kamayut. However, since that day, Maung Maung had remained by his side, unwilling to be apart from him. No matter how hard he tried, he couldn't convince Maung Maung to stay at the orphanage. Fearing that the boy might run away if left alone, he ultimately took him to Mandalay, where he worked. In Mandalay, he had to enrol Maung Maung in a school. Throughout Maung Maung's life, U Thet Lwin acted as both a brother and a father, raising him to this point.

Now, unexpectedly, U Thet Lwin had to deal with the fact that Yumisan, his sister, had appeared. He had to make Maung Maung understand and accept that Yumisan was his sister. This problem weighed heavily on his mind, leaving him confused and distressed.

Ko Thet Lwin couldn't sleep, burdened by his thoughts. He wanted to wake Maung Maung and tell him the good news about his sister's arrival. If Maung Maung accepted it, that would be wonderful. But if he didn't, and acted recklessly out of shame . . . Ko Thet Lwin dreaded the thought.

He believed that once he eased Maung Maung's existing distress, it would be easier to inform him about Yumisan. Restlessly tossing and turning in bed, he kept pondering and planning.

6

The time had arrived for a Saturday evening when Yumisan's wish would be fulfilled. Her face radiated a youthful glow, marked by smiles throughout the day. She was eagerly looking forward to finally meeting her younger brother, whom she had longed to see for many years. Her heart filled with joy and her appearance seemed more vibrant and light-hearted than usual.

As the afternoon approached, she sat in front of her mirror to prepare herself. She didn't just see her face; she saw a blank canvas ready for her artistic touch. She carefully applied various colours, shaping her eyebrows, accentuating her eyelashes, highlighting her nose, and applying a soft rose colour to her lips. She painted her cheeks with a delicate pink, meticulously crafting her face until it appeared as a beautiful figurine in the mirror. She perfected her make-up, ensuring her eyes, eyebrows, nose, and lips looked just right.

Yumisan wanted to present herself as a beautiful sister when she met her brother, believing that her beauty would foster a bond of affection. She trusted that people appreciated beauty and that being lovable would naturally attract love. After enhancing her natural beauty with make-up, she realized that a beautiful face alone wasn't enough. She needed to dress well too.

She chose to wear a soft pink silk dress from an array of colourful gowns. In the evening sunlight, the soft pink hue radiated gently. The fashionably designed pink dress fit her perfectly, accentuating her fresh and vibrant look. The dress was skilfully tailored to highlight her full bust, delicate waist, and gracefully curved hips.

After putting on the pink dress, she neatly styled her hair. She gathered her short hair at the back of her head, twisted it, and secured it with a small, black flower hairpin.

Feeling the need for some jewellery, she added a pearl necklace around her neck. Pearl white, delicate pink, and soft skin tones shimmered together in her dress, beautifully complementing each other and enhancing her overall radiance. Lastly, she sprayed a light, fragrant body mist and called out from her room:

'Obasan, it's half-past three. Is Sarmi here yet?'

'Yes, Ma Yu, he's already here,' Daw Aung May replied, entering the room. Taking in the fragrant aroma and Yumisan's appearance, she thought, *I've never seen her look this beautiful before*.

Smiling, Yumisan asked her the usual question, 'Do I look nice, Obasan?'

With a grin that revealed her even, white teeth, Daw Aung May responded, 'You look beautiful, Ma Yu. Today, you look the best! If you wore a kimono like a Japanese girl on a calendar, you'd be even more stunning.'

'I'm not very good at wearing kimonos. Modern Japanese girls don't wear kimonos well any more; they prefer gowns. It's only for big events that I wear a kimono,' Yumisan explained with a smile.

Daw Aung May, who understood that the traditional attire for a Burmese woman was *htinemathein* and for a Japanese woman, it was the kimono, did not think Western-style clothing suited any Eastern woman regardless of their nationality.

Yumisan put on her nylon gloves. Wearing white high-heeled shoes, she quickly left the room. Daw Aung May, wondering why Yumisan was so cheerful, closed the door behind her.

As she got into the car, Yumisan had to suppress her excitement and calm her racing heart. She would soon see the clear, vivid form of her little brother, who had been no more than a hazy image until now. The anticipation of meeting him filled her with nervous energy.

Following the address given by U Thet Lwin, the car entered the compound of a single-storey house on Guttalitt Road. Seeing the car enter the compound, U Thet Lwin rushed to open the door and stood ready to greet her.

'Please come in, Sayama. I've been expecting you. I haven't been back from work for long. Maung Maung should be back from school in about half an hour.'

With a multitude of emotions stirring within her, Yumisan smiled as best she could, bowed, and greeted. U Thet Lwin led Yumisan to the living room. The armchairs that were scattered haphazardly had to be moved for the guest. Newspapers were spread out on the table, and the bookshelves and desk were cluttered with books in disarray. Despite the disordered living room, a beautifully hung painting added a touch of elegance. The painting depicted the Mandalay Palace walls and its moat.

Upon reaching the living room, Yumisan noticed the painting. She approached it to take a closer look before sitting down.

'Who painted this?' she asked.

'It's been a long time, Sayama. I painted it,' U Thet Lwin replied.

Yumisan examined U Thet Lwin's handiwork. As she sat in the living room, she realized that no part of U Thet Lwin's house was tidy, leading her to think it might be a typical bachelor's home without a woman's touch.

'I also paint. I'll show you the paintings that I've drawn since I arrived in Myanmar,' she said.

Learning that Maung Maung was not yet home calmed her a bit, allowing her to speak more comfortably.

'What kind of paintings do you do, Sayama?'

'I've done a painting of the Shwedagon Pagoda, a landscape from the Bago region, a monastery, and a painting of the Ngapali beach.'

'What are your thoughts on Burmese art, Sayama?' U Thet Lwin asked.

Yumisan responded with an open smile.

'When I first arrived in Myanmar and saw Myanmar paintings, I was surprised. They use a lot of green, red, blue, and yellow colours. The Chinese paintings, Indian paintings, and Myanmar paintings look quite similar, Saya. Most of the Myanmar paintings I saw are realistic and resemble photographs. They depict everything in great detail without leaving anything out,' said Yumisan.

U Thet Lwin appreciated Yumisan's openness and said, 'They are quite different from Japanese paintings, Sayama. Japanese paintings are simple, straightforward, serene, and gentle. At first glance, they may seem plain, but their beauty and meaning gradually emerge and are quite profound.'

'Yes, Saya. The essence of Japanese paintings is like adding pepper to hot water; you can immediately tell it's pepper. However, if you mix it with ginger, garlic, and other ingredients, the pepper's presence might be lost. What I mean is that it's hard to immediately understand what is being emphasized.'

U Thet Lwin found Yumisan's mannerisms endearing and began to feel a growing sense of familiarity and affection for her. Her articulate way of speaking made it engaging to listen to her.

'When I first arrived, the embassy took me to Ngapali. There were five coconut trees on the beach, but in my painting, I only drew two instead of five. My friend asked why I only drew two when there were five,' Yumisan said.

U Thet Lwin laughed heartily before she finished talking.

'What do you think of the ancient paintings in Bagan, Sayama? Have you been to Bagan yet?'

'I haven't been to Bagan yet, Saya. I'll visit when the school is closed. I'm really interested in the paintings from the Bagan era, especially those on lacquerware. Line painting and curved style painting have a distinctive two-dimensional quality on both sides. These styles are reminiscent of Japan's Edo-period Ukiyo-e paintings.'

'Don't you see that there are many places to paint in Myanmar, Sayama?'

Yumisan nodded slightly and replied, 'Yes, there are many. I'll invite you to my house one day to show you the ones I've painted.'

'Where is your house?'

'It's in Inya Myaing. It's a nice house, and I live alone in a spacious place. Is this house yours, Saya?'

'It's not my house, Sayama. I'm renting it. I live here with Maung Maung and one of my students who is also my housemate. It's just the three of us.'

Yumisan nodded slightly while listening and glanced at her wristwatch.

'Maung Maung should be here soon, Sayama. I've been holding back my excitement to tell him about meeting you. When he arrives, you can see how he reacts, Sayama.'

U Thet Lwin saw Yumisan smiling brightly, but this made him feel uneasy. The thought of Yumisan having to meet Maung Maung as just another guest rather than as an older sister made him feel uncomfortable.

'I'll wait, Saya. When I see him, I'll be so happy. And if the day comes when I can tell him that I'm his sister, I'll be even happier. Isn't that right, Saya?' said the gentle voice, stirring compassion in U Thet Lwin's heart.

Feeling uneasy, U Thet Lwin nodded silently.

They heard a whistle at the gate, and the familiar sound of Maung Maung's military march filled the air. As usual, Maung Maung walked towards them in his reserve army uniform, damp with sweat. The sound of his march sharply reached U Thet Lwin's ears, making his head feel heavy.

'He's here, Sayama,' U Thet Lwin said as he got up to open the door.

'Oh, you're here already, Ahkogyi?'

Yumisan, with a pounding heart, looked at Maung Maung. To her eyes, her brother in his reserve military uniform looked not like a Myanmar soldier, but a true Japanese soldier, with his Japanese features shining through.

The blood in Yumisan's chest surged violently, as if it would burst out at any moment. Yumisan couldn't control her emotions or pretend otherwise. Her eyes were shining brightly, and her face simultaneously reflected both sadness and joy. She felt an intense urge to get up from her seat and hug Maung Maung, even wanting to kiss his forehead.

The shadowy figure that had always been a vague image in her mind now appeared vividly before her.

Though she saw him clearly, she couldn't verbally express that he was her brother and she his sister. Instead, her eyes did the speaking for her, focusing intently on him.

First, her gaze rested on Maung Maung's face and whole body. Then, she scrutinized each feature: his forehead, nose, eyes, lips, cheeks, and jawline down to his neck. His resemblance to her father, Major Yoshida, was so strong that she was reminded of him and felt a pang of nostalgia. She wished her father could see his soldier-like son. Her unwavering gaze lingered on the parts of Maung Maung that resembled her father.

Maung Maung, upon seeing the unfamiliar guest in the living room, froze in shock. Under Yumisan's piercing gaze, Maung Maung hesitated to enter the house, feeling like an earthworm sprinkled with salt. U Thet Lwin opened the door and spoke calmly, maintaining his composure.

'Come in, come in . . . we have a guest,' U Thet Lwin said, turning back toward Yumisan. Before reaching her, he controlled his voice and said, 'Sayama, this is my younger brother, Maung Maung. He's now in university.'

Maung Maung, who had been standing frozen, slowly approached when he heard 'my younger brother, Maung Maung'.

'Nice to meet you,' said Yumisan, standing up and gazing intently at Maung Maung.

'Maung Maung, this guest is a Japanese teacher named Yumisan from the Institute of Foreign Languages. She's come to ask for help in continuing her Burmese studies with me.'

U Thet Lwin placed a hand on Maung Maung's shoulder and introduced him to Yumisan.

Yumisan stared directly at Maung Maung, with tears welling up in her eyes and a sweet smile on her face.

Hearing the word 'Japanese' sent a chill down Maung Maung's spine. A deep-seated pain surged within him, and a lifelong feeling of shame surfaced. For a moment, his eyes went blank, unable to see anything. Overwhelmed with embarrassment, he forced a smile in front of his older brother's guest, despite feeling incredibly awkward. His smile was clearly strained and fake.

Yumisan observed every detail of Maung Maung's behaviour without missing a thing.

'Please, have a seat.'

U Thet Lwin introduced Maung Maung and then motioned for him to sit down. Maung Maung found it difficult to meet Yumisan's gaze, which was warm and inviting. Her overly friendly demeanour made him uncomfortable, and he couldn't look directly at her.

Before sitting back down, Yumisan moved a chair closer to her for Maung Maung. 'Please, have a seat,' she said. Her overly familiar actions made Maung Maung think, 'This Japanese teacher is quite bold; it's like she's in her own home.'

'She knows Burmese. She studied it in Japan,' U Thet Lwin said gently. Maung Maung averted his eyes, avoiding direct eye contact with Yumisan. He couldn't reconcile her appearance with that of a typical teacher; she seemed too friendly, too sweet, lacking the usual reserve. His gaze dropped to her legs visible beneath her gown. He had never been so close to a Japanese woman with her knees and thighs exposed before, causing him to avert his eyes.

Noticing Maung Maung's unease, U Thet Lwin spoke up to ease the tension. 'It's just the two of us brothers, Sayama. Our parents passed away a long time ago.'

'Really, Saya? Since you only have one younger brother, you must love him very much,' Yumisan said, her eyes returning to Maung Maung. He averted his eyes and turned his face back towards U Thet Lwin.

'Yes, Sayama, I only have him to love,' U Thet Lwin replied.

'Your younger brother is adorable. He's very lovable,' Yumisan said, her eyes fixed on Maung Maung, not moving away for a long while. The realization that he was her brother and her own blood tightened the bond in her heart.

U Thet Lwin felt a pang of emotion. Maung Maung's face turned red. He was embarrassed at being treated like a little child despite being in his twenties.

'What year are you in at the university, Maung Maung?' Yumisan asked sweetly. There was a hint of condescension in her sweet tone, which made U Thet Lwin's smiling face show a shadow of sadness.

'First year,' Maung Maung replied curtly, his face tense.

'What major are you taking, Maung Maung?' Yumisan continued to ask, her voice the sweetest and her smile the brightest.

'I'm majoring in Economics.'

Hearing Maung Maung's words and seeing his unfamiliar expression, Yumisan's heart began to pound.

'Wouldn't you like to learn Japanese, Maung Maung? You can take part-time classes at our language school while attending evening classes. You could become fluent in Japanese,' she suggested.

Maung Maung's previously bright face darkened. Though he understood that Yumisan was gently using 'Ma Ma' (older sister) instead of 'I' when she spoke, the word still stung him. He had no desire to meet Japanese people, let alone learn their language, which he didn't want to hear. Feeling deeply displeased, he had no desire to remain and wanted to leave Yumisan's side, but he stayed seated out of respect for his older brother's guest. His words, however, were blunt and direct.

'I'm Burmese, Sayama. I don't need to know Japanese, and I don't want to speak it.'

U Thet Lwin felt uncomfortable and embarrassed by Maung Maung's response, finding it difficult to sit still in front of Yumisan. However, he let Maung Maung speak freely, understanding that it was important for Yumisan to know his true feelings.

With all her might, Yumisan responded with a determined voice. Her eyes shone brightly as she spoke.

'At our school, only Burmese people attend Japanese classes, Maung Maung. They want to learn Japanese. I am Japanese, but I wanted to learn Burmese so much that I studied it in Japan. Now, I am continuing my Burmese studies with the teacher here. Isn't it good to know a foreign language, no matter which one it is?' Yumisan said, her bright eyes probing deep into Maung Maung's heart.

Maung Maung smiled back, but his smile was one of pride and defiance. 'I want to learn other languages, but not Japanese, Sayama.'

Yumisan noticed that he addressed her as 'Sayama' despite her previous efforts to have him call her 'Ma Ma'.

'Why? Do you think Japanese is difficult?' she asked, probing further.

Understanding the tension in Yumisan's questioning, U Thet Lwin smiled politely and remained silent, although he was internally anxious.

'We're just not interested in Japanese, so we don't want to learn it, Sayama,' Maung Maung responded definitively, signalling his unwillingness to continue the conversation on this topic. Not wanting to be rude, he turned abruptly to his older brother and said, 'Ahkogyi, I'm going to change my clothes.'

U Thet Lwin, realizing Maung Maung's discomfort thought that it was best to end the conversation, said, 'All right, all right, go ahead and change. He's a bit lazy with his studies, Sayama. Even with his schoolwork, he barely manages.'

Yumisan, refusing to back down, continued speaking to Maung Maung with determination. 'Learn when you're interested, Maung Maung. I was so interested that I learned Burmese. One day, you might be interested. Who can say you won't? Isn't that right, Maung Maung?'

Maung Maung, finding her words tedious, stood up lightly and left the room without fully listening.

After he disappeared, Yumisan's face turned pale, her lips stiffened. The sorrow and disappointment visible on her once cheerful face moved U Thet Lwin deeply, stirring feelings of compassion and sympathy within him.

'Isn't it just as I said, Sayama?' U Thet Lwin spoke softly, his voice tinged with emotion.

Yumisan nodded, unable to speak, overwhelmed by her emotions. She couldn't calm herself. Instead of feeling joy and pride at meeting her long-lost brother in a foreign land, she was disheartened and saddened. She had hoped for a warm reunion but faced Maung Maung's resentment. Overcome with inner pain, Yumisan lowered her head and let her eyes fill with tears.

In front of U Thet Lwin, Yumisan looked pitiable, her head bowed, exuding an air of helplessness. Concerned that their silence might arouse Maung Maung's suspicion, U Thet Lwin broke the silence.

'Sayama, did you learn Burmese poetry while studying Burmese?'

Yumisan lifted her face, her downcast eyes looking up. Her expression was a mix of sadness, disappointment, and hope. Tears welled up in her eyes.

Realizing that U Thet Lwin was trying to manage the situation, she did her best to steer the conversation.

'Yes, I learned poetry, Saya. I studied some contemporary poetry too.'

Their conversation felt strained and stilted, with each speaking out of politeness rather than genuine interest. They talked, but their hearts and minds were elsewhere.

Maung Maung avoided the front room and went to the kitchen after changing his clothes.

'How convenient, young man. The tea is ready for our guest. Take it to them. The rice pot here is about to boil,' called out Ko Mya Phay, handing the prepared tea tray to Maung Maung.

'Oh . . . I don't want to go. Why don't you take it?' Maung Maung responded.

'Oh . . . why is that?'

Ko Mya Phay looked at Maung Maung's sullen face in surprise and asked again, 'What's the matter?'

Maung Maung replied, 'The Japanese woman speaks Burmese in a high-handed manner, I can't stand listening to it. And she calls herself "Ma Ma".'

After speaking, Maung Maung shrugged his shoulders and made a face.

'Oh dear . . . you're something else. Why should you be bothered by that? If she calls herself "Ma Ma", let her. You already have a real older brother here,' said Ko Mya Phay, laughing.

'Hey, don't talk like that. Don't get my brother involved with this woman.'

'Oh . . . still hung up on that, huh?'

'Yes, my brother is Burmese, she's Japanese. Why bring this up? Don't mix it up with this.'

'I'm not making fun. I'm serious. I noticed earlier how pretty that Japanese girl is. You watch, your older brother has been picky about women, which is why he's still single. This time, he might really go for it.'

Ko Mya Phay never missed a chance to tease Maung Maung whenever a girl visited the house, always doing it deliberately to provoke him. Only when Maung Maung became visibly irritated, his large eyes blazing with anger, did Ko Mya Phay flash a mocking smile, pick up the tea tray, and walk out.

When Ko Mya Phay returned to the kitchen, he saw Maung Maung sitting on a stool, tapping the table with a meat slicing knife and playing.

'Hey . . . Saya is asking for you. Go,' Ko Mya Phay said.

'I don't want to go,' Maung Maung replied.

'Come on, who is this Japanese lady anyway? She's never been to our house before, and she speaks Burmese too,' Ko Mya Phay said, moving closer to Maung Maung's face with curiosity.

'She's a Japanese teacher from the Institute of Foreign Languages. She's coming to learn Burmese from my brother,' Maung Maung explained.

'Oh . . . so that means this teacher will be coming to our house frequently. Why are you so angry about it? It's just a language lesson,' Ko Mya Phay said.

'It's not that I'm angry. I just don't like the Japanese teacher's demeanour. I don't know how long my brother will be teaching her. She doesn't even look at me with a hint of modesty. She just stares and glares,' Maung Maung said.

Ko Mya Phay laughed heartily, unable to contain his amusement.

'You won't get hurt by her stare. If she looks at Saya like that, let her. It's like paying off an old debt,' Ko Mya Phay teased.

'What old debt?' Maung Maung asked, eyes wide.

'During the Japanese occupation, many Japanese soldiers married Burmese women. Some of those marriages were forced. This debt still exists,' Ko Mya Phay said with a sly smile.

As Maung Maung listened, a deep feeling of unease grew within him. While tapping the table with the knife, a sudden memory of the mother he had never known surfaced in his mind. He began to yearn for the mother he had only imagined. The thought that, as Ko Mya Phay suggested, his mother might have been wronged and had given birth to him under difficult circumstances troubled him deeply.

This realization filled him with a shame he wished to neither acknowledge nor dwell upon. Because of his ignorance of his past, he had always avoided confronting such painful thoughts. Now, it felt as if Maung Maung was tossing around the heart that had just been ripped out into his brain.

Ko Mya Phay, who was stirring the rice pot, noticed the chips and cuts Maung Maung had made on the edge of the table with the knife and exclaimed in surprise.

'Hey . . . hey . . . why are you cutting up my table like this?'

Ko Mya Phay couldn't see the emotional wounds in Maung Maung's heart, only the physical damage to the edge of the table, which was now marred with nicks and cuts.

'Sorry . . . sorry, I was just tapping and accidentally cut it up,' Maung Maung replied in an affected tone.

'Maung Maung,' U Thet Lwin called from the front of the house, his voice reaching into the kitchen.

Maung Maung straightened up reluctantly.

'You're being called, aren't you going to answer?' Ko Mya Phay said, prompting Maung Maung to get up from his place.

'Sayama is about to leave and wants to say goodbye to you,' U Thet Lwin informed.

Yumisan, deeply moved, stood by with a gentle smile, waiting to bid farewell to Maung Maung. She fought back her tears, her eyes becoming dull and lifeless as she struggled to hold them back.

'Yes, all right, Sayama,' Maung Maung replied in a flat, emotionless tone, showing neither a smile nor warmth. His response left U Thet Lwin feeling a pang of frustration. Despite this, U Thet Lwin forced a smile, though he wondered if it was more for Maung Maung's sake. His strained smile somehow made him look twenty-five years older.

Together with Yumisan, they walked out of the house. U Thet Lwin escorted her to the car, personally opening and closing the door for her.

Before the car left, U Thet Lwin conveyed his sympathy and sadness through his eyes, ensuring that Yumisan understood he shared her feelings, despite his inability to express them in words.

As the car was about to leave, U Thet Lwin's actions stood out sharply from within the house. He had never interacted with a woman so warmly before. Maung Maung wondered why his brother had allowed a Japanese woman into their home and if he had forgotten his resentment towards her people and their shared past. This unexpected behaviour ignited a new irritation in Maung Maung towards U Thet Lwin.

As the car drove away, Yumisan felt as if she was being punished by a cane, her entire body in pain. Overwhelmed by sadness, heartbreak, and intense suffering, she wanted to cry. She wiped away her tears and silently endured all the pain.

Upon returning home, she felt a sharp pang in her chest, her whole body trembling. She struggled to breathe properly and quickly changed her clothes before collapsing onto her bed. She told Obasan that she had a headache.

When Daw Aung May offered to massage her, Yumisan shook her head without speaking. When told that she had a telephone call, she raised her hand to decline.

Yumisan lay limply, her eyes tightly shut, feeling more distressed than necessary. Now that she had found Maung Maung, her deep affection for him revealed a binding attachment she couldn't escape.

Maung Maung's image appeared in front of her repeatedly. She felt a deep, tangible love for him, speaking with him in her thoughts as if he were truly there. In Yumisan's mind, they knew they were siblings, and they still felt a peaceful contentment together.

7

Yumisan spent the entire night consumed by these thoughts, unable to sleep. Before dawn, she got out of bed. This morning, she felt driven by a resolute plan and acted upon it. She opened drawers and wardrobes, carefully packing the boxes and bags she needed. She took a cold shower early in the morning and prepared herself, changing clothes. Before Daw Aung May woke up, she opened all the windows and doors in the house, boiled water, and made herself coffee.

'Hey . . . Ma Yu, up so early? Are you feeling better?' Daw Aung May asked, still drowsy from sleep.

'Oh my . . . you're making your own coffee already? You should have woken me up.' Daw Aung May was astonished to see Yumisan sitting at the breakfast table, drinking coffee so early. Seeing her dressed and groomed, she wondered if she was going out. Yumisan confirmed her suspicion.

'I'm waiting for seven o'clock. Once it's seven, I'll head out. Don't prepare breakfast for me; I'll have it at a friend's house who works at the embassy.'

Since it was Sunday, Daw Aung May simply assumed that Yumisan was going out for a visit.

'When will you be back, Ma Yu?' Daw Aung May asked.

Yumisan didn't hear her question. She was lost in thought, gazing longingly at the image of Maung Maung in his military uniform that was vivid in her mind.

Daw Aung May asked again, starting to find Yumisan's behaviour a bit strange.

'Did you ask me, Obasan? I think I'll be back by four in the afternoon.'

'Oh . . . oh.'

Yumisan then grabbed the bags she had placed on the table and stood up. Since Sarmi wouldn't come on Sundays, she drove the car herself. She headed straight to Maung Maung's house on Guttalitt Road.

Seeing Maung Maung yesterday wasn't enough; she couldn't stop thinking about him and wanted to see him again. She wanted to spend as much time with him as possible, especially on weekends when she had free time. During the weekdays, the school kept her busy, leaving her with little free time. She wanted to dedicate her available time to seeing Maung Maung.

It was still before 7 a.m., and she wondered if the household would be awake yet. If not, she planned to drive around until they opened the door. If the door was open, she would go inside. If they weren't awake, she would wait for them. She was excited because she had brought some Japanese sweets for them to enjoy together.

She thought about ordering shirts and pants for Maung Maung from Japan. She also planned to write a letter to her grandparents in Japan to share the good news that she had found her younger brother. In the letter, she intended to include detailed information about U Thet Lwin, who was a kind and caring person. She imagined how happy her grandparents would be.

Leaving early without considering whether she would disturb U Thet Lwin didn't bother her at all. She knew he was understanding and empathetic towards her feelings. He understood that Maung Maung's house was like her own, where she could come and go as she pleased. In her thoughts, U Thet Lwin was someone she felt very close to.

When she arrived at Maung Maung's house, she saw that not only the main door but also the windows facing the front were still closed. She reversed the car and drove towards the lake.

Parking the car, she walked to the lake's edge, where a mist hung over the water. As she looked at the calm surface of the lake, her anxious heart gradually began to settle. The cool breeze soothed her, and the peaceful surroundings brought a sense of tranquillity to her mind. Appreciating the serene atmosphere, she stood there quietly for a long time before finally leaving the lake.

As Yumisan's car came to a stop in front of Maung Maung's house, she noticed that both sides of the compound gate were wide open. The windows at the front of the house were also thrown open.

Yumisan slowly drove into the compound. After gathering the gift-wrapped packages, she stepped out of the car and glanced at the house. The small, single-storey building stood quietly under the morning sun.

Before Yumisan could reach the entrance, the doors on both sides swung open, as if someone inside had been expecting her. Maung Maung's head poked out through the narrow gap, just barely visible from the doorway.

Yumisan walked towards him, trying to remain calm, and smiled at him. Maung Maung didn't smile back. As she got closer and made eye contact with him, her steps faltered. Maung Maung's cold gaze made her throat tighten with emotion.

'Did you come to see my brother?' Maung Maung asked in a flat tone, still looking at her with those cold eyes.

Maung Maung's gaze, filled with a clear expression of resentment and anger, seemed to penetrate her very being.

'I came to see both you and Saya,' Yumisan's words slipped out automatically, without her even realizing it.

'Ahkogyi isn't here. He left early this morning,' Maung Maung said.

'I'll wait,' Yumisan replied.

Maung Maung smiled visibly, but it was a mocking smile, aimed at preventing her from entering the house.

'You can't wait here. Ahkogyi is out for the day, wandering around. I don't know when he'll be back. I'm about to lock up and leave too,' Maung Maung said.

Yumisan kept staring at Maung Maung. She realized it was futile to continue talking or to try to enter the house. Maung Maung's words and behaviour clearly indicated he wanted her to leave.

She still felt an urge to try and get into the house one more time. However, her resolve weakened as she thought about how pointless it would be. Maung Maung's actions showed that he did not want her there, and she couldn't decide whether to be angry or hurt by his rejection. Her love for him was a solid presence in her heart, unmoved and unyielding, like a mother's unwavering love for her child.

Softly and gently, she said, 'I brought gifts for you all. I'll leave them here. Please let U Thet Lwin know I came.'

She handed over the large package. Maung Maung quickly took it and promptly shut the door, bolting it from the inside.

He placed the package on the table and quietly tiptoed to the kitchen to avoid waking U Thet Lwin, who was still asleep.

Yumisan found herself unable to move from where she stood. The sound of the door bolt echoed loudly in her ears, as terrifying as a thunderclap. Gathering all her remaining strength, she forced herself to move and descended the steps.

She had no memory of how she walked back or how she got into the car. Yumisan's senses were numb, and she was in a daze, driving without awareness of her surroundings or direction. Her mind was consumed by a single thought: Why did Maung Maung hate her so much?

The realization that two siblings, living and interacting in close proximity, could be so emotionally distant from each other caused her immense pain. She wondered whose fault it was—her father's, her younger brother's, or someone else's. Ultimately, she concluded that it wasn't anyone's fault. It was the legacy of the past war, which had created deep-seated racial hatred and led to this situation. Even though the war had ended, the emotional wounds it inflicted on her heart remained raw and painful.

Maung Maung's acceptance of the gift from her hands was heart-wrenching. He neither appreciated nor acknowledged the gift, nor did he even say thank you. He did not recognize the gesture of someone who had come to his home early in the morning to present a thoughtful gift. To him, she was nothing more than an unwelcome ghostly visitor, not his own sister by blood.

As Yumisan thought about this, her heart grew heavy and sorrowful. Just as she had thought, Maung Maung was irritable at her early morning visit. He looked at her with disdain, frustrated that she had come back so early.

Soon, Ko Mya Phay returned from the market.

'Has Saya woken up?' Ko Mya Phay asked, putting down his shopping bag.

'No, not yet. Earlier this morning, that woman came again,' Maung Maung replied.

'Who was it?'

'The Japanese teacher who came yesterday. She showed up with a gift package. I told her that Ahkogyi wasn't home and had gone out.'

'You really are something.'

Maung Maung laughed, pleased with his own actions.

'She came here yesterday. This morning, too, she came back so early and asked me to allow her to wait inside the house.'

'Oh my . . . What did you say to her?'

'I told her I was going out and would lock the house, so she left. What else could I do?'

'She must be really tired now.'

'Let her be. It's not your worry. Is it?'

'It's not my worry, but your brother's. Ha ha ha.' Ko Mya Phay laughed uncontrollably. With each laugh, Maung Maung's resentment towards Yumisan deepened. Her boldness and lack of modesty made him increasingly concerned about potential complications in her relationship with his brother.

U Thet Lwin, who had just woken up, overheard Ko Mya Phay's laughter and peeked into the kitchen while on his way to the bathroom. Seeing U Thet Lwin, both Maung Maung and Ko Mya Phay fell silent.

'Ahkogyi, the Japanese teacher came by earlier.'

'Oh . . . really?' U Thet Lwin replied, his voice long and drawn out, his eyes widening. His entire face lit up with curiosity.

Maung Maung, watching his older brother's reaction, didn't say anything further, prompting U Thet Lwin to ask, 'So, what's up?'

'She brought a gift package,' Maung Maung said reluctantly, his voice betraying his reluctance.

'Really? Where is it? Didn't she ask about me?'

Maung Maung was put off by U Thet Lwin's overly quick reply. 'The gift package is on the table in front of the house. I didn't want to wake you up, so I told her you weren't home.'

U Thet Lwin's previously lively face suddenly darkened at Maung Maung's words. He realized it wasn't that Maung Maung didn't want to wake him up, but that he knew Maung Maung didn't like Yumisan. This realization made his face fall.

After leaving the bathroom, U Thet Lwin took the package from the table and opened it. Ko Mya Phay, who was standing nearby, frowned, baring his teeth and giving a mock nod. Maung Maung pursed his lips in response.

U Thet Lwin carried the large package to the kitchen table, and with a gentle expression, began untying the strings.

'It's cheese from Japan. And this is Japanese chocolate. These look like snack boxes.' As U Thet Lwin spoke, he opened one of the boxes. Inside was a beautifully crafted cake, shaped like soap and wrapped in multiple layers. The first was silver paper, followed by a layer of silk paper, and finally, a neatly crafted bamboo sheath. U Thet Lwin broke off a piece of the cake and tasted it, savouring the delicate sweetness.

'Just looking at how it's wrapped layer by layer, it seems like it's made to last long, with that subtle sweetness,' U Thet Lwin observed as he tried one of the candies. 'It's wrapped in so many layers, like preserved food. It's sweet and mild.'

As U Thet Lwin spoke, Ko Mya Phay suddenly interrupted with a loud clap. 'The way it's wrapped is so beautiful, Saya. Such lovely little things, too nice to eat! Hahahaha.'

'Japan has come a long way since the post-war days. It's impressive how they've turned things around, especially with so few natural resources. Their innovation and hard work really set them apart. Honestly, there's so much we can learn from them,' U Thet Lwin praised.

Ko Mya Phay nodded vigorously in agreement, his face still brimming with laughter.

Maung Maung, who had been watching the whole time, felt a growing irritation at Ko Mya Phay's impish expressions. U Thet Lwin's praise also grated on his nerves. Unable to bear watching any longer, he left the room without a word.

Although U Thet Lwin noticed Maung Maung leaving, he pretended not to and continued opening box after box of snacks, all the while envisioning Yumisan's sad, wistful face.

* * *

Yumisan drove nonstop until she finally parked in front of her house at 9 a.m.

Daw Aung May glanced over at Yumisan, who had said she would return in the evening, with wide eyes. Yumisan's frustration was evident on her face. She entered the house with a gloomy expression.

'Ma Yu, you said you wouldn't eat breakfast here today and would eat at the consulate house, and that you'd be back in the evening,' Daw Aung May remarked.

The words 'you said, you said' echoed in Yumisan's ears. Unable to muster the energy to respond, she collapsed onto the long couch, exhausted.

Daw Aung May stood there, watching with wide eyes. She couldn't comprehend Yumisan's behaviour. As she stood there, unsure whether to stay or leave, Yumisan looked over at her for support.

'Ma Yu, what's wrong? Are you feeling unwell?' Daw Aung May approached Yumisan. Seeing Yumisan's tear-filled eyes, she was startled.

Yumisan felt an overwhelming pressure in her chest. She wished she could expel the lump in her throat. She had so many things she wanted to say to unburden herself. Who could she talk to about her problems? If not to Obasan, then who?

‘Obasan,’ Yumisan called out in a trembling voice and sat up straight.

‘What is it, Ma Yu? Tell me. What’s the matter?’

Yumisan noticed Daw Aung May’s anxious demeanour and quickly grasped her hand, turning to face her directly.

‘Obasan, I want to wear a Myanmar htamein. Can you teach me how to put it on?’

Daw Aung May, initially startled, became even more surprised.

‘You want to wear a htamein? If you want to, I’ll teach you. But why do you suddenly want to dress like a Burmese woman? Tell me about it.’

Yumisan gently wiped away the tears forming in the corners of her eyes, struggling to speak as her heart pounded in her chest.

‘I have a Burmese younger brother, Obasan.’

Daw Aung May was momentarily at a loss for words, then finally managed to speak. ‘My goodness! A Burmese younger brother? Where did this Burmese brother come from?’

Daw Aung May, deeply moved, suddenly felt faint and nearly collapsed.

'He's the son of a Burmese woman who was my father's wife during the war.'

Daw Aung May pressed her palm against her chest and then spoke. 'My goodness! Is he still alive? Where is he? Have you met him?'

'We've searched for him, and I've finally found him. I've fallen deeply in love with him, but as for him . . .'

Yumisan raised her hand and curled her index finger to demonstrate.

Daw Aung May stared blankly, trying to figure out the meaning of the bent index finger.

'Do you mean he dislikes you . . . or that he doesn't love you?'

'He doesn't love me at all,' Yumisan replied, her voice tinged with bitterness.

Daw Aung May grew more confused and asked, astonished, 'Why doesn't he love you? Doesn't he know that you are his sister?'

'He doesn't know . . .'

'Oh . . . why haven't you told him?'

'I haven't had the chance to.'

'Why hasn't there been a chance, Ma Yu?'

Daw Aung May's head started to nod with understanding. She began to recall past moments when she had wondered if her half-siblings in

Myanmar would love or hate her, and now the truth was unfolding.

‘He resents Japan, Obasan. I’m afraid if I tell him, he’ll distance himself from me even more.’

How bad! Where is he now? This is such a sad situation, Ma Yu.’

‘Obasan, please don’t ask any more. You’ll find out later. Please don’t tell anyone about this.’

‘I won’t tell anyone, Ma Yu. I feel so sad hearing this. How old is he now? Does he look Burmese?’

‘He’s over twenty years old, a university student. When he dresses like a Burmese, he looks Burmese, but when he wears pants, he looks Japanese.’

‘What’s his name? Is his skin as fair as yours?’

‘His name is Maung Maung. His skin isn’t very fair. He looks a lot like my father; his forehead and chin are very similar. He’s incredibly lovable, Obasan. I can’t even describe how lovable he is.’

‘Is that why you want to start wearing the htamein? Tell me more.’

‘I’ll be visiting him often. I don’t want to go there in a gown anymore. I want to wear traditional Burmese clothes and show him that I’m a proud Burmese woman. I want him to know that I love Burma, Obasan.’

‘Oh, so that’s how it is. Well then, I’ll teach you. Just wait a moment.’

Daw Aung May then went into her room and came out with a new *batik longyi*. She unfurled it, shook it once, and said, 'Come on, try it on.'

Yumisan stood up and slipped her legs into the longyi, which Daw Aung May had prepared for her, pulled it up, and fastened it at the waist. As she tied it, the lower part of the longyi loosened and fell into a loop.

'Not like that, Ma Yu. Look here, spread it out like this, fold it here so the bottom doesn't come undone, pull it tight, and then tuck it in here. Look, it won't come loose any more.'

Daw Aung May demonstrated how to wear the longyi correctly, ensuring it stayed in place, and showed her how to do it on her own body.

Even though Yumisan tried to wear the longyi as Daw Aung May showed her, she couldn't get it right. It kept slipping, coming undone, and falling off. Daw Aung May stepped in to help her put it on properly.

'Once you put on the longyi, you look very much like a Burmese girl, Ma Yu. Try walking in it.'

Yumisan, feeling stifled by the tight longyi, tried to walk, but after just a few steps, it loosened and slipped off again. Daw Aung May, sweating but smiling through her exasperation, watched Yumisan persistently try again, picking up the longyi each time it fell and trying to wear it correctly. She walked a bit, it fell off, she picked it up and put it back on, over and over.

Watching Yumisan repeatedly put on the longyi and walk around the living room with determination, Daw Aung May wanted to laugh but held it in, knowing that Yumisan was determined and would keep trying until she succeeded.

'Obasan, what if I wear a belt around my waist?'

'Of course, Ma Yu. Until you get used to it, you can wear a belt. Once you get the hang of it, you won't need one any more. Do you have a belt?'

Yumisan picked up the fallen longyi, clutched it to her chest, and went back into the room. When she didn't come out for a while, Daw Aung May followed her into the room.

Yumisan was practising wearing the longyi in front of the full-length mirror. She repeatedly adjusted and tried it on until it fit snugly around her waist. Once the longyi was properly adjusted and she had a belt around her waist, she walked in front of the mirror to check her appearance.

In the mirror, she no longer saw the Yumisan who had come from Japan. Instead, she saw the reflection of Ma Yu, the sister of Maung Maung from Myanmar. Her appearance in the longyi looked pleasing to her, and she became satisfied with it.

'I still need a blouse, Obasan. I want to buy the fabric today and have it tailored within a week. Is that possible?'

'Yes, it's possible, Ma Yu. We can go buy it this afternoon. There's a good tailor shop on Maung Khaing Street. They have excellent designs. If you place an urgent order, they'll do it right away. Don't worry.'

'Do I look Burmese? Does wearing the traditional blouse and longyi suit me? Tell me honestly.'

'You look wonderful, dear. You look just like a real Myanmar girl. People from the East, no matter who they are, once their eyes aren't blue and their hair is dark, they look Burmese in traditional clothing. Fair-skinned people, when they wear Myanmar attire, their skin, hair, and features go perfectly with the traditional clothes. When White women wear Myanmar's traditional attire, their complexion, hair, and facial features don't quite match the Myanmar clothing.'

Encouraged by Daw Aung May's words, Yumisan felt confident wearing the longyi. She hoped that if Maung Maung saw her in Myanmar's traditional attire many times, he would change his mind. Wearing Burmese clothes was not enough; she also wanted to practise Burmese customs, traditions, and manners to fully embrace the Burmese way of life.

'I'll practise wearing the longyi all week. I don't like wearing a belt. Only when I can wear the longyi without a belt will I look truly Burmese. Next Saturday, I'll go to Maung Maung's place dressed as a Burmese.'

Daw Aung May looked at Yumisan with great compassion. The cute, fair face of Yumisan, filled with hope, blushed slightly and radiated with happiness.

8

At the Institute of Foreign Languages, besides the classrooms divided by country, there were also single-storey classroom buildings for first- and second-year students, separated by open spaces, at the back of the school.

Yumisan left the Japanese first-year classroom in a small building after class. During her break, she entered the large hall where international professors, lecturers, and teachers from various countries took their breaks and had tea.

At a table in the hall, Daw Khin Win Mu, who was drinking tea, approached Yumisan. She handed her an envelope from her hand.

'Do you need more money, Daw Khin Win Mu?' Yumisan asked in Japanese, given the public setting, while opening the small envelope.

Inside the envelope, Yumisan found a richly coloured golden, Mandalay Acheik longyi and exclaimed, 'It's so beautiful!'

‘I don’t need money, Sayama. It’s only 75 kyats. What’s it for, Sayama? Are you sending a gift to Japan?’ Daw Khin Win Mu inquired

Smiling, Yumisan replied, ‘It’s to wear.’

Daw Khin Win Mu’s eyes lit up with joy as she responded enthusiastically, ‘Are you going to wear it Burmese-style, Sayama? It will look wonderful on you. I’d love to see it, Sayama. Please wear it to school sometimes.’

Yumisan smiled and nodded. She realized that wearing Burmese attire would endear her to the Burmese people, fostering closer relationships and a sense of kinship. She believed it would make interactions easier.

Yumisan eagerly looked forward to the upcoming Saturday. It had been a week since she last visited Maung Maung’s house after returning from her previous visit. During that time, she called U Thet Lwin at work to ask about Maung Maung. U Thet Lwin mentioned that he had been home on Sunday. Realizing that Maung Maung had lied about U Thet Lwin being away that day, Yumisan felt deceived and thought of Maung Maung as a troublesome child.

U Thet Lwin called Yumisan to apologize to her for Maung Maung’s rudeness. Yumisan recognized that while Maung Maung’s behaviour was hard to forgive, her sense of kinship made her willing to forgive. She resolved not to dwell on the matter and remained hopeful that one day Maung Maung would recognize her affection.

The Mandalay Acheik longyi given by Daw Khin Win Mu was placed into her small basket. Although she wanted to try it on, she couldn't go home yet as she still had classes. She climbed back up to the school's upper floor.

There was still some time before the language practice session with the first-year Japanese class students. The language lab, which could accommodate about thirty to forty students, was a large hall equipped with a reciter machine. This machine helped students practise and perfect their pronunciation in languages such as French, German, Russian, Chinese, and English. Just like in other international language schools in independent countries, this language school prided itself on having such a facility.

The students entered the large hall one after another and took their seats at their assigned desks, which were numbered one, two, three, and so on. Each student had a reciter machine placed in front of them, separated by glass panels to the front and partition boards on either side, ensuring individual workspace and privacy.

In front of the students was a raised platform where the instructor sat at a large desk equipped with sound control devices, microphones, and tape recorders. The teacher would broadcast the sounds, and the students would listen and practise accordingly.

As Yumisan entered the room, the students stood up and greeted her in Japanese. From the platform, Yumisan greeted them back with her sweet voice. As Yumisan sat at her desk, the students put on their headphones, ready to listen to her instructions.

Yumisan's voice, broadcasted through the recorder, was heard by the students through their headphones. They had to listen attentively and respond to every question she asked. Yumisan, in turn, listened to each student's response through her own headphone to check for correctness. She would identify the student by looking at the number on their desk and listen to the recording to ensure the pronunciation was correct.

'*Anata wa nihon ni itta koto ga arimasu ka*?' (Have you ever been to Japan?)

'*Iie, watashi wa nihon ni itta koto ga arimasen,*' (No, I have never been to Japan) the students responded in Japanese.

'*Anata wa nihon no seihin o motteimasu ka*?' (Do you have any Japanese stamps?)

'*Nan-mai no nimotsu ga arimasu ka*?' (How many stamps do you have?)

'*Anata wa nihon no eiga o mita koto ga arimasu ka*?' (Have you ever watched a Japanese movie?)

'*Anata wa nihonshoku o tabeta koto ga arimasu ka*?' (Have you ever eaten Japanese curry?)

As the students answered her questions in Japanese, Yumisan checked their pronunciation for accuracy. She pressed the buttons for each student's desk number to listen carefully to their responses. Her ears were focused, her hands busy, and her mouth constantly asking questions to ensure comprehensive language practice.

In the large language practice room, air conditioners were installed to keep the entire room cool. The students stayed in their places, and amid the sounds of button presses and clicks, Yumisan's continuous, melodious voice filled the room with '*anata wa nihon no* . . .' and similar phrases, sounding like the serene flow of a spring.

After engaging the students in a Q&A practice session, Yumisan began teaching and reading a traditional Japanese folk tale. The story was about a young cowherd and a diligent weaving girl and their love story. They loved each other so much that they neglected their work, and as a result, the god became angry and separated the two lovers. They were allowed to meet only once a year, and their reunion in the Milky Way was marked by the celebration of the Tanabata festival in Japan, where people hang wishes on bamboo trees to commemorate the lovers' meeting.

As Yumisan taught this story, she couldn't help but compare it to her own situation. She wondered which powerful deity had separated her and her brother across different countries and forced them to live as humans. Why were they unable to recognize each other as siblings despite being allowed to meet? She pondered when they would be finally allowed to realize they were siblings.

During the Tanabata festival in Japan, people would write their wishes on paper and hang them on bamboo branches to celebrate and remember the lovers' story.

She wanted the world to know the story of their union as a folktale. Instead of teaching the traditional Japanese story of the Tanabata festival, she wanted to create a tale about her and her younger brother and teach that to the students. She believed the story of the siblings would be more interesting to the Burmese students than the Tanabata story.

After finishing the folktale, she gave the students a spelling test based on the story. The students listened to Yumisan's voice through their headphones, writing the correct spellings on their papers.

In her imagination, Yumisan saw Maung Maung through a glass opening, sitting and writing in the seat of an absent student. She thought about how joyful and peaceful it would be if she could teach Japanese to her brother while they were in Myanmar. She wished she could make her younger brother learn Japanese just like the students before her. She desired to teach him to speak Japanese. Reflecting on how she and Maung Maung both missed out on this opportunity made her feel a deep sense of sadness.

Yumisan stood up, feeling sad, and looked around at the students who were writing. Then she walked over to the student sitting in the far right of the last row and stood behind him. The student was writing nervously, aware that the teacher was standing behind him. Yumisan wasn't watching him because he was writing poorly; she stood there because he reminded her of Maung Maung.

After school, Yumisan returned home to find Daw Aung May preparing lunch.

'Look, Obasan, isn't this Mandalay Acheik longyi beautiful?' Yumisan said, taking the bundle from her basket and draping it over herself.

'It's very pretty! It would look perfect with your pale yellow blouse,' Daw Aung May replied.

Feeling satisfied, Yumisan went to her room and looked in the mirror. Since last Sunday, for six consecutive days, except for school hours, Yumisan had been practising wearing the longyi at home until she could wear it perfectly. She was preparing to visit Maung Maung the next day in traditional Burmese attire. She felt anxious and excited, getting ready as if for a special occasion. She wore a traditional blouse and longyi and shared her plans with Daw Aung May over lunch.

'I'm going to wear my Burmese-style blouse and longyi, and have my hair done in a simple style with bangs, like the one worn by Nu Nu, at the hair salon. What kind of flowers should I put in my hair, Obasan?'

Daw Aung May, just as eager as Yumisan, was excited to help her prepare.

'Don't say, "Put flowers in your hair," say, "Adorn your hair with flowers." I'll get some delicate yellow roses from the market for you. It will look perfect.'

'That's right . . . that's right. Adorn your hair with flowers. I'll take a camera too. I'll take a picture of Maung Maung and send it to Japan. Grandma and Grandpa will be so happy to see it, Obasan.'

'Will Maung Maung be okay with having his picture taken?' Daw Aung May wondered.

This was something to consider. Yumisan stirred her rice with her spoon, a bit hesitant. She realized it might not be as easy as she had thought. Seeing her hesitation, Daw Aung May encouraged her, 'Just try to be gentle and take the photo, Ma Yu.'

Yumisan took a bite of rice and, as she placed it into her mouth, she suddenly imagined Maung Maung's cruel face, gazing at her with cold eyes.

9

Yumisan's car pulled into the yard, and Ko Mya Phay opened the gate for her. He almost didn't recognize her. Yumisan was wearing a light yellow Mandalay Ahcheik longyi, with her long hair resting on her shoulders, adorned with a single yellow rose in her hair, and carrying a camera. Ko Mya Phay looked back at her, surprised and impressed.

'Is Saya here?' Yumisan asked merrily from the entrance.

Ko Mya Phay, still surprised, nodded his head and then smiled again as he remembered. He thought to himself how beautifully Yumisan had dressed in traditional Burmese attire, to the point where she looked more graceful than a typical Burmese woman.

Yumisan's long-sleeved, pale yellow blouse was perfectly tailored to fit her body, looking elegant and beautiful on her.

With a full chest and well-rounded arms, Yumisan looked graceful, her upper body appearing sleek and beautiful from both the front and back. The Mandalay Acheik longyi she wore around her waist was elegantly draped, fitting her slender figure perfectly. It would be challenging for an ordinary Burmese woman to achieve such a neat and balanced appearance. She wore it so gracefully that even a Burmese woman might want to imitate her.

'Saya is taking a shower. Please have a seat for a moment, Sayama,' Ko Mya Phay said, leaving Yumisan in the living room. Hearing Yumisan's voice from outside, U Thet Lwin realized she had arrived earlier than scheduled and before Maung Maung.

U Thet Lwin came out of his room after showering and changing clothes. Yumisan rose from her seat, bowing respectfully and smiling warmly. U Thet Lwin gazed at her, captivated by her presence. Yumisan's fair complexion and bright yellow outfit made her look like a celestial maiden. She was so elegantly dressed in traditional Burmese attire that he struggled to maintain his composure.

'Wow . . . you look so dignified in Burmese attire, Sayama. By wearing this Burmese traditional attire, you've truly highlighted all the beauty you possess. I'm being completely honest, Sayama,' U Thet Lwin exclaimed, genuinely impressed and praising her without holding back.

'Thank you, Saya.'

U Thet Lwin wasn't satisfied with just one compliment, so he spoke again.

'I've seen many foreigners in Burmese attire, but in my eyes, it's always the person and the clothes separately. I see foreigners dressed like Burmese, but I don't perceive them as truly embodying it. But when I look at you, even knowing you're a foreigner, I can't see you as separate from the attire. You exemplify how graceful and elegant our traditional Burmese clothing can be. It suits you perfectly.'

Yumisan smiled gracefully, maintaining a composed demeanour. Her manners and attitude, now dressed in traditional Burmese clothing, seemed more refined and sophisticated compared to the first time they'd met.

'When I put on Burmese attire, I realize how much I love it, Saya. When I see myself in the mirror, I forget I'm Japanese. I feel like a Burmese girl; I can't quite explain it.'

U Thet Lwin appreciated the way Yumisan expressed herself, especially the phrase 'I can't quite explain it,' and laughed warmly and openly.

'Isn't Maung Maung a Burmese person in Myanmar, Saya? If I were a Japanese person living in Myanmar, how could we ever connect closely? That's why I chose to dress like a Burmese.'

She spoke in a hushed tone, ensuring no one else could hear their conversation.

U Thet Lwin looked at Yumisan closely, feeling a deep sense of sympathy. He wondered if the Japanese also shared this trait, like the Chinese, who often feel a strong bond with their kin.

'Today, we need to wait and see how Maung Maung reacts when he comes back. I haven't mentioned anything about you to him yet. I've told him that you are my guest. I acted as if I didn't notice his rudeness towards you when you came here to give the presents. The challenge is figuring out how to address and resolve the lingering feelings in his heart. I'll keep thinking about it as long as I can, Sayama,' U Thet Lwin said softly, his face showing concern.

'Don't worry about us, Saya. No matter how difficult it gets, I won't give up. We're family, aren't we? I believe everything will turn out as I hope,' Yumisan said, encouraging herself and expressing her determination.

'I pray that things will be resolved quickly for you, Sayama. Maung Maung is a truly kind-hearted child. To this day, he has never done anything to cause me distress,' U Thet Lwin responded gently.

'Really, Saya?'

Yumisan felt proud and happy hearing the kind words about her brother from the person who had adopted him.

'If I don't look happy, he is restless. He listens to everything I say. From the moment I took him in,

I've always treated him like a child I took in out of compassion. But he doesn't see me the same way, Sayama. He sees me as his older brother. Since he was brought from the monastery, he hasn't taken his eyes off me. Wherever I go, he follows. When we went to Mandalay, I had to rent a room because of him. He won't eat unless I come home. He waits for me, even if he's hungry. He eats only when I return, and he sleeps only when I sleep. He's happy just being near me.'

Yumisan, with tears in her eyes, responded, 'He must be very downhearted, Saya? He has no father, no mother, no relatives. So, he must depend on you a lot.'

'Yes, Sayama. He clings to me because he has no one else. He loves me deeply, and because of that, I've developed a bond with him. What started as compassion turned into love, and over time, he became my little brother,' U Thet Lwin explained.

Yumisan listened with teary eyes. Through U Thet Lwin's words, she saw his noble character and compassionate heart. She admired and respected U Thet Lwin's qualities, finding him lovable, admirable, and reliable. She began to feel like she regarded and loved U Thet Lwin just as Maung Maung did, seeing him as an older brother.

* * *

Maung Maung was returning later than usual. In the evening, after the military reserve drills ended, the students hurriedly dispersed and went home. However, since it was Saturday, Maung Maung hesitated to return, thinking there might be guests at home whom he didn't want to see. Sweaty and exhausted, he went back into the ROTC building. A captain saw him from inside a room.

'Hey, Maung Maung, haven't you gone home yet?'

'I'm going now, Captain. I just came to get my bag.'

'My car still hasn't arrived yet.' As the captain spoke, he walked out of the office with Maung Maung. 'Did your family agree to let you attend officer cadet training?' The captain had a particular fondness for Maung Maung among all the students. He admired Maung Maung's agility, politeness, discipline, and determination.

'My elder brother wants me to be a teacher like him. He doesn't really want me to go to officer training, but I think if I insist, he won't object.'

The captain leaned against the tree to wait for the car and started speaking again. 'It's better if you get permission from home.'

'When you joined the military, did your family easily agree to it?'

'My family?' The captain paused and took out a cigarette, lighting it before he continued, smiling as he spoke with the cigarette in his mouth. 'Don't ask whether my family agreed or not. My family pushed me to join the military.'

'Oh, is that so?' Maung Maung responded.

The captain, leaning back against the tree with a thoughtful expression, continued to share his story.

'It's like this: our father was captured during the Japanese occupation and suffered terribly under their torture. During a battle, he escaped from captivity, but a Japanese soldier shot him with a rifle, and to this day, he has one leg missing. He's been through so much hardship. His belief is that a true man should know the art of war and become a good soldier for his country and his people. That's his ideology. Because of that, all of us brothers have ended up in the military one after the other.'

Maung Maung unexpectedly heard something he didn't want to hear. The captain's demeanour, as he spoke about his father's suffering at the hands of the Japanese, showed no signs of lingering hatred or resentment towards the Japanese who had caused his father's suffering. Instead, Maung Maung's own feelings of hatred and anger towards the Japanese flared up, burning fiercely within him.

Because he carried Japanese blood, Maung Maung felt a wave of shame wash over him in front of the captain, not knowing how to face him. He felt embarrassed and disgusted with himself and wished he could purge the Japanese blood from his veins right there in front of the captain.

'If you're joining the military, you need to have a purpose. Don't join just because you want to become an officer. The right way to join is out of love for your country and your people. What is your purpose?' the captain asked, flicking the ash off his cigarette and looking at Maung Maung intently.

'It's not because I want to be an officer, captain. It's because I want to protect and preserve the independence we've achieved,' Maung Maung replied, his eyes shining with determination. His face and eyes expressed the depth and sincerity of his words.

'That's the right attitude. With that mindset, you'll undoubtedly become a great soldier one day,' the captain said.

At that moment, the captain's car arrived, and he insisted on driving Maung Maung home.

Seeing Yumisan's car parked at the house, Maung Maung got off at the gate to avoid bringing the military vehicle inside.

While U Thet Lwin was conversing with Yumisan inside, he heard the sound of a car in front of the house and stood up to take a look. He saw Maung Maung get down from a military vehicle and then, instead of entering the house, head around to the back.

'Look . . . look . . . Sayama. Maung Maung didn't come in the front because he saw your car; he went around to the back,' U Thet Lwin said softly. He then resumed their conversation about Myanmar literature, trying to maintain a calm demeanour.

Yumisan felt her heart flutter with anticipation at the thought of Maung Maung's return, and she tried to steady herself, feeling a bit nervous.

'Hey, why did you come in from the back?' Ko Mya Phay called out to Maung Maung, who had just arrived at the back door.

'Why not come in from the front, Maung Maung? If you come in from the front, you'll see your beauty queen sister waiting for you,' Ko Mya Phay teased, raising his eyebrows suggestively.

'What sister? What beauty queen?' Maung Maung asked, looking at Ko Mya Phay suspiciously.

Ko Mya Phay, smirking, replied, 'Oh, you know . . . in the evening twilight, I saw a heavenly maiden descending from the sky, as beautiful as a goddess. Go and see for yourself. I think she came down from the heavens this evening.'

Realizing that Ko Mya Phay was teasing him on purpose, Maung Maung felt irritated and glared at him. He then hit him lightly with his elbow before heading to his room to change clothes.

From outside, U Thet Lwin called out to him.

'Maung Maung, are you back? Come out for a moment. Sayama is here,' U Thet Lwin called out, feeling relieved as he signalled to Yumisan and shrugged his shoulders.

Maung Maung, annoyed at having to face someone he didn't want to see, scowled as he changed his clothes. He didn't dare defy his older brother by not coming out. Even though he didn't want to see the Japanese teacher, he had to meet her as she was his brother's guest. Reluctantly, he emerged from his room.

In the living room, Maung Maung saw Yumisan, with her long bangs hanging over her shoulders, sitting quietly and smiling at him with an air of grace. Seeing her in traditional Myanmar attire caught him off guard. This must be the 'beauty queen' Ko Mya Phay had mentioned. The sight of Yumisan in Myanmar clothes made her look different from her usual appearance when she wore a kimono or skirt, and this newfound elegance struck Maung Maung as something special.

'Sit down,' U Thet Lwin invited Maung Maung to sit. Yumisan smiled at Maung Maung, her smile carrying an air of grace and poise unlike the forced smile she had previously given him when he'd said, 'Ahkogyi isn't here.'

'Doesn't Sayama look wonderful in our traditional Myanmar clothes? How beautiful and elegant she looks!' U Thet Lwin praised sincerely, though Maung Maung found it childish and annoying that his older brother would say such things. His irritation made him glare at Yumisan in her Myanmar attire.

Maung Maung sat in stony silence, offering no reaction.

'Maung Maung, don't you think I look nice in Myanmar clothes?' Yumisan asked calmly. Maung Maung didn't move, didn't answer, and avoided eye contact, staring instead at the table.

'Sayama asked you a question, answer her,' U Thet Lwin prompted, his heart pounding as he watched.

'Of course, not being Myanmar, how could she look as good as a real Myanmar woman in our traditional clothes? Our traditional attire looks best on Myanmar women,' Maung Maung replied, his tone dripping with sarcasm.

Both U Thet Lwin and Yumisan recognized his mocking tone. Yumisan's face turned pale, but she gathered her courage, lifted her head, and replied without showing embarrassment.

'Ma Ma really likes the Myanmar traditional dress, Maung Maung. Even if you think it doesn't suit me, I'll still wear it. I love the Myanmar people, don't I? And I like Myanmar very much, don't I? So, of course, I should wear Myanmar clothes.'

Yumisan's voice, though composed of Burmese words, did not sound pleasant to Maung Maung's ears. Instead, it felt harsh and jarring. When Yumisan noticed Maung Maung's forced little smile, she continued speaking without backing down.

'There's a saying. You know it, Maung Maung. "When in Rome, do as the Romans do." Since I'm in Myanmar, I should act like a Myanmar person. Isn't that right, Maung Maung?'

Maung Maung thought to himself how grandiose it all seemed. He criticized her for possibly trying to blend in as a Myanmar woman, wondering if she was forgetting her true self. His disdain for Yumisan, who was attempting to mimic being Myanmar, grew even sharper.

Seeing the tension between the siblings, U Thet Lwin felt uneasy and stepped in to smooth things over, saying, 'That's right, Sayama. When in Rome, do as the Romans do—it's a sign of a cultured and respectful attitude.'

Yumisan blushed and smiled with a flushed face and then thought of a way to change the subject.

'By the way, Saya, do you like Japanese snacks? Do you find them tasty?' she asked, looking directly at U Thet Lwin.

U Thet Lwin, feeling relieved by the change of topic, responded, 'Yes, they are quite tasty. I think they've been made to last long.'

'They can be eaten for a long time. In Japan, this snack is quite famous and very popular. It's called *yokan*,' Yumisan explained.

'What about Myanmar snacks? Have you tried a variety of them?' U Thet Lwin asked, trying to involve the quiet Maung Maung in the conversation.

'I have tried a variety. I don't particularly like *mont hinkar* (a traditional rice noodle soup), but I really enjoy *ohn no khauk swe* (coconut noodle soup). I like *shwe kyi*, *kyauk kyaw*, and *jim thoke* too,' Yumisan replied.

'How about this, Sayama? Tomorrow is Sunday, and I would like to invite you for a Myanmar meal. Please come and enjoy some traditional Myanmar dishes,' U Thet Lwin invited.

Maung Maung didn't like the idea of this invitation at all. He felt a surge of irritation, wondering why U Thet Lwin was being so hospitable to the Japanese teacher.

'I do eat Myanmar food. There's a Myanmar lady who lives with me and often cooks Myanmar meals for me. Now I can even handle a bit of spice,' Yumisan said.

Maung Maung smiled. It was a smile that seemed to hide something, a fleeting smile that quickly disappeared. Yumisan, thinking that Maung Maung might have appreciated that she could handle spicy food, felt pleased to express her fondness for Myanmar cuisine in front of him.

U Thet Lwin took the Japanese calendar that Yumisan had brought as a gift and started flipping through it. He pointed to it to draw Maung Maung into the conversation.

'Mount Fuji is really beautiful. Look here, Maung Maung, isn't this photo beautiful?' U Thet Lwin pointed to the picture of Mount Fuji. Maung Maung glanced at it and nodded without speaking. He sat quietly, not daring to move.

'Mount Fuji is a symbol of Japan. There's a traditional folktale associated with it. I recently taught it to my students.'

'How about us . . . Can we listen to the story, Sayama?' U Thet Lwin asked with a smile, knowing Maung Maung was restless but wanting him to stay and listen to the story.

'If you want to listen to that story, I'll tell you,' Yumisan replied. 'But my Burmese is not very good for long stories, so please forgive any mistakes,' she added.

'Please go ahead, Sayama. No problem, if you make mistakes, we'll correct them,' said U Thet Lwin.

Yumisan, contemplating where to begin, glanced at Maung Maung. She didn't catch his eye; instead,

Maung Maung shifted his gaze to the picture of Mount Fuji. Watching Maung Maung sadly, she began the story.

'A long time ago, there was an old bamboo cutter who lived by selling bamboo crafts. One day, while cutting a bamboo root, he found a little girl inside. The girl was very beautiful. In Myanmar, there are similar stories, aren't there?' she asked U Thet Lwin.

U Thet Lwin smiled warmly. 'Yes, in Myanmar folklore, there are stories of people being born from bamboo, lily bud, tamarind tree, and in mangrove fruit. We have many such tales.'

'So, "born from" means "to exist as a human", right?' Yumisan clarified.

'Yes, that's correct,' U Thet Lwin replied.

He felt delighted to see Maung Maung showing interest and listening attentively, hoping that these moments would help them bond.

Yumisan tried to maintain her composure. U Thet Lwin thought that her modesty in Myanmar attire only added to her beauty.

'The old couple who raised the girl loved her dearly. When she grew up, she became very beautiful. She was so beautiful that all the young men admired her, which caused some trouble.'

Yumisan's expressions and gestures were like those of a teacher telling a story to her students in class. Her voice varied in pitch and tone, making the storytelling enjoyable and engaging, and she captivated U Thet Lwin with her soothing, imperfect Burmese pronunciation, drawing him in to listen intently. Maung Maung, on the other hand, was still bothered by the words about men flocking to admire the girl, feeling uneasy and uncomfortable, as if her words were alluding to his brother.

'The girl in the story isn't a human, Saya. She's a fairy from the heavens, temporarily turned human inside the bamboo. Being a fairy, marrying a human is difficult, and so there are complications,' Yumisan explained.

Maung Maung thought to himself, 'This story may not be about Mount Fuji's ancient legend. Is this Japanese teacher pretending to be a fairy and speaking like one?' He misunderstood the tale's intent and continued to harbour suspicions. As Yumisan's eyes occasionally glanced at Maung Maung, he averted his gaze, avoiding eye contact.

'The girl told the men who admired her that if they truly loved her, they must retrieve a jewel from the dragon's mouth at the bottom of the ocean,' Yumisan continued.

'What kind of jewel from the dragon's mouth?' U Thet Lwin interjected.

Yumisan furrowed her brows and batted her eyelashes, thinking deeply about how to phrase it in

Burmese. 'How should I say it in Burmese? Should I call it a ball, like a jewel ball?' she pondered.

Unable to contain his amusement, U Thet Lwin laughed. He glanced at Maung Maung to see if he would join in the laughter, but seeing Maung Maung sitting with a stern expression, he stopped laughing and continued, 'It must be *padamyar myat shin* (ruby ball) if it's from the dragon's mouth, Sayama.'

'Hai, hai, it can be called "*par-tay-myar myat shin*",' Yumisan replied, slightly unsure of her Burmese pronunciation.

Due to her mispronunciation of Burmese, despite her apparent fluency, a Japanese-sounding 'hai hai' slipped out, making Maung Maung stifle a laugh. He felt an overwhelming urge to burst into uncontrollable laughter. However, as she was a guest of his older brother, he managed to restrain himself. Yet, despite his best efforts, his amusement at her mistake was unmistakable, his face betraying the laughter he tried to suppress.

Yumisan continued in a gentle tone, 'Another man came and confessed his love to her. She then told him that if he truly loved her, he should bring back a thing called *nghet taing* from the highest mountain in India. She promised to accept him if he could bring it. This mountain in India is one that no human can climb.'

'Is it Mount Himalaya, Sayama? It must be Mount Himalaya. What is nghet taing?' U Thet Lwin interjected, trying to clarify and asked again since the meaning of the word was not clear.

Yumisan smiled. She was thinking hard, trying to find the right Burmese word to explain the meaning of nghet taing.

'I don't know how to say it in Burmese, Saya. In Japanese, it's called "*subame no su*".'

'Is it a bird's sacred perch, Sayama? In Myanmar, the sacred perches are found at the top of pagodas.'

Yumisan did not immediately understand U Thet Lwin's mention of the bird's sacred perch. She only knew the Japanese term 'subame no su' and tried hard to convey its meaning.

'No, it's not something found in a temple, Saya. It's something you eat.'

U Thet Lwin, now more confused, tried to keep his composure and thought carefully. Maung Maung, meanwhile, was sceptical about the idea of eating a bird's perch and silently criticized the story's logic.

'I got it, Sayama. It's probably not a perch. If it's something that can be eaten and found on a high mountain, it must be *nghet thike* (bird's nest). Birds make their nests on high mountains.'

U Thet Lwin realized that Yumisan had difficulty pronouncing certain Burmese consonants, particularly 't' and 'th'. Maung Maung, unable to hold back, smiled at the realization. He found the misunderstanding and the mispronunciations amusing, causing him to smile.

Yumisan gazed fondly at Maung Maung's smiling face, captivated by its purity. His innocent smile and the way his eyes sparkled with laughter made her think how endearing he was.

'Is it called "nghet thike", Saya?'

Yumisan repeated the words 'nghet thike' several times to remember the term correctly.

'Sometimes, I want to speak, Saya, but in the middle of talking, I can't find the right word, and it becomes quite a struggle.'

Yumisan laughed, her eyes narrowing slightly as she spoke in a long, drawn-out manner, emphasizing the struggle. Her endearing effort evoked compassion in U Thet Lwin.

'Please continue, Sayama. It's not your native language, so it's natural to have difficulties. But if you make mistakes, there will always be someone to correct you. You can speak a lot of Burmese, Sayama. Please, go on.'

U Thet Lwin offered words of encouragement to prevent Yumisan from feeling disheartened by the language barrier. Motivated by U Thet Lwin's support, Yumisan continued the story with growing confidence.

'Another person came to confess his love, too. So, she told him that if he could bring her a tree from the depths of the Chinese sea and make a ring out of gold from that tree, she would marry him.'

U Thet Lwin was eager to understand what kind of tree it was that grew in the sea. He wondered if it was some kind of seaweed. While he pondered, Yumisan, looking hesitant, said, 'In Japanese, it's called "*sango*". I'm not sure how to say it in Burmese, Saya.'

A thought sparked in U Thet Lwin's mind, and his eyes brightened as he provided the meaning. 'Sayama, it's seaweed.'

'It's not seaweed, Sayama.'

Yumisan knew the word 'seaweed'. She was struggling to translate the Japanese 'sango' accurately into Burmese.

'If it's a tree from the deep sea, Sayama, it could only be coral. Does it have colours?'

Yumisan responded enthusiastically, 'Yes, it has. There are green and red colours. It's very beautiful for making gold rings.'

'Ah . . . Sayama, it must be coral.'

Yumisan's eyes sparkled with excitement. 'Yes, Saya, it is coral. My mouth just couldn't say "coral" quickly.'

They all laughed together. U Thet Lwin and Yumisan shared a moment of joy. Maung Maung, hearing the laughter, felt left out. The laughter seemed to linger in front of him, making him feel somewhat uneasy and excluded.

'She isn't human; she's a fairy who came down from the sky. Since it's hard to say that, she tells the people who love her to go to places that humans can't reach. This girl knows that she won't be staying long in the human world. On full moon nights, she looks at the moon and cries.'

As Yumisan spoke, her voice became clouded with emotion, and her face showed signs of sorrow, as if she was about to cry. Throughout her efforts to tell the story, Maung Maung remained uninterested and distant, avoiding eye contact and turning his face away, which made Yumisan want to cry.

Watching the siblings while listening to the story, U Thet Lwin, who never missed a detail, observed Yumisan's expression and understood the sadness she was feeling. Maung Maung, however, did not grasp its significance. He wondered why she was so sensitive, allowing herself to cry along with the fairy in the story, despite being a teacher. Silently, he mocked her in his mind.

'Her ageing parents were worried because they didn't know why she cried looking at the moon. When they asked her, she said that the moon would take her back one day and that she cried because she couldn't leave her parents. She was attached to her parents so much, Saya.'

How come a Japanese teacher is talking about such deep attachments? The word 'attachments' spoken by Yumisan sounded weird in Maung Maung's ears. He was surprised that she could use such profound words, even feeling a bit bitter about it.

'In the kingdom, the king knew she was the most beautiful, Saya. So, on a full moon night, he had soldiers surround her so no one could take her away. Her parents also stayed with her all night. But a celestial being came to take her away, and when he arrived, the soldiers became like lifeless bodies. Even though they wanted to fire their guns, they couldn't move. It was said that the celestial being used his divine power. Before the fairy followed the celestial being, she cried a lot and gave her parents a small bottle of medicine. She told them to take the medicine, saying it would make them live forever and never die. Only after the celestial being took the fairy did the soldiers regain their movement.'

At this point, Yumisan paused her story. She quickly tucked her hand into the hem of her htamein, adjusting the upper part to cover her knees properly. Maung Maung watched her as she fixed her htamein, her actions striking him deeply.

Her mannerisms are just like a real Burmese woman, he thought, reluctantly acknowledging her grace and Burmese-like behaviour.

U Thet Lwin gazed at Yumisan, fixated on how she arranged her htamein.

After adjusting her htamein, Yumisan placed her hands on her lap and continued the story.

'The old parents cried a lot and said that living without her would only bring them more suffering. So, to avoid living without her, they threw the medicine away to Mount Fuji. That's why, according to the traditional story, Mount Fuji will never die and is beautiful in every season.'

Yumisan concluded the story, but she felt a bit hesitant inside. She wanted to sit with her younger brother and tell him Japanese stories one after another, regardless of whether he was interested or not.

'Maung Maung, do you like this story?' she asked, eager for his response.

Maung Maung wanted to pretend he hadn't heard the question, but with U Thet Lwin present, he couldn't ignore it. He knew he had to respect his elder brother's foreign guest. Reluctantly, he answered.

'I like it.'

Yumisan was pleased. Whether Maung Maung truly liked the story of Mount Fuji or not, she was delighted by his simple reply of 'I like it' and her face lit up with happiness.

U Thet Lwin looked alternately at Yumisan and Maung Maung. Hearing Maung Maung's response made him feel relieved. Seeing Yumisan's face light up with a smile, he found it difficult to continue watching the two siblings interacting so formally. He pondered about what fate or circumstances had brought him to encounter these siblings.

'Traditional stories exist in every country, especially in the East. Our folktales are often crafted with some moral or meaning, making them appealing and charming. Your grasp of the Myanmar language makes these stories even more vivid,' he said.

'My Myanmar language skills are still weak, Saya. However, at Osaka University, I was the best in Myanmar language and passed all my exams with honours,' Yumisan replied.

'You are not weak at all; you are very good. Was your professor who taught Myanmar language very skilled?' he asked.

'Yes, Saya. When our professor speaks or teaches Myanmar, there is no Japanese accent at all. He was born in Myanmar before the war and went to school there. He spent a year at Yangon University when he was sixteen before returning to Japan just before the war.'

'That explains why he is so skilled, then,' U Thet Lwin said.

Yumisan, smiling, glanced at Maung Maung and then spoke.

'I really wanted to master the Myanmar language. I told my professor that I wanted to be as proficient as he was. He told me, "If you really want to be that good, go to Myanmar." Throughout all four years at school, my professor never spoke a single word of Japanese to me because he knew how much I wanted to learn Myanmar. He always spoke to me in Myanmar,' Yumisan said.

Ko Mya Phay brought in the tea set and glanced at the two siblings sitting together, listening to Yumisan's story. In his mind, Yumisan no longer seemed like a foreign Japanese woman but rather like the lady of the house, sitting and chatting with her family. Smiling to himself, he left the room.

Maung Maung was still plotting to leave the moment Yumisan and U Thet Lwin started drinking tea. Then, remembering something, Yumisan said, 'The sunlight is perfect, Saya. Let me take a photo of you and Maung Maung. I brought a camera.'

Maung Maung's face fell. He didn't want his photo to end up in the hands of a Japanese person and bitterly declined her request.

'I don't want to take a photo, Ahkogyi. You take it instead.'

'I want a photo of both of you together, Maung Maung. I want to have photos to remember my friends and loved ones in Myanmar,' Yumisan pleaded.

Maung Maung, his expression still sour, just shook his head.

'Come on, don't be shy. Sayama is asking you for a favour. It's just a photo with your older brother, me,' U Thet Lwin encouraged.

'I don't want to take it, Ahkogyi. You take it,' Maung Maung insisted.

Yumisan looked at Maung Maung with a sad expression, noticing his reluctance.

'Come on, why are you being like this?' U Thet Lwin spoke firmly, trying to prevent Maung Maung from refusing again. Eventually, Maung Maung reluctantly moved to the front veranda.

In the photo that Yumisan took, the two brothers stood side by side. U Thet Lwin's face appeared clear and bright, while Maung Maung's face showed a mix of hatred, disgust, and dissatisfaction, making him look unpleasant.

Yumisan, pleased to have gotten the photo, returned home happily. As she was leaving in the car, U Thet Lwin encouraged her gently, 'Take it easy, Sayama.'

When Yumisan returned home, Daw Aung May greeted her at the door.

'Ma Yu . . . did you meet them?' she asked.

'Yes, I did . . . Obasan,' Yumisan replied.

'How did they like seeing you in Myanmar attire?'

Instead of answering with words, Yumisan just raised her hand and slightly bent her finger.

Seeing Yumisan's weary face and the gesture of her bent finger, Daw Aung May asked again, 'What happened? Tell me.'

Yumisan sighed deeply, lowering her hand.

'The teacher who lives with him and adopted him said that I looked very beautiful in traditional Myanmar attire. But he said that Myanmar clothes look good only on Myanmar women. Then his face, Obasan, looked . . . like this . . . like this,' Yumisan said, lowering her eyebrows and pouting her lips, making her face look old before heading to her room.

Daw Aung May, feeling sorry upon seeing Yumisan's expression, followed her into the room. Yumisan stood in front of the mirror, looking at herself. She saw her disappointed reflection and clenched her lips tightly in frustration.

'What a pity, Ma Yu. He said you don't look good in Myanmar attire just to spite you.'

'Exactly, he said it on purpose. He really hates Japan,' Yumisan said, her face turning sad again as she changed her clothes. Looking at Daw Aung May, with tears welling up, she added, 'I took a photo of him, but his face didn't look like his usual self. I can't even describe how it looked. If you see this photo, you'll cry.'

After changing her clothes, Yumisan sat down on the bed. Daw Aung May, standing nearby with a concerned expression, asked, 'When will you visit him again?'

'They've invited me to have lunch at their house tomorrow. It would be good to eat with my hands, right? Please teach me how to eat with my hands,' Yumisan replied.

Daw Aung May set the dinner table and instructed Yumisan on how to eat with her hands. She demonstrated the gentle and refined manner of taking and eating rice, ensuring Yumisan practised until she could do it neatly and gracefully.

Yumisan tried to carefully imitate Daw Aung May's graceful manner of serving the soup, taking the rice, and eating without letting the grains stick to her hands.

* * *

U Thet Lwin was exhausted from spending the whole day preparing to host a foreign guest for a meal at his home. It wasn't until later that he realized he didn't have any nice dishes to serve. Then, he began noticing the cobwebs on the walls, dust everywhere, and the litter on the floor. He cleaned the dust, swept the floor, replaced the plates and glasses, and even cut up the Mudon gift tablecloth to make emergency napkins.

Whenever they hosted a guest for a meal at home, Ko Mya Phay took charge in the kitchen, with Maung Maung lending a hand. U Thet Lwin had carefully planned a menu featuring coconut rice, chicken curry, fried prawns, fried fish, *nga phay* salad, and soup. In a brief moment when Ko Mya Phay was away, Maung Maung couldn't resist a bit of mischief, tossing extra chilli into the chicken curry Ko Mya Phay was preparing. He also made sure to chop the hottest chillies for the nga phay salad. Then he muttered to himself while chopping, 'You said you like Burmese food. Now let's see how much you really like spicy food.'

'Hey . . . hey . . . Maung Maung, what are you doing?' asked Ko Mya Phay, shocked at the sight of the chopped green chillies.

'I'm chopping chillies. She said they can eat spicy food,' Maung Maung replied with a mischievous look.

'Even if she likes spicy food, this is too much. How can she eat it this spicy?'

Ko Mya Phay picked up the sliced green chillies that Maung Maung had prepared and tossed them aside. Realizing that forcing his plan wouldn't work, Maung Maung quietly let it go. He seemed to think there was no need for more chillies, as plenty had already been added to the chicken curry.

By the evening, when Yumisan arrived, Maung Maung's face showed no resentment but was rather calm and composed.

Yumisan greeted U Thet Lwin with a deep bow, expressing her respect with a warm smile. She was dressed in a traditional Myanmar outfit, a white blouse with a dark green *zim may* longyi.

Just like yesterday, Yumisan looked graceful, beautiful, and refined. She entered the living room, sat down, glanced at Maung Maung busily moving around, and smiled warmly. Maung Maung, pretending to be too busy to notice her smile, turned quickly and headed towards the kitchen.

'Maung Maung is quite busy today, Sayama. When we have guests over for a meal, he's the one who helps out. He can cook too. Sometimes, when there's no one else at home, he cooks for me,' said U Thet Lwin cheerfully before sitting down.

'Really? That's impressive. Without a woman in the house, it's good that he knows how to do these things,' Yumisan replied. She felt a sense of happiness at the thought of eating the dishes prepared by her younger brother.

'Next week, I'll be able to send the photos to Japan. My grandmother will be so happy to see her grandson. When she reads about him in my letters, she might feel sad though . . .' Yumisan trailed off, not wanting to say anything negative.

U Thet Lwin's house didn't have a separate dining room; they used the area outside the bedroom for dining, placing a table and some stools there. Therefore, the dining area was visible from the living room.

Maung Maung paced back and forth between the dining room and kitchen, busy arranging plates and glasses on the table. Each time he entered, Yumisan would fall silent, only resuming her conversation with U Thet Lwin once Maung Maung had left the room.

'I was thinking last night,' U Thet Lwin said, 'maybe we should tell him the truth. What do you think, Sayama?'

'Not yet, Saya. If we tell him now, he won't handle it well. I'm worried about how he'll react. It's better to wait for the right time. Please, hold on just a little longer,' Yumisan said, her tone filled with concern.

U Thet Lwin nodded but pressed on. 'Your grandparents already know about Maung Maung, don't they?'

'My father told them before he passed away, so they all know. Obasan is eager to meet him—she's never seen her grandson before, and since it's a boy, she's especially excited.'

'In Myanmar, there's a saying: "A son is loved, but a grandson is cherished twice as much." Did you write about him in your letter?'

Yumisan's expression turned solemn, her face paling as she gave a faint nod.

Meanwhile, Ko Mya Phay watched Maung Maung bustling around the kitchen and couldn't help but think how cooperative and good-natured he was being today. With a teasing smile, he asked, 'Is your beauty queen sister here dressed in traditional Myanmar clothes?'

'Yes,' Maung Maung replied, 'she's wearing a white blouse and a green zim may longyi. I wonder if she sees herself as a Burmese woman now.'

'In her Myanmar attire, she really matches well with your brother when walking together,' said Ko Mya Phay.

'Enough joking, man. Just do your work. It's almost time to set the table,' Maung Maung replied.

Ko Mya Phay laughed heartily as he stirred the chicken curry pot.

Maung Maung continued, 'I've stirred the pot, but the meat is not tender yet. I've already tasted it to know if the seasoning is right.'

'Is it still bland?'

'It's perfect,' Maung Maung responded with a serious demeanour.

When the dinner table was set, U Thet Lwin invited Yumisan to the table. The dinner arrangement, though not grand or lavish, was cleaner and more organized than usual, which U Thet Lwin felt proud of.

Before sitting down, Yumisan looked at the table. The simple and clean set-up made her feel genuinely thankful to U Thet Lwin.

'Won't you join us, Maung Maung?' she asked.

'No, Sayama, I don't want to eat yet,' Maung Maung replied calmly.

'You should join us for dinner,' U Thet Lwin insisted.

'Come eat with us, Maung Maung,' Yumisan added, urging him again.

Maung Maung, however, did not want to sit and eat with Yumisan.

'I won't eat yet, Ahkogyi,' Maung Maung repeated, declining the invitation.

'Even if you're not hungry, come and eat. If the guest wants you to join, you should,' U Thet Lwin urged again, making Maung Maung unable to refuse further.

At the table, U Thet Lwin and Maung Maung sat on one side, facing Yumisan on the other.

This was the first time in Myanmar that Yumisan was sharing a meal with her own blood, her younger brother, at the same table. She sat down in her place, a radiant smile lighting up her face.

Sitting across from Maung Maung, she felt as if her secret was laid bare before everyone. An intense feeling of love and affection for her younger brother surged through her body.

Seeing the utensils set for her, she expressed her preference. 'I'd like to eat with my hands.'

'Let's eat with spoons and forks, Sayama. We'll use them too,' U Thet Lwin suggested.

But Yumisan insisted. 'I'd prefer to eat with my hands, Saya.'

Yumisan washed her hands with the water that Ko Mya Phay prepared for her. Ko Mya Phay then served her coconut rice in her plate first. Once the rice was served, Yumisan placed her hands together in front of her chest, closed her eyes, and silently offered a prayer over her plate. Everyone watched her intently. After a moment of focused prayer, Yumisan smiled and explained, 'My grandmother taught me from a young age to offer a prayer and thanksgiving before eating. It has become a habit, Saya.'

'What kind of prayer is it, Sayama? Please share,' U Thet Lwin asked, feeling happy and proud to see the sibling connection between Maung Maung and Yumisan. His face was lit up with a genuine smile.

'We begin by thanking the Lord for placing us in the human world, where we have the blessing of eating rice. Then, we remember and thank the sun for giving warmth and the rain for nurturing the rice plants. We also express gratitude to the farmers who cultivate the grain and the workers who process it into rice. My grandmother taught me to remember and be grateful for everyone's contributions before eating.' Yumisan thus explained the meaning behind her prayer.

U Thet Lwin, who had been watching Yumisan intently with a smile on his face, clapped his hands on the table and, with a cheerful smile, said, 'Your prayer is very fitting for our Myanmar tradition, Sayama. Our children should also be taught to remember and be grateful to the farmers and workers who make our meals possible before they eat.'

Yumisan looked directly into U Thet Lwin's eyes and replied, 'Indeed, Saya.'

'Every time before eating, we should remember and be grateful for everyone's efforts. I should teach this to Maung Maung as well, Saya,' Yumisan said, smiling, before taking a small amount of rice from her plate with her fingertips and gently placing it in her mouth.

'Please teach him, Sayama,' U Thet Lwin said, laughing. Maung Maung, who had kept his eyes lowered since he sat down, seemed tense and uncomfortable with the conversation being about him. His posture was hunched.

'Maung Maung, did you hear what I said? Always remember to be thankful before you eat,' Yumisan encouraged. She hoped Maung Maung would at least respond with a smile or a glance, but he remained silent, his head hanging even lower, focusing on his food.

Seeing this, U Thet Lwin nudged Maung Maung's leg under the table and whispered, 'Sayama is talking to you. Why are you so shy, Maung Maung?'

Maung Maung finally lifted his head, forced a smile, and looked down again, pondering whether she considered him as a student from her class. U Thet Lwin, feeling relieved at Maung Maung's response, picked up the chicken curry dish and handed it to Yumisan, saying, 'Please, Sayama.'

Yumisan scooped a spoonful of curry and a piece of chicken onto her plate. Just as Daw Aung May had taught her, she gently mixed the curry with her rice, then delicately took a small bite. Almost immediately, her face turned red, and she felt an intense heat spreading from her tongue to her cheeks and ears. Unable to bear the spiciness, tears welled up in her eyes, and she struggled to hold back her reaction.

'Oh . . . Sayama, is it too spicy? What a pity! I thought you could handle spicy food, so I made this oily curry.

Would you like some water, Sayama?' U Thet Lwin asked, feeling concerned upon seeing Yumisan's reaction to the spiciness. He spoke softly, his voice tinged with worry. Maung Maung continued eating quietly, feeling a mix of satisfaction and amusement at Yumisan's inability to handle the spiciness. He felt a sense of pride, enjoying her struggle.

Although Yumisan had eaten Myanmar dishes many times at home, she had never encountered such spiciness before. U Thet Lwin himself hadn't yet tasted the chicken curry, so he didn't realize how spicy it was. 'I can handle a bit of spiciness, but this curry is very spicy,' Yumisan said, wiping her eyes and nose with a handkerchief. Her tongue was burning intensely, unable to relieve the heat.

'Sayama, switch plates. Eat the fried shrimp that doesn't have any chilli.'

U Thet Lwin instructed Ko Mya Phay to bring a new plate and added more rice for Yumisan. Ko Mya Phay just assumed Yumisan couldn't handle the spiciness. He had no idea how spicy the chicken curry actually was.

Maung Maung felt a guilty pleasure, watching Yumisan's discomfort. The satisfaction he felt was evident on his face. U Thet Lwin watched Yumisan closely, feeling a deep sense of compassion as he noticed her reddened face.

'Sayama, if the spiciness hasn't subsided, drink some water,' he said, handing her a glass of water.

Yumisan took the glass, her eyelashes fluttering, and sipped the water slowly. Embarrassed by her reaction, with tears streaming down her face, she smiled and said, 'It's alright, Saya. It's good. This meal will always be memorable for me.'

U Thet Lwin, relieved by Yumisan's ability to smile and speak again, added fried shrimp to her plate. He then tasted the chicken curry himself, realizing it was spicier than usual.

'Your dish has a bit too much chilli, Ko Mya Phay. Even I find it spicy,' he admitted.

Ko Mya Phay had added the usual amount of chilli, so he couldn't understand why he was being blamed. He looked suspiciously at Maung Maung, who had prepared the chilli paste. Maung Maung discreetly winked at Ko Mya Phay, revealing the trick he had played.

Though a foreigner, Yumisan ate rice with her hands as neatly and gracefully as a Myanmar woman, which impressed U Thet Lwin. Her refined and gentle manner of eating was pleasing to his eyes and added a sense of calm elegance to the scene.

Taking the plate of nga phay salad, U Thet Lwin intended to add some to Yumisan's plate but first asked Ko Mya Phay, 'Is there any fresh chilli in this?'

Maung Maung answered quickly, 'No.'

Ko Mya Phay, not entirely trusting Maung Maung, added, 'There's a little bit, Saya.'

U Thet Lwin took the nga phay salad plate back and offered Yumisan the fried fish instead, saying, 'Have some fried fish, Sayama.' He then asked, 'Do you like coconut rice?'

'Yes, I do, Saya. I also like fried prawns,' Yumisan replied, reaching for the fried fish plate and continuing to chat with U Thet Lwin. Meanwhile, Maung Maung shot Ko Mya Phay a displeased look, knowing that his comment about the nga phay salad having chilli wasn't true.

'Maung Maung, take some fried fish,' Yumisan offered, handing him the plate of fried fish.

'Maung Maung, is the food tasty?' she asked once he had taken the plate, catching his eye.

Maung Maung wondered if he was being treated like a guest in his own home, so he sarcastically replied with a spiteful grin, 'It's delicious.'

'Maung Maung, do you take your lunch with you when you go to school in the morning?' she asked.

'No, I eat before I go,' he replied.

'And what do you have for lunch?'

'I have tea.'

Seeing Maung Maung start to open up, Yumisan's face lit up with pleasure. 'What time do you go to school in the morning?' she continued.

'At eight o'clock,' he answered.

'Our school starts at seven-thirty. That's quite early,' she remarked.

When Maung Maung lowered his gaze again, Yumisan stopped asking questions. She focused on eating her rice, enjoying the meal while occasionally glancing at Maung Maung. His neatly parted hair, his neatly buttoned shirt, and his innocent lips and forehead made him endearing in her eyes. She took her time eating, savouring each bite while observing him.

Once everyone had finished eating, Ko Mya Phay cleared the table and brought out fruits and coffee for everyone.

'Sayama, is the lady who lives at home with you a good cook?' U Thet Lwin asked Yumisan as he peeled bananas for her.

'Yes, she cooks very well. She is very good at cooking snakehead fish. I'm planning to invite you and Maung Maung over for dinner next Saturday night. You can try her cooking then,' Yumisan replied.

Upon hearing the invitation for dinner on Saturday night, Maung Maung immediately decided he wouldn't go.

'Is she Burmese or Karen?' U Thet Lwin continued.

'She's a Burmese, Buddhist woman, Saya. She's very devoted and says long prayers. Her chanting voice is very pleasant to listen to. She offers alms every morning at home,' Yumisan explained.

'Do Japanese people also have the tradition of offering alms at the shrine?' U Thet Lwin inquired.

Yumisan smiled and replied, 'Yes, we do, Saya. Some people cook three times a day and they offer three times a day. In Buddhism, there are different sects like Shinto, Shinshu, and Zen. Obasan offers alms early in the morning, so I also join her in prayer.'

'How do you pray, Sayama? What do you say? Do you pray in Japanese or in Burmese?' U Thet Lwin asked, looking intently at Yumisan's face.

'I can't chant like Obasan, Saya, so when I pray in Burmese, I pray like this,' Yumisan replied. Yumisan put her hands together and touched her forehead, then began to recite: 'O Ahshin Phaya, I pray to you once, twice, and for the third time. Just know, I pray exactly the same way as those expert prayers in Myanmar—just like they do it, no difference, Ahshin Phaya, no difference . . .'

U Thet Lwin watched Yumisan's way of praying and laughed heartily. Maung Maung, thinking that Yumisan wasn't watching him, took the opportunity to glance at her. Seeing her actions and manner of praying, he couldn't help but laugh silently.

After finishing her prayer, Yumisan lowered her hands and smiled at Maung Maung.

'Maung Maung, do you pray every day?' she asked.

Maung Maung gave a shy smile and shook his head.

'Have you never prayed to the Buddha?' Yumisan asked, surprised.

'Not every day. Sometimes I do,' Maung Maung replied.

'Do you know the Five Precepts of Buddhism, Maung Maung?' she inquired further.

'Yes, I am from Myanmar, so I know how to pray and follow the Five Precepts,' Maung Maung said. After speaking, he realized the meaning of his words and felt a bit embarrassed as he glanced at U Thet Lwin.

U Thet Lwin observed Maung Maung's every word, his tone, and his expression.

'What about Thuyathadi, the goddess? Don't you pray to her, Maung Maung?'

Both U Thet Lwin and Maung Maung looked at Yumisan in amazement. U Thet Lwin's eyes sparkled brightly as he heard Yumisan mention Thuyathadi. He couldn't believe his ears and asked, half-smiling, 'Sayama, how do you know about Thuyathadi, the goddess?'

Maung Maung felt like laughing but held it in, waiting for Yumisan's response.

'At my house, my grandmother has a statue of Thuyathadi, the goddess, sitting on a *hamsa* bird. My grandmother told me about her. Thuyathadi is a goddess who guards the scriptures of Buddha, the

Pitakas. Praying to her brings wisdom and protection,' Yumisan explained.

U Thet Lwin couldn't contain his laughter and burst out, while Maung Maung, losing his urge to laugh, thought humorously, *If this Japanese teacher stays in Myanmar long enough, she might start reciting the* Kammavaca.

After his laughter subsided, U Thet Lwin asked Yumisan with interest, 'Do you have similar goddesses in Japan?'

Yumisan's eyes brightened as she answered, 'Yes, we do. In Japan, we have Kannon. We hang her image in our living rooms and pray to her.'

'Sayama, living with a Myanmar woman suits you well, and it helps you learn more about Myanmar.'

'I fit in well because I live with Obasan. She has taken me to almost every pagoda in Yangon. We've also visited astrologers and palmists. We watched traditional performances of *ah nyeint*: Shwe Man Tin Maung, Sein Aung Min, and Kanet Sein together the entire night,' Yumisan replied.

U Thet Lwin smiled broadly. His cheerful demeanour and wide smile seemed to convey a sense of enjoyment and contentment. Yumisan appeared to be a foreigner full of charm and likable traits in U Thet Lwin's eyes. However, in Maung Maung's view, she seemed like a Japanese woman who had become overly familiar with Myanmar, sparking feelings of envy and resentment.

'Which astrologers and palmists have you visited?' U Thet Lwin asked, squinting his eyes.

'I visited Astrologer Sandra. He predicted that my ambitions would not be easily achieved and that there would be significant challenges. I think he might be right,' Yumisan replied, staring at U Thet Lwin. A slight smile flickered on her face, a blend of genuine and bittersweet emotions.

U Thet Lwin seemed to understand the meaning behind Yumisan's faint smile. He recognized her unspoken struggles, acknowledging them with a look of sympathy before responding.

'Sayama, while you're in Myanmar, you should watch the Taung Pyone Nat festival. You'd find it fascinating.'

'Obasan promised to take me to Taung Pyone, Saya. She explained many names of the *nats*, like Mother Poppa, Mingyi, Mingalay, and U Min Kyaw, but I couldn't remember them all. I wrote everything down in my notes,' Yumisan replied.

U Thet Lwin couldn't help but admire Yumisan's extensive knowledge despite her short stay in Myanmar.

'Sayama, do you watch Myanmar dramas? Do you like them?'

'Why wouldn't I, Saya?' Yumisan responded, her lips parting into a gentle smile like a blooming rose, and she gazed intently at U Thet Lwin with a look of surprise, then covered her expression with a smile.

'I love them, Saya. When I watch dramas, I prefer sitting near the orchestra because I get to see both the musicians play and the actors up close. At the same timc, there's so much to see and hear. Sometimes, Obasan whispers explanations to me, and I have to split my attention between listening to her and the performance while taking notes. It's quite an experience,' she explained.

U Thet Lwin listened to Yumisan, enthralled by her every word, never tiring of her voice. He watched as her lips moved, her eyes sparkled, and her radiant smile shone, captivated by her lively expressions.

'Do you like the dance movements, Sayama?' U Thet Lwin asked, eagerly listening for more when Yumisan paused. Meanwhile, Maung Maung was anxiously waiting for the right moment to excuse himself from the table. He knew it was inappropriate to leave mid-conversation, but he was feeling increasingly uncomfortable and distracted.

'When the actress lifts her longyi hem and runs across the stage, Saya, I feel like I'm right there with her—lifting my own longyi and running beside her,' Yumisan said, her arms extending as she mimicked the motion with a broad smile. Her laughter, full of warmth and carefree joy, made U Thet Lwin irresistibly drawn to her.

'I especially love the court dances, Saya. The grace and artistry of the maidens is mesmerizing. Watching them, I can see why King Mindon had so many wives,' Yumisan remarked. U Thet Lwin burst into uncontrollable laughter, while Maung Maung's expression darkened, like a cloud heavy with impending rain.

'If you visit Upper Myanmar, you'll learn and see even more about Myanmar,' U Thet Lwin suggested.

'This December, during the school break, I'm planning to visit Bagan, Popa, and Mandalay,' Yumisan replied.

'What about Shan state and Taunggyi? Have you been there yet?' U Thet Lwin asked, increasingly fascinated by Yumisan. He noticed that her qualities seemed to shine more brightly with each passing moment.

'During the Thadingyut school holidays, I went to Taunggyi. I've been to Taunggyi, Inle Lake, Pindaya, and Kalaw,' Yumisan said.

'The weather is nice there, so you'll probably like Shan state, Sayama,' U Thet Lwin replied.

'I do like it. I want to go again. Maung Maung, have you ever been to Shan state?' Yumisan asked, trying to get Maung Maung to join the conversation.

'I have,' Maung Maung responded curtly.

'Maung Maung, do you like Shan state?' Yumisan asked, glancing at him.

Maung Maung, wanting to keep it brief, replied, 'I don't like anywhere except Yangon.'

Yumisan laughed. Sensing the deeper meaning behind Maung Maung's words, she found it amusing.

'I want to invite you to Japan, Saya. Have you ever wanted to go to Japan, Maung Maung? If you want to go, I'll take you,' Yumisan said, her question electrifying Maung Maung.

Being asked this question in front of U Thet Lwin caused Maung Maung intense pain. Without answering, he shook his head vigorously, blushing with embarrassment.

Realizing her mistake, Yumisan quickly backtracked, saying, 'Maung Maung only likes Yangon.'

She laughed again.

'How long will you stay in Myanmar, Sayama?' U Thet Lwin asked, sensing Maung Maung's discomfort and wanting to change the subject.

'I have a two-year contract,' Yumisan replied.

'Your desire to write a book about Myanmar and your curiosity are admirable, Sayama. There's so much to study here. What's your impression of Myanmar's people since you arrived?' U Thet Lwin asked.

Yumisan's eyes lit up, and she wanted to share her thoughts openly.

'Shall I tell you, Saya?' she asked.

'Please do,' U Thet Lwin encouraged.

'Myanmar people often look back at the past, Saya. For example, they haven't forgotten what happened during the wartime. From what I understand, there's still a sense of animosity towards Japan. In Japan, we don't look back at the past. What's done is done, and we don't dwell on it. In Japan, how devastating were the atomic bombs dropped on Hiroshima and Nagasaki by the Americans? But Japan doesn't look back; we accepted our loss in the war and formed friendly relations with the victorious country, with the mindset of rebuilding the nation together. This is the difference I notice between Myanmar and Japan,' Yumisan said, briefly glancing at Maung Maung. Her words seemed to be aimed directly at him.

Maung Maung turned his face away, looking somewhat downcast. U Thet Lwin, realizing that Yumisan's words were subtly directed at Maung Maung, hoped he would understand. However, Maung Maung couldn't accept Yumisan's words. In his mind, no one could surpass his resentment towards the Japanese. He believed he could never be swayed by anyone's opinions to change his feelings.

'Japanese people aren't naturally aggressive, Sayama. They treat each other with respect, almost like a religious observance. They are humble. In truth, they are a polite nation,' U Thet Lwin said, helping Yumisan make her point.

'War is truly cruel and brutal. Look at Hiroshima and Nagasaki in Japan, Saya. Within minutes, people turned to ashes. It's horrifying. For me, war is nothing but slaughter, and I hate war the most,' Yumisan added, with a hint of sadness, her eyes darkened with the bitterness she felt toward war.

Maung Maung remained silent. He was disheartened with U Thet Lwin due to their differing views about the Japanese. He didn't seem to support those taking the leading roles; in fact, he appeared to oppose them.

'When talking about the war, I remember a poem my father wrote, Saya,' Yumisan said, recalling the poem 'From Mingaladon' that her father had written from Mingaladon.

'Is your father a poet, Sayama?' U Thet Lwin asked, his heart racing with concern over what Yumisan might say next.

'My father was an artist. He wrote poems and painted. He served in the military during the war and even lived in Mingaladon, Myanmar,' she replied.

U Thet Lwin's eyes widened. Maung Maung glanced at Yumisan's face, filled with anger at the revelation that her father had been to Myanmar. On the other hand, U Thet Lwin looked at Yumisan with anxious anticipation of what she might reveal next.

'So, your father has been to Myanmar. What kind of poem did he write, Sayama?' U Thet Lwin asked, trying to keep his composure while his heart pounded.

'It's a simple poem, Saya. He wrote it and sent it to me from Mingaladon for my fifth birthday,' Yumisan replied, lowering her face slightly and thinking about how to translate the Japanese poem into Burmese.

During her time at the foreign language school in Osaka, Yumisan's Japanese professor had translated her father's poem, 'From Mingaladon', into Burmese prose for her. She had memorized the translated words and now recited them slowly and softly.

Today is Yumisan's fifth birthday.
At her party, she dances with a fan,
Graceful, light, full of joy.
I wish to paint her figure,
To show the truth of being human.
But no brush in my hand—
Only a gun I hold.

Yumisan's voice trailed off. After a brief silence, she said, 'This is the meaning of the poem in Burmese, Saya.'

Her translation had a profound impact on U Thet Lwin.

As Yumisan recited the professor's translation in Burmese, each word was clear and deliberate, earning her admiration. Her gestures, mimicking holding a paintbrush and a gun, added depth to the poem's meaning.

'The meaning of the poem is wonderful, Sayama. It's profound. Japanese paintings and poems are simple and clear, but they carry deep meanings behind the simplicity, like the contrast between the paintbrush and the gun,' U Thet Lwin said.

Yumisan wanted to reveal that this poem was written by Maung Maung's father, but she couldn't bring herself to say it. She felt a deep, unspoken sadness for her inability to share the truth.

'Is this translation your work, Sayama?' U Thet Lwin asked.

'No, Saya. It was done by my professor in Japan. He translated it for me. He asked me to bring a translated version of this poem in Burmese when I returned from Myanmar. Saya, could you teach me to write Burmese poetry?' she requested.

Maung Maung, who had been silent, suddenly jerked with surprise. He couldn't hide his displeasure about Yumisan asking U Thet Lwin to teach her poetry, which made him look around nervously, glancing at the plates on the table and the walls.

'I will teach you, Sayama. Let's find a suitable time for both of us. I will help you turn your father's poem into a Burmese poem,' U Thet Lwin said.

Although U Thet Lwin didn't sense Maung Maung's discomfort, Yumisan did. She felt saddened rather than pleased by U Thet Lwin's offer of help.

'Your father is not a man of war, Sayama,' U Thet Lwin said.

Yumisan felt a tightness in her chest at his words.

Noticing her silence, Maung Maung began to think, his thoughts turning bitter, *The Japanese only retreated because they lost the war; otherwise, the entire country would be in a far worse state.*

Yumisan, struggling to hold back her emotions, finally spoke up. 'At that time, Saya, every man in Japan was involved in the war. My father left for the war when I was just ten months old. My mother died on the day I was born. My grandmother raised me. I never saw my father. Even after the war ended, he became a hostage of war, and I couldn't meet him immediately. I only saw him when I turned fifteen. Even then, he didn't live long; he died due to sickness.'

As Yumisan spoke about her father to U Thet Lwin, it was also meant for Maung Maung to hear. Hearing about her father made Maung Maung remember his own mother. He felt a wave of sadness wash over him, pushing him away from the voices of U Thet Lwin and Yumisan. In his mind, he was engulfed by the incompleteness of his own life, and the memories he wanted to forget started surfacing again.

In truth, Maung Maung had never been able to fully come to terms with his life. After his mother passed away and until he was five, he considered his grandfather U Saing, who had raised him, as his real father. When U Saing passed away when he was five, Maung Maung ended up in the care of U Htun Maung, and his wife, Ma Pwe.

It was only while living with Ma Pwe that he started hearing from her and others, 'Your father is Japanese.' At that time, Maung Maung would respond with, 'No, he's not.' Whenever he was teased about it, he would either burst into tears or get angry and bang his head against the floor, crying. Those who wanted to see him do this would surround him, laughing and jeering.

Before U Htun Maung sent him to Kyaik Sakaw Monastery, he told Maung Maung, 'Your father is Japanese, and U Saing was your grandfather.' He also showed him a photograph. But Maung Maung didn't think of the person in the photograph as his father, or even a person; to him, it was just an image, devoid of any emotional attachment or recognition.

After U Saing's death in Kadote village, there was no one in the village who could clearly tell Maung Maung about his own life. He had no idea, like Yumisan did, that his parents had been married during the Japanese occupation. It was only after he came to live with U Thet Lwin and started attending school that he slowly began to learn completely about the Japanese era.

As his thoughts surfaced from the depths, he imagined his Japanese-speaking father violently pulling his mother as she struggled to break free. The vision blurred as he fought to confront the memories. The images overwhelmed him, and his heart pounded fiercely, like waves crashing against a cliff in a storm.

Suddenly, Maung Maung stood up abruptly from the dining table and quietly walked towards the kitchen.

As soon as Maung Maung stood up and left, Yumisan leaned forward slightly and spoke softly. 'Isn't it good that I've already given him a little heads-up, Saya?'

'It's fine, Sayama, it's fine,' U Thet Lwin said in agreement.

When Maung Maung reached the kitchen, Ko Mya Phay greeted him with an amused expression.

'Tell me, how many chilli peppers did you add? I only soaked three.'

'Seven . . .'

Maung Maung replied with satisfaction, smiling broadly.

'Oh, poor lady! She suffered unbearably from the spiciness,' Ko Mya Phay remarked.

Shuu-shay . . . Shuu-shay . . . Shuu-shay . . .

At the dining table, Maung Maung was playfully mocking Yumisan by imitating how she had been making hissing sounds after eating spicy food, unable to handle the heat.

10

Yumisan kept glancing at the clock, feeling anxious because her invited guests were an hour late for the appointment. She walked to the window and looked outside countless times, feeling weary.

That night, the moonlight shone softly outside the house. In the yard, the frangipani trees, heavy with flowers, were bathed in a soft glow of moonlight, their green leaves glistening. The peacock flowers adorning the fence were blooming brightly in white and various colours, gently swaying in the wind.

Yumisan missed the cherry blossoms that would be in full bloom in Japan at this time of year. She imagined the large branches of the cherry trees laden with delicate, pale pink blossoms. As she thought of this, she also remembered her grandfather and grandmother, their memories filling her heart.

'By now, *Obaasan* and *Ojiisan* would have seen Maung Maung's photograph,' she sighed, as a car sped noisily past the front of the house.

Because U Thet Lwin and Maung Maung were invited for dinner tonight at her house, everyone was prepared and waiting. Daw Aung May, eager to host Yumisan's younger brother, had cooked a variety of delicious Burmese dishes.

Yumisan had sent a car to pick them up, but as the scheduled time passed without the car returning, she became anxious, wondering if it had a flat tire or had broken down. To keep Maung Maung entertained, she had prepared a selection of English-Japanese magazines and photo albums of scenic spots in Japan, hoping he would see pictures of their grandparents among them.

She also planned to show Maung Maung their Burmese and Japanese-style guest rooms and play some Japanese songs she thought he would like. She had meticulously selected everything to ensure Maung Maung would enjoy his visit.

Though they were supposed to arrive at six o'clock, the car only entered the yard at half-past seven. Hearing the car, Yumisan quickly opened the front door. Daw Aung May, standing behind her, was breathing heavily in anticipation.

When U Thet Lwin got out of the car alone, Yumisan stared at him with fading hope and asked, 'Maung Maung . . .?'

She couldn't ask anything more.

'He was delayed, and we ended up running late, Sayama,' U Thet Lwin explained with a downcast face, standing by the door.

'Please, come in . . . Saya,' Yumisan, deeply disappointed that Maung Maung didn't come, struggled to regain her composure. She bowed slightly and respectfully led U Thet Lwin into the guest room.

Looking at Yumisan's sombre face, U Thet Lwin felt disheartened. The guest room, neatly and simply arranged, was Yumisan's Burmese guest room, unlike anything typically seen in Burmese homes.

The room appeared spacious due to the minimal furniture: two single armchairs, one double armchair, and a low dining table in the centre. The teak armchairs had an antique style, with low seats and high armrests, supported by intricately carved legs with curves and bends reminiscent of old designs from King Bodaw's times. The black polish on the teak made it gleam.

The double armchair, not really an armchair, was more like a lounging settee, with no backrest, and its top curled up to provide a headrest, supported by six curving legs. A bright red cushion was placed on it.

In the centre was a low dining table made of teak. A small silver vase with roses sat on it. Wooden carvings of elephants, horses, humans, and a princess were neatly arranged on the table. A red lacquer tray was separately displayed on one side.

Burmese traditional puppets, depicting prince, princess, *zawgyi*, and rope dancers, were elegantly hung on the walls. Two bronze cymbals adorned the upper corners of the walls. Beneath them, on another table, was a xylophone.

On a low table, an arrangement of old palm leaves coloured yellow with dye, stood prominently on a low table. The intricate Burmese puppets and other decorations gave the room a special elegance and charm.

On the large glass doors, pale gray Mudon curtains were hung with white hooks. At the top of the long curtains on either side of the wall were golden paintings of Bagan art: one depicting the birth of Lady Maya, and the other showing two goddesses, Lokanatha and Tara Devi.

When U Thet Lwin entered the guest room, he saw the simple yet distinct Burmese decorations and quietly sat down on one of the armchairs. He said softly, 'This morning, I reminded him to come home early so we could visit you this evening, but he didn't want to come. He refused, Sayama. I insisted, and told him we'd be waiting for him. He hasn't come home yet.'

Yumisan's heart was in great pain, so much that she could not respond and felt her chest tighten. She was on the verge of breaking down and crying in front of U Thet Lwin.

'In all the twelve years he has been with me, this is the first time he has ever disobeyed my words, Sayama.'

Even if Maung Maung expressed his hatred toward Yumisan with words, it would not be as clear and evident as this act of defiance. U Thet Lwin thought that Yumisan now truly understood the depth of Maung Maung's resentment.

'Please don't feel so sad, Sayama. Maung Maung will come to your house one day. Next time, I'll make sure to bring him along.'

U Thet Lwin, seeing Yumisan's unmistakable sorrow, tried to console her, but he couldn't bear to see her so heartbroken and quiet. 'I need to talk to him and explain how wrong his actions are when I get back.'

Yumisan remained still, overwhelmed by a sorrow so deep and incomparable that no other grief could match it.

'He'll be afraid that I'll scold him.'

Yumisan lifted her head, her voice tinged with worry.

'Please don't scold him, Saya. If you blame Maung Maung, he'll hate me even more, won't he? That's why please just tell him that I feel bad, Saya.'

Yumisan, unwilling to reveal her inner turmoil any further in front of the guest, seemed to pull herself together. She quickly masked the evident grief and distress that had been so clear on her face.

'I am not his enemy. I'm just a human being, an older sister like anyone else. I must make him understand that. Please, don't blame him, Saya,' Yumisan said.

Her words brought a sense of relief to U Thet Lwin, allowing him to ease the tension in his mind.

'Since he didn't come, I brought the portrait of your father that I had copied, Sayama. I had to hide it so he wouldn't see it.'

U Thet Lwin took out the portrait of Yumisan's father from the large envelope he had brought. Yumisan was amazed and stared intently at the painting of her father. The tender and gentle expression on his face was depicted so accurately that she praised U Thet Lwin's skilful work.

'You're very talented at drawing portraits, Saya. Could you draw a portrait of me before I return to Japan?'

Seeing a bright smile return to Yumisan's face, U Thet Lwin responded with joy, 'I will, Sayama. I want to draw you in traditional Burmese attire. Not just any traditional outfit, but something like the royal costume of old. Do you know what a htamein is?'

'Of course I do, Saya. It's what the bride wears at a wedding.'

'You must have attended a wedding ceremony before, right?' U Thet Lwin asked with a smile.

'I attended my student's wedding ceremony. I've also been to wedding ceremonies and novitiation ceremonies in Myanmar.'

U Thet Lwin wondered if there were still things Yumisan had not experienced in Myanmar.

'I had to combine two parts of this photo to draw the portrait, Sayama,' U Thet Lwin said, taking another photograph out of the envelope.

Yumisan saw that it was a replica of the photograph she had. Her father must have given her one photo and Maung Maung's mother another. Looking at the paper attached to the back of the photograph, Yumisan said.

'This . . . wasn't this torn up by Maung Maung, Saya?'

'Yes, it was. I'll never forget what happened the day I redrew this photo,' U Thet Lwin replied.

'Why not, Saya? I want to hear it. Please tell me,' Yumisan leaned forward on her chair, her face eager to listen.

U Thet Lwin recounted the unforgettable incident. He described how a group of buffalo boys surrounded and beat Maung Maung, blood streaming from his lips, his eyes swollen, and how he had to bandage him. As U Thet Lwin vividly recalled the events, Yumisan could almost picture the incident herself.

'He said he wanted to run away to a place where no one knew his father was Japanese. I didn't know how to comfort him. I had to promise not to tell anyone that his father was Japanese to bring him with me,' U Thet Lwin explained.

After hearing the complete story of Maung Maung's life and experiences from U Thet Lwin, Yumisan understood the depth of Maung Maung's pain. She realized how much patience, effort, and perseverance would be needed to console him.

'If I hadn't met the old man at Phayalay village, I wouldn't have been able to find Maung Maung in Myanmar,' Yumisan said, recounting Maung Maung's history as told to her by the old man, U San Aye, to U Thet Lwin.

U Thet Lwin listened with a warm face as Yumisan spoke about Maung Maung, whom he had raised as his brother for twelve whole years.

'Doesn't Maung Maung know his mother married my father in Phayalay village?' Yumisan asked, her question catching U Thet Lwin off guard.

'I only know about Maung Maung's mother and father's wedding because you just told me. How would Maung Maung know? I don't think he knows,' U Thet Lwin replied.

Yumisan looked at him intently and asked, 'During all the time he was with you, did Maung Maung never talk about his mother or anything related to her?'

U Thet Lwin shook his head slowly, 'From the day I brought him until today, I've been waiting for him to mention anything about his mother or himself. It's been twelve years, but he's never spoken about it, Sayama.'

Yumisan blinked and asked, 'Did you never try to bring it up yourself?'

U Thet Lwin sighed deeply and looked directly at Yumisan, who was staring at him without blinking, before responding calmly.

'I never had the heart to ask him, Sayama,' U Thet Lwin responded.

Both U Thet Lwin and Yumisan lowered their heads in silence. During this intense silence, Daw Aung May entered the living room.

U Thet Lwin looked up at Daw Aung May, who brought him a glass of orange juice.

'This is Obasan, whom I mentioned, Saya. Since there's no one else to talk to about Maung Maung,

I had to tell Obasan. She was really happy about Maung Maung coming today.'

Daw Aung May was smiling throughout Yumisan's explanation and joined the conversation once Yumisan finished.

'It's saddening to know about this situation. I was eagerly looking forward to meeting him today. Ma Yu was all smiles the whole day thinking of meeting her younger brother,' Daw Aung May said, standing upright. She spoke only these few words, knowing what was appropriate to say, and then returned to the dining room where she had work to do.

U Thet Lwin observed Yumisan's living room closely as he drank his orange juice. 'Your living room truly embodies the elegance of Burmese art. With its paintings, carvings, and literature, the beautifully and neatly arranged items make them seem even more valuable. By the way, what's that scroll, Sayama?'

Yumisan was proud to be seen by a Burmese as someone who valued Myanmar culture. In her home, she arranged traditional Myanmar items to make them look beautiful and meaningful in a distinctly Myanmar style.

'That's an old Burmese medical scroll from the past, a heritage item from Obasan's grandmother in Sagaing. She gave it to me,' Yumisan explained.

U Thet Lwin surveyed the entire living room, examining the items in detail with wide eyes, and then smiled as he spoke.

'These armchairs look so grand. They resemble the style from the ancient times. Where did you buy them?'

Yumisan laughed.

'They weren't bought, Saya. I've read about ancient Burmese history in French and English books, and I even found a photo in an Italian book showing Mingyi U Kaung standing by an armchair, with a golden sash draped over his shoulders. That photo inspired me, though I adapted it with my own imagination. A Chinese carpenter helped bring my ideas to life not long ago. I create one piece and purchase another each month for this living room. When I return to Japan, I'll take them with me.'

'Don't you collect ivories, Sayama?'

'I have a few ivory items in the dining room. They are very expensive, so I collect them gradually.'

After U Thet Lwin complimented the living room, Yumisan stood up, pointed at a painting and said, 'That's a painting I made.'

A large painting of Shwedagon Pagoda was hung high up on the wall behind U Thet Lwin. He stood up to take a closer look. The painting was done with muted colours, highlighting the golden stupa, which stood out vividly and brightly. While U Thet Lwin observed the painting, Yumisan brought out some paintings she had done in Myanmar from another room.

One painting depicted Ngapali beach with the sunset, another showed a small pagoda atop a mountain peak. U Thet Lwin examined the painting of the pagoda on the mountain with great interest as Yumisan stood by and explained her paintings in a mix of half English and half Burmese, with a Japanese accent in the Burmese words but not in the English ones.

'When I went to Ngapali, the plane flew over the mountains before I even caught a glimpse of the sea. Seeing those mountains from the plane really set the mood for me. Even when I got back to Yangon, I couldn't shake the image of those mountains from my mind. That feeling stayed with me, and it's what made the biggest impression. The mountains looked like waves, rolling one after another. They are so beautiful, Saya.'

As U Thet Lwin gazed intently at Yumisan's painting, he became curious to ask why she depicted Burmese landscapes using Japanese painting techniques.

'Why did you change the original colours, Sayama?'

Yumisan smiled and replied, 'Since Myanmar is a tropical country, why not paint it to give a cool feeling? I paint freely with my thoughts and feelings.

If you understand the rules of fine art, you can still create harmonious designs, right?'

U Thet Lwin saw more clearly through the painting the boldness in Yumisan's efforts to innovate and change.

'I control the colours because if I paint the trees green, they'll blend in with the forest and the painting will look like a poster. I don't want that. I express myself in green and in blue, so I don't want to paint the forest and mountains in such intense colours. I have to transform them. If I paint the trees bright green, it won't allow me to achieve the desired cloud colour transformation. Colours in a painting must be harmonious, right?'

U Thet Lwin looked at the muted, soft, dry colours of the trees on the mountains and responded, 'Just like rhythm in music, there's harmony in painting too. Your painting shows a unified colour harmony.'

'This painting was done using Japanese techniques and colours, but I've incorporated fine art theory. You see the pagoda on the mountain, don't you?'

Yumisan pointed at the small pagoda.

'Isn't it to show the height of the mountain?'

'Yes, Saya. In this painting, I wanted to highlight the trees, so I didn't paint many trees. With controlled colours throughout the painting, the trees stand out, don't they?'

'Saya, do you mostly do fine art? Do you not paint modern art?'

'I only paint fine art. Without a foundation in fine art and realistic painting, I don't accept the idea of jumping straight to modern art, Sayama.'

'That's right, Saya. Picasso painted a lot of fine art before transitioning to modern art, didn't he?'

'When I was learning fine art, my teacher was the great painter U Ngwe Gaing.'

Yumisan thought for a moment, rolling her eyes slightly.

'I saw a painting by U Ngwe Gaing at the embassy. I really like his realistic painting techniques.'

Through viewing Myanmar's gem paintings, U Thet Lwin learned that Yumisan had an understanding of colour blending in art. She wanted to express through colours her feelings about how beautiful and precious the gems hidden underground were. The painting spoke with colours, showcasing vibrant rubies, deep blue sapphires, and light green jade, with pearls included as well. The surrounding background with the mauve hues suggested the fiery glow of these gems within the earth.

'In Myanmar, I noticed that most painters are not confident in painting freely. They usually paint what appeals to the audience's eye. Why is that, Saya?'

'What kind of painting do you mean, Sayama?'

U Thet Lwin asked while wiping his face with a white towel.

'For example, a very poor Indian boy with no clothes, looking utterly desperate as he sucked on a piece of sugarcane. That kind of painting . . .'

U Thet Lwin laughed. 'A painting of a poor Indian child, looking utterly desperate as he hungrily sucked on sugarcane, wouldn't appeal to the Myanmar audience. For them, a painting should be beautiful, dignified, and emotionally moving. Pleasing the audience is part of the artist's goal. The kind of painting you described would likely remain in the artist's own home.'

At that moment, Daw Aung May entered the room. When U Thet Lwin and Yumisan paused their conversation about painting, she announced, 'Dinner is ready.'

U Thet Lwin and Yumisan got up from their seats.

In the dining room, one side of the rectangular dining table was set with a wooden chair. There was no tablecloth, but the table was covered with a white Formica surface. Beneath the plates placed on the table, intricately embroidered pink doilies were laid, arranged in size according to the plates.

On the wall, atop a china cabinet, a beautifully crafted statue of a *kinnari* made of ivory was displayed. Directly across from the cabinet, on a tall shelf along the opposite wall, two small statues of a lion made of ivory were positioned on either side of a table clock encased in glass. In one corner of the room stood a refrigerator. The dining room was neat and orderly.

According to the pre-arranged seating, U Thet Lwin was to sit on one side of the dining table, with the brother and sister on the other side. Since they were arranged to face U Thet Lwin, one chair remained empty. In Maung Maung's place, only a plate had been set. Before sitting down in the empty chair, Yumisan glanced at the plate meant for Maung Maung. A wave of pain surfaced in her eyes. She was unable to shake the feeling that Maung Maung's presence still lingered in that chair, as though he could never truly be absent.

The meal was beautifully arranged, with a variety of delicious dishes served on fine Japanese porcelain plates. U Thet Lwin felt a bit awkward as he looked at the grand spread, so different from the way meals were served at his own home.

'Please sit here, Saya. Make yourself at home and enjoy the meal.'

The dishes were so varied that it was hard to know what they all were. It was unclear whether the elaborate meal was meant to impress not only Maung Maung but also his older brother. It was an effort made with sincere intention.

Daw Aung May brought over a low rolling metal table beside U Thet Lwin. On the table were a water jug, a glass basin for washing hands, and soap. Daw Aung May poured water from the jug over U Thet Lwin's hands so he could wash them. She did the same for Yumisan.

'I miss Maung Maung so much, Saya. It would be wonderful if he were here.'

Yumisan washed her hands while thinking about Maung Maung, feeling an unfulfilled emptiness, a yearning for something unattainable in her heart. Hearing the longing in Yumisan's voice made U Thet Lwin feel heavy-hearted. He thought about how difficult sibling relationships must be. A warm feeling mixed with a sense of sadness enveloped his chest.

'I was thinking on my way here about how sad you must be with Maung Maung's absence,' U Thet Lwin said, his heart feeling heavy, even before he began eating.

'The sweaters we ordered for Maung Maung arrived today. Ma Yu was so happy. When one sibling loves deeply but the other holds so much hate, it really hurts us.'

Daw Aung May said this while serving rice from the pot onto the plates. Yumisan tried her best to suppress her sadness and smiled.

'Since there are visitors from Japan, I ordered two sweaters—one for Maung Maung and one for you, Saya. They've arrived, and I've wrapped them to give to you. Do you think he'll accept it and wear it?

Yumisan's voice trailed off at this point. She cupped her hands at her chest and, focusing on the plate of rice, offered a silent prayer.

As Yumisan lowered her hands, U Thet Lwin continued to speak.

'He will wear it if you give it to him, for sure, Sayama. Now that he has become a young man, he likes to dress nicely. However, he never asks for anything. He only wears what I buy for him. Even when I buy something for him, he always asks first if I've bought for me, too.'

U Thet Lwin seemed to enjoy talking about his brother more than the meal itself, smiling as he spoke.

'It's so endearing how he asks, isn't it, Saya? Isn't it lovely?'

Yumisan said this cheerfully, her face beaming, as she placed duck stew and mushrooms onto U Thet Lwin's plate.

'Indeed, Sayama. He has many endearing qualities. For instance, when it comes to food, if it's something I like, he won't eat it because he wants to ensure I get enough. Even if I had a blood brother, I doubt he would love and care for me as much as he does.'

U Thet Lwin's eyes sparkled with emotion as he spoke fondly about Maung Maung. He felt a sense of fullness in his heart as he ate.

'He's incredibly thoughtful, deeply understanding the challenges of a single mouse's life (solo living), and he possesses a truly compassionate heart, Saya.'

Hearing the Burmese phrase 'single mouse', U Thet Lwin laughed and turned to Daw Aung May, who was standing nearby, and said, 'Ah Daw, Sayama can use the expression "single mouse" from living with you.'

Daw Aung May, her face full of delight, responded with a big smile. 'It's not just because she was taught by someone; it's her eagerness to learn and her efforts that set her apart from others. Like a young parrot learning to speak, she asks questions eagerly and persistently. Except for the times when she is at school, she never sits still at home. If she wants to know something, she asks immediately; if she wants to see something, she goes right away. She doesn't waste any time. Even with the half day she spends at school, she makes use of the remaining half day by travelling to the rural areas of Dala, Thanlyin, Kyauktan, and Twante. She's been seeking knowledge from various sources in Myanmar for almost a year now; how could she not have learned anything by now?'

Yumisan smiled warmly at Daw Aung May, who was praising her.

'When I want to know something and ask Obasan, she not only answers my question but also provides additional information, two or three times more than what I initially asked. Isn't that wonderful, Saya?'

The atmosphere at the dining table became more pleasant with laughter filling the room.

U Thet Lwin glanced at Daw Aung May, appreciating her clean and dignified appearance. She wasn't just a housemaid; she was someone who managed and maintained the household with an air of authority, someone who could even engage with the lady of the house. He marvelled at the fate that had brought Daw Aung May and Yumisan together.

Daw Aung May was impressed by the graceful, traditional way Yumisan ate with her bare hands.

U Thet Lwin noticed that Yumisan wasn't eating pork, chicken, or duck dishes, but instead was focusing on dishes like pickled radish and grilled fish. He enjoyed the variety of flavours she had placed on his plate, savouring the different tastes.

Usually, he only had meals with Maung Maung, but now, eating face-to-face with Maung Maung's sister felt like a dream to U Thet Lwin.

Under the light, Yumisan's beauty was accentuated, making her look even more radiant. She wore a long-sleeved white blouse and a bright red Acheik longyi.

The small diamond earrings she wore glimmered, reflecting the light. Her even, white teeth gleamed under the light, perfectly aligned and radiant. She had her hair neatly tied into a bun at the back, with a puffed style that emphasized her high forehead. The neatly combed hair in the front, combined with her high forehead, gave her a distinguished appearance.

When her smile or laughter faded, her serene face reappeared, reflecting a calm and composed demeanour. On this serene face, her dark eyebrows and eyelashes, along with her prominent nose and thin lips, seemed perfectly arranged, like a carefully sculpted statue. For the first time, U Thet Lwin realized how truly beautiful Yumisan was, like a finely carved marble statue.

Daw Aung May spoke as she added more rice to U Thet Lwin's plate, 'Now, the young lady is learning the xylophone, Saya.'

'Is that so?' U Thet Lwin, surprised, raised his head and continued, 'I thought it was just for display in the living room. Can you play it well now, Sayama?

Yumisan blushed and lowered her eyes, smiling softly as she replied, 'I haven't learned it properly yet, Saya. I'm still at the beginner stage. Learning Myanmar music is very challenging for me.'

'Can you play the piano, Sayama?' U Thet Lwin asked.

Yumisan lifted her gaze slightly and responded, 'I can play, Saya. I love music, no matter what kind. From the moment I heard the sound of the xylophone, I was enchanted. I really like this sound. I have xylophone lessons twice a week, two hours each.'

'If you want to learn Myanmar music, it might take you a long time to master it,' U Thet Lwin replied earnestly.

'It's okay, Saya. I'll be satisfied if I can just play one Myanmar song,' Yumisan replied.

U Thet Lwin paused his meal, resting his hands on the edge of his plate, and looked intently at Yumisan as he continued, 'To really get to know Myanmar, two years might not be enough, Sayama. You might need to stay for about five years.'

Yumisan looked directly at U Thet Lwin, her face softening with emotion. In a quiet, gentle voice, she said, 'If I could stay in Myanmar with Maung Maung, I would love to stay for a long time, Saya.'

Yumisan, with her eyes full of expectation, kept gazing at U Thet Lwin, unable to look away. A sense of worry arose in U Thet Lwin's chest. The subject of Maung Maung was pervasive, permeating the atmosphere at the dinner table, where the earlier cheerfulness had now turned into sombre reflection.

After a moment, Yumisan asked, 'Does Maung Maung like music, Saya?'

'No, he doesn't.'

'What about painting, Saya?'

U Thet Lwin shook his head.

'What is his passion, Saya? Does he play chess?'

'He isn't interested in that either. He likes volleyball, gymnastics, and swimming. He has a strong passion for sports.'

In Yumisan's mind, Maung Maung stood out vividly. She pondered various ways to quickly become close to him.

'Ma Yu has arranged for a record changer and gramophones from a friend who works at the embassy. She said she'd play them to Maung Maung when he comes. She loves him that much,' Daw Aung May said as she collected the plates from the table.

U Thet Lwin was amazed at Daw Aung May's excellent English pronunciation.

'Sayama, what do your grandparents do in Japan?' U Thet Lwin inquired, not wanting Yumisan to stay quiet.

'My grandfather is a prominent doctor. He runs a clinic in Kobe. My grandparents are my father's parents. Since they only have one son, they didn't want to let me go far away, but they allowed it for Maung Maung.'

U Thet Lwin, not wanting to continue discussing Maung Maung, shifted his attention to Yumisan.

'Do you have any acquaintances in Bagan? Where will you be staying?'

'The embassy said there's a government guesthouse in Bagan.'

'My uncle lives in Nyaung U. He has a car and a ready house. If you need a place to stay, let me know, and I can help.'

Yumisan smiled as she asked, 'If I stay there, can you come along? Can Maung Maung join us too?'

She seemed eager to have Maung Maung accompany her. U Thet Lwin smiled and responded, 'Maung Maung won't be able to join, Sayama. His training unit will have to go on a trip when the university closes. But I can accompany you if you want.'

'If you could accompany me, that would be very kind of you. I want to learn all about Bagan.'

With the conversation about Maung Maung concluded, U Thet Lwin sighed softly and asked, 'Sayama, didn't you study Myanmar history in your Burmese course?'

'Yes, I did. We studied King Anawrahta, Kyansittha, Saw Lu, and Alaungsithu.'

'When you visit Bagan, you will encounter King Anawrahta and Kyansittha. With your knowledge of the historical background, Bagan will testify to how grand it was in Myanmar's history, Sayama.'

After dinner, they moved to the living room for coffee. As they sipped their drinks, U Thet Lwin spoke about the ancient culture of Bagan, describing the grandeur of temples like Ananda, Bupaya, Shwegu Gyi, Thatbyinnyu, Kan Taw Palin, Naga Yone, Manuha, Dhammayan, Gupyauk Gyi, Shwe Phat Leik, and Nge Phat Leik, as well as various caves and monasteries, until late into the night.

When U Thet Lwin left the guest room to go home, Yumisan invited him to show him her Japanese guest room.

Yumisan pushed open the door of a closed room. Moonlight streamed in gently, illuminating the room. The entire floor was covered with tatami mats from wall to wall. In the centre of the room was a low, square mahogany table, surrounded by small green cushions. On the wall was a large hanging scroll of a Japanese goddess and long inscriptions in Japanese calligraphy. In the middle, there was a circular plaque with white Japanese characters painted on it, hung with a red string. Two red tassels hung down from the ends of the string onto the plaque.

Beneath the circular opening of the door was a low bench with a vase neatly placed on it. The flower vase, treated as a piece of art, indicated its high value. It was a white porcelain vase, about a foot tall, with a white ceramic plate underneath. Inside the vase was a single, half-bloomed white rose.

The vase symbolized a blend of controlled elegance and gentle grace. U Thet Lwin quietly gazed at the vase bathed in moonlight. As he observed the flower, he found his mind entirely focused on it, free from distractions—a testament to his calm and controlled state of mind.

When U Thet Lwin arrived home, it was already midnight. Maung Maung opened the door for him and stood quietly in the doorway. Expecting to be scolded, yelled at, or lectured, he stood still like a stone statue, knowing he was at fault.

U Thet Lwin walked straight into the house through the door. After he passed, Maung Maung closed the door. Not hearing anything from U Thet Lwin, Maung Maung's head began to ache, unsure whether he should wait for U Thet Lwin to speak first or if he should start the conversation himself.

As usual, Maung Maung helped U Thet Lwin remove his clothes. He took the freshly removed longyi, folded it, and placed it at the foot of the bed. He also took the shirt and hung it on the hanger. Up to that point, U Thet Lwin hadn't spoken a word, making Maung Maung increasingly anxious.

'Ahkogyi, you were waiting for me, weren't you?' Maung Maung said hesitantly.

U Thet Lwin looked at Maung Maung. He saw a soft, young face that seemed as delicate as a leaf. The pale face and eyes appeared to be pleading for forgiveness.

U Thet Lwin, gazing at Maung Maung's face, felt his heart tighten. He had a lot to say to reprimand Maung Maung. Were he to scold Maung Maung for not accompanying him to Yumisan's house, it would end with Maung Maung admitting his hatred for Japan. That was the truth.

Maung Maung's past had been securely walled off for twelve years by a barrier as strong as steel. If they had to engage in an unavoidable long conversation, it would be like breaking through that steel barrier. U Thet Lwin knew only undesirable consequences would come out of their talk and decided not to say anything.

'It's late, Maung Maung. Go to sleep,' U Thet Lwin said with a disappointed expression as he headed towards the bathroom. Maung Maung was preparing the bed for U Thet Lwin by lowering the mosquito net when U Thet Lwin returned to the bedroom.

'In that bundle, there are two sweaters. Sayama gave them. Take the one you like,' U Thet Lwin said.

Maung Maung didn't even glance at the bundle on the chair. When U Thet Lwin got into bed and turned off the light, Maung Maung went to his own bed, feeling hurt that U Thet Lwin hadn't scolded him at all.

Maung Maung didn't pull down his mosquito net but lay down gently on his bed.

'I don't want to disobey you. I don't mean to be disrespectful. I just hate the Japanese teacher so much that I don't want to go with you to her house, Ahkogyi. Please don't be upset,' Maung Maung said quietly to himself, staring at the ceiling of the mosquito net.

11

Maung Maung didn't know about U Thet Lwin and Yumisan's trip to Bagan in advance. He only found out the night before when U Thet Lwin mentioned he would be leaving the next morning. Maung Maung had already packed his belongings for his training trip to the military camp, which was scheduled for the same day.

'I'm going to take the Japanese teacher to Bagan for three days.'

Maung Maung did not believe his own ears, his eyes practically popping out.

His bachelor brother was going on a trip with a woman. And the woman was Japanese. He felt a lump tighten in his chest.

He turned his face away, feeling both ashamed and sad about his brother's changed feelings. Maung Maung was only half-listening to U Thet Lwin's carefully delivered words of advice regarding his upcoming journey. He felt a sharp pang in his heart, a clear sense of the distance that had grown between him and U Thet Lwin.

Maung Maung couldn't sleep all night. U Thet Lwin also seemed restless and unable to fall into a deep sleep. Though they were in the same room, lying on adjacent beds, they felt distant from each other.

Maung Maung lay with his head resting on his arm, his whole body trembling slightly. He felt a growing sense of isolation, as if he were the only person in the world, which made him feel increasingly small and vulnerable. In his loneliness, his thoughts drifted towards his mother. He longed for her love and compassion, thinking of her with a deep yearning and teary eyes. Although he tried to recall her face, he couldn't picture it clearly as he had never seen her. He vaguely remembered her name mentioned by Daw Pwe, but he wasn't certain if it was correct. *Ma Htway Htway* he thought, unsure.

At 6 a.m., Yumisan was ready to leave for the airport. While U Thet Lwin was giving instructions to Ko Mya Phay, Maung Maung roamed restlessly around the house, unable to stay still.

'Maung Maung . . . remember what I told you last night. Military training is not child's play. Take care,' U Thet Lwin said in a tone that sounded both hurried and firm, noticing that Maung Maung was upset. Then, carrying his travel bag, he rushed out of the house and got into the car.

'How's it, little brother? Your older brother has already left with the Japanese teacher,' Ko Mya Phay said with a teasing tone, scratching his chest and giving Maung Maung a sly look.

Anger flared up inside Maung Maung. With eyes that couldn't hide his rage, he shouted back at Ko Mya Phay. 'I wouldn't care even if he doesn't come back to this house at all! I'm ashamed for my brother. That Japanese woman has really turned things upside down.'

Ko Mya Phay, wanting to further provoke Maung Maung's anger, taunted him with a sneer.

'*When a woman falls in love, she waits for her lover. When a man falls in love, he goes straight to her. When a woman falls in love . . .*'

Ko Mya Phay clapped his hands and sang loudly. Enraged, Maung Maung picked up a nearby book, ready to hurl it at him. Sensing danger, Ko Mya Phay ran straight into the kitchen.

Meanwhile, Yumisan and U Thet Lwin arrived at the airport. Yumisan, dressed in a white gown and white hat, looked every bit the foreigner. Beside her, U Thet Lwin, wearing a neatly pressed traditional shirt, checkered longyi, and sunglasses, looked like her interpreter.

Yumisan would one day return to Japan, and with time, U Thet Lwin would likely forget about her.

However, the trip to Bagan they took together would be an unforgettable journey in U Thet Lwin's lifetime.

Upon their arrival in Nyaung U, Uncle U Thann Saw, who had been informed in advance, was there to meet them with a jeep. U Thann Saw, about fifty years old, tall and thin with fair skin and greying hair, greeted them with a smile.

At U Thann Saw's single-storey house in Nyaung U, they were welcomed by Daw Tin Tin, his wife, who greeted them warmly with a bright smile and large diamond earrings sparkling in her ear.

U Thet Lwin introduced Yumisan and Daw Tin Tin to each other.

'Auntie, this is Yumisan, a lecturer of the Japanese language from the Institute of Foreign Languages. She's Maung Maung's sister.'

'What?'

Daw Tin Tin, surprised, leaned forward, her mouth agape. U Thann Saw and Daw Tin Tin were wide-eyed with astonishment. U Thet Lwin, seeing their reaction, smiled and turned to Yumisan.

'This is my aunt. Everyone here knows that Maung Maung was taken from a monastery and adopted by me. They don't know his father is Japanese,' he explained.

U Thann Saw and Daw Tin Tin were visibly shaken by the revelation.

Yumisan smiled, bent slightly at the waist in a gesture of respect, and greeted them. Daw Tin Tin, puzzled, looked back and forth between U Thet Lwin and Yumisan, as if trying to solve an unsolvable riddle.

'I'll explain everything tonight. We can only stay in Bagan for one day and must leave for Poppa tomorrow. We don't have much time. Right now, we're heading to Bagan. We'll come back for lunch at noon,' U Thet Lwin said.

After dropping off their belongings, he got Yumisan back in the car, and they drove off while Daw Tin Tin and U Thann Saw stood bewildered. As the car was about to leave, Daw Tin Tin muttered, 'He always does things like this,' prompting U Thet Lwin to laugh loudly as he drove away from the house.

U Thet Lwin first took Yumisan to see Shwezigon Pagoda. He parked the car on the south side of the road leading to Bagan, near the edge of Nyaung U.

Before getting out of the jeep, Yumisan excitedly took off her shoes and exclaimed, 'Saya, I've finally arrived in Myanmar, a thousand-year-old land!'

The first thing Yumisan saw at Shwezigon Pagoda were two large lion statues. She stared at them with wide eyes, moving back and forth to look at them from different angles. U Thet Lwin, watching her amazement, stood by with a smile on his face.

'Saya, these lion statues look a bit different from the ones at Shwedagon Pagoda. They don't have much decoration on their heads, their mouths are wider, and they have necklaces. They look unique,' Yumisan commented.

U Thet Lwin chuckled and said, 'Those are not necklaces, Sayama. They are chains.'

'This one is the father of Sihabahu, right?'

'What? Will you say that again, Sayama?' U Thet Lwin asked, quickly approaching Yumisan.

'Obasan told me the story of the lions at Shwedagon Pagoda, Saya. Sihabahu and his mother fled the forest, and his father, the lion, followed them, right? When they reached the towns and villages where people lived, the prince shot and killed the lion, fearing that his father would cause trouble. Deeply affected after killing his father, the son built a pair of lion statues in the pagoda as a sign of respect and reverence for his parents. Is this story true, Saya?'

U Thet Lwin laughed heartily and replied, 'Yes, Sayama, this story is true.'

Yumisan looked back at the two lion statues with undivided attention.

'These lions seem alive, Saya, as if they might leap and bite.'

The two of them, laughing and chatting, entered the pagoda precinct. It was quiet and clear, with few visitors around.

Yumisan gazed at the grand Shwezigon Pagoda with great admiration. She also compared it with the Shwedagon Pagoda, which was etched in her memory. The Shwedagon Pagoda's form was comforting and serene, while the Shwezigon Pagoda's presence was energizing and uplifting.

'Wow, Saya, the pagoda is so majestic and impressive. It was built by Kyansittha, right?'

'Yes, Sayama, it was started by *Shin* Arahan and King Anawrahta and later continued by King Kyansittha.'

As U Thet Lwin paid his respects to the pagoda, Yumisan took photos of both the pagoda and U Thet Lwin from various angles. After taking the photos, she stood upright, clasped her hands together on her forehead, and paid homage to the Shwezigon Pagoda.

U Thet Lwin found it intriguing to see Yumisan paying homage with such discipline while taking pictures of her. He wondered if she always maintained such formality even while praying.

After praying, Yumisan looked at each of the terracotta figures surrounding the base of the stupa. Whenever she found something interesting, she took a photo. She observed everything on the pagoda grounds with wide-open eyes, committing to memory what she saw. Despite her endless questions, U Thet Lwin explained without tiring that terracotta figures are made by moulding and applying glaze to baked clay, known as *sintkwin* (terracotta).

As there was a lot to show, U Thet Lwin quickly guided Yumisan around the pagoda grounds, showing her the various exhibits before leading her to the Kyansittha cave located to the southwest of Shwezigon Pagoda. Inside the cave, Yumisan's eyes were drawn to a wall painting of a monk threading beads.

'Is this a Chinese monk, Saya?'

'Yes, it is, Sayama. It was probably painted during the time when Kublai Khan's forces attacked Bagan. The wall painting depicts Chinese soldiers and military officers.'

Yumisan nodded slightly as if pondering Myanmar history. U Thet Lwin then led her from Kyansittha cave to Ananda Pagoda.

The sky was clear, and the sun was high. Yumisan took a deep breath of the cool air of the central plains. As they crossed Nyaung U and moved towards the outskirts, the magnificent view of Bagan unfolded before her eyes, a breathtaking sight filled with countless stupas and pagodas glowing in the sunlight, leaving her awe-struck and delighted.

The ancient stupas and large, ruined temples scattered across the vast landscape seemed to rival the sun's splendour in the sky, leaving a deep impression on U Thet Lwin. With a profound appreciation for art and ancient artefacts, Yumisan was instantly captivated by the imposing structures of Bagan, embodying the traditional Japanese sense of deep admiration. She gazed at them reverently, bowing slightly in respect, deeply moved by their majesty.

Everywhere she looked, stupas and temples filled her view. There were so many stupas and temples.

Amidst the lush green fields of corn and sesame, the Ananda Temple stood tall, its spires reaching for the sky, exuding a majestic and awe-inspiring presence. Yumisan had finally arrived in the land of Myanmar, a country with a thousand years of history and rich cultural heritage. The ancient pagodas and temples, gleaming with gold and vibrant colours, reminded her of grand palaces from the past. She gazed at them in wonder from the car, her breath taken away by the sight.

The two large statues at the entrance of Ananda Temple greeted Yumisan. These celestial statues, with lifelike features and smiling eyes, appeared to come alive, enhancing the sense of awe and wonder.

Yumisan gazed directly at the large statues and, for some reason, bowed slightly at the waist, showing her respect. U Thet Lwin took various photographs of Yumisan with the two large statues. Before entering the inner chamber of the Ananda Temple, Yumisan marvelled at the grandiose facade above the entrance.

U Thet Lwin pointed to a large statue of Makara made of cement at each corner of the vertical ornamental embellishments. Just as Yumisan was about to take a photo, she noticed something unusual and exclaimed in surprise, 'Saya, there's a lion standing in its mouth. Why is that?'

U Thet Lwin admired her keen observation and explained, 'The lion is carved standing inside the mouth of the Makara.'

Nodding slightly, as if understanding but still curious, Yumisan took the photo. She took pictures from different angles, both close-up and from a distance, as she wanted. After taking the photos, she touched the large wall of the Ananda Temple with her hand.

'This was built with ancient bricks,' explained U Thet Lwin.

As they entered the temple, they saw that it had a double-storied passageway surrounding the main hall. On the outer walls of the passage, they found various golden Buddha statues carved in stone.

'This picture shows Queen Maya being carried by deities to the Deva Dahan realm,' U Thet Lwin explained.

Yumisan gazed intently at Queen Maya's attire as she sat sideways on the palanquin.

'Saya, over there is a painting of Queen Maya from my home,' she said.

Her eyes remained fixed on the image of Queen Maya. The carved figures on the stone panel were so fascinating that she stared at them intently. She marvelled at the intricate details of the belt on Maya's figure, adorned with floral patterns and delicate decorations. U Thet Lwin patiently waited, allowing Yumisan to study as she pleased.

Yumisan couldn't get enough of the depiction of Queen Maya, who appeared exhausted and leaning on her mother-in-law, Gotami. Yumisan was deeply captivated and could not tear her eyes away, unable to show restraint.

'This image offers so many perspectives: the painter's view, the sculptor's view, the artist's view, the historian's view, the Buddhist's view. No matter how many people look at it, each will have a different experience and appreciation. The craftsmanship from ancient times is priceless,' she said, breathless with amazement.

Taking various photos, she reluctantly moved away from the statues, unable to completely part from them.

Upon entering, they were enveloped by a thick darkness that swept over their surroundings. In this void, Yumisan felt her mind being drawn in and held, unable to wander. As this enveloping darkness surrounded her, a profound sense of tranquillity washed over her.

As they walked straight towards the ancient, upright Buddha statue, they saw its face illuminated by the light offerings, revealing its serene expression. The Buddha's face appeared more distinguished and majestic to Yumisan than she had ever seen before.

Without bowing, kneeling, or averting her gaze, she walked directly to the base of the eighteen-foot-tall Buddha. There, she knelt down, bowed her head deeply, and paid her respects. The sight of Yumisan kneeling and bowing deeply before the statue was a moment U Thet Lwin would never forget from their journey to Bagan.

Yumisan, her white kimono softly spread around her in delicate folds, knelt gracefully at the base of the Buddha statue, keeping her head bowed for a while. U Thet Lwin photographed her from different angles, capturing the serene beauty of her posture. Seeing Yumisan bowing reverently before the Shwezigon Pagoda and now at the Ananda Temple, U Thet Lwin marvelled at how the ancient Bagan architects had skilfully designed these monuments to inspire humility and deepen faith in all who approached them.

With her hands clasped together at her chest, Yumisan lifted her face reverently. She gazed up at the entire statue with admiration, deeply moved by its majestic presence.

Bathed in the clear and pure light, the statue stood in perfect harmony, displaying the flawless and proportionate features of the hands, delicately extended fingers, the broad shoulders, and the serene, radiant face. Yumisan looked at the statue with unwavering admiration and devotion.

It was unclear what prayer or wish Yumisan was making. Her entire demeanour, filled with reverence and humility, showed her deep concentration and devotion as she prayed.

'Saya, where does the light on the Buddha's face come from?' Yumisan asked, standing up in awe after admiring the statue.

'The architects ingeniously directed this light. From a hidden skylight above the shrine, the light is directed onto the face of the Buddha. It's a hidden way of offering light,' U Thet Lwin explained.

'From now on, no matter which Buddha I pray to, this Buddha will always be in my mind,' Yumisan replied.

'It's truly awe-inspiring, Sayama. In ancient times, architects built such grand structures that have stood strong for over nine hundred years without using any metal reinforcements. Isn't it amazing? I believe the architects infused this pagoda with not just their skills but also their devotion and faith,' U Thet Lwin said.

Yumisan nodded and responded, 'Ananda is a very rare and exquisite piece of art from the golden era, Saya.'

'Sayama, what prayer did you make at this pagoda?' U Thet Lwin asked.

'I prayed as Obasan taught me, Saya,' Yumisan replied.

'Please tell me, Sayama, what did your Obasan teach you? I'm curious.'

'When visiting Bagan and praying at the pagodas, she taught me to say, "May I be freed from the suffering of *samsara*, Ahshin Phaya,' Yumisan explained.

'Samsara . . . You understand it, then?' U Thet Lwin asked in amazement.

'Samsara is the cycle of life and death, the endless repetition of suffering, isn't it?' Yumisan said.

U Thet Lwin laughed and said, 'Sayama, before you return to Japan, you should meditate at a meditation centre.'

'In Myanmar, when people practise Buddhist meditation, they engage in *samatha*, right, Saya?' Yumisan asked.

'Myat Swar Phaya . . . you understand *samatha* too, Sayama?' U Thet Lwin exclaimed with wide eyes.

'Yes, Saya, I understand samatha. It's quite similar to the zen Buddhist path in Japan. In zen Buddhism, we control the mind and aim for enlightenment by focusing and calming the mind. We concentrate fully on one thing to achieve peace and tranquillity. This is why Japanese tea ceremonies and garden designs embody the essence of zen,' Yumisan explained.

They continued to walk around, paying respects to the three remaining standing statues at the four faces of the Gandhakuti shrine. Yumisan noticed the statues of Shin Arahan and the kneeling Kyansittha in front of the large statue at the west. Her respectful posture and frequent bowing to Shin Arahan and Kyansittha were notable. She studied the details of the armour on Kyansittha's statue and sketched notes in her notebook. With great admiration, she also took several photographs of the Kyansittha statue.

Afterwards, they went outside the pagoda and observed the bas-reliefs on the brick walls. U Thet Lwin explained that these depicted the battle of Mara. Yumisan listened intently, her eyes wide with interest, and mentally noted everything. If she didn't understand something, she would ask many questions until she was satisfied. Explaining to her could be quite exhausting due to her thoroughness.

After that, U Thet Lwin took her from Ananda Cave to Thabbyinnyu Pagoda. Before climbing the steps, Yumisan gazed intently at the shape of the grand pagoda, and with a sense of deep respect and reverence for the ancient artefacts, she finally entered the pagoda. They then climbed to the upper levels using the brick staircase built into the side wall.

On the upper level, they saw the large, seated Buddha statue and bowed their heads in peaceful reverence.

U Thet Lwin showed her the views of Bagan from the top of Thabbyinnyu Pagoda. Yumisan carefully followed his pointed directions, gazing at each spot with unwavering attention.

Seeing the ancient landscapes that spanned many centuries, she felt a profound and deep admiration as she viewed them with an artist's eye.

'That hill over there is Tu Ywin Taung, Sayama. There's the Sularmuni Pagoda built by King Narapati, and over there is the Dhammayangyi Temple, built by Narathu,' he explained.

Yumisan stood silent as a statue.

'Over there is the Shwezigon Pagoda that we visited. Next to the Shwegu, you can see the Pitaka Library built by King Anawrahta. Can you see it? And to the north is the Kan Taw Palin Pagoda.'

'There's so much to study here in Bagan, isn't there, Saya?' she asked.

'One day isn't enough to visit all, Sayama.'

'I'll go to Popa Mountain next time. What if I stay here for an extra day, Saya?'

'Of course, Sayama. You can.'

Yumisan, breathing in the gentle breeze with a deep sigh, gazed beyond the pagodas and temples to the vast expanse of the Ayeyarwady River. The dim silhouette of the distant Tantkyit mountain range evoked a sense of nostalgia within her.

'How many times has Maung Maung been to Bagan, Saya?' she asked.

'I've been to Bagan four or five times, but Maung Maung has never been,' U Thet Lwin replied lightly, but Yumisan, displeased with his casual tone, raised her eyebrows and exclaimed, '*Oh*!'

'It will be good for Maung Maung to visit Bagan, Saya. Not just Maung Maung, but every tenth-grade student in Myanmar should visit Bagan. The government should arrange for every tenth-grade student to come here. Don't you think tenth-grade students should study Bagan, Saya? In Japan, even elementary schoolchildren have visited places like this.'

U Thet Lwin smiled at Yumisan.

'Don't any students come here to study in groups, Saya?'

'Yes, they do. Sometimes the university history clubs come for study trips.'

Yumisan frowned slightly and replied briskly, 'Nu Nu from the final year of the university history programme, the one who helped me contact you, said she has never been to Bagan, Saya. I was astonished. Not just history students, but all tenth-grade students should come to Bagan before they go to university. We have a saying in Japan: "Seeing once is better than hearing a hundred times."'

'That's true, Sayama,' U Thet Lwin commented, mentally noting that she was the type of teacher to have a strong bond with the students.

'Reading about Myanmar history in a book and seeing it with my own eyes is completely different, Saya. The value of this ancient Bagan site for people now and for future generations is immeasurable. After the Bagan era, was it the Inwa era or the Pinya era? I can't remember.'

'After Bagan, it was Pinya, then Inwa, Taungoo, and finally the Nyaungyan Alaungpaya era,' U Thet Lwin filled her in.

Yumisan continued enthusiastically, 'The Pinya, Inwa, and Taungoo periods that followed Bagan—how much did Bagan mean to those people, Saya? Wasn't Bagan the foundation for those kingdoms?'

'Yes, Sayama. Bagan was the foundation for establishing those great kingdoms,' U Thet Lwin said, smiling broadly, clearly impressed and in agreement with Yumisan's thoughts.

'A country suffers if there is excessive devotion and compassion, Saya,' said Yumisan.

U Thet Lwin did not understand her intention, so he asked, 'What do you mean, Sayama?'

'I'm quite disappointed with some temples in Myanmar. When I visited the Inle Pagoda, I couldn't see the original Buddha image; all I saw was a large gold-covered statue. It's very hard to distinguish the Buddha's face, Saya. The original face is gone. Earlier, at Shwezigon Pagoda, I didn't see any ancient artefacts because they were covered with gold leaf. It's not just me; any foreigner would be equally disappointed.'

Feeling disheartened by Yumisan's dismay, U Thet Lwin replied, 'The overzealous devotion and generosity have led to this, Sayama. It's indeed disappointing to see ancient statues and artefacts covered to the point where their original features are obscured. At Ananda, ancient Mon inscriptions on Buddha statues were covered with gold leaf, making them unreadable. The same goes for the Four-Faced Buddha. If you scrub the lime off the face of the image with a damp cloth, the inscriptions reappear.'

After speaking to Yumisan, U Thet Lwin wished that just as foreigners feel disheartened, so should the Myanmar people. He hoped they would learn to appreciate and value their heritage. They spent a considerable amount of time at Ananda and the Sabbanyu Pagodas.

Then, U Thet Lwin took Yumisan to the museum and the inscription hall.

Yumisan had a hard time leaving the museum. She was fascinated by the numerous wooden, bronze, and stone statues she saw. She closely examined the carved wooden figures. When she saw the inscription stone of the Myazedi Pagoda, U Thet Lwin mentioned that it was in its original location. Then they went to the Pitakat *taik* (library). Inside, they paid special attention to the murals of blooming flowers on the walls. They ended up having their lunch at 2 p.m.

After lunch, they didn't have time to rest at their lodging and immediately went out again. They visited the Shwegu Gyi Pagoda, the Thantawgya Pagoda, the Nat Hlaung Kyaung Temple, and the Nga-Kywel-Nar-Taung Pagoda.

When they arrived in front of the Thantawgya Buddha image, U Thet Lwin asked, 'Sayama, carefully observe this image. What's unique about it?'

Without hesitation, Yumisan focused on the statue and responded quickly to U Thet Lwin's question.

'It's the mouth, Saya. The mouth is prominent, as if it's speaking.'

U Thet Lwin laughed and replied, 'It's not just speaking; it's preaching. The Buddha is depicted delivering a sermon, which is why this image is named Thantawgya. When you observe carefully, doesn't it seem like you can almost hear the voice?'

'This is stone carving, right? What an exceptional artist! It truly seems like you can hear the voice. Preserving such masterpieces is crucial,' Yumisan noted.

'These bricks are not just ordinary bricks, Sayama; they are stone bricks,' U Thet Lwin explained.

As soon as Yumisan saw the Nat Hlaung Kyaung Temple, she exclaimed, 'Is this a Hindu temple?' Yumisan had a flash of recognition, thinking of the statues she had seen at the Mahapimnel Hindu Temples in Yangon.

'In ancient times, there were Hindu Indians living in Bagan, Sayama. They were likely merchants. This temple might have been built and donated by those who worshipped Vishnu,' U Thet Lwin explained.

Next, they went to the Nga-Kywel-Nar-Taung Pagoda, built with green-glazed bricks. From there, they visited the Pahtothamya Temple.

From there, they proceeded to Kandaw Palin Temple, built by King Narapati Sithu, and to Minnanthu, Dammayan, and Sularmuni temples.

Then, they went to Upali Sima Hall, Htilominlo Temple, and Mingalazedi Pagoda.

Upon reaching the Gubyaukgyi Temple in Myinkaba, Yumisan was captivated by the mural paintings on the walls. She observed the ancient frescoes depicting the Buddha descending from Tavatimsa Heaven after preaching the Abhidhamma to his mother, Queen Maya, surrounded by gods; the Mara war; and other scenes from the Buddha's life. The colours and artistry of these ancient paintings were astonishingly well-preserved. She noted how the paintings followed the traditional Indian style of drawing with single, continuous lines.

'Because of the ancient paintings here, this one wall alone would be worth millions of dollars in another country,' Yumisan remarked, recognizing the immense value of the Bagan murals through the eyes of a foreigner visiting Myanmar.

Yumisan couldn't help but appreciate the pricelessness of the Bagan wall paintings, which had survived countless centuries, embodying the skill and planning of King Anawrahta and Kyansittha, who had magnificently established and breathed life into Bagan. She marvelled at how the achievements of King Anawrahta and Kyansittha still provided inspiration and vigour to the present day. It was only upon arriving in Bagan that she fully grasped the greatness of Anawrahta's contributions, which she had studied in Myanmar history back in Japan.

'All the wall paintings show the Indian painting technique, Saya,' Yumisan observed.

'Originally, since Buddhism descended from India, the ancient Indian painting technique had reached Thiri Ketra and then to Thaton before the Bagan era, and then to Bagan,' U Thet Lwin explained.

Yumisan carefully studied not just the wall paintings but also the inscriptions, straining her eyes to take in every detail, even those on the ceiling. From the Gubyaukgyi Temple, they proceeded to the Myazedi Pagoda and the Myazedi stone inscription.

Yumisan took photographs of all four faces of the Myazedi stone inscription. She carefully examined each line of the engraved Pali, Mon, Pyu, and Myanmar script, which recorded the Rajakumara inscription. Unsatisfied with merely looking, she said, 'Please read it aloud, Saya. I want to listen.'

Assistant lecturer U Thet Lwin had taught this stone inscription to students countless times, so he could recite it from memory without even looking at it.

U Thet Lwin began by explaining that the inscription was engraved by Prince Rajakumara a year after his father, King Kyansittha, had passed away. He then read the inscription slowly, explaining its content in detail.

'The meaning of the inscription is as follows, Sayama: In the 1628th year of the Buddhist era, King Kyansittha ruled Bagan. He had a son, Prince Rajakumara, born to Queen Tilokawadamsaka Devi. King Kyansittha bestowed upon the queen three villages and valuable ornaments. When the queen passed away, these villages and ornaments were given to Prince Rajakumara. After ruling for twenty-eight years, when King Kyansittha became ill, Prince Rajakumara, in honour of his father, sold the queen's ornaments, cast a golden statue, sprinkled water (made a libation) before his father, and enshrined the statue in Gu Pagoda. The inscription records that he also donated the three villages.'

Yumisan listened intently and remarked at the end of U Thet Lwin's explanation, 'He must have loved his father so much.'

'He truly loved his father, Sayama. Prince Rajakumara was incredibly loyal. Despite Rajakumara being the legitimate heir, King Kyansittha did not pass the throne to him but to his grandson instead. Rajakumara fully supported his father's decision and never plotted to seize the throne for himself. He demonstrated his approval of his father's actions for the stability of the kingdom,' U Thet Lwin explained.

'Where is that Gu Pagoda located?' Yumisan asked.

'It's the very pagoda we just visited, the Gubyaukgyi Pagoda. It was built by Prince Rajakumara. The pagoda was already under construction before King Kyansittha passed away. After his father's death, Rajakumara enshrined the golden statue in the cave,' U Thet Lwin replied.

With a furrowed brow, Yumisan, appearing unsatisfied, asked, 'Why is the inscription pillar here at Myazedi Pagoda instead of the Gu Pagoda? Why is it called the Myazedi inscription?'

U Thet Lwin nodded and explained, 'The Myazedi inscription got its name because it is located near the Myazedi Pagoda. Nowadays, it is often referred to as the Rajakumara inscription. The Gubyaukgyi Pagoda and its surrounding area were quite expansive in ancient times. This Myazedi Pagoda was not built during the Bagan era. When comparing the construction styles of the Gubyaukgyi Pagoda and the Myazedi Pagoda, scholars generally accept that the Myazedi Pagoda was built during the Inwa period.'

'In Bagan, when building pagoda caves, the surrounding areas were vast, with large monastic compounds and double-layered fortified walls. This stone pillar remains in its original place. The land where the pillar is planted is part of the monastic compound land of Gubyaukgyi Pagoda. When they dug the ground, they found another stone pillar of similar nature. Earlier, I showed this at the Bagan Museum,' U Thet Lwin explained.

Yumisan, still standing near the stone pillar, seemed deep in thought, contemplating something she wanted to say.

'Saya, the inscription reveals the deep love of a devoted son. It's both touching and admirable. Prince Rajakumara truly loved his father and was filled with gratitude. That feels so natural. But Maung Maung, who has never even met his father or known his name, feels only hatred instead of love. Isn't that so unnatural? Isn't Maung Maung more to be pitied?' Yumisan's face showed a hint of sadness as she spoke.

Seeing Yumisan's sorrowful expression, U Thet Lwin felt a surge of empathy toward her, understanding her deep attachment to Maung Maung.

'One day, Maung Maung will come to love his father as a parent, Sayama,' U Thet Lwin gently comforted Yumisan, with feelings of compassion and sympathy.

'In the royal chronicles, Prince Rajakumara's mother was a country woman, right?'

'Yes, a country woman, indeed. Don't you know her name, Sayama? It's Thanbula. When she and her son came, King Kyansittha elevated her to a queen and bestowed upon her the title "*trilawka wadanthagadevi*". Translated into Myanmar, her title means "*thone-lawka u-sauk-pann*",' U Thet Lwin said with a smile.

'What does the name "thone-lawka u-sauk-pann" mean, Saya?' Yumisan asked, softly pronouncing each word in a slight Japanese accent.

'It means "flower crown of the three worlds". Three worlds refers to the human world, the celestial world, and the Brahma world. Flower crown signifies a flower placed on the top of the head. The king gave this queen a special title, Sayama, the highest title in all three worlds.'

'The name flower crown is beautiful, Saya, a flower blooming right at the top,' Yumisan expressed her delight upon understanding the meaning as explained by U Thet Lwin. Filled with gratitude and affection, she humorously remarked to U Thet Lwin, 'Wouldn't it be lovely if my Myanmar name was U-Sauk-Pann, Saya?'

Yumisan's laughter, melodious like music, lingered in U Thet Lwin's ears. They returned to their relative's house by sunset to stay. That night, tired from the journey, Yumisan went to bed early in her prepared room. Despite feeling sleepy, U Thet Lwin stayed up until midnight, narrating Maung Maung's tale to Daw Tin Tin's family.

The next day's plan to visit Popa was cancelled, and instead, they toured Bagan. U Thet Lwin guided her to many still-unseen Gu temples in Bagan.

They visited Manuha, Nan Phaya, Nagayone, Ahpay Yadana, Soemingyi, Ngwe Fet Leik, Shwe Fet Leik, Nandamannya, and Phaya Thone Su. They closely examined the wall paintings in Nandamannya Pagoda, depicting a group of young and old women dancing in line.

Today, Yumisan did not wear a gown but dressed in traditional Myanmar clothing. She wore a long-sleeved white blouse and a black longyi, with her hair neatly tied at the back. She had a long golden chain hanging down to her chest. U Thet Lwin noticed how well her Myanmar appearance suited the atmosphere of Bagan. The pilgrims were captivated by Yumisan and her friend, drawn to the sight of a foreigner in Myanmar attire.

Yumisan was fascinated by the paintings of a group of Bagan women, both young and old, on the wall. She observed the different hairstyles, the various headdresses adorned with jewels, the short skirts, tight-fitting blouses, chest bands, waistbands, belts, bracelets, and the golden jewellery hanging from their wrists. The traditional adornments of the ancient times intrigued her.

The features of the women depicted in the paintings included broad foreheads, prominent noses, beautiful eyebrows, round eyes, some with narrow eyes and delicate eyebrows, and others with large eyes and striking brows. Their necks were full and rounded, their breasts were well-developed, waists slim, and their legs slender and graceful.

'Saya, are these pictures of Bagan women?' Yumisan asked.

U Thet Lwin responded, 'What do you think?'

'I think they are Bagan women. Even though their clothing looks ancient Indian, you can't determine their ethnicity based on their clothes. I'm wearing a gown, aren't I? But just because I wear a gown, it doesn't mean I'm from a Western country. During the ancient times, Indian culture flourished, so it's not surprising that Bagan women dressed similarly to ancient Indian women.'

'Hmm . . . your opinion is reasonable and acceptable,' U Thet Lwin agreed.

Yumisan then took photos of the wall paintings inside the Phaya Thone Su Temple. She was delighted to find that the paintings of Lawkanat and Tara Devi, which hung in her living room, were actually reproductions of these original wall paintings.

Today's plan involved sketching the wall paintings they each liked and then painting them together for fun. They chose a spot to sit and began sketching the outlines of the wall paintings with pencils, drawing lines, and figures. The atmosphere grew quiet as they focused on their work.

After a while, Yumisan broke the silence. She continued painting as she spoke.

'I really like the green paint in Bagan's wall paintings, Saya. Even after so many years, the colours are still so vibrant and fresh. It's amazing,' Yumisan said, and then she fell silent again. She continued drawing quietly, deeply absorbed in her painting. Sitting next to each other, U Thet Lwin on her left, Yumisan leaned over, resting her painting on her knee as she worked. After a while, something crossed her mind, and she spoke up again.

'Coming to Bagan stimulates my imagination, Saya.'

Turning to face her, U Thet Lwin asked, 'What are you thinking about?'

Yumisan responded without looking up from her sketch, 'Coming to Bagan feels like coming back to my old place. Bagan has a way of drawing me back in. It's such a wonderful feeling.'

She smiled as she spoke. U Thet Lwin, still drawing, smiled back at her. 'In Buddhism, we believe in reincarnation, don't we? Maybe I was thone-lawka u-sauk-pann during the Bagan period. Who's to say I wasn't?'

Yumisan turned her face toward U Thet Lwin with a playful smile, making him laugh. He couldn't stop himself from smiling and looking at her as she painted with her legs curled up, her smile bright.

U Thet Lwin continued to laugh, amused by Yumisan's whimsical thought.

* * *

At that moment, Maung Maung was gasping for breath at the training camp, crawling across the searing ground as he strained to obey the sergeant's orders under the blazing sun. They had to push through thorny bushes and dense forests, descending from high to low ground. They practised shooting, spear thrusting, and tactical combat. The training included dividing eleven trainees into three groups: one defending and two attacking with spears.

From morning roll call to evening dismissal, Maung Maung rigorously followed the sergeant's commands without faltering. If the sergeant was not satisfied and ordered more drills, they had to repeat the exercises, leaving them utterly exhausted.

Maung Maung found no time to think about U Thet Lwin and Yumisan. The life of a soldier was undeniably tough, and the sergeant's commands felt as deafening as bomb blasts. Despite his exhaustion, Maung Maung remained determined. Mastering military skills and becoming a good soldier was essential for defending his country.

In tactical combat training, Maung Maung stood out from the rest. He was daring, energetic, and resilient, with a tenacity and spirit nurtured within him. When the defending group was firing at the enemies, Maung Maung's team received the signal to charge with their spears towards the enemies, giving a loud 'Charge!' signal.

In his mind, Maung Maung did not consider the training mere military drills; he felt he was engaged in real combat on the battlefield. He imagined the enemies as Japanese soldiers. Running to thrust his spear, Maung Maung shouted, 'Charge!'

His voice, full of fervour, resonated and echoed up into the sky.

12

After returning from Bagan, Yumisan rested for a day before leaving for Mandalay with Daw Aung May the following day. They returned from Mandalay at the end of the December school holidays. Letters from her grandparents in Japan had arrived. Both letters awaited Yumisan's return from Mandalay.

Upon arrival, Yumisan opened and read the letters. In her grandfather's letter, he advised that if sharing the truth would disturb his grandson, who resented and disliked Japan, it would be better to remain silent and let things pass rather than openly discussing it.

In contrast, her grandmother's letter was entirely different. She urged Yumisan to strive as much as possible to reconnect and understand her heritage, and to develop affection for her little brother.

The two letters reflected opposing viewpoints from her grandparents. Yumisan felt torn between accepting her grandfather's advice to remain silent or following her grandmother's urging to embrace her heritage and love her brother. This internal conflict left Yumisan feeling breathless and tense.

Considering her grandmother's wishes, Yumisan decided to visit U Thet Lwin's house not just Saturdays but also on Sundays, making it two visits per week. Once back from Mandalay, Yumisan began visiting U Thet Lwin's house twice a week.

Maung Maung's curiosity about Yumisan's increasingly frequent comings and goings grew sharper. One Sunday morning at eight o'clock, Yumisan and Daw Aung May arrived at Maung Maung's house. U Thet Lwin opened the door for them. From inside the house, Maung Maung peeked out and wondered who the elderly woman with Yumisan was, eventually realizing she was the woman living with Yumisan.

Recently, Yumisan had been moving around the house without interacting much with Maung Maung, acting as though she barely noticed him. Maung Maung, who had once treated Yumisan with distant politeness, now felt a sense of ease, treating her as just another guest of his older brother without any particular regard. When Yumisan visited, he no longer had to entertain the guests with his brother, which allowed him to feel more at ease.

Daw Aung May followed behind Yumisan, carrying a large leather bag and a package of food. While Yumisan greeted U Thet Lwin respectfully, Daw Aung May glanced over at Maung Maung, observing him closely. Having never met Maung Maung before, she couldn't take her eyes off him. Upon seeing him, she immediately felt a sense of affection as if recognizing Yumisan's blood relation and experienced a fluttering in her heart.

As Daw Aung May and Yumisan entered the house, Maung Maung hurriedly slipped into the kitchen. 'The Japanese teacher is here with an older woman from her house. I don't know what they're planning to do, but they've got a big leather bag and a lacquer bowl,' he whispered quietly to Ko Mya Phay.

Ko Mya Phay smiled at Maung Maung before replying softly, 'You still don't know, do you? Your brother is going to draw a portrait of your beautiful sister. Early this morning, Saya told us that he and the lady would come to paint and asked us to prepare coffee.'

Yumisan had borrowed a long-sleeved htaingmathein blouse and plain sarong from a recently married student from her school, trying them on at her house in preparation for painting. After trying on the clothes at home, she packed them in a leather bag and brought Daw Aung May along to help her get ready.

'May I use the room to change, Saya?' Yumisan asked for permission to enter the room and change clothes. Despite feeling embarrassed about the cluttered room, U Thet Lwin allowed her in.

'Please go ahead, Sayama,' he said.

Yumisan and Daw Aung May entered the bedroom. Inside U Thet Lwin's bedroom were two single beds, a cluttered writing desk covered with books, two wardrobes, and two large chests. Books were scattered on the floor, haphazardly placed in piles.

The bedroom was in complete disarray, cluttered and untidy, with nothing in its place. At the foot of the beds were various piled-up longyis, and each bed had a jumble of clothes. The clothesline was draped with face towels, old shirts, and sarongs, all haphazardly hung.

U Thet Lwin entered the room and asked, 'Sayama, do you need a mirror?' Yumisan had already noticed a small hand mirror about an inch wide on the cluttered desk.

'A larger mirror is in the chest, Saya. I don't need anything else. Please prepare for painting; I'll change my clothes and come out.'

After U Thet Lwin left, Daw Aung May wrinkled her nose at the unsightly clothesline and motioned towards it. They both smiled sheepishly.

Yumisan had worn her hair in a single braid, neatly coiled into a bun, ever since she left her home. With only the task of changing clothes left to do, they shut the door behind U Thet Lwin as soon as he stepped out.

Yumisan reached up to grab Maung Maung's regular black and red checkered shirt from the clothesline. Pulling a measuring tape from her leather bag, she measured the shirt's dimensions, quickly noting them down in her notebook. She then took Maung Maung's military uniform jacket from the foot of the bed and measured it the same way, noting the details.

Daw Aung May watched Yumisan's meticulous movements and softly murmured, 'Compassion . . . compassion,' as she sighed gently.

It was only when Maung Maung came out of the kitchen that he realized Yumisan and her companion had entered the bedroom. From outside, the faint sound of their conversation could be heard. He felt disgruntled by their intrusion into his bedroom and returned to the kitchen.

'They've entered the bedroom,' he said.

'What . . .?' Ko Mya Phay replied, widening his eyes in confusion. 'Is she with your elder brother?'

'Stop it! How could she be with my elder brother? It's the woman from their house. They're getting ready for the drawing.'

'And your elder brother?'

'He's also getting ready for painting.'

Maung Maung sat down at the kitchen table, with a furrowed brow and a sulky expression.

'Go help them outside,' Ko Mya Phay suggested.

'They're already in the bedroom; what help could they need?'

Ko Mya Phay chuckled at Maung Maung's disgruntled expression. While making coffee, he instructed Maung Maung to take the coffee pot and cups to them.

'You go take them,' Maung Maung grumbled.

Meanwhile, Daw Aung May was helping Yumisan get ready. She leaned close to Yumisan and whispered softly, 'That boy is adorable.'

Yumisan signalled with her eyes, bending her index finger.

'I know. He has such a serious face and doesn't even say a word,' Daw Aung May added.

Yumisan leaned closer to Daw Aung May's face and whispered back.

'He only talks when spoken to. He never initiates a conversation with me or greets me,' Yumisan said.

After helping Yumisan put on the traditional jacket, Daw Aung May held up a large mirror for her.

Yumisan looked in the mirror, pleased with what she saw. Daw Aung May then placed a three-strand pearl necklace around Yumisan's neck. After putting on the long-sleeved jacket, Yumisan was adorned with a pearl bracelet, a sapphire bracelet, and a ruby bracelet that Daw Khin Win Mu had sent her.

Daw Khin Win Mu helped Yumisan gather everything she needed for the painting, as Yumisan planned to pose wearing the htaingmathein. But the diamond ring, diamond hairpin, diamond necklace, and diamond chain that Daw Khin Win Mu had prepared were all returned by Yumisan without wearing them.

'If I wear all these, I'll look like a modern-day bride. To match the ancient style of the painting, I need to focus on the traditional attire,' Yumisan explained, making Daw Khin Win Mu laugh at her reasoning.

On Saturday morning, before going to U Thet Lwin's home, they had already tried dressing Yumisan in the traditional attire at her home. Daw Khin Win Mu took various photos of Yumisan in thc outfit. Daw Khin Win Mu wasn't aware that Yumisan's younger brother was staying at U Thet Lwin's house. She only knew from Yumisan that Ma Htway Htway's son had been found.

Daw Aung May helped Yumisan put on the pink embroidered longyi, ensuring it fit perfectly. She adjusted the side hooks of the longyi, which were bordered with white lace, making the garment flare out gracefully at the bottom. As Yumisan wore the longyi, her heart pounded with excitement. She had never dreamed of wearing traditional Myanmar royal attire, and the thrill made her sweat.

Daw Aung May then instructed Yumisan to tug at the edge of the longyi and practise walking around the room, worried that she might not walk gracefully outside. As Yumisan elegantly lifted the bottom edge of the longyi and walked without stumbling, Daw Aung May felt reassured.

Yumisan then touched up her make-up and decorated her neatly styled hair with tiger-lady flowers, arranging them to her liking. She felt a tinge of shyness and hesitance about stepping outside. Before opening the door, Daw Aung May draped a long, sheer pink shawl over Yumisan's shoulders and then opened the door.

Holding the side of the longyi with one hand, Yumisan gracefully stepped out of the room, with Daw Aung May following behind, holding up the shawl to keep it from dragging on the floor.

Ko Mya Phay, who was setting the coffee table in the front guest room, was stunned by Yumisan's appearance as she emerged from the room, his mouth agape in disbelief.

'Come, come . . . Sayama, come,' U Thet Lwin called from the guest room.

'Saya, do I look okay in this court dress, this htaingmathein?' Yumisan asked shyly, laughing.

U Thet Lwin gazed at Yumisan's beauty, captivated and entranced. He was reminded of the court maidens from the royal palaces during the Mindon and Thibaw dynasties and wondered which one Yumisan resembled.

'Sayama, you look stunning in this attire. You truly embody grace. Now you really resemble u-sauk-pann,' U Thet Lwin remarked.

Both U Thet Lwin and Yumisan burst into laughter.

Daw Aung May handed the lacquer bowl (*soon-oak*) to Yumisan.

'Sayama, stand here. Ah Daw, could you drape the shawl over one of her shoulders to make the soon-oak more prominent?' U Thet Lwin instructed Daw Aung May.

U Thet Lwin positioned Yumisan in various poses, preparing her for the painting. Daw Aung May carefully placed the long shawl over one shoulder, adjusting the folds of the longyi to make sure it draped elegantly. She continually made small adjustments to ensure everything was perfect.

Yumisan held the soon-oak, trying to strike a natural pose, but her shyness was evident.

Ko Mya Phay, in awe, stared blankly at the scene. Then, remembering he had more work to do, he left the guest room and briskly returned to the kitchen.

'Yo, Maung Maung, Saya's calling you,' he said, his face impassive.

Still absorbed in his school lesson at the kitchen table, Maung Maung responded, 'What does he want?'

'I don't know, but he just asked me to tell you,' Ko Mya Phay replied.

Maung Maung didn't move at all.

'You'd better go, Maung Maung. I'm not sure what he wants you to do,' Ko Mya Phay urged.

Maung Maung reluctantly got up and left the kitchen with an unhappy look.

As soon as Maung Maung saw Yumisan's figure in the front guest room, he trembled as though struck by lightning, overwhelmed by intense bitterness. Jealousy and irrational thoughts flooded his mind, stirring confusion as pride began to surface.

Oh dear . . . why is she wearing those clothes? His unvoiced question echoed in his chest, resonating deeply.

In his eyes, Yumisan looked unbearably awkward in the traditional attire. Overcome with growing frustration, Maung Maung struggled to control his anger, wanting to tear off Yumisan's traditional htaingmathein outfit. His face tightened, and in a tense, sharp voice, he blurted out, 'Ahkogyi, did you call for me?'

U Thet Lwin, noticing Maung Maung's tense demeanour, responded calmly, 'No, I didn't call for you.'

Maung Maung turned abruptly to leave. Yumisan, still holding the soon-oak, watched him intently. Daw Aung May smiled at Maung Maung, her gaze fixed on him, but inside, she felt a strong urge to grab and shake him for behaving so distant and rigid.

As soon as Maung Maung entered the kitchen, Ko Mya Phay, anticipating his arrival, remarked, 'Hey, you must have seen a vision of heavenly beauty in the front room, didn't you?'

Maung Maung glared at Ko Mya Phay, unable to form a coherent response. 'It wasn't Ahkogyi calling . . . What . . .'

Unable to finish his sentence, he stood trembling with rage, his entire body shaking uncontrollably.

Knowing that Maung Maung was upset, Ko Mya Phay softened his tone.

'Don't be mad, little brother. I just wanted to show you the royal beauty in the front parlour,' he said, spreading his palms in a placating gesture and apologizing with a sheepish grin before adding sharply, '*Tsk* . . . your elder brother's up against a tough challenge, Maung Maung.'

Maung Maung grabbed the nearest chair and sat down heavily. He slammed his open textbook shut and tossed it back onto the table.

'What an awkward sight! What's the connection between that Japanese lady and this attire anyway?

Jeez,' Maung Maung muttered irritably, his anger simmering.

Ko Mya Phay, sensing Maung Maung's growing anger, added fuel to the fire. 'Don't even talk about it. I can't stand to look at it either, Maung Maung. Until this painting is finished, we're going to see that scene. Why not paint her in a simple, traditional Myanmar dress? But, wow, she's really beautiful. She looks completely transformed.'

While Ko Mya Phay spoke, Daw Aung May entered the kitchen. She glanced at Maung Maung and Ko Mya Phay with a single sharp look before speaking. 'Can I get a glass of water?'

Ko Mya Phay immediately straightened up and smiled broadly, showing all his teeth. 'Sure . . . right away, Ah Daw.'

He poured a glass of water from the kettle and handed it to her. Daw Aung May, still watching Maung Maung, took a few sips.

'Ah Daw, are you living with the lady teacher?' Ko Mya Phay asked as he reached for the glass.

Maung Maung opened his book and stared at it miserably without lifting his head.

Daw Aung May glanced at Maung Maung before responding to Ko Mya Phay.

'Yes, I'm living with her. Saya wanted to paint the young lady in traditional attire, but she didn't know how to wear it, so I helped her dress.' Aware that Ko Mya Phay and Maung Maung were gossiping before she entered the kitchen, Daw Aung May explained calmly and walked out.

* * *

Yumisan stood holding the soon-oak the whole time. U Thet Lwin watched her intently, looking around and sketching her, silence reigning in front of the house as if no one was present.

Sitting on a chair at the entrance to the guest room, Daw Aung May watched Yumisan, all the while recalling Maung Maung's angry, sullen expression from earlier.

When Yumisan and the others drove off, Maung Maung came out to the front of the house.

U Thet Lwin greeted him warmly, 'Look here, Maung Maung. Does my drawing look like her? Sayama looks so beautiful in this traditional dress?'

Unable to contain his frustration, Maung Maung replied curtly, 'She doesn't look beautiful at all, Ahkogyi. What does this dress have to do with her?'

U Thet Lwin felt a pang of annoyance but answered calmly while packing away the painting, 'It's not about matching, Maung Maung. It's about capturing beauty.'

Maung Maung, curious but still upset, asked, 'Will she take this painting with her when she leaves, Ahkogyi?'

With a soft smile, U Thet Lwin explained, 'Of course, she will. The canvas and paints are her materials. Her forehead and nose are so prominent that I wanted to paint her in traditional attire.'

Maung Maung couldn't shake off the word 'prominent'. He couldn't bear to look at the sketch of Yumisan, feeling an urge to slash the painting to pieces with a knife.

Thus, Maung Maung couldn't stand to look at Yumisan, and Yumisan couldn't bear not seeing Maung Maung. From December to the summer break in March, time passed with this tension.

When summer break arrived, Yumisan planned to return to Japan for a short while. She frequently visited Maung Maung's house, hoping to become closer to him before her departure, but her efforts were in vain. Instead of growing closer, Maung Maung's hatred towards her only intensified.

On the day her exams ended, Yumisan went to see a Burmese movie. After the movie, she spotted Maung Maung in the crowd. Maung Maung also caught a glimpse of Yumisan in a yellow dress. As soon as Yumisan saw him, she called out to Daw Aung May, saying, 'There's Maung Maung,' and pushed through the crowd to greet him, wanting to give him a ride home in her car.

Despite having heard someone call his name, Maung Maung pretended not to hear Yumisan's voice. Without even glancing back, he forced his way through the crowd to avoid her. Yumisan stood still, tears streaming down her face amid the people. Daw Aung May approached, took her by the hand, and led her to the car.

As the school term drew to a close and her departure for Japan approached, Yumisan's face became clouded and unhappy. At home, she was no longer cheerful, and even at Maung Maung's house, she looked despondent, her face downcast and her demeanour subdued.

'Sayama, wouldn't it be better if we told him the truth?' U Thet Lwin suggested cautiously.

Yumisan shook her head slightly and replied gently, 'It's not the right time to tell him now, Saya. There's still another year left. I'll try harder when I return.'

U Thet Lwin sighed deeply, quietly admiring Yumisan's unwavering determination with a nod.

'Before I go back to Japan, I'd like to invite you all over for dinner at my place. Could you please bring

Maung Maung along, Saya?' Yumisan asked, tears welling up in her eyes.

Observing Yumisan's hesitant demeanour, U Thet Lwin, feeling a bit uneasy, reassured her, 'I'll make sure to bring Maung Maung, Sayama. Just let me know a day in advance.'

Though it was easy for Yumisan to get a promise, she didn't realize how difficult it would be to bring Maung Maung. Every day, U Thet Lwin gently and persistently tried to persuade Maung Maung to go with him to Yumisan's house.

'This is the last time I'm asking you, Maung Maung. If you don't want to go after this, that's fine. But just this once, come with me. She invited us because she's leaving soon. I already told her we'd both come, so please, for my sake, come with me.'

Maung Maung would rather sleep in front of a tiger than go to Yumisan's house. His heart was filled with bitterness, and he refused firmly without giving any reason. U Thet Lwin, with no room for compromise, insisted forcefully. He was now at the point where he felt he had to beg Maung Maung to come along.

'It's just the two of us at home. They invited both of us. Would it be right for only one to go? Think about it, and let's just go this once,' U Thet Lwin pleaded, his face growing stern as he spoke.

Maung Maung, still unwilling to comply, found it difficult to look at U Thet Lwin's darkening face or to admit that he would go along. Overcome with sadness, he retreated to his room and sat in silence, feeling increasingly uncomfortable. After a while, with a heavy sigh, he bit his lip, swallowed his reluctance, and finally stepped out.

After Maung Maung retreated to his room, U Thet Lwin sat on a nearby wooden chair with his eyes closed, lost in thought and feeling disheartened. He was troubled by the fate of the brother and sister, his mind swirling with confusion.

'Ahkogyi, I'll come with you this time,' Maung Maung finally said.

U Thet Lwin suddenly opened his eyes wide. He understood his brother's reluctance to visit Yumisan's house and realized that Maung Maung was only acquiescing to his wishes to keep him happy. This awareness made him feel weak in the face of Maung Maung's struggles. With half-closed eyes, U Thet Lwin managed a hesitant, uncertain smile as he looked at his brother.

'Do you understand me, Maung Maung? I'm asking you to come this time because I really need you to.'

Maung Maung, feeling a burning pain in his chest, lowered his head.

The next day, U Thet Lwin called Yumisan's house from school and told her that he and Maung Maung would come on Sunday.

'Thank you so much, Saya. I really appreciate it,' Yumisan's trembling voice could be heard through the phone.

13

On the day Yumisan was set to host dinner for U Thet Lwin and Maung Maung, she immersed herself in preparations. She asked Daw Aung May to take the day off from cooking, opting to handle the meal herself. Yumisan decided on a Japanese menu, with Daw Aung May assisting her from the sidelines. Though Daw Aung May was curious about what inspired Yumisan's choice of cuisine, she decided against asking.

At four o'clock in the afternoon, Yumisan's Japanese friend from the Japanese embassy arrived and helped her put on her kimono. Daw Aung May, with tears in her eyes, said in a trembling voice, 'You look so beautiful, Ma Yu.'

Dressed in a stunning white silk kimono with silver flowers, a stone-grey sash around her chest, and a matching *obi* tied at the back, Yumisan seemed completely transformed, prompting Daw Aung May to gaze at her in wonder.

The kimono made Yumisan look taller, and her slender figure in the pure white garment was gracefully proportioned and irresistibly charming. Her hair, styled in a traditional Japanese manner, was adorned with a single elegant red hairpin. Her delicate face and soft, gentle demeanour, complemented by the kimono, radiated a refined beauty.

Daw Aung May gazed at Yumisan's exquisite appearance, perfectly complemented by the kimono, with a tender and appreciative heart, unable to get enough of the sight.

At exactly seven in the evening, a car entered the yard. Daw Aung May opened the front door and welcomed the guests at the entrance.

U Thet Lwin arrived with a cheerful face, while Maung Maung, who followed beside him, appeared hunched, his face dark and sombre.

'Please come in, everyone. Today, the young lady will host you in the Japanese guest room,' Daw Aung May said, ushering them inside.

Daw Aung May escorted U Thet Lwin and Maung Maung to the Japanese guest room where Yumisan was. When they reached the entrance of the guest room, they were both struck with amazement at the sight of Yumisan.

Yumisan was kneeling on the tatami mat, facing the room's entrance, sitting gracefully with her knees together. As soon as U Thet Lwin and Maung Maung entered, she extended her hands forward, touching her index fingers and thumbs together on the mat, and bowed deeply, her forehead touching the floor in the traditional Japanese greeting.

They couldn't see Yumisan's face. Instead, they were captivated by the sight of her white kimono with its faint, delicate patterns, the bright red obi tied at her back, and the way one foot was slightly lifted off the other, covered by white socks.

U Thet Lwin didn't know how to respond properly. He was unfamiliar with this deeply respectful Japanese tradition, leading to a moment of awkwardness.

Yumisan then straightened herself and spoke gently, 'It's just simple Japanese food. I wanted to cook it myself because I really wanted to serve you. I hope you enjoy it.'

After these kind words, she bowed deeply again, her forehead touching her hands on the mat. 'I don't know if it will taste good or not,' Yumisan said in a gentle voice, then bowed her forehead back onto her outstretched hands on the tatami mat.

Maung Maung, who had never witnessed Japanese customs first-hand, was suddenly confused, wondering if Yumisan was bowing to them.

Despite speaking in Burmese, Yumisan's actions were so aligned with Japanese customs that it almost seemed like she was speaking in Japanese to U Thet Lwin.

Each time Yumisan lifted her head, U Thet Lwin bent slightly at the waist and smiled at her. Maung Maung had seen Yumisan in Western dresses and traditional Burmese attire, but the sight of her in the kimono captivated him in a new way, as he couldn't take his eyes off her. The kimono highlighted her cultural heritage, and he found it appealing.

U Thet Lwin often used his artistic eye to envision Yumisan as a Japanese doll in a kimono, the traditional attire of Japan. Now that the doll had come to life right in front of him, he watched her with admiration, almost forgetting to breathe.

After formally welcoming them in the Japanese tradition, Yumisan smiled sweetly and said, 'Please, Saya, sit on this cushion, and Maung Maung, sit here on this cushion.'

U Thet Lwin and Maung Maung took their seats on the small cushions arranged around the low table in the centre of the room. Unsure of how to sit on the floor cushions, U Thet Lwin awkwardly folded his legs and sat down, with Maung Maung mimicking his posture. Once they were seated, Yumisan gracefully kneeled on a small cushion.

At the dining table, U Thet Lwin and Maung Maung faced each other with Yumisan in the middle. A warm light shone on Yumisan. In a corner of the room, a

Japanese doll with a fan pinned to its chest seemed to be asking who was more beautiful, Yumisan or the doll, while tilting its head slightly.

'Thank you for accepting my invitation before I return to Japan, Saya. Thank you, Maung Maung,' Yumisan said.

U Thet Lwin smiled as he watched Yumisan. Maung Maung, trying to look modest, seemed to wonder where he had ended up.

In the living room, the beautiful flowers in the vase captivated Maung Maung's attention. He had never thought flowers like orchids were beautiful on the plant, but seeing them in this glass vase without any leaves, surrounded by bare stems, he appreciated their beauty.

On the papered wall, a Japanese scroll with gold and silver letters and black ink was hanging. In the middle of the wall, an ornament featuring white Japanese characters tied with a red string hung from a small round hook, with two bright red blossoms attached to the white characters.

On one side, there was an embroidered image of a Japanese goddess. The goddess, with a bun on her head, had a small statue of Buddha perched on it. Her clothes seemed a blend of Chinese and Japanese styles, making it hard to distinguish. A small, white cloth extended over both arms, with both ends gracefully hanging down. At the foot of the goddess's statue was a small doll. The goddess appeared to be pouring water from a bottle with her right hand over the doll, while her left hand held a wooden staff.

U Thet Lwin looked at the image of the goddess and the letters on the wall, curious about their meaning.

'Sayama, what does that Japanese writing mean?' he asked.

Yumisan smiled, revealing a set of evenly-spaced teeth. She gently looked at the writing, then back at Maung Maung, and replied.

'The meaning is, "The time that passes from day to day and year to year is extremely fast, like an arrow shot from a bow",' Yumisan explained.

'The phrase has a deep meaning and is quite admirable,' said U Thet Lwin, looking at the hanging inscription with appreciation. Yumisan, lowering her face, thought about how, over the past year, she had not yet developed a close bond with Maung Maung.

'What does the Japanese character on the round plaque in the middle mean, Sayama?' asked U Thet Lwin.

Sitting on the mat with her knees folded, Yumisan placed her hands gently on her lap and, with her eyes downcast in tranquillity, lifted her gaze in response to U Thet Lwin's question.

'It means "love", Saya. Just one word, "love".'

With a serene smile, Yumisan glanced at both U Thet Lwin and Maung Maung in turn.

'I like that too, Sayama. In Buddhism, "love" is very important. If we cultivate love continuously, day and night, anger and hatred will disappear from within us, Sayama.'

'In Burmese, isn't there a saying, "If one shows loving-kindness to another, that person will respond with loving-kindness"?' Yumisan asked with a gentle smile.

'Yes, there is, Sayama. No matter how much someone hates you, if you hold on to love and pure affection, one day, the power of that love will be undeniable, Sayama.'

Maung Maung sat quietly, gripped by insecurity, wondering if U Thet Lwin and Yumisan were speaking ill of him as someone who despised Japan.

'What about that statue of the goddess, Sayama?' U Thet Lwin asked, feeling a special kind of joy at being able to speak about the concept of love in front of Maung Maung.

'This statue represents the Japanese goddess Kannon-*sama*, Saya. In one hand, she holds a stick that, to explain in a way that Burmese people would understand, is akin to an *aung thabyay* (Eugenia) stalk. In her other hand, she pours water from a bottle onto the child below, symbolizing the act of sprinkling pure love. This child figure represents a child born on any day of the week.'

Daw Aung May brought in a tray with three baskets made of bamboo. She smiled at Maung Maung from behind U Thet Lwin and left. Inside the baskets were small, neatly folded, colourful hand towels.

'Saya, please use this to wipe your hands and face if you're sweating. According to Japanese custom, people wipe off sweat with this cloth before eating. It's called "*oshibori*" in Japanese.'

Yumisan unfolded a damp hand towel from one of the baskets and wiped her small hands gracefully. The scent from the handkerchief suddenly intensified and permeated. U Thet Lwin followed her example. Maung Maung didn't wipe his hands and shook his head with a reluctant smile.

Daw Aung May returned to the room, this time carrying a tray with bottles of Japanese *sake*, sake cups, and three small porcelain cups.

Yumisan leaned over from where she was sitting, arranging the sake cups in front of each person.

'Please have a little sake, Saya,' she said, picking up the bottle to open it.

'I don't drink, Sayama. I can't even stand the smell of cigarettes,' U Thet Lwin replied with a smile, declining the offer.

As Yumisan poured a small amount of sake into his cup, she smiled sweetly and apologized.

'It's not strong alcohol, Saya. It's light. Just a sip or a touch to your lips, please,' she insisted.

'I'm not used to drinking, Sayama,' U Thet Lwin said, still trying to politely refuse.

'Just a touch to your lips, Saya. It's part of Japanese custom, and I'm hosting you,' Yumisan said, continuing to pour the sake.

Watching this scene, Maung Maung was reminded of an English movie he had seen. He vividly recalled a scene where a Japanese geisha served sake to men during a meal. This memory made him perceive Yumisan in the same way, seeing her as a geisha in his mind's eye.

Fearing it would be rude to refuse Yumisan's request again, U Thet Lwin reluctantly picked up the sake cup, touched it to his lips, and then set it back down.

As U Thet Lwin picked up the sake cup, Maung Maung felt a deep, uncomfortable sensation in his chest. He wanted to avoid looking at anyone's face and, if possible, leave the room altogether.

'What about you, Maung Maung?' Yumisan turned to him with a sweet smile.

Maung Maung, his heart aching with frustration toward U Thet Lwin—who had never touched alcohol in his life yet still went along with Yumisan's wishes—shook his head bitterly when she turned to him.

Yumisan took the covered porcelain soup bowls brought by Daw Aung May and placed them in front of everyone. She clasped her hands together and said, 'This is *ozoni* soup. Please enjoy.'

Even though it was soup, U Thet Lwin was left unsure how to eat it with chopsticks, as the spoon was nowhere to be found. At that moment, Yumisan demonstrated, saying, 'Like this, Saya,' lifting the bowl to her palm, and drinking the broth slowly while using the chopsticks to pick out the solid ingredients.

U Thet Lwin followed her example, sipping the soup and using the chopsticks to eat the pieces. Maung Maung reluctantly drank a little only after seeing U Thet Lwin watching him.

Fresh fish, sliced thinly and arranged beautifully on a plate, was served next, along with green ginger, coriander, and Japanese soy sauce.

'Saya, *doe zoe*. Maung Maung, doe zoe,' Yumisan urged them to eat.

With uncertainty in his eyes, U Thet Lwin asked, 'Is this raw fish, Sayama?'

Yumisan laughed in response.

'That's right, Saya. It's thinly sliced raw fish, called sashimi. If you eat it with ginger powder and soy sauce, it's very tasty,' Yumisan explained.

U Thet Lwin was hesitant to eat it. Just hearing about eating raw fish made Maung Maung feel queasy.

Yumisan insisted that they try a piece. U Thet Lwin apologized and declined, while Maung Maung wrinkled his nose and shook his head.

Yumisan picked up a slice of raw fish with her chopsticks, dipped it in soy sauce and ginger paste, and ate it. She then encouraged, 'Please try a little, Saya.'

'This green paste is called "*wasabi*". It's very strong, and you need to mix it with a few drops of water. It's so strong that if someone with a stuffy nose smells it, their nose will clear up immediately. The raw fish, when combined with wasabi, becomes a bit cooked because it's so hot. What looks raw on the plate actually tastes good when eaten with soy sauce. Please try a little, Saya.'

Yumisan encouraged U Thet Lwin and Maung Maung to eat the raw fish through explanation. Reminding himself that he had even eaten sour shrimp and fish before, U Thet Lwin decided to give it a try. He picked up a small piece of fish with his chopsticks, dipped it in wasabi and soy sauce, and swallowed it without chewing.

Just watching U Thet Lwin handle the raw fish with chopsticks made Maung Maung feel nauseous and want to vomit.

'Maung Maung, try a little,' Yumisan encouraged.

Maung Maung replied bluntly to Yumisan without showing any signs of hesitation, 'I don't eat raw meat or fish, Sayama.'

Yumisan laughed and said, 'All right, Maung Maung, you can eat the cooked food.'

A large grilled hilsa fish, garnished with pine leaves, lay spread out on a big plate. Another large plate held whole fried shrimp, placed on paper. There was also a dish of sliced cucumber, and white and red radishes, marinated with soy sauce, vinegar, sugar, and sweetener. The vibrant colours of the cucumber, white radish, and red radish were visually appealing, creating a striking contrast.

'These dishes shouldn't serve as food; they are so beautifully presented that they are a feast for the eyes,' U Thet Lwin laughed as he admired the beautifully arranged dishes.

'In Japan, food presentation is important, Saya. First, you enjoy the food with your eyes, and then you taste it with your tongue,' Yumisan explained as she used chopsticks to serve pieces of fish from the grilled hilsa dish to U Thet Lwin and Maung Maung's plates.

'Maung Maung, eat up. This is grilled and cooked. In Japan, we grill golden fish like this, which we call *yakizakana*. It's delicious. We Japanese eat fish raw to enjoy its natural taste, but we also grill it. The natural taste of fish is better enjoyed when grilled rather than cooked with chili, oil, and onions. Grilling brings out the natural flavour of a fish, be it a carp or a hilsa. Eat it with the sweet and sour radish,' Yumisan encouraged.

'Saya . . . doe zoe. Please enjoy,' she said, offering the grilled fish.

They found the grilled hilsa delicious. It wasn't grilled the usual way with salt; instead, it was marinated with a mixture of soy sauce and sugar, resulting in a slightly sweet flavour, as Yumisan had described. The natural taste and aroma of the hilsa fish were wonderfully brought out.

Not only the hilsa but also the fried shrimp was very tasty, and U Thet Lwin ate heartily. Since no one was drinking from the sake bottles, they just sat on the table, looking somewhat out of place. Yumisan, thinking that Maung Maung didn't like alcohol, did not insist on him drinking again.

The fact that Maung Maung ate the rice she served made Yumisan feel very happy. Seeing Maung Maung enjoy the food made her feel satisfied, as if she had eaten it herself.

'This shrimp is called "*tempura*" in Japanese. It's made with eggs. Eat more, Maung Maung.'

Although Maung Maung seemed to eat reluctantly, he enjoyed the fried shrimp, which made Yumisan happy. She also liked the way he skilfully used his chopsticks.

Small pieces of chicken, fried until red, were served on plates with whole tomatoes.

Yumisan dipped a piece of chicken in soy sauce and ate it. Maung Maung followed suit, using his chopsticks to dip a piece of chicken in soy sauce before eating it. Watching Maung Maung eat brought Yumisan great joy, making her feel warm and light-hearted, and she felt an immense sense of happiness.

Next, they were served skewers with grilled meat. The skewers didn't just contain meat but also included onion tops and tofu.

'This is beef, Saya. Before grilling, it was marinated several times with miso, sugar, and lemon juice, giving it a delicious flavour.'

Yumisan gently pulled back the sleeve of her kimono with one hand and reached over to serve the grilled meat. The way she gracefully managed her kimono sleeve while serving was both adorable and elegant.

'Maung Maung, don't you like beef?'

Maung Maung merely nibbled at the grilled meat, not really eating it.

'I don't like beef much.'

Focusing too much on Maung Maung, Yumisan forgot to eat herself. She smiled sweetly, facing Maung Maung.

U Thet Lwin, however, ate the grilled meat heartily. Maung Maung just ate enough to say he ate, not really enjoying the Japanese dishes except for the fried shrimp. He thought the food looked good but didn't find it tasty.

What Maung Maung found the most funny was the final serving of rice with pickled radish. Along with the rice, there was a small piece of green paper-like garnish.

Yumisan explained that Japanese people finish their meal with plain white rice and pickled radish.

'After eating all the meat, fish, and fatty foods, we eat this rice and pickled radish to cleanse our palate. The rice is cooked with rice brought from Japan.'

By now, Maung Maung only wanted to eat this rice with the earlier side dishes. The rice was made from a variety of sticky grains, white and shiny. U Thet Lwin, however, didn't know how to eat just the plain rice with pickled radish and felt at a loss.

Yumisan picked up a small piece of green, paper-like flake and started eating it. U Thet Lwin asked, 'What kind of paper is that?'

'That's seaweed, Saya. It's called "*yakinori*" in Japanese. It's made to look like paper and is very tasty,' she replied.

U Thet Lwin ate the delicious Japanese rice without the pickled radish, finishing half of his plate with just the plain rice.

'Try it, Maung Maung. Japanese rice is very tasty,' U Thet Lwin encouraged.

Maung Maung, however, wasn't interested in trying the rice from Japan and simply responded, 'I'm full.'

After the meal, they were served Japanese canned pineapples as dessert, followed by Japanese *yokuro* green tea. That was such a particularly flavourful green tea that they had two or three cups each.

Yumisan showed Maung Maung pictures of Japanese landscapes and photographs, trying to catch his interest. While Maung Maung listlessly flipped through the photos, Yumisan pulled out two photos from the album and showed them to him.

'These are pictures of my grandparents,' she explained.

As Maung Maung looked at the photos, Yumisan and U Thet Lwin exchanged glances.

Looking at the photos, U Thet Lwin commented, 'Your grandparents must be waiting eagerly for your return.'

Yumisan smiled faintly to hide her inner pain and spoke coolly, 'My grandparents are longing to see me as I've never been away from them this long, Saya.'

'When are you coming back, Sayama? Just before the school reopens?'

Maung Maung was secretly happy at the thought of Yumisan leaving when the school closed. If Yumisan didn't come home, he would be able to stay home undisturbed. He felt an unexpected surge of unwanted feelings.

'I'll be back in May. Maung Maung, is there anything you want from Japan? If you need something, let me know, and I'll get it for you,' Yumisan offered.

Without looking at her, Maung Maung replied, 'I don't need anything.'

'What about a camera? Don't you want one?' she asked.

Maung Maung shook his head.

'A wristwatch, maybe?'

'I don't want anything,' he said, closing off the conversation to avoid any further lengthy talks.

U Thet Lwin changed the topic. 'How are things at the school? Are you satisfied with teaching there?'

'I'm very satisfied, Saya. The students are eager to learn Japanese and study hard. I'm happy to have the opportunity to teach Japanese to Burmese students,' Yumisan replied.

'Did you visit many places in Mandalay?' U Thet Lwin asked.

Yumisan responded energetically, 'I did, Saya. After visiting Bagan, I went to Mandalay. Bagan is a place to long for, but Mandalay felt like a recent event, warm and vivid in my mind. It's dustier and hotter than Bagan, but it cools down once you reach Pyin Oo Lwin.'

While Yumisan and U Thet Lwin were having their pleasant conversation, Maung Maung picked up the magazines she had given him, flipping through them and looking at the pictures to pass the time.

The magazines with pictures helped Maung Maung become aware of and interested in the high level of Japanese culture and traditions, and the way of life in modern Japan. However, even as he looked closely at the images, his mind felt distant. The essence of Japan could not captivate Maung Maung. He saw the Japanese and himself as belonging to two distinctly different worlds and flipped through the pages with this sense of detachment.

Upon Yumisan's request, Daw Aung May brought a record player and records. 'Let's listen to some Japanese music, Saya. In Japan, there are modern popular songs, classical songs, and a mix of tango, jazz, and *shanko* music.'

Yumisan selected records and played them one by one. Modern melodies were realized as Japanese songs only because Yumisan mentioned that they were, but the music resembled the kind played by the grand orchestras of world music. After playing each record, Yumisan would ask Maung Maung if he liked it. As Maung Maung listened to the contemporary beats, he thought the Japanese music was not much different from English and French music.

Before playing the final record, Yumisan selected it with a serious demeanour and spoke softly, 'Saya, listen to this song first. Feel it in your heart as you listen. Then, I will explain its meaning. After that, listen to it again, and you will understand how beautiful it is.'

Intrigued by Yumisan's words, U Thet Lwin paid close attention, expecting an emotional experience. He prepared himself to feel deeply as Yumisan started the record.

The music was exceptionally soothing, evoking a deep sense of longing and sadness through both the vocals and the instrumental. Although the lyrics were incomprehensible, the female singer's voice initially brought a sense of calm to the listener. The music, combined with the sound of ocean waves, gradually evoked a feeling of melancholy as if it were stirring the listener's heart.

The sound of large waves crashing and then receding from the shore blended with the music, creating an emotional experience that, even without understanding the words, made one's heart ache with a sense of longing.

'That was amazing, Sayama. The sound of the ocean waves mixed with the music makes it even deeper and more emotional. What song is this, Sayama?' U Thet Lwin wasn't the only one; Maung Maung, too, was curious and focused, eager to know more about the song.

While Yumisan was intently gazing at Maung Maung without blinking, she heard U Thet Lwin's voice and shifted her gaze to him. With a gentle and tender look, she explained, 'The name of this record is "Tokiniwa Haha no Nai Ko no Youni", which translates to "A Child Without a Mother" in Burmese. It's a song about an orphan child longing for his mother.'

Yumisan paused for a moment, took a soft breath, and continued, 'The meaning of the first stanza of the song is . . .

'The motherless child is silently sitting and gazing at the vast, tumultuous sea.

'As he watches the sea, feelings of wanting to wander aimlessly alone arise within him. His mind becomes restless. He struggles with the thought, "Where can I run away to?" and ends up containing his own feelings.

'Imagine being a child without a mother. A child without a mother can no longer experience the taste of maternal love. He can't even accept the compassion of others and can't speak words of love with anyone.'

Maung Maung, who was deeply engrossed, kept his eyes fixed without moving, absorbing every word.

U Thet Lwin attentively listened to Yumisan's translation with his mouth slightly open. As he grasped Yumisan's earnest presentation of the record, he felt deeply moved, with a heavy heart and a sombre demeanour. Yumisan, hoping the record would have an impact, silently prayed for its effectiveness.

'The next stanza, Saya,' Yumisan said quietly, her voice trembling slightly. She struggled to let the words escape her throat.

'Sometimes, the child wants to write a long letter that he doesn't know who to send to,' she continued. 'And sometimes, he feels like shouting, "Mother, mother," from one end of the sea to the other. The child warns others not to blame him for the emotions happening inside him. He ponders how a child without a mother can understand love.'

Finishing her translation, Yumisan lowered her eyes, her emotions evident as she momentarily fell silent with a sorrowful heart.

Maung Maung, your life and my life are the same. We both have no parents and have never experienced a mother's love. But remember, my love for you is equal to the love your mother would have had for you, Yumisan thought, unable to verbally express these words to her brother but feeling them struggle to break free from her lips.

Pushing past what she couldn't say, she managed to convey what she could. 'I've never seen my mother. Imagine how I feel every time I play this record, Saya,' she said. Yumisan then replayed the record.

Maung Maung felt an overwhelming surge in his chest, to the point where he wanted to block the music and melodies around him. They echoed the translation Yumisan provided. He couldn't help but remember his motherless life, feeling his heart ache. As the sound of crashing waves grew louder, Maung Maung, deeply moved, clenched his hands tightly, the pain of his longing for his mother evident. The waves from the record seemed to crash into his heart, intensifying his emotions. He clenched his teeth so hard that he felt they might crack.

14

That evening, the sky wasn't clear. Clouds gathered, blanketing the entire sky. As school let out, Maung Maung glanced up at the sky. The overcast sky, darkening with rain clouds, seemed to threaten a downpour. Wondering if he could escape the rain without an umbrella, he got on a readily available bus.

Before long, the wind picked up, and the darkening rain clouds began to pour. Raindrops started to spatter into the bus. 'It's going to rain heavily,' Maung Maung muttered. The bus turned toward Guttalitt Road and stopped at the bus stop before reaching the corner.

As Maung Maung jumped off the bus, rain poured down on him, drenching him with its roar. True to the saying that it pours in the months of *Warso* and *Warkhaung*, the heavy rain was so intense that Maung Maung couldn't even see his feet. He had to wade through the water covering his ankle as he walked. The wind pushed against him along with the rain.

Not only was Maung Maung soaked to the bone, but the bag carrying his books was also entirely wet, resembling a drenched rat, and he trudged on looking bedraggled. As he turned the corner, he spotted Yumisan's little white car in the yard.

It had been about three months since Yumisan returned from Japan. Since returning from Japan, Yumisan's schedule had changed. Previously, she only visited on Saturdays and Sundays. Now, she came to the house whenever she had free time in the evenings when she was not on duty at school, making it impossible to predict her visits like before.

Maung Maung glanced at Sarmi sitting inside the white car with its windows closed, then turned towards the back. Not seeing Ko Mya Phay in the kitchen, he stopped briefly under the eaves to shake off the rain.

'Ko Mya Phay . . . Ko Mya Phay . . .'

Maung Maung's voice was muffled by the rain.

'Ko Mya Phay . . . Ko Mya Phay . . .'

Holding his bag tightly, he shivered. He thought Ko Mya Phay might have gone to the front to serve coffee to guests, so he waited a moment. When Ko Mya Phay didn't appear, Maung Maung hung his wet bag in the corner to drain and stood under the eaves, shivering from the cold as he waited.

As the rain lessened, Ko Mya Phay finally heard Maung Maung's repeated calls and emerged from the kitchen door. Smiling, Ko Mya Phay walked towards Maung Maung, stepping over the stream of water flowing from the soaked bag hanging in the corner, and handed him a dry loincloth from the clothesline.

After changing out of his wet clothes, Maung Maung joined Ko Mya Phay in the kitchen.

While Maung Maung was taking out the wet books from his bag and spreading them out, Ko Mya Phay beckoned to him. With light footsteps, he walked into the room. Maung Maung watched, bewildered, not understanding Ko Mya Phay's actions.

'Come here,' Ko Mya Phay called out, popping his head out of the room door, and then went back inside. Uncertain, Maung Maung followed him into the room.

Ko Mya Phay pressed his ear against the wall, facing it closely, and motioned for Maung Maung to do the same. Maung Maung moved closer to the wall and placed his ear against it.

In the living room at the front of the house, U Thet Lwin was teaching Yumisan poetry. After finishing one poem, he started reciting another.

'The golden gong that spun around
With melodies of a Nirvana song
Has now grown still, its echoes fade.'

U Thet Lwin recited the poem loudly and clearly. Maung Maung and Ko Mya Phay had to prick their ears to make sure it could be heard even over the sound of the rain. Yumisan was sitting crouched on a chair with her hand resting under her chin.

U Thet Lwin prepared to explain the meaning of the next stanza, but Yumisan interrupted by raising a hand and saying, 'It will lose its charm, Saya. I understand the meaning. Please continue reading.'

Ko Mya Phay, who was secretly listening by the wall, stuck out his tongue slightly and nodded with a mischievous look. Maung Maung, pulling away from the wall, roughly opened the wardrobe to get a vest.

Before starting the next stanza, U Thet Lwin turned his head towards the room due to the loud noise coming from it. This noise made Yumisan realize that Maung Maung had returned from school.

As U Thet Lwin recited the next part with emphasis:

'In radiant clarity, the oil lamp glows,
spinning in its circle, humbling its pride.
It has bowed in devotion; its flame has dimmed.'

Yumisan looked intently and quietly at U Thet Lwin while he recited it with rhythm and intonation.

'"In radiant clarity, the oil lamp glows" refers to the brightly shining oil lamp, Sayama. Do you understand?'

Yumisan nodded.

'The part "spinning in its circle, humbling its pride. It has bowed in devotion; its flame now dimmed." means that the oil lamp placed near the Buddha's feet is offering its light in reverence, humbling its pride by bowing, and its flame has dimmed, signifying it has gone out. Do you understand the meaning, Sayama?'

Yumisan, resting her chin on her hand, said with interest, 'Yes, I do, Saya.'

U Thet Lwin continued reading:

'The faint smell lingers, the smoke rises gently, to the peaceful land of Nirvana, free from harm, it shall seek, with unwavering effort, As the blue fragrant smoke ascends . . .'

'Okay, Sayama. Look at this stanza. Which word do you not understand?' Yumisan took the book and started reading it almost silently. U Thet Lwin watched her while she was reading.

Since Yumisan's return from Japan, she seems to become more beautiful day by day, he thought. She often wore traditional Myanmar clothes in various colours and styles, carefully choosing matching outfits with an artistic eye. Today, she was wearing a dark blue blouse and skirt. Without any make-up, her soft, fair skin seemed to glow against the dark blue outfit. Her face, focused on the book, looked fuller and more vibrant.

'In this stanza, I understand everything, except for one phrase. I can't quite figure out the meaning of "fragrant smoke",' Yumisan said, looking into U Thet Lwin's eyes, which were fixed on her.

'The meaning of "fragrant smoke" refers to the smell of incense or something that emits a pleasant fragrance. "Smoke" here implies incense smoke, so "fragrant smoke" refers to the smoke that carries a pleasant scent. Now, please explain the stanza as you understand it.'

Looking back at the book, Yumisan explained as she understood it, 'The oil lamp has extinguished, but the pleasant-smelling smoke, which is blue in colour, is rising up to the sky, striving to find the safe haven of Nirvana. Is that correct, Saya?'

'Exactly, you've got it. Now, try to visualize it clearly in your mind,' U Thet Lwin responded.

'I can appreciate poetry well, Saya. I particularly enjoy the poems written by the poet who wrote this and those by the poet Zawgyi. I can truly savour their essence.'

'Which poem by Saya Zawgyi do you like?' U Thet Lwin asked, curious.

Yumisan replied promptly, 'The "Veda Flower" (water hyacinth) poem, Saya.'

'Have you ever seen a *veda* plant, Sayama?' U Thet Lwin asked, smiling, waiting for her response.

'Yes, I have, Saya. When I went to Twante, I saw veda plants floating in the river,' Yumisan answered.

'You can truly appreciate the essence of the poem when you've seen the plants and flowers floating in the water yourself, Sayama.'

'In the history of Burmese poetry, many poems have been written about flowers on land, but this poet is the only one who has written about the veda flower in the water. Right, Saya?'

U Thet Lwin laughed, finding Yumisan's question amusing.

'Yes, he is the only poet who has written about it, Sayama. The "Veda Flower" poem is not just one poem, though; there are quite a few others about this flower by him.'

'I was taught at Osaka University that Zawgyi is the pioneer of modern Burmese poetry. I want to read all the veda poems. Please teach me, Saya.'

'I will teach you. The veda plant, floating in the river, embodies a life that is not only adorable and admirable but also resilient, enduring the waves and winds without giving up. It has been praised for its perseverance and strength. The poems about the veda plant not only offer comfort to the human world but also serve as an inspiring example.'

'I am very interested, Saya. Please teach me the veda poems.'

U Thet Lwin continued, 'All right, listen up.'

'A fragrance column, from the aromatic gathering,
a pleasant scent, never-ending, always lingering.'

'Sayama, the fragrant smoke from earlier becomes more profound when connected with this stanza. Does it make sense?'

'It makes perfect sense, Saya. I can almost smell the fragrance. Does "gathering" mean collecting various fragrances to make an incense stick?'

U Thet Lwin laughed and nodded in agreement.

'Crossing the left side, with a travelling companion,
smiling sweetly with shared joy, earnestly wishing to be near,
striving upwards to the fragrant incense,
where the smoke never ends, where the fire never ceases,
a place beyond count, it has reached.'

U Thet Lwin's face flushed with emotion as he recited the poem, a little smile playing on his lips. At the end of the poem, he looked at Yumisan with gleaming eyes. Yumisan, taken aback by U Thet Lwin's intense gaze, suddenly blushed, her usually fair face turning slightly red. She stared back at him with a dreamy, dazed look.

U Thet Lwin quickly realized his lapse in composure and immediately pulled back, regaining his calm demeanour. He then asked, in a steady voice, 'All right, Sayama, look at this stanza. Is there anything you don't understand?'

U Thet Lwin handed the book to Yumisan, preparing to explain the meaning of the poem to her.

Yumisan stared at the stanza for a long while.

'In this stanza, I understand the meaning of "travelling companion", Saya. But what kind of "left side" does it refer to?'

U Thet Lwin no longer looked at Yumisan. He gazed straight ahead, answering with a serene and clear face.

'This "left side" refers to the cycle of life, samsara, Sayama. Next part . . .'

'I still don't quite understand "beyond count, it has reached", Saya.'

'Do you notice the spelling for the Burmese word "*seik seik kalay*" Sayama? This phrase means that it's close, not far apart, indicating closeness or attachment. "Beyond count, it has reached" means that the number of times you've wished to be near your companion cannot be counted. It's continuous and unwavering.'

Yumisan smiled and said abruptly, 'This is such a beautiful love poem.'

U Thet Lwin nodded in agreement, trying to look as modest as possible.

'Have you finished writing the poem for my father's "From Mingaladon", Saya?' Yumisan interjected, asking before moving on to the next stanza.

U Thet Lwin smiled and replied, 'I just wrote it last night, Sayama. Since I'm not a poet, it took me quite a while to compose a poem.'

'Show me, Saya. I want to see it.'

U Thet Lwin got up and went into the room. He found Maung Maung curled up sleeping under the blanket on the bed. Thinking he was cold and curled up, he quietly opened the desk drawer without making a noise. Then he took out some papers from the drawer.

Yumisan read the Burmese poem aloud, enunciating each word clearly:

'*My beloved daughter,*
five years old today,
happy and youthful, Yumisan,
your graceful, delicate demeanour, came to mind.

This lovable image, inspires deep emotions to paint a picture.

Feeling excited,

But alas, as a soldier, I do not hold a paintbrush, only a gun in my hand.'

The sound of Yumisan's recitation softly entered U Thet Lwin's heart. Feeling both content and passionate, she exclaimed joyfully, 'I love it, Saya!'

'My professor will love it too, Saya,' she added enthusiastically.

U Thet Lwin was pleased to know that she liked his poem.

'I wrote it as best as I could, Sayama. It doesn't have as many words as your father's original Burmese version, nor does it capture the lively essence of human life.'

'I like this one more. The meaning of my father's poem and this one are equally close, Saya.'

Yumisan smiled happily.

'It seems like in Japanese poetry, just like in Myanmar, we have four-syllable verses. How many syllables do your poems have?' U Thet Lwin asked, maintaining a modest tone.

'In Japanese, we have five-syllable, seven-syllable, and five-syllable poems called "haiku". Another type is five-syllable, seven-syllable, five-syllable, seven-syllable, five-syllable, and seven-syllable poems, known as "waka". Composing in the haiku style is difficult, Saya, because you have to say everything with very few words. The waka style, with its five-syllable and seven-syllable structure, allows for a bit more, so it's easier.'

As Yumisan and U Thet Lwin were having a pleasant conversation, Ko Mya Phay entered the living room.

'Saya, Maung Maung is running a high fever.'

'What?'

'He got caught in the rain earlier. He drank some medicine with hot water and didn't come out of his room. When I went to check on him, he had a high fever, so I covered him with more blankets. Now, when I checked again, he didn't respond.'

'Oh no . . .'

With a trembling voice, Yumisan shouted and rushed out. U Thet Lwin also stood up quickly. They both hurried to the room, with U Thet Lwin leading and Yumisan following.

'Maung Maung . . .'

U Thet Lwin leaned over Maung Maung, who was slouched and shivering uncontrollably. As he checked on him, he noticed that Maung Maung was barely conscious.

Yumisan bent her body from below Maung Maung's waist and looked up at his face. Seeing

Maung Maung's unresponsive expression made her heart race. U Thet Lwin felt Maung Maung's forehead, while Yumisan held his hand. Maung Maung's skin was burning hot.

Not satisfied with just holding his hand, Yumisan moved closer to U Thet Lwin and bent down to check Maung Maung's forehead. She gently brushed his hair aside. Her face turned pale with worry, and her eyes reflected her deep concern. She turned to U Thet Lwin and said, 'Saya, I have a car. Call the doctor.'

U Thet Lwin hurried out of the room and rushed down the stairs. Ko Mya Phay followed him and closed the door behind him.

Ko Mya Phay returned to the room and pressed his body over Maung Maung's. Yumisan, standing at the foot of the bed, anxiously asked, 'Does Maung Maung often get sick like this?'

'He gets fevers, but it's never been this bad. This might be malaria,' Ko Mya Phay replied.

Yumisan personally wanted to press her body against Maung Maung's to help ease his chills and fever on behalf of Ko Mya Phay. She felt as though Ko Mya Phay's presence in the room created a barrier between her and Maung Maung. She stood there, watching Maung Maung's unconscious face in the dim light, unable to take her eyes off him, her heart filled with worry.

Soon, they heard the sound of a car entering the yard. Dr Kyi Soe, U Thet Lwin's friend from Hermetic Tharthana Yeikthar Street, had arrived. Ko Mya Phay got up to open the door, leaving the room. Yumisan didn't realize how she had approached Maung Maung's side. She pressed her cheek lightly against Maung Maung's forehead. The heat from his forehead swiftly transferred to her cheek, burning intensely. Quickly, she withdrew her cheek, but the heat had already reached her heart.

Before others entered the room, she quickly moved to the foot of the bed. She didn't know how fast she had moved, but her heart was pounding hard.

The doctor administered an injection to Maung Maung and stayed until his fever subsided. Then he left. U Thet Lwin did not accompany him. Sarmi drove him back. Yumisan asked Sarmi to come and fetch her only after he had dinner.

U Thet Lwin and Yumisan watched over Maung Maung in the bedroom. Yumisan still felt the lingering warmth on her cheek from when she discreetly checked Maung Maung's forehead with hers while Ko Mya Phay was making coffee.

Standing behind U Thet Lwin, who was sitting on the bed, Yumisan watched Maung Maung's face closely, unable to take her eyes off him.

When Maung Maung regained consciousness and opened his eyes, he vaguely saw U Thet Lwin's face hovering over him. The room was brightly lit. He tried to discern the face standing behind U Thet Lwin, straining to see who it was. As his vision cleared, he recognized Yumisan's face.

'Maung Maung . . . are you awake?' U Thet Lwin asked, shaking Maung Maung's shoulder and leaning in closer.

Not wanting to look at the face he saw, Maung Maung tightly shut his eyes again.

'Maung Maung,' U Thet Lwin called again.

'Yes,' Maung Maung replied without opening his eyes.

Maung Maung heard his heart pounding loudly in his chest. He remembered he was sick when he heard U Thet Lwin's voice reciting, '*Smiling sweetly with shared joy, earnestly wishing to be near,*' echoing in his mind.

Disliking Yumisan's presence in his room, Maung Maung mentally tried to push her away.

'Why did you come in? Leave . . . get out . . .'

Anger caused sweat to pour down Maung Maung's body.

'You're sweating a lot, which means the fever has gone down,' U Thet Lwin said, noticing the beads of sweat on Maung Maung's forehead. Maung Maung kept his eyes tightly shut.

'Change Maung Maung's shirt, please,' Yumisan's voice echoed in Maung Maung's ears like molten iron being poured, making him unbearably hot.

'Mya Phay . . .'

U Thet Lwin called out to Ko Mya Phay, who then came into the room from behind.

'Wipe the sweat and change his clothes.'

Ko Mya Phay began removing the blankets from Maung Maung, who clung to them tightly.

'Go on . . . you two go outside first, I'll change him,' Ko Mya Phay said, prompting U Thet Lwin and Yumisan to leave the room.

Although Maung Maung's fever had gone down, Yumisan was still worried since he hadn't opened his eyes. She wanted to wipe his sweat herself, change his clothes, give him medicine, and stay by his side all night. Thinking about their lives, their situation, and their hardships made Yumisan's heart ache.

That night, even though she didn't want to leave, Yumisan reluctantly returned home from Maung Maung's house. Before leaving, she repeatedly reminded U Thet Lwin to feed Maung Maung warm powdered milk.

Looking at Yumisan's overly worried face, U Thet Lwin reassured her with a heavy heart and told her to go home.

The next day, at noon, Yumisan came back from school, changed into traditional attire, and headed to Maung Maung's house.

At 10 a.m., Yumisan had called U Thet Lwin from school to ask about Maung Maung's condition. U Thet Lwin replied that Maung Maung's fever had not returned and that his body temperature had cooled down. Nevertheless, Yumisan couldn't shake her worries and came by in the afternoon, anxious that the fever might spike again.

While Maung Maung was sitting up in bed, leaning on pillows and sipping rice porridge, there was a knock at the front door. Though he hadn't noticed the sound of a car entering the yard, the knocking made Maung Maung suspect who it might be.

'It sounds like Sayama,' Ko Mya Phay said, turning his head and listening towards the source of the sound.

Maung Maung, who had been half-heartedly eating the rice porridge, put the bowl aside and spoke firmly to Ko Mya Phay.

'Go and tell her . . . tell her Ahkogyi isn't here. If she asks about me, say I'm asleep. Don't open the door for her.'

After speaking, Maung Maung lay back down on the bed. Ko Mya Phay took the rice porridge bowl through a back opening that led to the kitchen, then went outside.

Yumisan stood waiting at the door, carrying bags. When Ko Mya Phay arrived at the door, he smiled and greeted her.

'Is Maung Maung still sick?'

Unable to dismiss Yumisan rudely without opening the door while she stood there with her hands full of bags, Ko Mya Phay, out of habit, reached for the door latch as he responded.

'No fever, Sayama. Maung Maung is asleep.'

Hearing the front door open from his room, Maung Maung grew angry at Ko Mya Phay for not managing to keep Yumisan away.

Not wanting to face Yumisan and having no time to shut his room door, Maung Maung pulled the thick blanket from the foot of the bed and covered himself completely.

Instead of sitting in the living room, Yumisan placed the bottles of Horlicks, tins of milk powder, and boxes of snacks she had brought on the dining table. From there, she could see Maung Maung lying in bed through his open room door.

'Oh . . . why is he wrapped in that big blanket? Does he have a fever again?'

Ko Mya Phay stood at the threshold of the room, trying to prevent Yumisan from entering, and spoke back politely.

'No fever, Sayama. He's just sweating it out.'

Ko Mya Phay spoke softly, barely audible. Yumisan replied loudly and insistently.

'How can he breathe under such a thick blanket, Ko Mya Phay? Lift it up and check. We can't tell if he's running a fever or unconscious like this.'

Maung Maung was both fully awake and increasingly angry, but he could do nothing. With his head covered by the blanket, he clenched his fists tightly, gritting his teeth. Seeing the worried expression on Yumisan's face, Ko Mya Phay found himself at a loss. If he didn't lift the blanket, Yumisan would likely do it herself.

Ko Mya Phay, assessing the situation, entered the room and gently grasped the blanket covering Maung Maung's face. Yumisan simultaneously entered the room from the doorway. Maung Maung realized Yumisan had entered the room from inside the blanket. To get her to leave quickly, he decided to pretend to be asleep.

'He's sleeping,' Ko Mya Phay said softly. Maung Maung, keeping his mouth shut, breathed rhythmically and kept his eyes closed, feigning sleep. Yumisan stood at the foot of the bed, observing him. 'He's sweating a lot,' she remarked quietly.

Ko Mya Phay then covered Maung Maung's face again with the blanket. Approaching closer, he whispered to Yumisan, 'He didn't sleep at all last night. Let him rest.' He then tiptoed out of the room, followed by Yumisan, who couldn't stay behind.

'How can he breathe with that blanket over him?' Yumisan expressed her displeasure to Ko Mya Phay in the living room, her face showing concern.

'This is a Burmese custom, Sayama. When someone has a fever, we cover their face with a blanket to make them sweat.'

Yumisan glanced at her watch. It would still be a while before U Thet Lwin returned. She thought that if Maung Maung's fever spiked again in U Thet Lwin's absence, they might need to call a doctor and would need the car ready.

Leaving Yumisan in the living room, Ko Mya Phay went back to Maung Maung's room. Maung Maung pulled off the blanket and glared angrily at Ko Mya Phay.

'What am I supposed to do? Since she brought milk powder and snacks, I had to open the door,' Ko Mya Phay whispered to Maung Maung.

Maung Maung gestured for Ko Mya Phay to close the door. Ko Mya Phay shook his head quickly and approached Maung Maung, whispering an apology.

'It's not a good idea to close it right now. Just pretend you're sleeping. She won't come here.'

'Do I have to keep this blanket over me all the time?' Maung Maung's voice was intense.

Worried that Yumisan might overhear from outside, Ko Mya Phay pressed his finger to his lips and signalled Maung Maung to keep quiet.

'I'll stay here and keep watch. When she comes in, I'll cover your face,' Ko Mya Phay whispered.

Maung Maung was so annoyed at being disturbed by Yumisan that he wondered if his fever might even run away in fright. He was sweating profusely, and his whole body felt cold.

Yumisan sat calmly on the chair, recalling the events of the previous day. She realized that if Maung Maung had not lost consciousness, she would not have had the chance to touch him. Imagining how he would react harshly if she tried to touch him made her tremble. She felt deeply sad about not being able to care for her brother in a normal, affectionate way because he didn't recognize her as a sibling.

Even though she was sitting quietly outside, Yumisan was not at ease. She was waiting for the time when Maung Maung might wake up.

From what Ko Mya Phay had told him that morning, Maung Maung knew that Yumisan had checked his temperature and touched his forehead the previous day. The thought of her touching his skin made him feel both angry and pained.

Maung Maung was constantly worried that Yumisan might enter his room. Because of his anxiety, he wanted to close the door to prevent her from coming in.

Maung Maung gestured to Ko Mya Phay for a glass of water. Ko Mya Phay left the room through the doorway leading to the dining room.

While Ko Mya Phay was fetching water, Maung Maung got up from the bed and went to close the door. When Ko Mya Phay returned with the water, he saw Maung Maung closing the door.

Ko Mya Phay sternly asked Maung Maung, 'Why did you close the door?' giving him a disapproving look.

Hearing the door close, Yumisan came out of the living room and approached the dining table. Seeing the closed door, she assumed that Maung Maung was awake and that Ko Mya Phay was wiping his sweat.

Instead of returning to the living room, Yumisan quietly paced around the dining table, trying to make no sound.

Flies were swarming around the dining table, making it look dirty. Observing the messy and untidy state of the house, she thought it might be causing Maung Maung's poor health. She made a mental note to come back and clean the house thoroughly once Maung Maung was well.

Ko Mya Phay came out from the kitchen area. Yumisan intercepted him with a question.

'Did he change clothes, Ko Mya Phay?'

'Yes, yes, Sayama. He wiped off his sweat and changed clothes. He didn't want any drafts, so he asked to keep the door closed. He doesn't have a fever any more,' Ko Mya Phay said, but his words didn't match his expression. Yumisan realized that Maung Maung had asked to keep the door closed to prevent her from entering the room.

Yumisan went to sit in the living room. She pondered and criticized herself for why she felt such affection for her younger brother, who seemed to detest her. She wished Maung Maung understood that in this vast world, they were the only family they had, as their parents were gone.

Ever since she learned that Maung Maung was in Myanmar, her body might have been in Japan, but her heart and mind were always in Myanmar. She reminisced about the efforts she put in to understand Burmese literature and culture before coming to Myanmar. She thought about how much she cared for Maung Maung and how hard she had tried to come to Myanmar with a deep sense of attachment.

Those thoughts were deeply alarming for Yumisan. Sitting alone outside, she wrestled with her unsettling emotions. Curled up in her chair, she alternately bent and stretched her fingers, her eyes darting aimlessly. Trembling and shaken, she struggled to ease the overwhelming turmoil within her.

Before 4 p.m., U Thet Lwin returned home. Yumisan opened the door and greeted him with a respectful bow. Without pausing in the living room, he went straight to Maung Maung's room. From outside, he knocked and called out.

'Maung Maung . . . do you still have a fever this evening?'

There was no response from Maung Maung inside the room. Ko Mya Phay came out of the kitchen and said that Maung Maung had gone to the bathroom. As soon as Yumisan heard U Thet Lwin being let in at the front door, Maung Maung had hurriedly rushed into the bathroom.

Since it was getting close to her time to teach in the afternoon at school, Yumisan could not wait for Maung Maung to come out of the bathroom. She bid farewell to U Thet Lwin and left with a somewhat displeased expression.

15

Though the season shifted from the rainy season to winter, only the weather changed; Maung Maung's mindset stayed the same. The relationship between Maung Maung and Yumisan had deteriorated further over time.

Whenever their eyes met, Maung Maung's eyes would flash with a harsh and hateful expression. Every time Yumisan saw those eyes, it hurt her deeply, as it affected the sibling bond she held within her heart.

Maung Maung's hostility always frightened Yumisan, making her too afraid to think or act. His constant animosity disrupted and hindered her, making it impossible for her to reveal the truth between them.

The situation had reached a point where she had to be cautious, fearing Maung Maung would notice their relationship. She wanted to show that her interactions were solely with U Thet Lwin and had nothing to do with Maung Maung, so she avoided speaking to Maung Maung altogether. When they did speak, it was only about trivial matters like asking if he was feeling well or if he was back from school.

During the summer school break when Yumisan returned to Japan, the gifts from the grandparents for Maung Maung had to be kept at home, waiting for the right time to be given to him. Their grandfather had sent a cassette recorder for Maung Maung, and their grandmother had sent a Canon camera, a wristwatch, and several ready-made shirts, pants, and jackets. All these gifts were still packed in a bundle at home, waiting for her return from Japan to give them to Maung Maung.

Their grandfather had told her to convey to Maung Maung that these were gifts from his Japanese grandfather. Their grandmother had also instructed her to tell Maung Maung that these were gifts from his grandmother, who hadn't met him yet.

Yumisan had been waiting for the right moment to give these gifts to Maung Maung, as she could not bring herself to explain to him as the grandparents had wished. It was becoming increasingly difficult to write to the grandparents about the situation.

Writing to her grandparents repeatedly to assure them she was doing her best to improve the situation had become a frustrating and discouraging task, as she had to address the same issue again and again. She was losing the motivation to write.

Recently, U Thet Lwin and Yumisan had been going out together frequently: to movies, art exhibitions, the Tazaungdaing festival, and even dining at Chinese restaurants. Their frequent outings together were causing increasing jealousy and resentment in Maung Maung, whose face grew gloomier by the day. His eyes were filled with a fearful intensity, and he began to harbour ill feelings towards U Thet Lwin.

Yumisan often returned home late at night, necessitating the door to be opened for her numerous times. On such nights, Maung Maung couldn't help but feel that U Thet Lwin's affection for him was waning, filling him with a deep sorrow.

U Thet Lwin often urged Yumisan to open up and face the reality of their situation, rather than silently endure the pain. However, she feared that speaking openly would only make things worse.

The first semester exams at Rangoon University were approaching, and the Institute of Foreign Languages where Yumisan worked was also demanding her attention with busy exam preparations.

One morning, after finishing her task of distributing exam papers, Yumisan had some free time and decided to visit Maung Maung's house.

She knew that both U Thet Lwin and Maung Maung were away at that time. Her purpose for going was to clean Maung Maung's cluttered house for health reasons. Although she had intended to do this earlier, her exam preparations had kept her busy. Today, she was determined to ensure it got done.

At 10 a.m., Ko Mya Phay was in the kitchen eating breakfast when Yumisan arrived at the front door. She walked to the back and asked Ko Mya Phay to open the front door.

'They are not here, Sayama,' Ko Mya Phay said with a smile as he opened the door. Before entering the house, Yumisan called out to her driver, Sarmi.

'Sarmi, tell Obasan that I will have lunch at one o'clock. You can come back to pick me up at that time.'

Ko Mya Phay couldn't understand why she needed to stay here for an hour when no one else was home. After Sarmi left, Yumisan entered the house and closed the front door.

Ko Mya Phay left Yumisan in the living room and went back to the kitchen to continue eating.

Yumisan took out two pieces of clothing from her bag that she had placed there earlier in the morning. She wrapped one piece of white cloth around her head and tied it, and the other piece she tied around her waist, fastening it behind her.

Yumisan waited for Ko Mya Phay to come out of the house. When he appeared, she asked him for a dust cloth. Ko Mya Phay, still confused by Yumisan's headscarf and waist cloth, fetched the dust cloth.

'Ko Mya Phay, I'd like to clean this house, so please give me a broom and a dustpan.'

Ko Mya Phay, understanding her intention, responded with a broad, somewhat embarrassed smile, revealing his teeth.

'Oh . . . it's okay, Sayama. I'll sweep it.'

'Ko Mya Phay, do your own tasks. I'll take care of the cleaning.'

'No, I mean it. I'll do the sweeping, Sayama.'

Yumisan started cleaning the front room. She had noticed the cobwebs on the windows and walls and the dust on the floor during every visit, but she could no longer bear to see them. Determined to tackle the mess today, she began her task.

Ko Mya Phay reluctantly joined in the sweeping. While he swept the windows and walls, Yumisan took the books off the table, dusted them off, and put them back one by one.

After cleaning the spider webs and dust from the window screens and walls, they dusted the dining table and chairs in the living room. Although Ko Mya Phay usually returned to his home in Bahan after having breakfast and closing the door, today he was unable to. Instead, he mopped the floor with water and scrubbed it with a coconut fibre brush, as Yumisan wished.

'Sayama, don't do anything. Your clothes will get wet. Tell me what to do, and I'll do it.'

Yumisan was about to assist Ko Mya Phay so that the work could finish quickly but was firmly stopped from helping. Ko Mya Phay was astonished by Yumisan's unexpected visit to clean the house. He was surprised and somewhat amused to see a respected lecturer sweeping and scrubbing the floors. He especially missed Maung Maung and wondered how he would react.

'Please mop the floor with a dry cloth.'

Ko Mya Phay wrung out Maung Maung's old longyi and used it to scrub the floors, making them shine. Once the floors were spotless, Yumisan rearranged the living room, making it tidy and pleasant. She separated the two armchairs and the dining table into one area and the living room chairs and tables into another, making the front room spacious and visually pleasing.

After finishing with the front room, they moved on to clean the dining area. Yumisan personally swept and cleared away all the trash from between the roof and the beams. Ko Mya Phay mopped the floor.

'Ko Mya Phay, please don't be upset about being busy because I came here to clean up. I'm doing this because I consider the people in this house, like my older brother and younger brother . . . my relatives,' Yumisan said with a smile.

'It's no problem at all, Sayama. When Saya comes back in the evening, he'll feel very uneasy about your work here. Since it's just us men in this house, as you can see, things get a bit untidy. I come in the morning to cook, go home at midday, and return in the evening, so I don't have much time to do household chores,' Ko Mya Phay explained.

Yumisan asked, wide-eyed, 'Don't you live here?'

'No, my wife and children are in Bahan,' Ko Mya Phay replied.

'Have you been staying with Saya for a long time?' Yumisan asked curiously.

'I only started staying with him when he moved to Yangon, Sayama. Initially, he lived in Mandalay. I met him after he moved to Yangon. He didn't want to get married, so I ended up working here,' Ko Mya Phay replied with a cheerful smile, just to keep the conversation going.

'If Saya gets married, will you leave?' Yumisan asked, her eyes sparkling with curiosity.

Ko Mya Phay just smiled in response.

'Saya won't get married, Sayama. He's very close to his younger brother. Maybe he's afraid that if he gets married, it will cause a rift with his brother,' Ko Mya Phay said, half-laughing and half-serious, while working energetically.

Yumisan continued cleaning the house efficiently, seeing exactly what needed to be done. In no time, the dining room was spotless and neatly arranged, looking different from how it was earlier.

'I want to clean the bedroom. Do you have the key, Ko Mya Phay?' Yumisan asked.

Although Ko Mya Phay wasn't keen on her cleaning the bedroom, he couldn't refuse because Yumisan was now more like part of the household rather than just a guest. He handed her the key.

They both started cleaning the bedroom. Yumisan removed all the bed linens and pillowcases, and Ko Mya Phay brought out fresh ones from the wardrobe. While flipping the mattress, an old karate uniform of Maung Maung's was found underneath.

Ko Mya Phay unfolded the karate uniform and noticed it was crumpled and tucked away. He felt both surprised and puzzled, recalling how Maung Maung used to practise in it every evening. It had been a long time since he had seen him wear the uniform. Now, seeing it in such disarray, he understood why it was hidden. He hurriedly took it to the bathroom to conceal it.

Yumisan worked so quickly and efficiently that Ko Mya Phay couldn't help but admire her silently, thinking that Japanese women were quite fast at cleaning houses.

In Maung Maung's bedroom, the books and magazines scattered on the floor were gone. Nothing was left hanging on the clothesline either. Everything, old and new, was put back in its place. The previously messy room now looked like a neat and inviting bedroom, clean and beautiful.

'Take a break, Sayama. Have some coffee,' Ko Mya Phay suggested.

'I'm done with the work. I don't need any coffee. I'll return home for lunch now and bring a flower vase from my house this evening,' Yumisan replied.

It had been about half an hour since Sarmi's car arrived. Yumisan removed the cloth tied around her head to keep dust out and untied the cloth wrapped around her waist to protect her dress.

'Do you like how the house looks now, Ko Mya Phay?' she asked, smiling before leaving.

'I do, Sayama. Thank you so much. When Saya and Maung Maung come back, they'll think they walked into the wrong house,' Ko Mya Phay replied.

After Yumisan drove away, Ko Mya Phay closed the door. He no longer had time to return home.

Looking at the neat and tidy front of the house, Ko Mya Phay thought about the mess in the back kitchen, realizing it needed to be cleaned next. He spent the whole day cleaning the kitchen, a task he had never tackled before.

At 3.30 in the afternoon, he heard the sound of Maung Maung's whistle from the back. Ko Mya Phay couldn't help but smile at the sound. Maung Maung was astonished to see Ko Mya Phay covered in dirt and grime from head to toe.

'What have you been doing, Ko Mya Phay?' Maung Maung asked, seeing the exceptionally clean kitchen for the first time. With curious eyes, he looked at Ko Mya Phay again.

'Before you enter the house, make sure to wipe your feet clean. Your graceful sister has cleaned the entire house,' Ko Mya Phay instructed.

'What . . .?' Maung Maung exclaimed loudly.

Despite being exhausted, Ko Mya Phay glanced at Maung Maung with a teasing look.

Maung Maung walked into the dining room, then to the living room, and finally to the bedroom. The dining room, living room, and bedroom had all been transformed, looking completely different from their previous state.

Noticing how clean and tidy the house had become, Maung Maung couldn't help but observe the remarkable change. Despite Yumisan's thorough cleaning, the new look of the house didn't sit well with him, and the transformation weighed heavily on his heart.

The old house where he and his elder brother lived seemed to have disappeared, replaced by a new home shared with Yumisan. The drastic change left him overwhelmed.

As Ko Mya Phay scrubbed the handle of a tiffin carrier, he talked to Maung Maung without glancing in his direction.

'Did you see it? Your beauty queen sister Yumisan's handiwork is top-notch,' he said, then turned to Maung Maung with a broad smile. Seeing Maung Maung's eyes blazing with anger, he was taken aback.

'Why did she come and clean this house? Is this her house?' Maung Maung retorted angrily.

'She regards this house as her own, given how she feels about it,' Ko Mya Phay replied calmly, ignoring Maung Maung's anger, and continued to rinse the handle with water.

'All right. Let's see whose house this is anyway,' Maung Maung stormed out of the house in anger.

Soon, loud noises could be heard from the front of the house, prompting Ko Mya Phay to rush outside.

Maung Maung had thrown the neatly arranged books from the table onto the floor and was pushing the table back to its original place.

'Hey, hey, Maung Maung, what are you doing?' Ko Mya Phay exclaimed.

Overwhelmed by anger, Maung Maung roared like a wild tiger, his tone growing increasingly harsh. He destroyed all the cleaning and tidying that Yumisan had done. Every item she had organized was deliberately scattered and thrown around. He pulled and pushed the chairs in the living room, moving them far from their places.

Ko Mya Phay initially planned to restrain Maung Maung, but he was intimidated by Maung Maung's intense anger. Instead, he tried to calm him down with a soothing tone.

'Please don't do this, my little brother. I beg you to stay cool. It's she who came and cleaned; let it be. You're still living in your own style. It's enough . . . enough . . .'

Ko Mya Phay's words didn't reach Maung Maung at all. Blinded by fury, Maung Maung ignored Ko Mya Phay's presence. He continued to disrupt and move things around in an effort to restore the disarrayed state of the front room to how it was before he left in the morning.

'Please listen to me, Maung Maung. She worked the whole morning to clean up. If she returns and sees this mess, how do you think she'll feel?'

'I'm doing all this so she can see it when she comes here. You don't need to worry at all,' Maung Maung, trembling with anger, shouted back, his voice echoing through the room.

Ko Mya Phay sighed in frustration, failing to calm Maung Maung. 'How bad! It seems like bad luck has taken over this house.'

Maung Maung moved the dining table and chairs in the dining room back to their original positions, creating a mess and scattering everything around. Then he went into the bedroom. He looked at the newly decorated room where they were supposed to sleep, his expression one of disgust. The sight of the bed, neatly made up by Yumisan, ignited such intense anger in him that it twisted his heart, filling him with unbearable pain.

Maung Maung's resentment and bitterness towards Yumisan grew so intense that it clouded his usual thoughts, filling his mind with wild and aggressive impulses. He didn't even realize what he was doing. While he was throwing books on the floor in the bedroom, Yumisan's car pulled into the yard.

Yumisan had returned to place a beautifully decorated vase in the living room before Maung Maung and his brother got home. Standing at the door with the vase in one hand, she paused. Ko Mya Phay opened the door for her with his head bowed, unable to meet her gaze.

'*Oh!*'

Yumisan was stunned the moment she saw the living room, standing still as if turned to stone. The sound of books being thrown onto the floor in Maung Maung's bedroom echoed loudly in her ears, amplifying the chaos.

Ko Mya Phay stood there with a downcast expression, unable to utter a single word, his lips merely quivering.

'Ko Mya Phay . . . this is Maung Maung's doing, right?' Yumisan said softly, pointing her finger at the messy living room and turning her head slightly towards him.

'Yes, I did it,' Maung Maung said, emerging from the room in a rush. He stood with his hands on his hips, staring defiantly at Yumisan.

Yumisan's face softened as she looked at Maung Maung. She gently placed the vase on the table, then turned back to him with a calm expression.

'Maung Maung, why are you feeling this way? Didn't I clean the house to make it tidy?' she asked gently, trying to keep her voice steady.

'Is this your house?' Maung Maung retorted.

Yumisan felt a sharp pang in her chest. She forced a smile and replied calmly, 'No, it's not my house, Maung Maung, but don't I have the right to care for a house I hold dear?'

Despite the sting in her heart, Yumisan kept her face kind and sweet.

'What are you talking about? Who are these people that care about you? Haven't you been trying too hard to win our favour?' Maung Maung replied harshly, his face twisted with anger and bitterness.

'Hey . . . hey, Maung Maung.'

Yumisan motioned to Ko Mya Phay to stop him from speaking.

'Are you trying to say that no one in this house cares about me?' Yumisan asked calmly, her voice and gaze steady.

'Well, you'd better understand that yourself. Don't you realize that the people in this house see you as just a guest, a stranger?' Maung Maung's voice dripped with resentment.

Yumisan's expression remained increasingly serene as she looked at Maung Maung. She wanted to show that no matter what he said, she wouldn't be shaken. She stood there, firm and unyielding.

'I think it's just your view that I'm a guest, a stranger, Maung Maung. Saya doesn't see me that way. And I didn't come here like some guest or stranger,' she replied.

Maung Maung scoffed, mocking her with a sneer. 'Oh? Then in what capacity did you come here?'

'Maung Maung, don't you have the sense to understand in what capacity I came and why I'm cleaning this house?' Yumisan's demeanour was exceedingly gentle, and her words were succinct. Her behaviour was like that of a teacher disciplining a student. Seeing this, Maung Maung's anger flared even more.

'Naturally, I have sense, Sayama. I did wonder why you were so eager to gain our favour. I'm not an idiot,' Maung Maung replied sharply.

Yumisan understood the implications of Maung Maung's words and wanted to correct his misconceptions. She calmly responded, 'I'm glad you understand, Maung Maung. I deeply respect Saya and think of him as my elder brother. I also consider you my dear younger brother. You know that, right?

'Ha ha ha ha!'

Yumisan's face flushed red. The mockery and sarcasm in Maung Maung's laughter embarrassed her to the point where she didn't know how to maintain her composure. Despite her embarrassment, she steeled herself and looked at Maung Maung with a gentle gaze.

'You have no family ties or friendships in this house. As a guest, it would be better if you came and went as a guest. My brother and I don't need you to do anything in our home. I don't like others handling things from my home,' Maung Maung said sharply, pouring out his innermost frustrations.

Yumisan remained calm and collected, though she felt a lump rise in her throat from the emotional turmoil. She looked at Maung Maung's angry eyes and listened to his furious voice, filled with bitterness. Despite her sadness, she gazed at him gently, seeing beyond his anger to the pain in his heart. She recognized that his rage stemmed from deep-seated pain, not just towards her but towards the entire Japanese race.

Reflecting on their encounters from the day they met until now, Yumisan realized that this was the longest and most heated conversation they had ever had. It was filled with hostility.

Facing the enraged Maung Maung, she struggled to find a way to calm herself. Even as she sought peace, she couldn't find it.

'If you don't like it, Maung Maung, I won't do it any more. But please, don't speak so harshly to anyone like you did just now,' said Yumisan.

Maung Maung sneered in response. 'I'm not harsh to everyone, Sayama. Understand this: I can be kind when I need to be and harsh when I need to be. Remember that.'

After saying this, Maung Maung turned and went back to his room, leaving Yumisan staring after him. Watching him walk away, she felt a deep sorrow for Maung Maung, who was so consumed by anger that he didn't recognize his own sister. Overcome with compassion, Yumisan's eyes filled with tears. She held back her tears in front of Ko Mya Phay and gently descended from the house with a serene expression.

As Yumisan was coming down from the house, U Thet Lwin entered the yard. Instead of heading to her car, she paused on the staircase, waiting.

'When did you arrive, Sayama?' U Thet Lwin asked.

Yumisan, her eyes still glistening with unshed tears, merely smiled at him without saying a word. Seeing the tears in her eyes, U Thet Lwin was confused.

'What happened, Sayama? Are you leaving now?' he asked.

'I'll call you tomorrow, Saya,' she replied.

Unable to control her emotions any longer, Yumisan quickly walked to her car and got in. U Thet Lwin waved gently to Yumisan, who had bowed her head with quiet respect from inside the car, and then, with a heart weighed down by emotion, made his way up to the house. He saw Ko Mya Phay's distressed face. He also caught a glimpse of Maung Maung's tense face as Maung Maung walked out of the room towards the kitchen.

'Sayama doesn't look happy. Mya Phay, what happened?' U Thet Lwin asked as he approached Ko Mya Phay, who was leaning against the dining table, head bowed.

'They had an argument, Sayama and Maung Maung,' Ko Mya Phay replied without looking up.

'What kind of argument?' U Thet Lwin, feeling uneasy, wondered if Yumisan had already told Maung Maung about their relationship.

'Sayama came in the afternoon and cleaned the whole house. When Maung Maung came home and saw everything cleaned up, he threw a fit and just messed the place up again. When Sayama returned to drop off a vase, she saw the mess and they argued.'

'*Maung Maung*!' U Thet Lwin called out.

Maung Maung emerged from the kitchen, his face still flushed and tense with anger.

'What happened with Sayama? Tell me,' U Thet Lwin said softly, though his face remained stern.

'She cleaned the house without asking the homeowners. She just came in and did whatever she wanted. I told her off, angrily,' Maung Maung replied.

U Thet Lwin's expression softened, and he forced a smile as he spoke.

'Wait, Maung Maung. Did she come to your house to make a mess or to clean? If she was making a mess, you can say you don't like it. But is it worth getting angry over her cleaning? She's a respectable lecturer who came to our house and cleaned up for us. Don't you realize that you should be grateful, Maung Maung? Don't you feel any shame, Maung Maung?' U Thet Lwin gently chided.

'I'm neither grateful nor ashamed. I can't even stand to look at her, Ahkogyi,' Maung Maung retorted, his voice growing harsher.

'Why can't you stand to look at her?' U Thet Lwin blurted out.

'In a house with men, I can't stand a woman who comes and goes so boldly at any time, Ahkogyi,' Maung Maung replied in an upset manner.

U Thet Lwin, though agitated, kept his composure and spoke calmly.

'She comes here because she's not Burmese. In their country, they don't differentiate between men and women like we do. They come and go freely with friendliness and simplicity. It's not unusual. You're just being overly sensitive,' U Thet Lwin explained.

Maung Maung's eyes glinted with defiance as he replied.

'This woman doesn't come here for ordinary reasons, brother. She comes because she likes you.

Do you think I'm not aware of it? I am, Ahkogyi,' Maung Maung said, averting his gaze from U Thet Lwin.

'Hey, Maung Maung, stop it. Why are you saying such things? Do you realize how shameful it would be if she heard such accusations? She comes here with innocent intentions, understand? Take back your words.' U Thet Lwin's voice grew stern.

Being reprimanded harshly, Maung Maung felt deeply wounded. Due to his hurt and anger, he firmly refused to retract his words.

'I'm not a child, Ahkogyi. I've been pretending not to notice for a long time. I told her I know she's trying to capture your heart.'

'What!' U Thet Lwin trembled with sudden anger. He jumped towards Maung Maung, grabbing his shoulder. His uncontrollable rage brought words pouring out of his mouth.

'What are you saying, Maung Maung? She's not just anyone; she's your sister. Understand? Your sister!' U Thet Lwin's voice shook.

Maung Maung's eyes widened in shock as he wrenched himself free from U Thet Lwin's grip. His whole body trembled uncontrollably, as though under a strange possession. Words he wanted to say stuck in his throat. Inside, he was overwhelmed with unbearable shame and sadness.

U Thet Lwin stood speechless, staring intensely at Maung Maung's tense face. Ko Mya Phay, who had been hanging his head, looked up, mouth agape.

'Is that what you want to tell me, Ahkogyi? So, just because you like that teacher, you've decided to make her my sister? You've already told her everything about me. You did tell me no one will ever call me . . . *a Japanese kid* again . . .'

Maung Maung stuttered, unable to finish his sentence, then covered his face with his hands and sobbed bitterly. U Thet Lwin couldn't bear to watch Maung Maung crying in front of him. It felt as if a burning spike had been driven into his chest, causing unbearable pain. Aware that he had already let the cat out of the bag, he painfully revealed all the secrets within him.

'It's not because I told her anything. She's been looking for you ever since she got the address your father left before he passed away. She went to Phayalay village, where they directed her to Kyaik Sakaw. When she arrived there, the abbot told her you were here with me, and that's why she came. I told her not to mention it to you until the time was right, so she kept it a secret.'

'Stop it, Ahkogyi. Just stop talking. I don't believe it. I can't believe it.'

Maung Maung uncovered his face, shouted loudly, and ran towards the kitchen, crying. U Thet Lwin took a deep breath and remained standing there, unmoving. Ko Mya Phay, stunned by the unexpected revelation about Maung Maung, stood frozen in shock, like a statue.

After a while, Ko Mya Phay came to his senses. He approached U Thet Lwin, bowed slightly, and spoke apologetically.

'Saya . . . please sit down.'

U Thet Lwin, regaining awareness at Ko Mya Phay's words, sat down on the dining chair Ko Mya Phay had pulled out for him. Leaning on the table with both hands, he ran his fingers through his hair and lowered his head, his face dark and sombre.

'Water . . . Saya, please drink some water.'

Ko Mya Phay brought water from the dining room filter. U Thet Lwin, suddenly feeling thirsty, reached for the glass and drank it down. After drinking the water, he got up from the table and threw himself onto the armchair in the living room, closing his eyes to rest. Seeing U Thet Lwin quiet, Ko Mya Phay went to the kitchen where Maung Maung was supposed to be.

Finding no sign of Maung Maung in the kitchen, he realized Maung Maung must be in the bathroom.

Since dinner wasn't cooked yet, Ko Mya Phay put rice into a pot and started to wash it under the tap water. As he was washing the rice, a suspicion crept into his mind, so he stopped and went to open the bathroom door from the outside.

Maung Maung was not in the bathroom. Realizing this, Ko Mya Phay's eyes widened in shock. He rushed out of the kitchen into the yard, but Maung Maung was nowhere to be found. Frantically, he ran back into the house and upstairs.

'Saya . . . Maung Maung is gone.'

U Thet Lwin sat up abruptly, his eyes wide with alarm.

'Where did he go? Where did he go?'

'I thought he was in the bathroom. When I went to check, he wasn't there any more.'

U Thet Lwin, his eyes wide with shock, stumbled out of the armchair. He checked the bedroom and the kitchen, realizing that Maung Maung was no longer in the house. His head spun with dizziness, making him feel faint. Like before, he found himself standing motionless by the dining table, lost in thought.

'He'll come back, Saya . . . He just left in his school clothes. He'll come back,' Ko Mya Phay said softly, trying to reassure U Thet Lwin, before hurrying back to the kitchen to tend to the soaking rice, worried it might spoil.

U Thet Lwin sank back into the armchair, closing his eyes tightly as his chest felt so tight with anxiety. He regretted revealing everything in front of Ko Mya Phay, which caused Maung Maung's shame. He felt remorse for his thoughtless revelation, for unmasking the secret he had kept hidden all his life. Standing up from the chair, he wondered where Maung Maung could have gone and if he would come back.

He stood by the front door, looking towards the yard entrance. Then, thinking that Maung Maung might have gone to the kitchen, he returned there.

'Don't worry, Saya. He'll come back soon,' Ko Mya Phay reassured, noticing U Thet Lwin's anxiety.

U Thet Lwin stood at the kitchen door, looking outside, his chest tight with worry, and let out a deep sigh. 'I made a mistake, Mya Phay. It's like I told him he was half-Japanese right in front of you. Sayama is his sister, same father, different mother. I adopted him when he was a little boy, promising him I'd never tell anyone his father was Japanese. I broke that promise.'

U Thet Lwin's voice trembled. His breaths came in gasps as he struggled to speak, while Ko Mya Phay listened intently to each word, trying to understand their significance. When U Thet Lwin stopped speaking, Ko Mya Phay looked up with a sorrowful expression and responded, 'I always thought he was just your younger brother. I can hardly believe it, Saya. I feel sorry for Sayama too; she came here to see her brother. I just realized that. But it seems Maung Maung doesn't believe she's his sister, Saya.'

Overwhelmed with emotion, U Thet Lwin could no longer speak and stepped outside the house again. The evening turned into night, and by ten o'clock, Maung Maung still hadn't returned. Ko Mya Phay waited until ten before he had to leave for his own home.

U Thet Lwin, wanting to hear Maung Maung as soon as he knocked, didn't go to his bedroom. Instead, he stayed in the armchair in the living room, waiting and waiting, well past midnight.

As midnight passed, U Thet Lwin felt heavy in his mind. He became increasingly worried. U Thet Lwin couldn't even imagine how Yumisan would react upon hearing this news. Maung Maung's absence at home made him feel as though all his internal organs were gone, leaving him empty and filled with unbearable sorrow.

He began to envision Maung Maung, and the sight of him in his imagination deepened the ache in his heart. *Poor Maung Maung. Adorable Maung Maung.* He was overwhelmed with regret over the turn of events that had made him appear cruel, unable to forgive himself.

Where could he have gone? Did he go to a friend's house? Where will he sleep tonight? Does he have money in his pocket? Where will he eat tonight? Will he be hungry? At whose house might he be staying?

Lost in endless, anxious thoughts, U Thet Lwin stayed awake until dawn.

That morning, U Thet Lwin couldn't go to work. Early in the morning, after Ko Mya Phay arrived, U Thet Lwin went to two or three houses where he thought Maung Maung might have gone.

At 9 a.m., Yumisan called U Thet Lwin. Upon hearing that U Thet Lwin was unwell and couldn't come to work, Yumisan felt a heaviness settle in her chest, without understanding why.

After finishing her morning classes, Yumisan asked for permission from the principal to leave and returned home without waiting till noon. Once home, she changed her clothes and went back out to U Thet Lwin's house.

Unable to find Maung Maung anywhere, U Thet Lwin returned home, and sat in the armchair, exhausted. Ko Mya Phay opened the door for Yumisan. Seeing U Thet Lwin in the armchair from the doorway, she bent slightly at the waist and greeted him before asking, 'Are you not feeling well, Saya?'

'Please have a seat, Sayama,' said Ko Mya Phay, pulling a chair over to U Thet Lwin. As soon as Yumisan sat down, U Thet Lwin began to speak.

'Maung Maung is gone, Sayama.'

'Oh . . . where did he go, Saya?' Yumisan asked, her face paling with shock, her heart pounding.

'He quietly left the house last night, Sayama,' U Thet Lwin said, not meeting her gaze, his voice heavy with regret.

'Why did he leave the house quietly? Tell me, Saya . . . Where did he go, Saya?' Yumisan asked, her concern growing.

U Thet Lwin remained silent. He had anticipated her distress and worry, and the compassion he felt for her made it difficult for him to speak.

'Did he get upset with you, Saya?' she asked, her face showing signs of distress.

Unable to bear the sight of her troubled expression, U Thet Lwin apologized for his mistake before explaining further.

'It's my fault, Sayama. When I found out that he was being rude to you, I lost my temper in front of Mya Phay and blurted out that you are his sister. Now Mya Phay knows his father is Japanese.'

'Oh . . . Saya, oh . . . oh . . .'

Yumisan felt a surge of intense sadness and regret in her heart, and tears began to flow uncontrollably. U Thet Lwin couldn't bear to look at the tearful Yumisan and turned his face away. Yumisan, unable to control her emotions, wiped her streaming tears with a handkerchief and asked, 'Saya, when you told him that I am his sister, what did he say?'

'He didn't believe it . . . Sayama.'

After speaking, U Thet Lwin clenched his teeth tightly and took deep breaths.

'Oh, he didn't believe it. Right, Saya? I'm saddened by that. It's obvious he doesn't want to be associated with the Japanese bloodline. His resentment towards the Japanese is very apparent. Just let it be . . . When is his exam, Saya?'

'His exam is just three days away, Sayama.'

Yumisan lowered her head. Unable to hold back her emotions, tears welled up in her eyes. U Thet Lwin, struggling with what to say, tried his best to offer comforting and encouraging words to her.

'I believe he'll come back, Sayama. He didn't take any of his clothes with him. He left wearing the same clothes he returned from school yesterday evening.'

'I don't think he'll come back, Saya. That's why I couldn't bring myself to open up to him. What's important to him now is the exam. Isn't the exam the most important thing for a student, Saya?'

Yumisan's soft voice echoed gently in U Thet Lwin's heart, reverberating with a quiet tenderness.

'It's definitely important, Sayama. If he doesn't take the exam, there's no hope for him to pass the exams this year.'

'We'll have to keep looking for him until we find him. Please keep searching for him, Saya.'

'I searched for him in the morning. In the evening, I'll go to Insein with one of his friends.'

Yumisan was deeply worried that Maung Maung might not be able to take the exam. If he failed and suffered the consequences for the entire year, she felt it would be solely Maung Maung who would bear the loss just because of her. She found herself overwhelmed with indescribable emotional distress as she struggled to figure out how to help her brother avoid any educational setbacks.

Her immense love, concern, and worry for Maung Maung grew so profoundly that she was ready to give him her flesh, her blood, and even her life. She was willing to do anything for him.

16

In the early morning, the tar road glistened with dew. The cold northern wind gently blew through the fog, bringing a refreshing and invigorating chill. The slight cold was delightful when combined with the renewed freshness of the tiny dewdrops.

In the distance, the roofs of the monastery in Hlegu village, sheltered by trees and covered in a light layer of fog, stood out sharply. Every object in sight seemed serene and beautiful in the clear, bright light. A car sped past the serene Hlegu village.

Yumisan, on her way to Kyaik Sakaw, recalled the early morning of her previous trip and felt a deep sadness. She had been unable to sleep the entire night due to intense emotions. If Maung Maung was not in Yangon, he must have rushed to Kyaik Sakaw, she guessed. Unable to inform U Thet Lwin or anyone else, she embarked on the journey alone.

Yumisan was certain that Maung Maung would go to Kyaik Sakaw Monastery and nowhere else.

Having left home, Maung Maung would seek to verify the truth of what his brother had said. *Only after confirming the truth or falsehood could he decisively cut ties with his brother*, Yumisan thought.

Yumisan had no other place to think of where Maung Maung might go besides Kyaik Sakaw. If he went somewhere else, she wouldn't know where to look for him. She set out to search for him at the place she thought he might be.

Yumisan was deeply concerned about Maung Maung's exams. She believed that if a student failed to take his exams, the loss would be unlike any other. She valued the importance of the exams highly.

She had planned to reveal everything to Maung Maung herself after his final exams before the summer break and before returning to Japan. However, U Thet Lwin had revealed the truth in advance, leading to a situation where Maung Maung might miss his exams. Yumisan was worried and distressed about the potential impact on Maung Maung's education.

She prayed to find Maung Maung at Kyaik Sakaw Monastery. The number of times she had wished for this was countless.

Yumisan had learned the morning after that Maung Maung had left the house the previous evening. He hadn't returned that day, nor the next day. Maung

Maung had been missing for two days now, and the exams were set to start tomorrow. Deeply worried, Yumisan had left the house early this morning to search for him.

If she found Maung Maung at the monastery, she planned to persuade him to take his exams with the help of the abbot. Sarmi drove Yumisan towards her destination as she wished, putting in all his effort. They arrived at Bago before 6.30 a.m.

As the morning light began to shine, they saw the golden stupa of Shwe Mawdaw. Yumisan clasped her hands together and prayed to find Maung Maung at Kyaik Sakaw.

They arrived at Kyaik Sakaw at 8 a.m. Yumisan instructed Sarmi not to drive the car up the hill to the monastery, but instead to take the cart path. She asked Sarmi to stop the car in the shade of distant trees near an old and dilapidated pagoda.

Concerned that Maung Maung might recognize the car and flee, she concealed it from view. To blend in as a local woman, she dressed in traditional Burmese attire, donning a Mudon shawl from Daw Aung May's collection, wrapping it around her head and neck and covering part of her body before exiting the car.

With her heart pounding, Yumisan climbed up the hill toward the monastery. She saw no one on the hill. She then headed toward the monastery compound she had visited before, looking around as she climbed, hoping to see Maung Maung.

On the upper floor of the monastery, she found the abbot of Kyaik Sakaw sitting quietly on a chair. He knew that a laywoman had come to the monastery but didn't know who she was yet. Yumisan removed the shawl that covered her head. She placed it on her shoulder and bowed to the abbot.

When she uncovered her face, the abbot realized she wasn't Burmese. He gazed at her intently, wondering if she was the Japanese teacher who had visited the monastery before.

'Do you remember me, Phaya? I am the Japanese teacher who visited this monastery last year,' Yumisan said.

The abbot smiled and looked at her with recognition.

'Yes, yes, I remember. Have you met Maung Maung yet?'

Yumisan's face lit up, and her eyes sparkled with excitement.

'Is Maung Maung here, Phaya?'

The abbot looked at Yumisan and replied calmly, 'Didn't you see him below? Maung Maung is here. He's been here for two days. He said he ran away from home. I've been urging him daily to return.'

Yumisan felt relieved and joyful upon hearing that Maung Maung was at the monastery.

'What did he say, Phaya? Did he ask about me?' she inquired eagerly. The abbot listened intently to her Japanese-accented question.

'He asked about you. He asked if a Japanese teacher had come, and I told him that you had. He also asked if you had said you were his sister, but I didn't tell him that. Instead, I said he was the son of your friend.'

Yumisan replied, smiling slightly.

'He isn't a son of my friend, Phaya. Maung Maung is my father's son. My mother gave birth to me in Japan and then passed away, and my father remarried in Burma. Maung Maung and I are siblings. When I first came to Burma, I looked for him without telling anyone about our relationship. It was only when I met that university teacher that I revealed we were siblings.'

The abbot interrupted her.

'Why didn't you tell him that you were his sister right away?'

Yumisan's face turned sorrowful, and she sighed deeply.

'I wanted to tell him as soon as I met him. But Saya asked me not to tell him immediately and to wait and see because Maung Maung has a strong resentment towards Japan. So, I haven't told him yet.'

The abbot fell silent, looking at Yumisan with eyes full of compassion and regret.

'Maung Thet Lwin was right, *Dagamalay*. It's not just that he hates Japan; he deeply resents it. When he lived here, he hit anyone who said his father was Japanese. Maung Thet Lwin said he'd raise him like his own brother and never told anyone he was Japanese. But now, Maung Thet Lwin mentioned that he was Japanese in front of his student. Maung Maung felt ashamed and hurt, which is why he ran away from home. He said he wouldn't go back home and planned to go to Mandalay instead.'

Yumisan was alarmed to hear that Maung Maung wouldn't return home.

'Where is Maung Maung now, Phaya? His exam is tomorrow. If he doesn't take it, he won't pass this year. That's why I've come to fetch him. Please tell him to come back with me.'

The abbot now realized that Yumisan and Maung Maung were siblings. He felt a deep compassion for Yumisan, understanding her great love and concern for Maung Maung.

After leaving home, Maung Maung had come to Kyaik Sakaw by bus from Bago. He came to ask the abbot about U Thet Lwin's statements, which he couldn't believe. When the abbot said Maung Maung was not the brother of the Japanese teacher, but just the son of her friend, he felt even more hurt and kept on staying at the monastery instead of returning home. He was still planning to go to Mandalay to find a job and build his future there.

The abbot rang a small bell by his side. A monastery boy quickly arrived and bowed to the abbot.

'Where is Maung Maung?'

'He's in the dining hall, Phaya.'

'All right. Go and fetch him. Tell him I want to see him.'

The boy nodded and left promptly.

Before Yumisan arrived at the monastery, Maung Maung had already left the dining hall and was walking towards the railway tracks. He sat at a sloping area, staring at a train coming in from Yangon. At that moment, two young men approached him.

'Hey, Japan! I heard you're back at the monastery.'

Maung Maung turned to see who had tapped his shoulder and spoken to him.

'It's me! Don't you recognize me? It's Htun Shein. I heard you're back at the monastery. How's it going? What did your Japanese father give you? I've heard some things about you.'

Tun Shein, the grandson of *kappiya* U Sa (attendant in the monastery), was now about twenty-five years of age. Having not seen each other in years, Maung Maung almost didn't recognize him. Tun Shein's face was visibly affected by heavy drinking, with red, swollen eyes. His voice was rough and hoarse. He had his longyi reversed and wrapped around him, revealing his black trousers underneath.

Another young man, similar in age to Tun Shein and also appearing to be drunk, was with him. This man wore a *pasoe* wrapped around his head and was shirtless, with a short longyi tied around his waist. He was strong, dark-skinned, and had the look of a manual labourer.

Maung Maung glanced at Tun Shein. Realizing they were drunk, he assessed the situation to avoid conflict and then spoke.

'Don't talk to me like that, Tun Shein. Just go your way peacefully.'

Tun Shein laughed loudly and then kicked Maung Maung in the back. Maung Maung quickly stood up.

'What's this, you Japanese bastard? I'm just asking. What do you think of yourself, living in Yangon? There is only one Tun Shein at Kyaik Sakaw. Understand, you, the son of a shorty!'

Tun Shein's face became arrogant and aggressive, showing his rough nature. Maung Maung swiftly kneed Tun Shein in the waist, causing him to fall to the ground. As Tun Shein lay there, his companion lunged at Maung Maung.

The monastery boy, unable to find Maung Maung in the dining hall, ran up the hill and briefly watched the fight. He then sprinted back to the monastery to report.

'Maung Maung from Yangon and Tun Shein from the village are fighting, Phaya.'

Yumisan stood up quickly, alarmed, and asked urgently. 'Where? Where are they fighting?' Yumisan asked.

The abbot also inquired, 'Hey, is it that drunkard Tun Shein? Where exactly?'

'At the rail tracks,' the monastery boy replied before running back down from the monastery. Yumisan followed closely behind, sprinting down the hill despite the sharp stones that pricked her feet, trying to keep up with the boy.

What Yumisan saw from atop the hill was Maung Maung falling flat on his back while fighting with Tun Shein's companion. She ran towards them. Maung Maung kicked Tun Shein's companion, and as the companion fell, he pinned him down, holding both of his arms in place. Just then, he thought he heard Yumisan's soft voice calling from behind, 'Maung Maung . . . Maung Maung.'

As Tun Shein, who had been lying on the ground, got up and grabbed a short stick nearby, he swung it forcefully at Maung Maung's head from behind. However, before the stick could land, Yumisan intervened, grabbing the stick from behind. This caused Tun Shein to spin around in surprise. Enraged, Tun Shein tightened his grip on the stick and, blinded by anger, swung it at Yumisan's head.

'Hey, Tun Shein . . . Tun Shein!' The monk's authoritative voice boomed from the top of the hill.

Tun Shein's strike landed hard on Yumisan's temple, making her stagger and collapse to the ground, unconscious. Maung Maung, who was twisting the arm of Tun Shein's companion, turned to see Yumisan fall. He released his grip on Tun Shein's companion and quickly rushed to Yumisan's side.

Seeing the monk running towards them, Tun Shein and his companion fled the scene.

Maung Maung knelt beside Yumisan, whose face was smeared with blood from the wound on her head. 'Sayama . . . Sayama!' he called out repeatedly in a panic, unsure of what to do.

The monk arrived, his voice trembling with concern. 'Oh dear . . . that's a lot of blood. Check her wound. How bad is it? Those drunk fools have harassed people and then run off.'

Seeing the blood, the monk became deeply worried. As more students gathered around, he instructed one, ‘Get some medicine . . . quickly, get some medicine!’

Maung Maung cradled Yumisan’s head in his lap, gently moving her hair aside to examine the wound. ‘It’s about two inches long, Phaya,’ he said.

The monk crouched beside them, saying, ‘Wipe the blood away.’

Maung Maung pulled a handkerchief from his pocket and began to clean the blood from Yumisan’s face.

‘She came here worried about your exam tomorrow,’ the monk said. ‘She was afraid you wouldn’t take it, so she came to get you. She’s your sister, you know . . . your sister. She got hurt because of you.’

The abbot examined the wound, muttering continuously under his breath. Maung Maung was extremely anxious, feeling completely responsible for Yumisan’s condition and trembling all over.

A monastery boy arrived with some medicine, and they applied it to Yumisan’s wound. She remained unconscious. The abbot suggested moving her downstairs, and Maung Maung carefully carried her downstairs, laying her on a mat.

'The bleeding won't stop; it needs stitches, Phaya,' Maung Maung said, his face tight with worry.

'Where can we get stitches in this village? Should we take her to the Bago hospital?' the monk replied.

'She can't be treated in Bago; she needs to go directly to Yangon,' Maung Maung insisted.

The monk sighed deeply, shaking his head. 'How are we going to get her to Yangon? There's no car available.'

'There is a car near the embankment over there,' one of the monastery boys interjected.

'I'll get the driver,' Maung Maung said and dashed out of the monastery yard.

Sarmi was dozing in the car. Maung Maung knocked on the window and said urgently, 'Hey you! Sayama has a head injury. Please come quickly.'

'What happened? How did she get hurt?' Sarmi asked, his eyes wide with surprise.

Seeing Maung Maung unexpectedly in the village, Sarmi was taken aback. Maung Maung, gathering himself, explained, 'A drunk person mistook her for someone else and hit her.'

Sarmi and Maung Maung rushed up the hill together.

'Sayama . . . Sayama,' the driver called, kneeling beside Yumisan and trying to rouse her. As the monastery boys crowded around, the abbot shooed them away. He instructed Maung Maung to moisten a towel with water and gently dab Yumisan's face to help revive her. Maung Maung followed the monk's instructions, carefully applying the damp cloth to Yumisan's face.

'This won't do . . . We need to get to Yangon immediately,' Sarmi said anxiously. Maung Maung also realized that Yumisan needed urgent medical attention in Yangon. He gently lifted Yumisan and carried her down from the monastery. Since Maung Maung couldn't carry her alone, Sarmi helped him. Together, they carefully carried her to the car.

In the car, Maung Maung sat in the back seat, cradling Yumisan's head on his lap. Once they were inside the car, Yumisan let out a small groan. Maung Maung and Sarmi called her to check if she was regaining consciousness. However, after that brief sound, she remained quiet and still.

The abbot brought Yumisan's shawl and handbag from the monastery and handed them over. Maung Maung tightly wrapped the shawl around Yumisan's head.

'Make sure you take the exam,' the monk reminded Maung Maung as a final instruction before the car departed.

Even though Sarmi was speeding at fifty miles per hour, it still didn't feel fast enough to him. Maung

Maung began to worry if Yumisan was still alive, as she wasn't moving. He held her hand to check for a pulse and placed his hand in front of her nose to feel if she was still breathing.

Maung Maung frequently glanced at Yumisan's face. It was pale and lifeless, appearing as if she was enduring an inevitable fate. He was surprised that Yumisan had come along to find him instead of his elder brother. Maung Maung felt deeply troubled that Yumisan had to bear the consequences in his place.

Previously, when he learned from the abbot that he was just the son of Yumisan's friend and not a blood relative, he harboured resentment, wondering why she had pretended to be his sister while deceiving his elder brother. Now, with the abbot's assertion that she was his sister, he questioned if they were indeed siblings.

Maung Maung felt increasingly disturbed as he watched Yumisan lying unconscious with her head resting on his lap—a person he had once hated so much that he couldn't even bear to look at her. In the past, she had seemed so distant, as if he could never meet her gaze. He hadn't known they were related by blood. But now, here she was, with her head on his lap. The shocking realization that she was his sister unsettled him even more. He tried to accept this truth, forcing himself to see her as his family. Yet, despite his efforts, he couldn't fully embrace her as his sister.

Yumisan was Japanese, while he was Burmese. The difference in their blood was just one of the reasons why he felt an insurmountable barrier to loving her. He found it impossible to accept her Japanese father as his own in any conceivable way, a realization that became increasingly clear to him. Even if Yumisan's father was also his, he couldn't reconcile with the idea of accepting a Japanese man as his father.

As they drove, Sarmi kept glancing back at Yumisan, checking if she had regained consciousness. 'When we get to the hospital, can we say she was mistakenly hit by a drunk person?' Sarmi asked Maung Maung with a serious look.

'What should we say?' Maung Maung responded.

'If we say she was hit by a drunk person, Sayama won't like it. It's better to say she fell and got hurt accidentally.'

Passing Bago, Maung Maung began to think intensely about his elder brother. He realized that Yumisan must have convinced his brother that she was his sister, which explained why his brother had gone to such lengths to favour her. Feeling ashamed of his earlier accusations and misunderstandings, Maung Maung silently apologized to his elder brother.

He grew up without parents, raised like a brother by U Thet Lwin, who rescued him when he was just a young boy at the monastery. U Thet Lwin was responsible for his education until he reached university. Holding Yumisan, Maung Maung deeply reflected on the gratitude he owed to his elder brother. The pain in his heart, triggered by his elder brother's revelation about his origins in front of Ko Mya Phay, subsided with these thoughts.

Yumisan moved slightly, interrupting Maung Maung's thoughts, and he turned to look at her. Gently, he wiped away the blood trickling from her ear with the handkerchief he had used earlier. As he cleaned the blood, he gazed at Yumisan's face, remembering how she had travelled all the way from Japan to Kyaik Sakaw to find him and how worried she had been about his exam. Being a blood relative, she treated him like a younger brother, calling herself 'Ma Ma' (his elder sister) as soon as they met.

Maung Maung reflected deeply on Yumisan, revisiting every detail from the very beginning. No matter how much he pondered, he realized his affection lay with his elder brother. He didn't know how to reciprocate Yumisan's sisterly love. In his heart, Yumisan felt distant, like the sister he saw in his dream. When he compared Yumisan to his older brother, he found that no one else mattered as much as his brother.

Reflecting on how he had been mistaken and harsh with Yumisan, Maung Maung felt deep shame and could not bear to look at her face. His face burned with embarrassment.

They arrived at Yangon General Hospital at 1 p.m. Maung Maung and Yumisan were left in the emergency room while Sarmi went to get Daw Aung May. Yumisan was placed on a stretcher and taken to rooms 3 and 4 for head injury treatment. While her wounds were being stitched, Maung Maung called a nearby house with a telephone and asked them to contact his elder brother.

It was Sunday. Someone from the neighbouring house informed U Thet Lwin urgently that there was a telephone call for him from Maung Maung. U Thet Lwin, upon hearing it was from Maung Maung, rushed to the neighbouring house and picked up the telephone.

'Hello . . . is that you, Ahkogyi?' Maung Maung's voice came through the telephone, and U Thet Lwin felt a wave of relief.

With a voice trembling with happiness, U Thet Lwin responded, 'Yes, Maung Maung. What happened?'

'Sayama came to Kyaik Sakaw in the morning. While I was at the monastery, I got into a fight with Tun Shein, Bagyi Sa's grandson. Sayama tried to intervene and grab the stick, but Tun Shein hit her with it.'

'*Oh dear*! Where did she get hit? Where is she now?'

U Thet Lwin, who had initially felt relief, now trembled with a heavy heart as fear and worry surged through him.

'She got hit on the head, Ahkogyi. She's at the general hospital now,' Maung Maung said.

'Is it serious?' U Thet Lwin asked.

'It's a bit serious, Ahkogyi.'

'Okay . . . I'm coming right now,' U Thet Lwin responded.

He was shocked to learn that Yumisan had followed Maung Maung to Kyaik Sakaw. Overwhelmed with concern for her, he felt his blood pressure rising. He had assumed Maung Maung would stay in Yangon, especially after hearing from one of Maung Maung's friends in Insein last evening that he had seen him near Theingyi Market. He figured Yumisan must have decided last night to follow Maung Maung. With rising worry over the seriousness of her injuries, U Thet Lwin hurried to the hospital.

At the hospital, Maung Maung waited anxiously for U Thet Lwin. Before he arrived, Daw Aung May showed up first. Upon seeing Maung Maung, she immediately gave him a stern look and questioned him. 'What happened? Fill me in.'

Daw Aung May was the only one who knew Yumisan had followed Maung Maung. Maung Maung felt cornered by Daw Aung May's gaze, and explained in a calm and steady voice, 'I was in the middle of a fight when she came near and tried to take away the stick. The man was so drunk he didn't recognize her and hit her, thinking she was someone else.'

Daw Aung May pursed her lips, her face creased with frown lines around her mouth and looked at Maung Maung with hatred in her eyes.

'Well, it serves her right. She became a scapegoat. Last night at ten o'clock, she decided to go to you. I tried to stop her because I didn't want her to go, but she wouldn't listen. I've never seen anyone as reckless as you. Your sister has such a strong bond with you. Where is she now?'

The words 'your sister' from Daw Aung May made Maung Maung's face flush with heat. He detested Daw Aung May for her harsh and cutting words, delivered with narrowed eyes. Biting his lower lip hard, he tried to suppress his anger and simply told her that Yumisan was in rooms 3 and 4.

Daw Aung May's emotions swirled within her, a tumult of anger and hatred directed at Maung Maung.

Struggling to maintain her composure, she made her way to rooms 3 and 4, following the directions she had received. Meanwhile, U Thet Lwin had faced his own challenges; unable to find a three-wheeler, he had taken a series of buses to reach the destination, arriving much later than Daw Aung May. When Maung Maung spotted U Thet Lwin, a wave of guilt washed over him. With a heavy heart, he lowered his gaze and guided him to Yumisan in rooms 3 and 4.

After Yumisan's wounds were stitched, she was moved to a special room in a two-storey building at the back of the hospital. Since it was not visiting hours and only one person was allowed to go up, U Thet Lwin went in alone.

Yumisan had regained her consciousness, but the pain from the tightly wrapped bandage on her head made her eyes blur. When Daw Aung May said that U Thet Lwin had arrived, she opened her eyes.

She saw the worried face of U Thet Lwin, who was looking pale.

'I feel so bad, Sayama. When Maung Maung called, I was very surprised. I didn't know you were going to Kyaik Sakaw. I was so shocked. Are your injuries severe, Sayama? Are you feeling better?'

In U Thet Lwin's gentle and soothing voice, there was an outpouring of sympathy, worry, sadness, and concern. Yumisan tried to respond, but her lips trembled, and tears welled up.

Daw Aung May interrupted, saying, 'The wounds required two stitches.'

'How about Maung Maung?' Yumisan asked, with a faint voice.

'Maung Maung is downstairs, Sayama. Since only one person was allowed to come up, I came up. Please rest well and don't talk much.'

Yumisan closed her eyes again. Daw Aung May gently wiped away the tears that fell when she closed her eyes.

'Sarmi declared the case as an accident to prevent it from dragging on. Ma Yu also didn't want to pursue the case, so she was pleased with Sarmi's decision,' Daw Aung May explained.

While Daw Aung May and U Thet Lwin were quietly conversing, the doctor arrived to administer an injection. Daw Aung May consulted with U Thet Lwin to arrange for Sarmi to report to the authority about the situation. Needing a thermos flask with ice for Yumisan, Daw Aung May requested U Thet Lwin to go with Sarmi and collect it from the house, handing him the house keys. While the doctor and Daw Aung May were talking, U Thet Lwin returned from the hospital ward.

'Sayama's awake and asking for you,' U Thet Lwin said, glancing at Maung Maung's weary state and letting out a deep sigh. 'She can't speak well yet, though.' The moment Maung Maung heard that Yumisan had regained consciousness, a spark ignited in his eyes, and his whole demeanour brightened, a change that didn't go unnoticed by U Thet Lwin.

'I'm going to Sayama's house now. Wait here for a while,' said U Thet Lwin.

'I want to go home, Ahkogyi. My whole body feels filthy,' replied Maung Maung.

'All right, all right. You go now. Come back in the evening. I will be right here,' said U Thet Lwin as he got into the car, and they parted ways.

In the evening, the hospital opened, and people started to come in. A professor and the principal from Yumisan's school arrived. Maung Maung did not come. As the time for the professors to leave approached, Maung Maung still hadn't arrived, making Yumisan worried and prompting her to ask, 'Maung Maung . . .'

'He said his body was smeared with blood and went home, Sayama. He didn't go anywhere, just went home,' U Thet Lwin explained to calm Yumisan.

'There's an exam tomorrow,' Yumisan muttered and then she fell silent. U Thet Lwin waited anxiously for Maung Maung's arrival, constantly glancing at the door with hopeful eyes, trusting that he would show up. When it was time to leave, U Thet Lwin bid Yumisan farewell. As he said goodbye, Yumisan felt a lump rise in her throat, and with tear-filled eyes, she managed a slight nod.

When U Thet Lwin got home from the hospital, he felt relieved to find Maung Maung opening the door for him. Before questioning Maung Maung about why he hadn't come to the hospital, he observed him first. Maung Maung's behaviour was the same as always, showing no signs of having gone anywhere but home. Feeling awkward about asking, U Thet Lwin finally spoke. 'Sayama can't speak properly yet. They said they would need to do a brain scan to see if there's any damage. We were waiting to see if you would come. Why didn't you come, Maung Maung?'

Despite knowing full well his duty to go and meet Yumisan, Maung Maung felt a great burden. He was ashamed to face her because of his previous cruelty, jealousy, resentment, and disdain toward her, and his mockery and sarcasm toward his elder brother. He did not dare to face Yumisan or meet with Daw Aung May. Since he had already taken her to the hospital, he felt there was no need to visit again and thus refrained from going.

Maung Maung could not look U Thet Lwin in the eye and averted his gaze. He felt so embarrassed and disgusted with himself in front of U Thet Lwin that it changed his demeanour, making it difficult for U Thet Lwin to understand him. U Thet Lwin asked about how Yumisan got beaten, and Maung Maung explained the situation. Ko Mya Phay remarked, 'She loves you so much,' after hearing about her adventure. Maung Maung lowered his head in shame in front of U Thet Lwin and Ko Mya Phay.

Maung Maung kept his head down, his face flushed red with embarrassment. Seeing this, Ko Mya Phay signalled U Thet Lwin, pointing out Maung Maung's behaviour. U Thet Lwin, thinking Maung Maung was just feeling shy, gestured with his eyes for Ko Mya Phay to stop talking, signalling him not to continue.

At 9 a.m., U Thet Lwin called from work to inform Daw Aung May, who was going to the hospital, that Maung Maung had taken the exam and to share the good news with Yumisan.

In the evening, Yumisan waited for U Thet Lwin and Maung Maung at the hospital, eagerly anticipating Maung Maung's arrival and imagining various expressions on his face. She pictured him looking sad, worried, embarrassed, and felt a mix of emotions. Throughout the day, she imagined him standing at her bedside with various expressions, feeling deeply moved.

Every time the wound on her head throbbed with pain, Yumisan would alleviate that suffering by thinking about the fact that Maung Maung had managed to take the exams. As evening approached, Yumisan was anxious, filled with joy and anticipation of Maung Maung's kindness, gentleness, and love.

Remembering Tun Shwe's stick, which had helped her and Maung Maung get closer, she felt grateful and excited for Maung Maung's arrival. When U Thet Lwin arrived without Maung Maung, Yumisan's face fell. She asked U Thet Lwin if Maung Maung had been able to take his exams.

'I haven't seen him yet, Sayama. I came here straight from work. I think he can handle the exam. He stayed up all night studying and didn't sleep,' said U Thet Lwin. Because Maung Maung didn't come to see her, she concluded that he did not accept her as his sister. Consequently, she realized that the things she thought were possible earlier—getting closer, and being successful—were no longer feasible.

Yumisan's face turned pale. U Thet Lwin looked intently at Yumisan. She stared straight ahead, her delicate face clouded with sadness.

'Saya, doesn't he believe I'm his sister?'

'It's not that he doesn't believe, Sayama. He only knew you were his sister when he came back from Kyaik Sakaw. Just this morning I told him I was going straight to the hospital from work and asked him to come. He'll come, Sayama.'

Yumisan sighed softly and calmed down.

'How are you doing, Sayama?' U Thet Lwin knew that Yumisan was upset because Maung Maung hadn't come, so he changed the subject.

'They took an X-ray. As long as the brain isn't affected, they said I should be able to leave the hospital within four or five days.'

U Thet Lwin felt relieved that Yumisan had started speaking. To make Yumisan feel better, he talked about how miserable Maung Maung looked yesterday and how cheerful he became when he was told Yumisan had regained consciousness. He explained that Tun Shein, who attacked Yumisan, was the same person who once hit Maung Maung so hard that he bled. This time, too, he called Maung Maung names and kicked him, trying to provoke a fight.

Yumisan thought that if she couldn't snatch the stick from Tun Shein's hand, she would be the one who came to the hospital now to ask after Maung Maung. This thought caused a sharp pain in her chest.

Yumisan had spent a week in the hospital, but Maung Maung hadn't visited even once. U Thet Lwin urged him to go see her, but Maung Maung simply kept his head down. Although U Thet Lwin considered forcing him, he chose a gentler approach.

'Maung Maung, as her brother, it's your duty to visit her. You shouldn't treat her coldly, especially since she got hurt protecting you.'

U Thet Lwin looked at Maung Maung, who had his head lowered in front of him, and continued speaking. 'As for her, even before she saw you, she made up her mind to find you and came to Myanmar. She searched for you tirelessly and even found out more about your life than you know yourself. Her father came to Myanmar after her mother died, and married your mother in Phayalay village. The old man from that village told her all about you. It was from her that I knew about your story. Think about how deep her love and regard for you must be, Maung Maung,' he said, trying to make Maung Maung understand. Maung Maung's head drooped even more.

The thought that a Japanese officer had forcibly taken his mother and that he had suffered shame and pain throughout his life changed when he heard that his mother had married the Japanese officer. Although it changed, this new feeling was even more shameful than the original.

He couldn't forget the chant-style song that went:

Sein Kyi, oh Sein Kyi,
wed without a clue, oh my,

master went back to Tokyo,
left her with a belly round.
Birthed a boy, small and short,
Monastery's now his retreat.

He remembered it vividly and felt his face flush with shame.

U Thet Lwin explained again to make Maung Maung understand clearly, but Maung Maung did not react at all, remaining with his head hung low the entire time. After observing Maung Maung's motionless state for a while, U Thet Lwin sighed deeply and called out.

'Maung Maung . . .'

Maung Maung did not respond and kept his head down.

'Tell me, Maung Maung. Aren't we going to the hospital this evening?'

Maung Maung did not lift his head but gave a slight shake of head. He bowed his head even lower to hide his sorrowful face from U Thet Lwin. Seeing Maung Maung's demeanour, U Thet Lwin got tired and stopped speaking, giving up.

After Yumisan left the hospital, she did not come to Maung Maung's house any more. She explained her reasons to U Thet Lwin over the phone so he would understand her decision.

'Saya, I won't be coming to your house any more. It is not appropriate for me to meet Maung Maung. He now knows that I am his sister, doesn't he? Didn't I also get injured because of him? But he does not want to see me, nor does he want to acknowledge me as his sister. I understand this now. I realize how much he resents Japan after I was beaten up and had my head broken. Please don't urge him to come to me. I want him to come to me out of his own desire.'

Listening to Yumisan's incessant voice over the phone, U Thet Lwin couldn't respond and let out a heavy sigh.

'Please come to my house once a week, Saya. Even though I don't see him, talking to you about him feels like meeting him.'

With no response from U Thet Lwin, Yumisan gently hung up the phone, tears welling up in her eyes.

17

Maung Maung noticed that U Thet Lwin was never home on Saturday evenings. U Thet Lwin also noticed that sometimes Maung Maung would stare blankly for no reason.

Ko Mya Phay, who used to tease Maung Maung about Yumisan and U Thet Lwin, felt embarrassed when he discovered that Yumisan was actually Maung Maung's sister. After that, he avoided bringing her up in conversation unless Maung Maung mentioned her first.

On Sundays, whenever Maung Maung heard the sound of a passing Volkswagen, he would immediately look out the gate.

Every Sunday, Maung Maung's behaviour differed from his usual routine. He started singing songs, finding unnecessary tasks to do, and even laughed louder than usual.

Sunday after Sunday passed by. Since Yumisan was discharged from the hospital, she hadn't come home even once, which Maung Maung found unusual. Maung Maung began to notice that U Thet Lwin avoided talking about Yumisan in front of him and even avoided mentioning her. It wasn't just U Thet Lwin; Ko Mya Phay also kept silent about Yumisan. This peculiarity continued for several weeks. As weeks turned into months, the peculiarity became so unusual that it hurt Maung Maung's feelings. Though he realized that his family knew he didn't love Yumisan and therefore didn't talk about her, he was still surprised by the extent of their silence. He felt uneasy as if he were a villain or a stranger in his own home.

Because U Thet Lwin didn't mention why Yumisan wasn't coming, Maung Maung's curiosity grew, but he found it difficult to ask directly. He decided to ignore her absence, thinking that if she didn't want to come, it was fine. But as time went on, he began to wonder if U Thet Lwin and Ko Mya Phay were mocking him behind his back.

Ko Mya Phay couldn't tell if Maung Maung's indifference was because he genuinely didn't care about Yumisan or if he was just pretending. So, he subtly tested Maung Maung. 'Maung Maung, what happened to the snack package from Yumisan? Haven't you seen it?' Ko Mya Phay deliberately asked about the missing snack package from Yumisan. He didn't directly ask Maung Maung face-to-face but instead casually mentioned it behind his back, as if it had just crossed his mind while he was busy with something else.

'I ate it,' Maung Maung replied.

Ko Mya Phay liked Maung Maung's response, closed his eyes, and smiled contentedly before daring to speak again.

'That Japanese snack isn't like the usual ones. Its packaging is beautiful, and the taste is quite good, isn't it?'

With his mouth slightly open, Ko Mya Phay's eyes were fixed, waiting breathlessly for Maung Maung's reply from behind him. Maung Maung stared at Ko Mya Phay's back, hesitating as if choosing which answer to give, before finally speaking softly.

'Not that much, it's salty.'

Ko Mya Phay listened attentively to Maung Maung's response, wanting to continue but seeing his hesitant demeanour, he stopped. Maung Maung seemed eager to hear more about Yumisan, waiting to see if Ko Mya Phay would continue the conversation. Since Ko Mya Phay remained silent, Maung Maung abruptly turned towards the front of the house.

Every Saturday, U Thet Lwin and Yumisan would meet at Yumisan's house. Although she didn't see Maung Maung, seeing U Thet Lwin provided some comfort. Due to Yumisan's strong reason for not coming to his house, inviting Maung Maung home was difficult. Since Yumisan didn't come, U Thet Lwin lacked the courage to invite Maung Maung to go with him to Yumisan's house, nor did he dare to forcefully bring him there. He faced the difficulty of not being able to mediate between the siblings.

U Thet Lwin deliberately mentioned that Maung Maung ate the food offered by Yumisan unlike before. At that moment, Yumisan's face brightened. Seeing Yumisan's now cheerful face, U Thet Lwin felt an urge to invite her to his house once more.

'Sayama, I thought Maung Maung might be too shy or afraid to meet you. We wanted to understand his feelings, so we kept observing him without mentioning anything about you. Sometimes he just remained silent, and we watched to see if he would say anything if we didn't. Does he really not want to meet you, or does he want to but just isn't coming? It's quite troubling to ponder over. Please come to our house once, Sayama, so we can understand him better.'

Yumisan's face noticeably dulled and softened. After a moment of silence, she replied with a saddened voice.

'No, Saya. Let him be at peace. My grandfather once wrote to me. He said not to ruin his life or disturb him; just let him be. Since he stopped coming to the hospital, I understand that he doesn't accept me as his sister. Even if he acknowledges me as his sister, it is evident that he has no other attachment in his life except you. Isn't this good for him too, Saya? When the school closes for summer vacation, I'll be returning to Japan for good.'

Unable to bear looking at Yumisan's tearful face, U Thet Lwin turned away. He sympathized with her when he realized how much self-control she had exercised to stay away from his home for so long. He fell silent and did not press further. As Yumisan believed, he, too, wondered if Maung Maung had severed emotional ties with Yumisan despite knowing she was his sister.

This thought sent a shiver through U Thet Lwin's entire body. When urging Maung Maung to go to the hospital, he imagined Maung Maung with his head bowed, motionless, and never looking up, reinforcing the thought that he might have severed ties. This caused U Thet Lwin deep sorrow. He felt profound sympathy for both Yumisan and Maung Maung. Wondering who was responsible for the siblings' tragic situation, he concluded that it was not due to anyone's actions but the result of the past war. This realization caused him great pain and sorrow.

As the final exams approached, Maung Maung spent his time studying at the table without breaks, while U Thet Lwin was also busy with work, making it difficult for him to visit Yumisan's home weekly as usual.

One afternoon, Nu Nu paid an unexpected visit to Yumisan's house when she got back home from work. Yumisan warmly welcomed her and led her into the living room. As soon as Nu Nu sat down, she spoke.

'Sayama, do you remember Ko Phoe Thike from the Phayalay village?'

'Of course I remember, Nu Nu. What happened to Ko Phoe Thike?' Yumisan said, smiling slightly, though her eyes looked tense.

Nu Nu took a large envelope out of her bag.

'When I returned to Bago yesterday, I met Ko Phoe Thike at my house, Sayama. He had recently visited Pyin Pone Gyi village and saw a photograph of a Japanese officer with a Burmese woman on the wall at his friend's house. When he asked whose photo it was, the house owner took it down and explained that it was a photo of his acquaintance U Saing's daughter, Ma Htway Htway, taken at her wedding to a Japanese man. Ko Phoe Thike asked for the photo, and they gave it to him. He brought it and gave it to me, Sayama.'

Yumisan, tears welling in her eyes and struggling to breathe, watched Nu Nu pull a photograph from the envelope and hand it to her.

'What a surprise, Nu Nu,' Yumisan said, looking at the old, yellowed photo that showed her father standing tall next to a woman seated in a chair. Yumisan stared intently at the woman's face, her eyes beginning to blur with emotion.

Ma Htway Htway in the photo could be about twenty-five years old. She had Maung Maung's eyes and nose. Her nose was sharp, her face was round, and she had tied her hair back with a small gold clip on top of her head. She wore a pearl necklace and had wrapped a scarf around her neck. She wore a black wristband on one hand and a watch on the other. On one wrist, she also wore five or six gold bangles. She wore a floral-patterned longyi with silk. On her feet, she wore velvet sandals.

In the picture, her father was wearing a military uniform and had a sword strapped to his side, smiling gently, his face full of contentment. Despite Yumisan's efforts to stay composed in front of Nu Nu, her eyes glistened with tears. With a sweet smile, she said, 'Ma Htway Htway is pretty, isn't she? So cute. Is this for me?'

'I brought it to show you. If you want it, you can take it. Or you can give it to Ma Htway Htway's son, who lives with Saya U Thet Lwin,' Nu Nu replied coolly.

Yumisan smiled even wider and responded with a sweet expression, 'Yes, Nu Nu. When U Thet Lwin comes, I will give him this photo for Ma Htway Htway's son to look at. I thank Ko Phoe Thike. Please tell him I am grateful. Let me give Ko Phoe Thike an umbrella as a gift through you.'

Yumisan then gave Nu Nu the umbrella, a gift from Maung Maung's grandmother to Maung Maung.

That evening, since there were no classes for the students, they watched a film in a dimly lit room about Japanese culture, including tea ceremonies, weddings, and the art of making and wearing kimonos—topics Yumisan had taught earlier that morning, allowing them to see these traditions with their own eyes.

Yumisan sat in the dark without watching the images on the screen, unable to hold back the tears flowing from her eyes. Suddenly, she saw the face of her stepmother, Daw Htway Htway. The longing to see Maung Maung overwhelmed her to the point where she couldn't control her feelings. She felt hurt for Maung Maung by the fact that she saw his mother before he did.

How would Maung Maung feel if he saw this photo? Would he be satisfied or able to forgive his mother, who married a Japanese soldier? Such confusing thoughts swirled in Yumisan's mind, making her head ache.

When Yumisan returned home from school, Daw Aung May handed her a letter sent from Japan. Recognizing her grandmother's handwriting on the envelope, Yumisan immediately opened the letter. Reading it, Yumisan's tears flowed, causing Daw Aung May to become worried and panicked.

'Ma Yu, what's wrong? Where is the letter from? What is it about? I'm worried; tell me, Ma Yu.'

Yumisan, with tears streaming down her cheeks, looked at Daw Aung May and then began to speak in a choked voice.

'Grandmother found the poem my father wrote on his deathbed and sent it to me.'

'What kind of poem was it? What was it about?'

Daw Aung May asked as she took the two sheets of paper written in Japanese. Not knowing what they were, she handed them back.

'Father wrote two poems, Obasan. One is about Maung Maung's mother and Maung Maung, and the other is about Maung Maung alone. Grandmother found them among the books when she was cleaning the house and gave them to show Maung Maung.'

'Don't show them, Ma Yu. Just throw them away. I've never seen someone so callous towards their own sister,' Daw Aung May said angrily.

'Grandmother gave them to show him, so they must be given to him.'

‘Even if given, it’s useless. Just throw them away. It’s hard to understand him. From what I see in the picture of his mother, she doesn’t seem to have such a harsh appearance. Surprisingly, he didn’t have a loving nature.’

Watching Daw Aung May’s angry demeanour, Yumisan sighed heavily.

‘A child without a mother is like this, Obasan. Never experiencing a mother’s love, he doesn’t understand love from others and doesn’t know how to love either.’

Daw Aung May looked at Yumisan, who was tearfully explaining in support of Maung Maung, and felt her anger dissipate. She felt so much compassion for Yumisan that she too almost started to cry.

The next day, Yumisan called U Thet Lwin from work. Since there were no evening classes that day, U Thet Lwin came to Yumisan’s house straight from work after the afternoon classes ended.

As Yumisan bowed in greeting at the doorway, U Thet Lwin paused before entering the house. Her eyes looked as though she had been crying, and the sight weighed heavily on his heart. Yumisan led U Thet Lwin to the living room, had him sit down, and then briefly left the room. Soon after, she returned to the living room with a large envelope.

'When is Maung Maung's exam, Saya?' Yumisan first asked about Maung Maung before mentioning what she intended to say.

'Next week, Sayama,' U Thet Lwin replied.

'The university will close right after the exams,' Yumisan said as she opened the envelope sombrely.

'The university will close right after the exams, Sayama,' U Thet Lwin repeated, looking at both the envelope and Yumisan. He then asked with concern, 'Is something the matter, Sayama?'

'Yes, there is something,' Yumisan replied. 'Nu Nu brought me a photo of Maung Maung's father and mother. Phoe Thike from Phayalay village gave it to her.' She handed U Thet Lwin an old photograph without a frame from the envelope.

U Thet Lwin looked puzzled and looked at the photo in silence. Seeing Maung Maung's mother's photo affected him deeply, even more than seeing his father's photo. He knew Maung Maung had never seen his mother's photo before. He stared at the picture, wondering how Maung Maung would react if he saw it, and became so absorbed in his thoughts that he forgot Yumisan was right beside him.

'Sayama, aren't you going to show this picture to Maung Maung?'

'I will give it to him before I return to Japan. Maung Maung's mother was beautiful and she was very young.'

U Thet Lwin looked at the photo again and said, 'Maung Maung resembles his mother, Sayama.'

'The eyes and nose are like his mother's, and the forehead and mouth are like his father's. Maung Maung's face is a blend of both,' Yumisan said with tears welling up. 'Moreover, there's something unusual, Saya,' she continued, pulling out two sheets of old paper written in Japanese from the envelope and handing them to U Thet Lwin. She moved her chair closer to him and passed the sheets, but U Thet Lwin, though he could see the Japanese writing, couldn't understand the content.

'Saya, this is a poem handwritten by my father. One is about Maung Maung and his mother. Another specifically talks about Maung Maung. The letters have faded over the years. My grandmother found it while cleaning the house and sent it to me. It arrived yesterday. I'll read it out and explain its meaning.'

When Yumisan recited the Japanese poem, she read it slowly, one line at a time, in a traditional recitative manner.

'Tsu mako bo shi
koite makurao
nura suyo no
ikuto senaruka
yamaifu su mini.'

Yumisan's recitation was sweet and pleasant to listen to.

U Thet Lwin took the fountain pen from his shirt pocket and wrote the sound of the poem in English letters on the back of poem sheet:

TSU MAKO BO SHI
KOITE MAKURAO
NURA SUYO NO
IKUTO SENARUKA
YAMAIFU SU MINI

'The first line "tsu mako bo shi" means "woman, son, star", Saya. The nature of Japanese poetry is such that if you look at each word separately, they might seem meaningless but listen to the whole thing.'

Yumisan continued to recite and translate the poem.

'The meaning of the second line "koite makurao" is "longing and wet pillow". The next line "nura suyo no" means "wet night".'

U Thet Lwin translated the words in Yumisan's language as (1) wife, son, star; (2) longing and wet pillow; (3) wet night. In sequence, he kept the meanings numbered in his head.

'The next line "ikuto senaruka" means "how many months, how many years, how many nights has it been", Saya. The last line "yamaifu su mini" means "my life spent lying down due to illness".'

U Thet Lwin reflected on the meaning of the Japanese poem.

'In summary, the meaning is: "In his life, lying in bed unable to get up, he looks at the stars in the sky, missing his wife and son so much that his pillows are soaked. How many months, how many years, how many nights has it been?" The Japanese poem shows tears without expressing them, yet you can see the tears, Saya.'

Even though words seem meaningless when looking at them separately, they bring profound meaning when they are connected appropriately in their places.

Yumisan wrote the sound of the Japanese words in English on the back of the second poem sheet. After writing, she read it out loud with the intonation of a poem.

'Tsukuzukuto
waga kono su ga ta
egakitaru
tsumani nise mita
ko ko ro kanashiku.'

U Thet Lwin listened to the poem excitedly, completely absorbed in it.

'The meaning of this poem is: "Tsukuzukuto" means "making various changes to make something as clear and complete as possible", "waga kono su gata" means "my son's figure", "egakitaru" means "painted or drawn", "tsumani nise mita" means "no matter how it is drawn, it always resembles my wife's face". "Kokoro kanashiku" means "this situation that is too hard to bear".'

Yumisan explained as clearly as possible, carefully observing U Thet Lwin to ensure he understood, and clarifying further until he grasped the meaning.

Seeing that U Thet Lwin still seemed confused, Yumisan repeated her explanation patiently.

'The meaning of this poem is like this, Saya. He tried to imagine his son's face vividly, wondering how it would look, how the eyes would be, how the nose would be. The poem's meaning lies in imagining this way. Because he longed so much to see his son's face and figure, he tried drawing the image in various ways. However, no matter how he tried to depict it, the image of his son never came out clearly and instead always resembled his wife's face. Therefore, this reality is very painful. Do you understand the meaning now, Saya? He has expressed the feelings of longing for the unseen image of his son through this poem.'

U Thet Lwin not only understood the meaning but also felt the emotions of Yumisan's father as if they were his own. The significance of the poem quietly and deeply resonated within U Thet Lwin, leaving him speechless.

U Thet Lwin vividly saw Major Yoshida lying in bed, tears streaming down his face. Maung Maung had not grown up under the care of his father, Major Yoshida, but had instead been raised by U Thet Lwin. With this thought, he felt a deep, unspoken pain in his heart for Major Yoshida, much like the sentiment expressed in one of Yoshida's poems.

'Before I leave, I will give this photo and the poem to Maung Maung, Saya,' Yumisan repeated softly with a choked voice.

U Thet Lwin looked at Yumisan gently, with a heavy heart.

Will you give it to him yourself? How will you give it to him?

These questions remained stuck in U Thet Lwin's throat, unable to leave his mouth.

18

It was 27 March, Revolution Day.

After Maung Maung finished his exams and the university closed, he boiled water, made tea, and performed other early morning chores before Ko Mya Phay returned from the market.

While making the table ready for this morning, he went outside to get the delivered newspapers. Every year, after Myanmar gained independence, newspapers published special editions on 27 March, Revolution Day.

These special editions recounted the hardships of the Japanese occupation, the story of resisting the fascist invaders, and the revolutionary activities of General Aung San and General Ne Win. They also featured speeches, photographs of these leaders together, and historical images of the 'three comrades' taken during their military training in Taiwan. These special issues included articles and photographs about the March Revolution and revolutionary experiences.

Maung Maung looked at the special edition newspaper cover featuring a painting that symbolized the revolution. Although it had been over twenty years, when Revolution Day arrived on 27 March, he eagerly flipped through newspaper after newspaper, drawn to the historical accounts of the Japanese era revolution, revolutionary experiences, and rare photographs of the revolution. In the latest issue of *Lanzin Party News*, which he picked up and looked through, he came across a poem titled 'Prayer on the Revolution Day'. The person who wrote that poem was Saya Zawgyi, and it piqued his interest upon discovering it in the newspaper. Driven by a strong desire to know what kind of poem Saya Zawgyi might have written in the Revolution Day special edition, he continued reading with enthusiasm.

Prayer on the Revolution Day

My brother, bright and radiant,
they have changed their minds, and so have we.
What begins badly, ends in ruin.
In the month of Tabaung, they reason,
the village of Kazaung rises in rebellion.

Because of this news,
Nippon police encircle the town,
spears gleaming in the light.
With strength and thunderous voices,
they advance, displaying their might.
'O Asian youths,
our soldiers, armoured in valour—
who dares to challenge our might?'
They march toward Kazaung, prepared for the fight.
The townspeople remain behind,
parents, children, and the newlywed—
all weary, their faces shadowed with sorrow.
I could hardly bear the sight.

Day after day passes,
five days, then six,
yet the Japanese troops never arrive.
Ten more days,
and still, no trace of their footsteps.
'Listen, sisters—
with modern weapons in the hands of our youth,
they march toward Kazaung,
advancing without pause,
facing hardships,
while hearing words of praise.
In Tokyo and beyond,
ageing parents and their children,

even the housewives—
all weary, their faces shadowed with sorrow.
Seeing their tired and troubled faces,
it breaks my heart.'
My brother, bright and radiant,
I don't want them to become hunters,
embracing the spirits of conquerors,
nor do we want to be subdued,
or become victims of war.
Under the cool shade of Shwedagon,
I offer five bunches of brown lilies,
along with joss sticks,
in prayer for blessings.

Maung Maung read the poem from beginning to end and then, excitedly, read it again. The next time he read it, he vividly visualized the imagery of the poem. After reading, Maung Maung stared at the poem. The stanza that moved him deeply was the one about the desire to neither become conquers nor victims of war.

Maung Maung felt a strong emotional reaction as he read about the hardships faced by the town elders, noblemen, and housewives in Tokyo, which made him sympathize deeply. This stanza made him think about the poet's inner turmoil and sorrow, stirring strong emotions within him.

As Maung Maung read the poem, a realization came to him that he had never considered before. This realization led him to contemplate the true causes of the war. He started to see that wars happen due to the ambitions of those in power, desiring conquest and dominance.

He reflected on how the Japanese promised independence to Burma before they arrived, only to change their minds and seek control once they were there. Maung Maung realized that the Japanese soldiers who died in the Kazaung battle were not responsible for the occupation; it was due to the high-ranking officials who desired conquest. Through the insight provided by the poem, Maung Maung clearly understood this.

The Japanese soldiers, who were trained to follow the rules of war, always obeyed the orders of their superiors. According to the orders of their superiors, they carried guns and fought, killed, bombed, burned, and displayed military might. The Japanese soldiers personally committed all these acts of war. They did so not because of their own desires, but because they had to follow the orders of their superiors without hesitation. With a poetic sense of understanding, Maung Maung saw this distinction clearly.

Maung Maung harboured a deep-seated hatred for all Japanese due to the painful and bitter experiences of his life under Japanese rule. However, through the awareness conveyed by the poem, his feelings of animosity shifted towards an anti-imperialist stance, and he began to resent the imperialist system itself.

Maung Maung saw that his life, filled with unpleasantries and misfortunes, was unavoidably intertwined with the schemes of imperialist aggressors. This realization was even more vivid than seeing the entire imagery of the poem. Reflecting deeply, like the poet who was also anguished, Maung Maung felt a profound sorrow in his heart. Overwhelmed by grief, he prayed fervently along with the poet that such a situation would never occur again.

Afterwards, Maung Maung continued to think intensely about his life and circumstances, which had unfolded in the era of Japanese occupation.

While sitting alone and thinking deeply, it seemed to him as if Yumisan was near him. Maung Maung saw Yumisan's face and heard her voice. He imagined hearing the conversations they had had. The scene came to mind where he destroyed everything she had cleaned and arranged as he said, 'Whose house do you think this is, and who do you think loves you?' He remembered Yumisan's sorrowful expression as he spoke those words. Although he constantly hurled baseless accusations and behaved harshly, Maung

Maung gradually came to understand the immense patience reflected in Yumisan's calm face, as well as the great love that had caused her to collapse onto the ground due to the injury she had sustained to her head for his sake.

He remembered Yumisan's unconscious face, bloodied and still. Maung Maung realized how immense and cruel his harshness had been—he hadn't even visited her in the hospital once. Clenching his fists and gritting his teeth, he muttered, 'I was harsh . . . terribly harsh.'

After saying these words, Maung Maung wondered to whom he was speaking, as he realized Yumisan would no longer come to this house. He turned his face towards the path Yumisan used to take and gazed at it.

At that moment, U Thet Lwin entered the living room where Maung Maung was sitting. Maung Maung quickly changed his expression, pretending to read a newspaper in his hand.

On that day, Maung Maung's behaviour was exceptionally gentle and calm, unlike his usual demeanour. He also spoke less. After breakfast, Ko Mya Phay returned home, and U Thet Lwin left for Yumisan's house. Maung Maung was busy cleaning the house alone the whole afternoon, something he had never done before.

He rearranged and cleaned the living room in the style that Yumisan had previously set up. He also cleaned and tidied the dining room, attempting to replicate Yumisan's handiwork as closely as possible.

Ko Mya Phay returned at 4 p.m. He was initially surprised by the cleanliness of the house, wondering what had gotten into Maung Maung. Seeing the living room and dining room arranged and cleaned in Yumisan's style, Ko Mya Phay was overwhelmed with emotion. He clutched his chest, breathing heavily as his heart raced. To avoid facing Maung Maung, he distanced himself and acted as if he didn't remember Yumisan's touch at all.

In the late afternoon, when U Thet Lwin returned from Yumisan's house, Ko Mya Phay greeted him and said, 'Look, Saya, Maung Maung is acting a bit different today. I don't know what got into him. He spent the whole day cleaning the house in his sister's style while I was away. It hurt me so much that I had to pretend not to notice.'

U Thet Lwin looked intently at the newly cleaned and organized living room and dining room in the house and then asked, 'He did all this without telling you anything?'

Ko Mya Phay replied with a disgruntled face, 'Since I came back, he hasn't said a single word, Saya. He worked silently, took a shower, changed clothes, and left, saying he was going to meet a friend to watch the lighting festival at the Revolution Park.'

U Thet Lwin, gazing once again at the living room, thought to himself, *Maung Maung . . . your sister won't be seeing your work; she's leaving.*

19

Maung Maung rose from the bed, the morning breeze drifting through the sunlit window. In the kitchen, Ko Mya Phay had just returned from the market. As Maung Maung freshened up, upbeat music floated in from a neighbour's radio.

'Oh no . . . it's already half past eight,' Maung Maung said as he walked towards the front of the house. Not seeing U Thet Lwin there, he turned back towards the kitchen.

'Ko Mya Phay, where is Ahkogyi?'

Ko Mya Phay looked at Maung Maung while he was pounding chilli.

'He went out when I got back from the market.'

'Did you make the coffee on the table?'

'Your brother made it himself after boiling the kettle early in the morning before I got here.'

Maung Maung felt bad because he had woken up late, and his brother had to boil the kettle himself.

'If only he had told me last night he had to go out early, I would have gotten up and made it for him. I was up late reading a novel, and I finished it near dawn,' Maung Maung said as he walked towards the dining room and sat at the table. While he was sipping the coffee left in the kettle for him, he heard the sound of a car from the front of the house.

Maung Maung instantly recognized the sound of the car—it was Yumisan's, a sound he hadn't heard in about five months.

He couldn't bring himself to look at the car entering the yard. His face, which he didn't dare show Yumisan, was stricken with fear, his heart racing. The sound of the car coming to a stop sent goosebumps crawling up Maung Maung's back and tingling across his scalp.

Confused to the point of not knowing what to do, Maung Maung ran into the kitchen.

'Ko Mya Phay, there's a car in front of the house. Please go and open the gate.'

Ko Mya Phay was astonished by Maung Maung's anxious behaviour.

'Whose car is it? Is it Sayama's car?'

Maung Maung nodded quickly. He was so nervous that he couldn't find a place to hide, trembling and not knowing what to do.

'Really?'

Ko Mya Phay exclaimed happily and ran straight out of the house.

Maung Maung stood still in the kitchen. He heard the sound of the door opening. Breathing heavily and with trembling lips, Maung Maung heard Ko Mya Phay calling from outside.

'Maung Maung.'

Ko Mya Phay's voice from the front of the house thundered like a storm, jolting Maung Maung and making his heart race with fear. He quickly turned his head in the direction of the voice, a chill creeping down his spine.

'Maung Maung, come here for a moment . . . come here.'

Ko Mya Phay's voice grew louder. After Ko Mya Phay's voice, Maung Maung faintly heard the voice of Sarmi.

Maung Maung timidly stepped out to the front of the house. Yumisan was not there. Only Sarmi was bringing packages from the car into the house.

'Sayama has left a letter and some packages for you,' Ko Mya Phay said before Maung Maung reached him.

Handing the items to Maung Maung with a smile, Sarmi gave him a large envelope. The envelope was sealed and had 'Maung Maung' written on it in Burmese.

'Sayama gave me this for you. She asked me to hand it to you. These items are also for you,' he said.

Maung Maung took the envelope with trembling hands and looked at the packages scattered on the floor with a worried look.

'She's leaving. Sayama is going back to Japan. I'll take her to the airport by ten o'clock.'

Maung Maung quickly looked up at Sarmi's face. His eyes were wide with disbelief. Ko Mya Phay interrupted with a troubled look on his face.

'What? Sayama is leaving? Is she leaving today . . .? Really . . .? Is she leaving for good?'

Ko Mya Phay was speaking in a trembling, shaky voice, as if he were delirious. Maung Maung stood still with wide-open eyes like a lifeless puppet.

Sarmi nodded his head and went back down from the house. Soon after, he drove off.

Maung Maung and Ko Mya Phay stood motionless up to this moment, only coming to life when they heard the sound of the car leaving.

'What are these things?'

Ko Mya Phay was the first to pull open the large paper box. Maung Maung just watched oddly.

'This one is recorder.'

Ko Mya Phay pulled out a recorder from the box and opened another package.

'Here is a camera. Canon . . . Canon.'

Continuing to unwrap the packages one by one, he exclaimed excitedly as he identified the items.

'Shirts, pants, a wristwatch, and this is a fountain pen.'

Maung Maung watched in fascination as one item after another emerged from the packages, not even blinking. After all the items were unwrapped, Ko Mya Phay noticed Maung Maung staring blankly at the envelope, almost in a trance.

'What's in the big envelope in your hand? Open it and see.'

At this, Maung Maung seemed to come alive, moving to sit on a nearby chair. With trembling hands, he opened the envelope by peeling off the seals. The first thing he pulled out was a folded letter, followed by a six-inch photograph.

Before unfolding the letter, Maung Maung stared at the photograph. Seeing the image of a Japanese officer and a Burmese woman, he immediately thought it must be a picture of his father and mother. His hands shook even more as he held the photo. Standing behind Maung Maung and looking over his shoulder at the photograph, Ko Mya Phay asked, 'Whose picture is this, Maung Maung? Is it a picture of your father and mother?'

Maung Maung nodded silently without answering verbally, staring intently at his mother's picture with unblinking eyes. Curious about the photograph, he placed it on the table briefly and quickly opened the letter. Ko Mya Phay's eyes remained fixed on the photograph on the table, staring in amazement.

Maung Maung noticed that Yumisan's Burmese handwriting was neatly and perfectly written with precise, rounded strokes.

Maung Maung, my little brother, you now know that you and I share the same father. I understand that you don't want to accept me as your sister. Look at the photograph I gave you. It was taken during the wedding of my father and your mother at Phayalay village. Recently, Ko Phoe Thike from Phayalay village found this photograph in a house in Pyin Pone Gyi village, where his friend lives, and he sent it to me through someone.

At this point, Maung Maung's eyes widened, and he could no longer read the letter. He picked up the photograph and stared at it again. Seeing his mother's image for the first time in his life, Maung Maung's heart ached with unbearable pain.

Oh, this is my mother. Mother . . . Mother . . . Mother, he cried out in a voice that echoed within him. His mother's youthful and beautiful face, with an honest and kind demeanour, was clearly visible in the photograph.

Whenever he felt weak throughout his life, he often thought of his mother and missed her deeply. It was more heartbreaking to yearn for her vividly while seeing her image in his mind than to miss her without ever having seen her picture. After staring at his mother's photo for a long time, his eyes slowly shifted to the image of his father standing beside her. The owner of the gentle smile seemed to wave lovingly at his son from within the photograph, as if greeting him. With the dignity and grace of a noble army officer, he stood tall, maintaining his poised posture, while carrying a soft, serene smile. Tenderness, compassion, and loving-kindness radiated not only from his eyes and his smile but also illuminated his entire face with a sweet and tranquil glow. As Maung Maung stared at the pictures of his parents, who were no longer in this world, he realized that apart from his sister Yumisan, there was no other blood relative left for him. He became aware of the reality that he and his sister were the only close blood relatives left in this world.

Because of this knowledge, he was overcome with emotion and had to put in considerable effort to continue reading.

Haven't you seen Daw Htway Htway, your mother? I've left the photo with you so you can see her. When you look at the photo of your father standing next to your mother, I want you to set aside your hatred for a moment.

Accompanying this letter were two pages written in Japanese. One was a poem your father composed after he became bedridden, expressing his deep longing for you and your mother upon his return to Japan. The other was a heartfelt message he wrote about you, filled with the yearning to meet the child he had never seen.

To ensure you understood the essence of the poem, I've provided a translation into English at the end.

Maung Maung took the two sheets written in Japanese by his father and, after briefly glancing at the English words written by Yumisan, continued reading the letter.

The meaning of the first poem is about his looking at the star in the sky, feeling an overwhelming longing for his wife and son, and how many years, months, and nights he had spent with his pillow soaked with tears, lying bedridden. Maung Maung, I want you to understand the sentiment behind this poem.

The meaning of the next poem is that he was thinking about what you would look like. Whenever he thought about it, your face resembled your mother's. He couldn't figure it out. This feeling hurt him deeply in his heart.

No one knew that Father wrote this poem on two sheets of paper before he died. Recently, my grandmother at home found it tucked between the pages of a book and sent it to you from Japan.

The packages that Sarmi handed over were also gifts from your grandfather and grandmother for you when I went back to Japan. They loved their son very much since he was their only son. I could even say they love you, their grandson, more than they love me, Maung Maung.

If you're unable to hold any affection for anyone any more and want to tear up this photo just like before because your father's photo is in it, I want to make one last request before you tear it up, Maung Maung.

Before you tear up your father's photo, please take this photo and the poem to the Shwedagon Pagoda. When you get there, you will see a big lion in front of the pagoda.

In the traditional folktale called Thihabahu, *the father, a lion named Thihabahu, lost his human wife and son, so he ran after them to search for them, didn't he, Maung Maung? Just as the lion, a wild animal, has a loving heart, your father, a human being, also has a loving heart for his wife and son, Maung Maung. May these two poems stand as a testament to how deeply your father cherished, loved, and was bound to both you and your mother.*

Look at the large lion statue in front of the Shwedagon Pagoda and then look at this photo and poem again. When you do this, compare the image of your father with the large lion statue. When you compare them, I hope you realize that your father is not a wild lion from the forest but a human being, Maung Maung. I pray this realization comes to you.

Didn't the son have to kill his father, the lion, to prevent him from harming humans while he was searching for his wife and son? Because of this act, the father lion was depicted as a sacred figure, worshipped alongside the Buddha. This story, as I understand it, shows that even though the father was an animal, the son still held him in such high regard, placing him on the same level as the revered Buddha, with a heart full of devotion and respect.

I've never failed to pray every time I saw lion statues in front of temples in Myanmar, wishing that you may have the heart to love and cherish your human father as a parent.

If, as I have prayed, you could develop a loving and compassionate heart towards your father, then my search for you in Myanmar would have been worthwhile.

After finding you in Myanmar, the distress I felt was not because of you. Nor do I blame it on our father for creating it, Maung Maung. It's the world war that separated us and made us suffer, Maung Maung. Because of this war, you were unfortunate, and I wasn't exactly lucky either.

My mother passed away right after giving birth to me. I barely saw my father until long after the war had ended. I lived with my father for almost fifteen years, and then he passed away, leaving me in this world with you. When I finally found you, you didn't want to look at me, and that's why I say I am not lucky, Maung Maung. In reality, you and I are siblings who were affected by the aftermath of the recent war. I want you to deeply think about this truth.

If you can deeply reflect on this, accept your father as Father, recognize my efforts to find you and acknowledge me as your sister, I have one last request for you.

After reading this letter, will you call me 'Ma Ma', even though I won't be able to hear it? Please, just call me 'Ma Ma' once, Maung Maung. Just once . . .

With much love,
Your sister,
Ma Ma

Maung Maung, unable to contain his sorrow even though Ko Mya Phay was right beside him, continued reading while tears streamed down his face.

As soon as he finished reading, Maung Maung tossed the folded letter onto the table, then stood up with a loud whoosh. He dashed into the room. Ko Mya Phay, startled, was at a loss even to ask what was going on.

Maung Maung ran into his room, grabbed a 10-kyat note from his drawer, and dashed out of the house, quickly climbing down from the upper floor.

'Hey . . . Maung Maung . . . Maung Maung . . . where to? Where to?'

Upon hearing Ko Mya Phay's voice, Maung Maung turned around from the yard and replied, 'To the airport . . . to the airport,' before running off down the street.

Maung Maung paused briefly at the end of the road, waiting for a three-wheeled vehicle. Growing impatient and unwilling to waste time waiting, he sprinted to the intersection of Kaba Aye Road.

As the four-wheeled vehicle rolled away from the gas station, it slowed at the intersection where Maung Maung stood waiting. With a quick motion, he signalled for the driver to stop.

'Brother, please! It's urgent. Please take me to the airport. I'll pay you as much as you want,' he pleaded breathlessly, on the verge of tears.

Seeing Maung Maung's desperate demeanour, the driver felt a pang of compassion.

'Come on . . . get in,' he said, opening the door.

'Hurry, brother . . . please drive fast.'

'Don't worry . . . don't worry,' the driver reassured.

Maung Maung felt as if he were staring death in the face. Restless in the speeding car, he couldn't shake the fear that the tires might come off at any moment. Each time the car swerved dangerously close to the vehicles ahead, his heart pounded, and he closed his eyes, bracing for a crash. As the driver took sharp curves without slowing down, a sense of impending doom gripped Maung Maung. Though terrified, with his heart racing and breath unsteady, he couldn't shake the worry of whether he would reach the airport in time. Despite the danger, he found himself wishing the driver would accelerate even more.

20

Before Maung Maung left the house, Yumisan and Daw Aung May headed to the airport as soon as Sarmi returned from Maung Maung's home. After hearing Sarmi had handed the presents to Maung Maung, Yumisan spent the entire ride in the car with tears streaming down her face.

U Thet Lwin had left home early to arrive at the airport on time. Knowing Yumisan's plan to send the items to Maung Maung, he wanted to avoid witnessing the final handover.

When Yumisan entered the airport building and saw U Thet Lwin, she went straight to him. She smiled faintly, bowed slightly, and greeted him.

Yumisan, dressed in a pink gown and high-heeled slippers, instantly brought back vivid memories for U Thet Lwin of the day she first visited his home wearing that exact outfit.

'When did you arrive, Saya?'

Yumisan's sadness over her impending separation from Maung Maung and U Thet Lwin far outweighed her feelings about leaving Myanmar today, and the distress was clear on her face.

'I left my house early in the morning before Maung Maung woke up, Sayama,' U Thet Lwin said. These words were all he could manage to say, feeling a tightness in his chest that made it difficult to speak further.

Yumisan turned her face away from U Thet Lwin, lowering her gaze as she said, 'I've sent all the presents to Maung Maung, Saya. Sarmi also delivered the letter I showed you yesterday. Please write to me if he tears up the photo after reading my letter.'

U Thet Lwin felt an intense, piercing pain in his heavy heart, as if it were being struck repeatedly by a lance. He had already read the letter Yumisan sent to Maung Maung the previous day.

When the two of them visited Bagan, she had looked at the lion statues by the Shwezigon Pagoda and asked, 'Isn't this . . . the lion, the father of Sihabahu?' He remembered how she had recounted the story of Thihabahu. Back then, the light-heartedness of the moment brought him laughter. But now, those same words stirred a deep pain in his heart, without a trace of laughter. U Thet Lwin, unable to speak any more, could only express his emotions through his eyes.

At that moment, the principal, professors, students, and Yumisan's friends from the Japanese embassy arrived at the airport. Yumisan left U Thet Lwin's side to greet each of them, unable to return quickly. Daw Aung May and Sarmi watched over Yumisan's belongings. Daw Aung May, her tear-streaked face and swollen eyes revealing her grief, managed only a sad smile at U Thet Lwin from a distance, unable to approach him because of her sorrow.

U Thet Lwin, aware of time passing second by second, could hear his heart pounding intensely without pause, echoing loudly in his ears. Though his eyes longed to take in one last look at Yumisan, who was bidding farewell to her friends, his heart was too heavy with sorrow to bear it. Overwhelmed by grief, he averted his gaze, unable to look directly at her.

The time for Yumisan to enter the international departure lounge was drawing near. Before she went in, she bid farewell to everyone and finally approached U Thet Lwin. The sound of her heels approaching felt like a prelude to their separation.

As Yumisan walked towards U Thet Lwin, her demeanour shifted dramatically. Her gait, facial expression, and overall presence changed as she realized that her intentions and hopes for coming to Myanmar did not align with reality.

Yumisan, her face composed and her mind collected, met U Thet Lwin's gaze with a smile. Of all the times Yumisan had smiled, he had never seen one so full of pity before.

U Thet Lwin forced a smile, moving only his lips.

'I have to go into the room, Saya. I have to go,' said Yumisan, trying to hold back the tears that were welling up. She stopped talking and fluttered her eyelashes to regain composure, then looked back into his eyes.

U Thet Lwin's sorrow was so profound, it felt unforgettable, as if it would linger into the afterlife. It wasn't just a farewell to her beloved brother before leaving Myanmar; it was a poignant reflection of Yumisan's unfulfilled hopes and efforts. U Thet Lwin felt her sorrow acutely, his heart weighed down by the heavy burden of sadness.

Yumisan fluttered her eyelashes to wipe away her tears and, with a small laugh, said her final words:

'When I reach Japan, I will throw all the love and affection I have for Maung Maung towards Mount Fuji, Saya.'

She used laughter to mask her grief, knowing she would cry if she spoke plainly. She struggled to balance between laughing and crying.

She took one last look at U Thet Lwin's tearful face, which was too choked with emotion for him to speak. With her sparkling eyes, she bowed her head and said, 'Thank you so much, Saya.'

While at home yesterday, U Thet Lwin was showered with words of gratitude. Since it felt like she hadn't thanked him enough, she kept expressing her thanks.

'Just as you always love and care for Maung Maung, please remember to always love and care for me too, Saya,' said Yumisan. After she spoke, she bowed her head and bent her waist in respect once again.

Watching her final goodbyes, U Thet Lwin felt as if Yumisan and he had disappeared inside the airport terminal and only their deep sorrow remained within the building.

'*Sayonara.*'

At that moment, U Thet Lwin, coming out of his dazed state, looked at Yumisan with a deep, serene gaze and gently nodded in acknowledgment.

After respectfully bowing and saying goodbye to U Thet Lwin one last time, Yumisan turned back and extended her small hand to U Thet Lwin.

As Yumisan extended her hand, U Thet Lwin's eyes seemed to come to life, glowing as he gently took her small hand. Holding her soft, delicate hand in his, U Thet Lwin felt a sudden urge to not let go, gripping it for a moment longer. When he finally let go of her hand, Yumisan withdrew her small hand, turned around briskly, and walked into the departure lounge without looking back.

As they had never held hands while saying goodbye before, the fact that Yumisan had held his hand for the last time made U Thet Lwin feel as though her small hand was still left in his grasp. So, he clenched his hand tightly, as if in delirium.

With his mind in turmoil, U Thet Lwin clutched one hand with the other as he walked towards the stairs leading to the upper floor of the airport. After climbing four or five steps, he glanced down through the large window and saw Daw Aung May standing there, watching Yumisan emerge onto the field below. He paused for a moment, emotionally affected, before continuing up to the upper floor. On the less crowded edge of the veranda, he stood and watched Yumisan come out with the passengers. Looking down from above, he saw her walking briskly with the crowd, tears filling his eyes. At that moment, Maung Maung came running into the airport building.

He didn't search anywhere inside the building and ran towards the international departure lounge. He pushed the door open, but the guard inside told him that entry was not allowed. He turned back and ran up the stairs in one swift motion. Upon reaching the upper floor's veranda, he was stopped in his tracks as he saw the large airplane parked in the field through the big glass door. He squeezed into the crowd and looked out from the veranda's edge.

When he saw Yumisan nearing the centre of the field, Maung Maung's vision blurred. Cupping his mouth with both hands, he yelled out with all his strength.

'Ma Ma . . . Ma Ma . . . Ma Ma . . .'

Maung Maung's earnest call from deep within him reached *bha wag* (pali), the highest realm of the existential world. It was a piercing sound that almost deafened those around him. U Thet Lwin, who was intently watching Yumisan, was shaken by Maung Maung's voice and looked in the direction of the sound. That was Maung Maung, shouting loudly enough for the entire field to hear:

'Ma Ma . . . Ma Ma . . . Ma Ma . . .'

This time, the call, made with sincere remorse and a pleading heart, was to ask for forgiveness for his past cruelties and harshness.

In the field, Yumisan, while walking quickly in high heels, suddenly stopped as if someone had grabbed her from behind.

'*Ma Ma . . . Ma Ma.*'

In this very call, the sound broke apart with trembling confession in his heart, 'Ma Ma, you are my sister. Father is my father.' Yumisan stopped in her tracks.

Maung Maung energetically kept shouting, 'Ma Ma . . . Ma Ma,' filling the whole airport with his loud calls. With her heart pounding, Yumisan turned around and looked back at the airport building, hoping the distant calls of 'Ma Ma' she heard were indeed true. From afar, she recognized Maung Maung wearing his usual black and red checkered shirt among the crowd.

As she looked back, she loudly shouted, 'Maung Maung . . . Maung Maung,' while raising her hand and waving frantically.

'Oh . . . oh . . . Maung Maung . . . Maung Maung . . .'

The moment Yumisan saw Maung Maung clearly, she let out a loud cry and turned around completely, running back towards the airport terminal where Maung Maung was. She stopped after running for a while, quickly estimating the distance between where she was and the airport building.

At the same time, she quickly turned to look at the large plane docked nearby. All the passengers who had come out with her were already near the airplane stairs, ready to board. It was impossible for her to run back to where Maung Maung was.

The vast field before her seemed to stretch farther with every second, as if an ocean were forming between them to prevent her from running back to him. Yumisan, with tears streaming down her face, hesitated, her heart heavy. She stood still and nodded firmly, signalling to Maung Maung that she had heard his cry of 'Ma Ma'. Then, slowly stepping backward, she raised her hand one last time in a final wave before turning away.

Yumisan had no choice but to leave as time wouldn't stand still. She glanced towards the airplane, still wanting to pause just a few seconds longer. All the passengers were already boarding the plane. She couldn't be left alone in the middle of the field.

'Sayonara . . . sayonara,' Yumisan called out to Maung Maung at the top of her voice, knowing he couldn't hear her. She then ran back to the airplane after waving goodbye. She paused for a moment, turned around, raised her hand to wave once more, and then ran back to the plane.

A large crowd on the veranda watched Maung Maung jumping and waving, while turning to see the Japanese girl standing in the field, as if they were watching a grand spectacle without understanding what was happening.

U Thet Lwin was gasping for breath, consumed by deep sorrow. He couldn't bear to look at Yumisan, who seemed to be in a frenzy, running back and forth like a madwoman. He could hardly hear Maung Maung's loud shouts. His mind was in turmoil, overwhelmed by uncontrollable anguish.

Yumisan hurriedly ran to the stairs. Before she climbed up the airplane stairs, she turned back, raised her hand, and waved. Since she was the only passenger arriving late, she felt embarrassed and apologetic as she climbed the airplane stairs. The flight attendant was waiting at the door to close it. At the top of the stairs, before entering the airplane, she waved one last time to her beloved younger brother to say goodbye and then entered the plane. The airplane door closed.

Maung Maung closed his eyes, leaning against the balcony railing with his head bowed as tears streamed down his cheeks. The airplane engines roared to life, its intense sound reverberating through the air and making the ground tremble slightly. Each roar pierced Maung Maung's heart deeply before the plane ascended into the sky.

'Ma Ma, you're leaving. I don't have the guts to look at the lion statues in front of the temple any more,' Maung Maung sobbed out loudly.

Maung Maung couldn't afford to feel ashamed—not of anyone. With his head bowed, he sobbed incessantly, lost in his grief.

As the large airplane soared into the sky and vanished from view, U Thet Lwin watched anxiously from the veranda, imagining Yumisan in tears aboard the flight. 'It's okay, Sayama. Your kindness is not in vain. You did achieve what you wanted,' he whispered reassuringly, as he gazed up at the sky.

When the large airplane finally disappeared, everyone turned their attention to the inconsolably weeping Maung Maung before heading downstairs. The veranda gradually emptied. It became silent as no one remained. Once it was quiet, Maung Maung's sobbing stopped. He wiped his tears. As he gently turned his head back, he saw U Thet Lwin, standing there with a compassionate and empathetic gaze, silently offering solace.

Maung Maung tearfully looked at U Thet Lwin. Then, step by step, he slowly approached him.

'Ahkogyi.'

Maung Maung, who had neither parents nor any blood-related sisters, called out 'Ahkogyi' in a voice filled with even more affection and reliance than before, and then leaned his head into U Thet Lwin's chest. U Thet Lwin gently released the hand he had been gripping all along and patted Maung Maung's back softly, comforting and encouraging him with all the love and compassion he could muster.

'Stop crying, my little brother. Just stop crying. Your sister isn't gone forever; she will return one day,' U Thet Lwin whispered as he held Maung Maung close. In that moment, he felt not just Maung Maung in his arms, but both siblings enveloped in his loving embrace.